*"To Char"*
*Hope.*
*Latest*
*Bes...*

## GURNEY LEAFMOULD

# THE MINISTRY
# OF DISRUPTION

*Paul Gait*

BY

## PAUL GAIT

Grosvenor House
Publishing Limited

This book is published by
Grosvenor House Publishing Ltd
Link House
140 The Broadway, Tolworth, Surrey, KT6 7HT.
www.grosvenorhousepublishing.co.uk

This novel is entirely a work of fiction. The names, characters and
incidents portrayed in it are the work of author's imagination.
Any resemblance to actual persons, living or dead, events or localities
is entirely coincidental.

A CIP record for this book
is available from the British Library

ISBN 978-1-78623-953-2

Dedicated

To **Stuart**

(Former HGV driver and friend - 'black dog' advisor.)

And

The Consultants and Staff of the Urology Department
Cheltenham General Hospital

# Thanks

To my wife Helen, for allowing me to spend countless
hours to develop yet another story;

To family and friends for continued support and
encouragement.

To Janet for again spending many hours proof reading
my manuscript.

**Note:** Like any large organisation, especially the civil service, the 'Ministry of Disruption' use codes in its everyday business jargon; for clarity at any time, see the glossary at the end of the story.

# *Foreword*

During the Second World War the Ministry of Defence set up a guerrilla force who, in the case of an invasion, would go underground and harass any army of occupation.

The imperative for quickly setting up the force, was the mass evacuation of British forces from Dunkirk, and an anticipated follow up invasion by the German army.

Although occupation was an unthinkable outcome for Churchill, Auxiliary Units were nevertheless secretly established across the country just in case.

Large quantities of weapons and explosives were secreted in hidden bunkers throughout the British Isles to support this clandestine army.

Many of the secret regiment's soldiers were recruited from 'Dad's Army' volunteers. Elderly doctors, farmers and drivers were included as well as young men from 'reserved' occupations.

The order 'that there will be no withdrawal' meant that the volunteers were ordered to fight guerrilla warfare to the last man i.e. suicide missions.

At the end of WW2 all units were disbanded.

However, the following story, is based on a fictional assumption that the 'Auxiliary Units' still exist and continue to undertake training exercises manipulating our daily lives, but in a non-combative role.

So, if you've been held up in a traffic jam; been stuck at an airport, delayed on a rail journey, the cause of which you could never establish…then it's likely you have been an unwitting 'casualty' of a Ministry of Disruption (MOD) exercise.

# CHAPTER 1

'Hotel Alpha, Hotel Alpha calling Whisky November five one. New immediate over.'

The radio interrupted their night shift nap. Groggily the patrol man reached for the microphone button.

'Whisky November five one go ahead over,' he said, clearing his soporific throat.

'Whisky November five one, we have reports of an rtc, lorry turn over between junction 1 and 2 on the m50 alpha. Can I show you making? Over'

'Whisky November five one show me stat 5.'

The driver started the Shogun and rammed it into gear.

'Another Black Dog incident?' he suggested cynically.

'You might be right at this time of the morning,' his shift partner chuckled, switching on the vehicles flashing lights.

'I told you not to use the Q word earlier.'

Gurney Leafmould gazed out of the window at the crisp winter morning. The frozen grasses stiffened by Jack Frost's nocturnal visit were thick with rime, the waking sun creating a heavenly diadem in the ice crystals.

He had to admit that at last he felt better. He had now rallied from the dark place where he'd been thrust.

The previous year had been a disastrous twelve months that he was keen to forget, although the list of his misadventures would be difficult to erase.

As an avid DIYer, he had to admit he'd been overconfident in his abilities, and consequently, failure had become his constant bedfellow.

Amongst the many 'cock-ups' he'd engineered, was the demolition of his own house that had to feature as his worst and most monumental DIY catastrophe.

Media misreporting and paparazzi intrusion had made his angst worse as they exaggerated stories about him whilst digging in to his personal cloud of chaos.

Although it was the consequences of his unintentional vandalising of his Mother-In-Law's house that had actually been the tipping point which sent him over the edge.

He was an emotional butterfly and had become depressed by his inability to break the cycle of failure, with the prospect of losing his wife as well, he made a terrible decision...to end it all.

Fortunately, his inability to execute anything successfully saved his life. His poor car maintenance, his chosen method to end his days, let him down and the attempt failed.

Following his abortive suicide attempt he had been pitched into a 'strange' adventure which started with a brief period of incarceration by an irate 'lady' farmer.

Eventually his short detention ended when he persuaded her that he was no threat but could help her modernise the farm.

So with her help, he exorcised his DIY 'demons' by the successful creation of an ensuite bathroom in the old Devon farmhouse.

It was a pity then, that the farm was subsequently

gutted by a fire, arguably not initially of his making, although his poor electrical design was the cause behind the electrical overload.

However, the near death experience of his Mother-in-law drowning in slurry, was attributable to him, because he'd forgotten to replace the cesspit manhole cover.

Unfortunately, the Devon episode had left him with a health problem; for having being tied hand and foot to an old farmhouse bed for several days, he'd developed a condition that had weakened his bladder, necessitating frequent visits to the loo.

His recovery had been a long, emotionally taxing journey, but he'd slowly regained his self-confidence and, with his wife Iris's help, he had restored his self-esteem.

Now he was showing signs of 'normality', Iris's sympathy had come to an end and she decided that in this new year, that they needed to move on with their lives.

'Right Gurney. If you want to stay married to me, your DIY days have now come to an end,' she said firmly.

'You can't be serious,' Gurney said, in shock.

'Yes I am. I've had enough. I've already forgiven you for demolishing our home and nearly killing my mother. Now it's up to you.'

'What do you mean, up to me?'

'I will support you in whatever you want to do, so long as it doesn't involve DIY.'

'But DIY is my 'passion',' Gurney argued.

'Well then, you'll have to choose your mistress. It's either DIY or me.'

'But...' Gurney racked his brains to think of a compromise.

'Your side of the bargain,' Iris told him firmly, 'is to get rid of all of your DIY tools.'

'No. That's going too far,' Gurney retorted, 'What if I promise not to use them again? Is that good enough?'

'No. I know you. As soon as my back is turned, you'll be working on another special project.'

'No I won't. Honest,' he pleaded.

'Take it, or... leave ME,' Iris threw down the ultimatum.

'You can't be serious, Iris? I've built up my tool collection over a long period of time. I'm emotionally attached to all of them,' Gurney's eyes filled, as a tear rolled down his cheek.

'What's the point of keeping them, if you're not going to be using them again?' Iris argued.

'Well...I...I,' Gurney searched for a feasible reply. 'Sentimental value,' he said finally.

'Sentimental value? How can you get sentimental over a set of tools?'

'They and I have created great things together,' Gurney announced proudly.

'Yes. Great chaos,' Iris added witheringly.

'No, that's not fair. When I use them...why it's like... it's like an artist creating a DIY masterpiece,' he said, making a sweeping gesture with his hand.

'Yes, a masterpiece of mayhem,' Iris countered.

'Please Iris, I beg you.'

'OK. I'll agree not to throw them out, so long as they're under lock and key. And I hold the key,' she proposed.

'Well...I suppose...that's better than nothing,' he reluctantly acceded.

'Besides which, legally you can't use them anyway,' she reminded him.

'What's the law got to do with it?' he quizzed.

'You have a convenient memory haven't you?' Iris suggested.

'What?' Gurney puzzled.

'The court injunction, granted to the utility companies?'

'Oh that nonsense,' he said dismissively.

'Nonsense or not, the court banned you from using your tools anyway,' she reminded him.

'They're just using corporate might, to bully me,' Gurney whinged.

'Isn't it more about the repetitive damage that you caused to their equipment and underground plant? Iris pointed out.

'Well I guess I did have a few minor accidents involving their services, I suppose,' he agreed, reluctantly.

'Minor! You call repeated damage to gas, water, telephone and broadband infrastructure, costing thousands of pounds, some minor damage?'

Mrs Eyes, Gurney's Mother-In-Law arrived with a tray of teacups and clearly had been eavesdropping for she joined in the conversation, much to Iris's dismay.

'Yes. You should be ashamed of yourself. You're the first person ever, to be given an Anti-Social Behaviour Order for doing DIY.'

'Mother, please. This is a discussion between Gurney and I.'

But the old woman ignored her daughter's plea.

'Just remember, that you're a guest in my house and I'll jolly well say what I want.'

'Yes, whatever,' Iris acknowledged.

'I mean, they've even sent his mugshot to DIY stores, to install in their face recognition software,' the old woman continued.

'Mother, please.'

'Yes and the courts have even ordered them to refuse to serve him,' she added. 'With special dispensation to eject him from their premises, too.'

'That's enough Mother, now please leave us.'

'I was only stating the facts. But, if you want to ignore them, then carry on. You'll soon regret it, my girl.'

The old lady shuffled her way out of the room, muttering.

'Thank heavens she's gone,' Gurney said

'Just ignore her.'

'Ignore who?' Gurney said, disparagingly. 'If you're banning me from doing DIY, can we talk about my other plans?' Gurney asked.

'What other plans? Iris asked suspiciously.

'You know! Journalism,' he reminded her.

'I thought that was just a passing whim.'

'No. I'm deadly serious,' Gurney affirmed.

'You'll never cope with it. It's hard work and long hours,' Iris said, seeking to bring him back to earth.

'You're the one who keeps moaning about me getting under your feet,' he reminded her.

'So what are you suggesting?' Iris asked, reluctantly.

'There are some journalist classes being run at the local College,' Gurney informed her.

'Go on,' she encouraged, wondering where his next fad would take them.

'It'll cost to join the course,' he admitted.

'So how do you propose we fund it?' Iris quizzed.

'Mother-In-Law?' Gurney said doubtfully.

'You've got to be joking. After what you've done to her?' Iris reminded him.

'What then? I'm not working,' Gurney threw his hands up.

'I suppose we could use money left from the insurance claim on the old house,' Iris suggested.

'Great, thanks. And there's a BA in Journalism and the news industry too that I could undertake,' he added enthusiastically.

'Don't push your luck. Let's see how you do first with this local course. Knowing you, it will be just a passing fad,' she forecast.

'Thanks,' he said, attempting to give her a hug and a kiss.' I'm keen to start.'

'I'm sure I'll regret it,' Iris said, moving away from his attempted embrace. 'So now that I've agreed to that, you can now forget DIY, right?' she proposed.

'If I'm doing the course, I won't have time to do it anyway,' Gurney accepted.

'Exactly,' Iris smiled, smugly.

And there's no lock that will keep me away from my precious tools,' he thought.

# CHAPTER 2

Gurney was bubbling over with excitement as he made his way to room M18 at the technical college to start his journalist's course.

He had hardly slept the previous night because of his childlike anticipation of the day to come, which also meant several nocturnal trips to the loo.

Suitably equipped with a reporter's notepad, and with several pens and pencils in an over- the- shoulder bag, he felt really up for the next chapter of his life.

He followed several others entering an unloved, shabby room and sat on one of the wooden chairs laid out in a semicircle.

At the front of the class a white board still showed half rubbed out formulas where permanent marker pens rather than wipeable ones had been used.

Shortly after Gurney had taken his seat, the lecturer arrived and stood in front of the five students.

'Welcome to this 12 week intensive course on Journalism here at the Brunswick college. I hope everyone is in the right room for this course?'

The students all nodded.

'Good, well that's a great start. I apologise for the environment, but this building was due to be knocked down when the new University was opened.

Unfortunately, the university project is running two

years behind and is a million pound over budget,' the course tutor advised.' That's a scandalous story, I've yet to write.'

The lecturer looked most odd Gurney thought, he was shiny bold on top of his head but with a thick black bushy beard; it was almost as if his hair had slipped from his head to his chin, Gurney concluded.

'As a result, you might have an occasional visit by a rat or two. But just ignore them, unless they start nibbling your feet,' he joked.

Several people unconsciously lifted their feet and looked nervously around.

'In the journalism world, you will encounter some horrible things. So just use this environment as an acclimatisation exercise.

In fact this will be a walk in the park, compared to some of the real life situations that you will encounter.'

Gurney swallowed hard. His dreamy vision of journalism was being despoiled by an unwelcome reality check.

'Nice to see it's a small course, for that means I can spend more time with each of you.

Let's start by introducing ourselves. My name is Peter Watts. I shall be your lecturer for the duration of the course. I am a former journalist, from a now 'closed down' newspaper.

I want you to write your name and aspirations on the whiteboard. And at the end of the course we'll see how close you've got.'

At the tutor's invitation an immature looking adolescent stood up and slouched his way to the board,.

'*John Cloud - Sports Journalist;*

'Hello John. Do you play sport yourself?' the tutor asked, as John returned to his place.

'No. Only table football.'

'Do you support a team or go to sporting events?'

'No. I don't like crowds.'

'OK. Well, I think you might have a challenge meeting your aim then,' the lecturer said, thinking he's going to be a waste of space. 'And the next.'

A grey haired lady, in tweeds, made her way to the board and wrote:-

*'Sarah Cliff - Writing in the local church magazine';*

'Sarah, why do you think this course will help you?'

'I will be writing for the parishioners, and some of them are former teachers. Most of them are very critical about anything and everything. So I'm hoping that you can teach me how to rise above their criticism and become a 'hard bitten' reporter.'

'You'll get a lot of criticism as a journalist for sure. Just spell their names correctly and that will be a good start. And the next.'

A studious looking, twenty something year old, minced his way to the board and wrote:

*'Sheldon Sands - Drama Critic Broodsheet journalist.'*

'Sheldon nice to see that you have great expectations of the course. Unfortunately, you will have to start as a 'cub reporter' on a local paper doing Am Dram and Scout Shows and the like, before the broadsheets will take you on.'

'Not so. I have been educated privately and my father is well connected,' he advised, in an 'upper crust' voice. 'I have already been promised a place at a well known newspaper, as soon as I complete this course.'

'Well best of luck with your network. '

'Do you have a pen I could borrow sir?' Sheldon asked.

'How are you going to be a journalist, if you don't carry a pen, for heaven's sake?'

'I usually use a tablet or record something on my mobile.'

'So why not today?'

''My batteries are flat.'

'In both of them?'

'Yes.'

'So if you were reporting something today, how would you get your copy printed?'

'My father's PA. She normally types it up for me.'

'Heaven help us,' the lecturer seethed, handing him a pen. 'Let me have it back at the end of the lecture.'

'Do you have some paper too?' the student asked.

Reluctantly he gave the ex-public schoolboy some paper, already classifying him as a lost cause.

'Incidentally you might like to check the spelling of broadsheet,' the tutor pointed out. 'And the next.'

A large middle aged man, waddled his rounded frame to the board, wheezing as if he'd just run a marathon and wrote:

'*Reuben Fence - Another qualification to add to my CV*'.

'Reuben. Another qualification?' the lecturer wondered.

'Yes, that's right. I don't apply for jobs. I'm a professional course taker.'

'So what's the point of choosing Journalism, if you aren't going to use it?'

'I'm always looking for ways to expand my knowledge,' Reuben replied.

'OK, that's novel.'

'Anyway, I'm surprised you haven't said you've seen me on television. I'm a serial quiz show contestant too.'

'Well everyone to their own,' the lecturer muttered under his breath. 'I'm still learning about students, that's for sure.'

And finally, he gestured to Gurney, who wrote;

*Gurney Leafmould - Investigative Journalist. Crusading journalism to help change the world for the better'*

'That's a tough one to go for Gurney. You realise that in order to get an investigative scoop, you might have to put your life on the line.'

'Really?' Gurney 'buttock clenched' in fear.

'You also have to consider the Public right to know over the privacy of the individual.'

'Oh!'

'You have to decide if it's your own personal sense of right, i.e. are you expressing a personal view or grievance? Or, is it really the 'public's right to know?'

'Well I...'

'Are you expecting that the lawyers will sort it, if you get it wrong?'

'I ummm...It's a bit grown up,' Gurney thought, 'getting lawyers involved because of something that I'd written.'

'Do you realise that people will get angry if you expose their 'dodgy' activities,' the tutor counselled.

'Will they? I hadn't thought of that,' Gurney confessed. 'But I'll be helping to get rid of corruption and evil,' he suggested. 'It might even make me rich and famous too,' Gurney thought, dreamily. Hoping sometime to secure a scoop.

# CHAPTER 3

'Now we know who we all are, and what we're aiming for,' the Journalism Course lecturer continued. 'I want you to show me and to each other, your current ability.

This first exercise will take, about fifteen minutes and I want you to write a newspaper article about the legendary Gloucestershire tradition of rolling a Cheese down a steep hill in your own style,' the lecturer explained.

'When you have completed the exercise, I'll get you to read your version out to the class.'

After the allotted fifteen minutes, the lecture asked for a volunteer to be first to read their article to the class.

Sarah Cliff was the first to read out her story.

'*It was love at first sight, her heart beat madly as she tended to his injuries. She leaned close to him, her breath coming in short pants. I think I've got something in my eye he said. I can't see anything she said. You'll need to come even closer he implored as their lips touched and...*'

'Well very good Sarah, but not that I was expecting a bodice ripper from rolling a cheese downhill,' the lecturer admitted.

'John, I think you're next.'

'I haven't done much but here it is. *They donned their 3D glasses and waited for the signal. The hill looked steep, but at least they knew that they'd not suffer broken bones like the real competitors on a real hill...* that's all I had time for.'

'Well at least that's another perspective I wouldn't have thought of. Sheldon, your article please.'

'*Lord Severn graciously allowed the peasants access to his land to pursue their ancient ritual of cheese pursuit. This primal activity was reputed to appease the hill gods. However poor direction and hapless performances disappointed the near capacity audiences.*'

'A critique of the 'staged' show, unusual but OK. And the next, Reuben please.'

'*The eight pound double Gloucester cheese is rolled down a 1 in 2 hill. Since 1988, the cheeses have been hand-made by Mrs. Diana Smart of Churcham, using milk from her herd of Brown Swiss, Holstein and Gloucester cows.*'

'OK, a very factual account. And finally last but not least, Gurney.'

Gurney cleared his throat and read his article.' *Competitors come from all over the world to take part in the downhill race chasing a local Double Gloucester cheese. The legendary annual event, held each spring bank holiday on Coopers Hill Gloucester, attracts entrants and visitors from far and wide. Rugby players from the local area help to catch the competitors before they collide with fences at the bottom.*' ...sorry that's all I had time for.' Gurney apologised.

'No need to apologise. You've all done very well. Can you see how your story is biased to your own viewpoint whereas in my view, Gurney has produced an easy to read article without overdoing any one aspect, but has successfully got behind the facts and produced a good story.

'Gurney, you seem to have a flair for this,' the lecturer encouraged. 'You've got a good feel for the story.'

'I think it's because I'm sensitive. I can empathise with the people and their situation.'

'Well don't get carried away. You need to work on your grammar. At the moment it's letting you down.'

'My wife is helping me to sort that out.'

'Good. Well so long as she's not also writing the stories for you?'

'No, I assure you that all the ideas and words are my own. But not necessarily in the right order.'

The class looked at each and smirked.

'I would encourage you all, to engage with your local newspapers. Get some practical experiences doing low level reporting such as fetes and kids events. Just observe and write.'

'You will hear me say this many, many times. Writers write; Reporters report. The more you write, the better you'll become.'

The Tutor listed types of articles that they would be considering over the period of the course:

- *News headlines*
- *International News*
- *Politics*
- *Crime and court reporting*
- *Health*
- *Investigative Journalism*

- *Humorous Articles*
- *Sports*
- *Animal, domestic and wild life*
- *Celebrity interview*
- *TV and Film reviews*
- *Specialist projects e.g. DIY*

Gurney relished the idea of working on the last category, although he felt guilty about even considering it, having promised Iris his commitment to DIY celibacy.

'Right, let's start off with a look at headline writing. Here's some bad headlines. Remember that a poor headline will render your article invisible. Here's a few examples:

- *'Students, cook and serve Grandparents';*
- *'City unsure why sewer smells';*
- *'Girls school still offering something special';*
- *Planes forced to land at airports';*
- *'Cop makes arrest in bathroom after smelling crack' ;*
- *'Viagra Con man hit with stiff sentence';*
- *'Slowdown continues to accelerate';*
- *'New study of obesity looks for larger test group.'*

'Behind the headlines, someone would have spent hours investigating and writing their articles. And to what avail? To lose the reader with an incompetent headline.

Clearly some headlines are deliberately funny, but others are just pathetic and wouldn't invite readers to even look at the article. So make sure you get your headlines right.

Over the next 12 weeks Gurney consistently came 'top of the class'. And particularly found the talk by a well-known crusading Investigative Journalist fascinating.

The Journalist had gone 'undercover' on a sheep farm, at shearing time and had 'blown the whistle' on an animal welfare issue.

The reporter had written an article entitled 'Sheep Shiver Scandal',

*A gang of contract shearers had been scheduled to shear a flock of sheep, but unseasonable weather caused the temperatures to suddenly plummet. However, as the shearers were working to a tight schedule with other farmers, no allowance could be made for the cold weather and the sheep were duly, 'robbed' of their woollen coats in spite of the conditions.*

*And, shock horror, the farmer had rejected the undercover journalists suggestion of temporarily refixing their fleeces with cable ties until the temperature had improved.*

*Thanks to his public exposure, an animal welfare organisation became involved and took the sheep away to be...slaughtered!*

On the final day of a very intensive course, Peter Watts sat in the staff room to review the students' progress against their original course aims.

'*John - Sports Reporter*, - Too immature. Better suited for the virtual world, rather than the real one,' he decided. 'However, he has the possibility of a job reviewing computer games for the local paper,' he conceded.

'*Sarah - Parish magazine*, sacked from editing the Parish magazine for the racy articles that she'd written about ladies of the parish. But threw off her tweeds and had become a novelist writing about shocking goings on in her 'fictional' village. Good for her,' he thought.

'*Sheldon* - failed the course because he never submitted anything, as expected,' the tutor recalled. 'Glad I refused to award him a 'special' certificate in spite of the college principal's insistence. Sand's father's promise of financial 'sponsorship' failed to move me; However, in spite of his incompetence, he still became a theatrical critic for a broadsheet. The old boys network. Huh!'

'*Reuben - CV person;* was average on the course and able to get by with his ability to 'bullshit', Consequently, he never did proper research and his articles were factual but weak,' Watts recollected. 'I'm glad he was caught cheating on that quiz show though. It turned out that his 'so called' hearing aid was found to be a radio receiver linked to an accomplice. And he was charged and is facing jail for fraud. Serves him right,' the lecturer smiled.

'*Gurney - investigative journalist* - The surprise of the course. Excelled in his final article which won him the best course article accolade. Keeping to the 'KISS principle --i.e. keep it simple stupid'.' Peter recalled. 'Based on his investigations of a 'scandal' involving a village fete cake competition. Genius. Now what was it?' he checked his notes and found the article.

'That's right, one of the members of the women's guild had been accused of entering a cake that she had bought rather than one she'd made herself.' He read the article again.

*'Best baker award fraud.'*

*'Villagers in Nether Upton are divided over the accusation that an elderly member of the women's guild, had won a coveted 'Best Baker' award with a cake that she is alleged to have purchased rather than making it.*

*This journalist has obtained a slice of the cake and sent it away for analysis.*

*It has been proven that the chemical makeup of the flour used in the cake, is the same type used in the baking industry.*

*This type of flour is not available at local supermarkets.*

*The woman, Mary Raspberry (83), former school cook, when confronted by the results, confessed to bribing a bakery employee to sell her flour from the bakery, but insisted that she made the cake herself. The jury is still out.'*

Finally, he re-joined his reduced class of students, who were sitting in the dingy classroom.

'Well, that's it folks. The course is over. For those of you who have passed, you have been awarded a diploma in Journalism. The presentation will be a 'cap and gown' session at Swansea University.

Best of luck with writing the next 'column inches' of your life.'

Gurney was beside himself with joy. His self-confidence shot off the scale. The course had 'flushed out' his natural ability to write. His life of creating mayhem was over, forever.

He was a 'born again' human being. No more guilt about things he'd cocked up.

He hugged the tutor and sobbed with joy, all over the other's shoulder.

'Thank you. Thank you so much,' he wept. 'I feel enabled to crusade for justice and the downtrodden.'

'Best of luck Gurney,' the tutor replied, equally emotional. 'You'll need it.'

# CHAPTER 4

The lorry driver was starting to feel tired. The five hour motorway journey had been boring and uneventful. The constant, even sound of the engine was like a lullaby which even the music from the radio failed to counter.

Although he enjoyed night driving, staring into the darkness for several hours caused him eye strain and now the wispy banks of localised fog were making him feel sleepy.

'I'll stop at the next services,' he said to himself. 'I could do with a coffee.'

He yawned and rubbed his heavy eyes with the back of his hand.

As he returned his focus back to the road, he suddenly saw them. Right in the middle of the motorway.

He stamped on his brakes, the wheels immediately locking, smoke erupting from the skidding tyres.

Frantically he turned the wheel to avoid running them over.

Then the lorry driver's nightmare occurred. He felt the trailer starting to jack-knife.

In a cacophony of noise, he was a passenger on the way to an accident. He had lost control of his vehicle and the crash was inevitable.

Forced along by the errant trailer, the cab crashed backwards off the motorway, tipped over and everything went black.

When he regained consciousness, the huge articulated vehicle was lying on its side in a ditch.

Although shocked by the accident, his only injury was a small bump on his head.

'Are they alright? Did I hit them?' he wondered.

Kicking away the crumpled windscreen, he climbed out through hole he'd created. As he stood on the edge of the motorway another lorry stopped by him and put on its hazard lights.

The driver quickly jumped down from the cab and rushed over to the other.

'Are they dead?' he asked the new arrival.

'Who?'

'On the motorway. Back up there,' he said, pointing. 'A child and a ...black dog.'

'A child? A black dog? You must be dreaming. There's nothing up there.'

As they spoke, a small convoy of vehicles squeezed past the lorry without stopping.

Undaunted by the other's explanation, the lorry driver wandered along the empty motorway looking for the child and dog.

Within a few moments of starting his frantic search, a police car and fast response paramedic arrived, their blue lights punctuating the night sky. Quickly they were at his side.

'Alright 'drive'? the paramedic asked. 'What you doing in the middle of the motorway?'

'I'm trying to find them. To see if I hit them,' he said frantically

'Hit who?' the first responder asked.

'A child and a black dog.'

'Oh! Black dog eh? Come and take a seat in my car. Did you bang your head?' the paramedic probed.

'Yes,' the lorry driver admitted, rubbing the lump on his forehead.

'Sounds like you might be suffering from a bit of concussion,' the first aider suggested.

'No, I swear. They were there,' the lorry driver insisted.

But the subsequent sweep of the area, by the emergency services found no-one.

# CHAPTER 5

They had been in the hot car for three long hours, returning from the award ceremony.

Gurney was in good spirits, but Iris, his wife, and Delores Eyes, his Mother-In-Law were far from happy. They had been forced to stand at the back of the hall during the two hour long presentation and didn't even get to see Gurney receiving his award.

After the ceremony Gurney had taken them for a celebratory meal at a nearby garden centre café, but at the checkout, found that his wallet was missing from his back pocket.

'Damn,' he cursed. 'Sorry Iris, but I appear to have left my wallet at home. You wouldn't mind paying for the meal would you?'

'This is getting to be an expensive day out,' his wife moaned. 'I've already bought the petrol for the trip.' Reluctantly she paid the bill and they made their way to a wooden topped table with a cast iron base.

'This would be nice on our patio,' Gurney observed stroking the table.

'If we had one,' Iris said tersely.

'I could always...' Gurney stared to say.

'Oh no. You're not going to make one either. Remember you're banned from DIY.

'Quite right too,' Mrs Eyes chipped in. 'The man's a danger with any tool in his hand.

Consequently because of the obvious tension, they ate their meal in stony silence.

As they left the café, Mrs Eyes spotted a cost saving deal on bags of potting compost.

'Oh that's a good price. I could do with a bag of that,' she said.

'How are we going to get it home?' Gurney questioned. 'It's a hundred litres. It's much too big for the metro's boot.'

'You've got a roof rack haven't you?' the old woman pointed out.

'Well, yeah, but it's very heavy stuff. Anyway, I can't lift that up on to the roof rack, he protested.'

'I'll do it,' Iris said. 'We could do with a bag of that as well.'

'But the weight,' Gurney protested.

'Stop making excuses. The weight will keep it on the roof.'

After a struggle, they managed to put the heavy bags of potting compost on the roof rack and tied them firmly on.

'That's going nowhere,' Iris said, completing the final knot. 'Thank goodness for my knot tying badge at Guides.'

Finally they left Swansea for the homeward journey. But within a few miles Mrs Eyes started complaining about the unseasonal heat.

'Can't we have some fresh air in here, she moaned.

'I'll open a window if you like,' Gurney said, trying to be dutiful.

'Don't you dare. We'll all be sent mad from the traffic noise and fumes.'

'Just concentrate on your driving, Gurney,' Iris said, quietly. 'She'll doze off in a minute.'

After another five minutes, Iris's prediction came true.

'Thank goodness for that! She's gone to sleep,' Gurney said, looking at the reflection of the comatose woman in the rear view mirror.

The old lady's head lolled on her chest as she snored loudly and dribbled onto her thin, sweat soaked, floral frock.

'Oh, it's so hot in here,' Iris complained, flapping her hand in front of her face. 'These temperatures are more like summer than spring.'

'This is the result of global warming. And you can't blame me for that,' Gurney added, quickly.

'Yes but you haven't helped with providing air conditioning in here.'

'Air conditioning.?' There isn't any.'

'Well the cooling fan or whatever it is. Stop splitting hairs,' Iris fumed. 'Instead of messing with it yourself, why didn't you get the garage to repair it?' she whined. 'You know how useless you are at...' she stopped in midsentence. 'Well, you know...I mean it is complicated isn't it?' she back-tracked, recalling her promise not to undermine his newly restored confidence. '

Gurney ignored her dig and carried on driving.

'I shouldn't have had that second cup of coffee though,' he jiggled.

'I told you. But you knew better didn't you?' Iris berated.

'I was celebrating my success,' he pointed out.

'Anyway, you're driving too fast,' she criticised.

'I'm not. I'm keeping to the speed limit.'

Gurney's concentration wavered as he switched off

from Iris's prattling and started dreaming about his future journalistic career now he'd got his diploma.

But as they topped the brow of a hill, he was jerked back to reality, for in front of them was a line of stationary traffic.

'Oh shit!' Gurney said, flooring the foot brake.

'We're going to crash,' Iris screamed, stamping on an imaginary pedal, on the passenger floor pan.

Anticipating the impact of a collision, she thrust out her arms and braced herself against the hot, sun baked, plastic glove compartment.

'Swerve around it,' she instructed. 'Go right. Not that way! The other right!' she ranted.

Her screams of command added to Gurney's confusion as he 'sawed' at the wheel. His mouth dried, surely the crash was inevitable.

The Metro was not fitted with cadence braking and the locked wheels and smoking tyres wrote a black signature on the hot tarmac.

The back of the stationary Daimler loomed larger in front.

# CHAPTER 6

Mrs Eyes, woken by the sound of her daughter's screams and the squealing tyres, joined in the ear-piercing noise that filled Gurney's head.

The silver haired barrister in the Daimler, looked in horror as his rear view mirror filled with the image of the skidding metro.

Although Gurney had scrubbed 65mph off his speed, the impact of 5 mph into the back of a stationary Daimler, was enough to demolish the front end of the overloaded Metro.

The Daimler's pneumatic rear bumpers lessened the impact and the Metro bounced off the bumper like a tennis ball off a racquet.

The barrister's smug satisfaction of his investment in the special bumpers, was quickly replaced with anger, when the over-burdened metro roof rack broke free and smashed through the Daimler's rear window, filling his back seats with 200 litres of potting compost.

A geyser of steam shot up from the Metro's split radiator and immediately enveloped the front of the car.

The front two airbags, that Gurney had fitted himself, had miraculously worked, but with a slight snag. Collateral damage.

'Oh my face stings,' Iris said, looking in the mirror attached to the back of the sun visor. 'Oh my god! What have you done to me? I look like a chimney sweep.'

'It's only soot from the explosive cartridges,' Gurney said, looking at his own blackened face in the rear view mirror. 'I think I bought the wrong sort off eBay. These are obviously high power ones. We've got mild flash burns,' he confessed.

'I'll give you flash burns, you idiot,' she ranted.

He was now close to breaking point himself. 'Next time, I'll replace the front passenger airbag with a plastic carrier bag. That'll stop your whining,' he thought.

In the back of the car, Mrs Eyes had been hit by a plastic cover from one the airbags and was sporting an egg shaped lump on her forehead.

Fortunately for Gurney, the usually verbose lady had been silenced by the shock of the crash.

'Quick, quick get out, get out,' Iris screamed, spotting the steam from the broken radiator. 'The cars on fire! The cars on fire!' Forcefully she threw open the door and grabbed her mother's arm.

As the trio scrambled out of the car, the owner of the Daimler emerged rubbing the back of his neck.

'What the bloody hell do you think you're doing? You bloody maniac. You could have killed somebody. '

As he strode purposefully towards Gurney, to confront him, Mrs Eyes stepped forward and her stare cut him dead.

The other driver paused in mid expletive, mouthed wordlessly and slid back into the Daimler, quickly locking the doors.

Gurney helped his Mother-in - Law up the embankment and out of harm's way as other cars skidded and crashed into the stationary queue.

'You bleedin maniac,' Mrs Eyes, shouted. 'First you try to kill me in a cesspit and now you deliberately crash the car when I'm asleep.'

Gurney walked away from the pair.

'Now where's he going Iris?'

'I think he needs to commune with nature,' she informed her mother.

'I'll give him communing with nature. He's a menace on the roads.'

'It wasn't his fault Mother,' Iris said, coming to his defence. 'He wasn't to blame.'

'I knew I should have stayed at home,' the old woman moaned.

'Come on it's been a nice day seeing Gurney collecting his Diploma, hasn't it?'

'If we'd been able to see what was going on, it might have been.

Now he's got it, what's he going to do with it? It's a waste of money if you ask me,' her mother complained.

'Well now he's got that qualification, he can start applying for newspaper jobs.'

'What, delivering them?' the old woman said sarcastically.

Gurney re-joined them feeling 'relieved.'

'Hello, I am actually here, when you two have finished 'slagging me off',' Gurney exclaimed. 'Anyway, the award ceremony was nearly cancelled.'

'Why was that? Had they heard about your reputation?' Delores Eyes jibed.

'Don't be so awful to him Mother.'

Gurney ignored the comment and continued, 'No, the college had run out of money.'

'Somebody probably had their hand in the til,' the old lady said, cynically.

'Mother, you can't say things like that,' Iris admonished.

'Course I can. Nobody can hear me up here. So why wasn't it cancelled?'

'I told them that they were in breach of contract and a scathing press article would damage their finances even more, if they didn't sort it,' Gurney advised.

'You didn't? I didn't know you had it in you,' the old woman admitted.'

'It sent the university into a financial rebalancing act. And the ceremony was reinstated,' Gurney proudly informed them.

Behind them the M50 was growing into a scrap yard as more and more vehicles ploughed into the tangled mass of shunted cars.

Within minutes of them evacuating the damaged Metro, several fire engines and a convoy of recovery trucks arrived on scene.

In a white Range Rover on the opposite carriageway, the driver was making a hands free call.

'Cabbage, who's calling?'

'Hello Eunice. This is CJ.

'CJ?'

'Yes, it's Carrington. Just a quick call. I'm on my way to my office, from your meeting at Elmley. I'm just now going through one of your roadwork schemes. Wonderful job. Long tailbacks. Lots of chaos. Congratulations to you and your team. Another brilliant job. Well done.'

'Thank you,' she beamed.

# CHAPTER 7

'Well, do you like it Mother?' Iris asked, waiting for her Mother's approval of her new home. For up until now, Mrs Eyes had always found an excuse not to visit them.

'Well if you like two bedroom bungalows, I suppose it's alright. But I wouldn't have bought it myself. Wrong part of the city for me,' she said, critically.

Iris didn't rise to the bait.

Following the multivehicle crash on the motorway, they had been brought home on the back of a breakdown truck as the metro was undriveable.

'Would you like another cup of tea? It's good for the shock.'

'Yes please. I must say the lounge is…is different,' the old lady said, looking around.

'We've been able to completely furnish it with new furniture and goods from the house insurance pay-out.'

'I'm amazed they paid up. Especially as your husband was the cause of its destruction. Undermining the foundations! I mean, what was the idiot thinking of?'

'We were lucky that a developer bought the old plot of land from us,' Iris volunteered.

'Whatever is he going to do with that 'bomb site'?' the old woman asked.

'I believe he intends to build a block of flats on it.'

'Tut. Further lowering the tone of the neighbourhood.

If your useless husband hadn't demolished your home, none of this would be necessary. Has he got a job yet?' Delores Eyes probed.

'No. But it's not from want of trying. He's written off for lots of newspaper jobs, Sent off his CV, but got no replies yet.'

'Iris, how many times have I got to tell you, the expression is, he hasn't received any replies' Anyone would think you were dragged up, not sent to the best Public school I could afford.'

'Sorry Mother.'

'I should think so too.'

'Apparently that additional online Diploma Course that he passed, is not recognised by the industry anyway.'

'Well, that was a waste of money then wasn't it? her mother retorted.

'Yes but it kept him out of mischief for a while. And writing those DIY articles for the Parish magazine attracted some good comments.'

'They were all probably pleased that his pen was the only thing in use. The community is safe, so long as that's all he does with DIY... just write about it.'

'His tools are safely locked away now,' Iris informed her.

'You mean his tools of mass destruction.'

'Mother! You make him sound like Rambo.'

'Dumbo, more like.'

'Mother!'

'Well at least you're not living with me anymore. I've got my home back at last.'

Iris, too, was thankful for moving out. Living again with her house-proud Mother had been like walking on egg shells. Whenever she attempted to do anything to help, it was 'not done properly'.

'He's driving me mad hanging around the house though. Can you think of anything that we can do?'

'Let me think now. How about getting him sectioned?'

'Oh Mother, be serious.'

'I am. The man was clearly born with cranial deficiencies.'

'Do you know anyone in the newspaper industry?' Iris asked.

'I used to know someone who worked at the local paper. I don't read it, do you?'

'Yes. Gurney gets it to criticise the articles. He reckons he could do better than any of their reporters.'

Iris foraged around the tidy lounge and found a copy of the previous day's edition. She handed it to her Mother.

'What are you looking for?'

'Seeing if I could spot his name amidst all these articles. But I don't know if he's still there or even if he's still alive,' Mrs Eyes said leafing through the paper.

After checking the names of the reporters against each article, she closed the paper.

'No he's not there.'

Iris took the paper from her. 'Let me check. You might have missed it.'

'Are you suggesting I'm too blind to spot a name, young lady?'

'No mother. Sometimes two heads are better than one. I suppose I mean four eyes are better than two, that's all.'

'Don't get ahead of yourself my girl. I might be old but I'm not stupid.'

Iris ignored the opportunity to remind her Mother that she was the one who had fallen down a manhole, into a cesspit in the dark and that her driving was the cause of major traffic disruption.

'What's his name?'

'Who?'

'The man you were looking for in the paper.'

'Gordon...or was it Graham. No, it was definitely Gordon. Yes that's it. Gordon Moss.'

'Oh well. No need to look any further. He's the editor of the paper.'

'My! He's done well for himself. I would have thought he was nearing retirement age.'

'How do you know him?'

'In the sixties, when I was a nurse.'

'Oh yes,' Iris winked, knowingly.

'Now I come to think of it. I might well have a bargaining chip that could help get your husband out from under your feet.'

'Great!'

'I'll see what I can do. But I'm not promising anything. In the meantime, is your kettle broken?'

'No. Why do you ask?'

'Well there's a shortage of tea in the teapot.'

# CHAPTER 8

The Security guard escorted Delores Eyes to the Editors 'office', irreverently called the 'pigpen' by his staff.

At the entrance of the corral formed by temporary office partitions, the security guard cleared his throat and announced. 'Mr Moss, I have your visitor, sir.'

No reaction.

'Mr Moss .... '

The old woman barely recognised the bald, 'rotund' man sitting behind the cluttered desk. It was three decades since she'd last seen him and clearly his unhealthy habit of snacking at his desk had not been kind to him.

'Sit,' the editor directed, without looking up and gestured to a chair the other side of his desk.

'Gordon Moss, I am not a dog to be ordered around at your command. Is this how you greet all your visitors?' the old lady demanded, without moving.

'I'll leave you then sir...with your visitor. You'll see her out won't you?' the Security guard asked, relieved to be leaving the cranky old woman.

'Is this your office?' Delores said, looking disparagingly around. 'Well I don't think much of it. I was expecting an executive office with a large mahogany conference table beholden to your status as an editor,' she commented, disdainfully.

'It's a coral. Open plan offices is what we do these days,' the editor said without looking at her. 'Now what can I do for you? I can spare you two minutes. I have a deadline to meet,' he said, scribbling over sentences on a printed piece of paper.

'Will you stop that infernal writing and pay me the courtesy of at least looking at me,' she demanded.

The editor dropped his pen, annoyed at the interruption and looked at her. He was clearly uncomfortable with the sight of the old woman with the red gash of lipstick on her pale, wrinkled face.

'Delores. How nice to see you. I see the years have been kind to you,' he lied. 'What brings you here today?'

'I'm sure you don't want to know which bus I came on. You're obviously a busy man so I'll cut to the chase.'

'I appreciate that, as you can see I'm...'

'A busy man! Yes, we've already established that. But not too busy to remember those raucous nights in the nurses home?'

A broad smile burst across his stress filled face. 'Do I ever,' he beamed. 'They were fantastic weren't they? The best days of my life. I thought I'd died and gone to heaven.'

'Some people really enjoyed their share of free love, didn't you?'

'The swinging sixties. Making love on the sheepskin rug, in front of the roaring coal fire. Brilliant parties you used to host. Excellent memories.'

The years dropped off him as he took a step back into his joyful memories.

'Then you'll probably also remember an unfortunate encounter in a mini?'

The smile turned to a grimace.

'Where they had to cut the roof off the car? The woman's husband's car? Where they had to take you on one stretcher to the hospital?', stacked one on top of the other?

'Yes, well best forgotten,' he said, slumping back in his chair.

'And so you should. The newspaper owner never did find out that it was one of his own cub reporters who was servicing his wife that day, did he?'

'It was a youthful adventure. There was nothing in it.'

'That's not the rumour I heard. I believe there was plenty in it, and that was the main cause of the problem. Big boy.'

'That was a long time ago and he never found out, so let's let sleeping dogs lie, shall we?'

'No. He obviously didn't find out, otherwise you'd be talking several octaves higher now, wouldn't you?'

'It's all water under the bridge. We all did things then that we regretted later.'

'Well, the frenzy of confessions about things that happened decades ago are coming back to bite people. As you newspaper people are only too keen to expose. What do the headlines say? No time limit. No hiding place?'

'What are you getting at?'

'It's perhaps not too late for the owner to find out about certain things?'

'What are you suggesting? Are you blackmailing me?'

'How dare you suggest that I would do such a dreadful thing?'

'So what's the purpose of you raking all this up, then?'

'However, I could ensure that if I wrote my memoirs, the part involving the owner's wife and car could be excluded.'

'In exchange for what? he asked cautiously. 'What are you after? Money?'

'Don't be so vulgar. Money! Blackmail! I think the other papers might be interested in my memoirs after all,' she said, starting to get up off her chair.

'OK. You've made your point. What do you want?'

'Well it pains me to do this. My son-in...My daughter's husband, has just completed a journalism course and is looking for a job.'

'Oh is that all?'

'Yes. I hate to use this trump card on such a trivial matter, but he needs to be kept busy, otherwise he gets into all manner of mischief.'

'Such as?'

'Doing DIY.'

'DIY!' The editor looked at her in disbelief.

'Yes. In his case it stands for Demolish it yourself,' the old woman explained.

'He's not the one who demolished his house is he?'

Yes. 'That's the idiot.'

'And you want me to take him on as a reporter? You must be joking. I have enough stress as it is with my current workforce, without taking on more ulcer causing hassle.'

'When he's away from tools he's...I'd like to say fine, but the reality is, that he only becomes a danger to himself and not others.'

'I suppose I've got no choice?' the editor said, submissively.

'If you don't want to sing falsetto, probably not,' Delores Eyes smiled.

The editor thought for a moment, assessing his options. 'The only job I can give him is as a reporter at the Magistrates court. There's a lot of hanging around there.'

'That's sounds just the job for him. You won't regret it. Your past is safe with me.'

'What always puzzled me was, how come the owner didn't track me down at the time,' the editor observed.

'You have me to thank for that.' Delores said smugly.

'Why?'

'As you know, I worked in the hospital and I amended the records of the incident. I changed your name to someone else's. I never did find out what happened to Mr Dobbyrash.'

# CHAPTER 9

Shortly after Mrs Eyes' visit to see the editor, Gurney found himself sitting in front of the newspaper man.

'Right Leafmould. I've read your CV and while it's not perfect. I see some merit in it. I can offer you a job as a Court Reporter. Take it or leave it,' the editor said dismissively.

'I'll take it, please Mr Moss,' Gurney beamed.

'Good. Well I'll get my sub editor to tell you all about the details of the job.'

'Thank you sir. You won't regret it,' Gurney said excitedly.

'I hope not, I sincerely hope not. Tell me, just out of curiosity, what sort of relationship do you have with your Mother-In-Law?'

'Does the job depend on my answer?' Gurney asked, apprehensively.

'No. You've got the job, subject to a satisfactory three month probationary period, of course.'

'Well to be honest. It's a bit strained. She's a bit of a ...'

'Tyrant?'

'And dictator. We don't often see eye to eye,' Gurney confessed.

'Well you need to know that it's her recommendation that has got you this job. So don't mess it up.'

'Oh. That is surprising. Perhaps she's weakening in her old age.'

'Now clear off, I've got a schedule to meet,' the editor dismissed him.

'Thank you sir. I will make you proud.'

'I doubt that,' the harassed editor muttered, as Gurney left.


The sub editor, Harry Rolling, took Gurney into a small meeting room.

'I see you have a notebook with you,' the newspaper man observed.' Do you do short hand?'

'No. I tried, but gave up after a while. I was thinking of buying a recorder. Is that OK?'

'Yes perfectly, so long as the person you are talking to doesn't object and of course, you mustn't use it in court,' the sub editor informed him.

'Oh that's a pity,' Gurney said, thwarting his plans to purchase a machine.

'So stick with trying to learn short hand, or to scribble quickly. I suggest you start today. Make notes as we talk through your role.'

'OK.' Gurney flipped open his 'reporters' notepad and patted his pockets to try to find a pen.

After watching for a few minutes as Gurney flapped around trying unsuccessfully to find a writing instrument, the sub editor pulled a pencil from behind his ear and gave it to him.

'Here. You'll soon get into the habit of having several pens and pencils secreted everywhere on yourself.'

'Thank you,' Gurney replied, inspecting the pencil for ear wax and surreptitiously wiping it in his trousers. 'I usually do, but the wife has taken them out for some reason.'

'When you're observing a case in court, whatever you do, don't become Judge and Jury. You are there to report what goes on. Not to create a fantasy around it,' Harry Rolling advised.

'What if it's obviously wrong?' Gurney asked.

'Whether there's a blatant miscarriage of justice or not, you report the facts and only the facts. Do you understand? '

'Yes.'

'It's called Fair, accurate and contemporaneous media reporting of proceedings,' the sub editor explained.

'Oh!' Gurney was taken aback by the jargon and starting to feel the pressure of having to learn a new vocabulary.

'The courts and Parliament have given particular rights to the press to give effect to the open justice principle, so that we can report court proceedings to the wider public, even if the public is excluded. So Gurney, you have a very responsible job to do.'

Gurney beamed. At last somebody was going to take him seriously.

'However, it will be my job to edit all your copy?'

'Oh! So I won't have the freedom...of the press?'

'No, you'll have the opportunity to submit reports.' Rolling confirmed. 'I will be your judge and jury.'

'Oh!' Gurney's enthusiasm dropped a notch.

'Son, you'll soon realise that there is an awful lot of politics in the newspaper business and at times it's like walking on thin ice. Just report the evidence as it's explained. Don't try and glamourize it. You understand?'

'Yes, I think so.'

'Right. Now you need to be familiar with the way courts work and the types of legal restrictions that might apply to the reporting of cases in those courts.'

'Why?' Gurney asked naively.

'Breach of these restrictions can be a criminal offence and can lead to fines. It can also lead to other serious consequences, such as the collapse of an ongoing trial.'

Gurney suddenly felt ill at ease. Unintentionally, he could have the full weight of the law on his shoulders, just for getting a few words wrong.

He recalled how devastated he'd been getting a school detention just for writing a story. Although he had to admit that his fictional article, about the school secretary and the caretaker had been a bit salacious.

The headmaster had called it scandalous and subversive, whereas his peers though it was great and it earned him a lot of 'street cred'.

'If you've never been in a crown court and watched proceedings, you should try to do that,' the sub editor continued, breaking into his daydream.

'No, I've never been to Crown court, only Magistrates. Perhaps I should do that,' he agreed.

He recalled the indignity of being punished with his DIY ASBO at the Magistrates court and the laughter from the public gallery when it was awarded.'

'It's important to get the feel of court procedures. Also you'll soon get used to hanging around with some dodgy characters.'

'Dodgy characters!' Gurney's stomach tensed.

'Well, people who go to court are there usually because they have done something wrong. You'll see a side of society you never knew existed,' Rolling revealed.

'Oh!' Gurney's heart rate increased at the thought of mixing with villains and drug dealers.

'Covering court cases is fascinating and absorbing. On a good day, there will be more real human drama in the hearings, than on any of the main TV channels.'

'Crikey!' Gurney said nervously, as butterflies filled his stomach.

'In theory the rules are straightforward, but they can trip up careless journalists,' the sub editor continued. 'Before a verdict is reached, court reports may cover only what a jury has seen and heard, and must be accurate and fair.'

'Accurate and fair,' Gurney repeated, scrawling the words in his notebook.

'However, there is a vast mountain of words and complexity surrounding court cases that you'll have to sift through, because lawyers often use mysterious and very specific language.'

Gurney was starting to think that this wasn't the job for him. He had only achieved three passes in his GCSE's and none contained the word 'English' in their title.

'If you are reporting a court case, you should make a few simple preparations,' the sub editor advised. 'Begin with a quick call to the court asking for the listing office or the relevant administrative team for that particular court.

For larger, more complex or high-profile cases, it is often worth checking with the Judicial Communications Office.'

'Judicial Communications Office,' Gurney repeated, licking the pencil 'lead'.

'This will usually get you the date, time and type of hearing. You'll also be able to find out what facilities are available for the press and whether any specific reporting restrictions are in place.'

In his haste to capture every single word of advice, Gurney broke the lead in the pencil.

'Sorry, he said awkwardly. 'Have you got a pencil sharper? I appear to have...'

The other had already dug a sharpener out of his waistcoat pocket and proffered it to his new 'apprentice'.

He watched in frustration as Gurney wound the pencil around in the sharpener, peeled a long strip of shavings from the cutting blade and then carelessly broke off the newly exposed lead.

Eventually, after creating a pile of shavings on his lap and reducing the pencil length by an inch, Gurney had a useable pencil.

'OK, ready to go again.'

'My sharpener please,' the Subby demanded, holding out his hand. Gurney retrieved it from his pocket.

'Sorry,' Gurney replied, colouring up and handing the small device back.

'Not returning it to its rightful owner, is how I got it in the first place,' Harry informed him. 'Right! Maintaining contact with the court can also keep you alert to any court orders imposed by judges that can affect what you can report.

This is essential if you are dipping in and out of a case. You should make enquiries with court staff and look out for any orders that might have been posted on the doors of the court.'

'Orders on doors of court,' Gurney wrote, not understanding why he'd done so.

'Remember, that it's your responsibility to find out if

any orders have been made. The consequences of being in breach of those orders can be very serious.'

Gurney squirmed in his seat. 'I didn't realise there was so much to the job.'

'You'll soon get used to the rules. It can be good fun, at times,' Harry added smiling.

'I hope so. It doesn't sound a lot of fun yet.'

'It pays to arrive at court having researched background information on the case. But you need to be very careful, that your research doesn't taint your reporting of the evidence.

And you should not publish your background information, while a case is being heard without asking me.'

Gurney wrote in capital letters, '*SPEAK TO HARRY first*'.

'You can only report what has been produced in court as part of the evidence. Otherwise you're at risk of contempt.

Keep reminding yourself what is background and what is evidence.'

Gurney underlined his notes. '*Background and Evidence separate*'.

'There is a library downstairs that you ought to peruse, to get up to speed with the legal world and how the Courts function.'

'OK thanks. I see I shall be busy. What do I do if I spot something out of a court case that needs further investigation, that perhaps could lead to a scoop?'

'Scoop! You'll be lucky in a Magistrates court!'

'Yes, but if I do?'

'In the unlikely case of uncovering a scoop story, you need to discuss it with me, before you do anything. Is that understood? We can't afford any loose cannons upsetting the judiciary. We've built up a good relationship with the courts.'

'OK understood,' Gurney nodded.

He happily headed off to the library and felt he was on cloud nine. At last, he was a journalist, a reporter.

# CHAPTER 10

A few days later, Gurney arrived at the Magistrate's Court to report on his first hearing.

Already overawed by the judicial atmosphere in the wooden panelled room, he apprehensively eased his way in to the press box, after first taking Iris's advice '*to visit the little boy's room, first.*'

He was very self-conscious as he sat on the hard wooden bench waiting for the case to start. Nervously he fished a notebook and pen out of his pocket, his hand trembled as he revealed its first blank page.

As the court filled with the various players in the case, Gurney's mind was in a whirl. 'Would he be able to capture all the information and accurately report in an unbiased way?' he wondered.

As the clerk read out the name and address of the accused, Gurney, his head in a whirl, struggled to hear and simultaneously write down what was being said.

'Are you John Horatio Stibbins of 22 Flashers Row?' the clerk asked.

'Yes,' the person in the dock replied.

Gurney looked at the creepy looking individual and tried to second guess what he was being accused of and nearly missed the actual charges.

'The accused is charged with five counts of indecent exposure,' the clerk informed the court.

'How do you plead, guilty or not guilty? the clerk asked.

'Guilty,' Stibbins replied.

'The magistrate addressed the lawyers. 'Have you had time to gather your respective evidence?' he quizzed.

'Yes,' the lawyers chorused.

'Right Mr Seapess, let's hear the case for the prosecution.'

The CPS lawyer summarised the background.

'The accused was observed sitting in his car near a school exposing himself.

Following a series of complaints, the police had 'staked' out the road and caught him in the act.

Other young people came forward and further evidence was obtained.

The accused asked for four other instances to be taken in to account. The accused has admitted all charges.'

'Sir, my client has been suffering stress and has had matrimonial problems in the bedroom department.'

'Are you saying he works in a bedding store? If so, what relevance has that got to do with this case?'

'No sir, I believe he has conjugal problems and exposes himself for personal gratification.'

'Yes I note he has been before this court on several other occasions,' the magistrate observed. 'Normally we would retire to consider our verdicts, but it is clear to me that, Stibbins, you are a habitual 'flasher' and in need of help.

I order a report to be compiled and hope that suitable psychiatric and medical treatment will result.'

Sentencing postponed for four weeks.'

'Phew, that wasn't too bad,' Gurney thought, until he

looked at his scribbled notes and realised they were in a hopeless jumble. 'Christ, I hope I can decipher them later on.'

The court emptied ready for the next case and Gurney went to the coffee machine in the reception area and got himself a black coffee.

As he was picking his cup from the dispenser, he overheard a Solicitor talking to a thuggish looking man.

'Put this badge on before you go in to court,' he instructed. 'And I'll see you inside.'

Gurney was puzzled by the conversation and returned to his place in the press box.

The court filled again and Gurney was not surprised to see the thuggish looking man in the dock.

After the usual court preamble, the clerk asked. 'How do you plead?'

'Not Guilty.'

The Prosecution outlined the case of an unprovoked street assault and got permission to show CCTV footage covering the vicious incident.

At the end of the screening the Prosecutor said, 'I think that's fairly clear. The defendant can be seen kicking the victim and is therefore clearly guilty as charged.'

The Solicitor, who had been in reception talking to the thug, stood up and addressed the bench.

'I appreciate how it must seem, but my client was not kicking the man in the head,' the solicitor informed an astonished court.

'But the CCTV images are quite clear,' the Magistrate pointed out.

'With respect your honour...'

'Whereas I appreciate your recognition of my legal rank, I am a magistrate not a judge.'

'Yes, sorry. I thought I was back in Crown Court. What the CCTV pictures do not show, your worship. Is that my client was trying to step on a cigarette butt, that somebody in the crowd had thrown and it was in danger of burning the, so called victim, while he was having a fit.'

'Really?' the Magistrate asked naively.

'Yes, my lud, sorry sir. While he was trying to help the man on the floor, his foot accidentally came in contact with the other persons face as the, so called victim, was convulsing.'

'I see,' the Magistrate said stroking his chin in thought.

'As you can see, from his badge, my client is a member of the tree huggers foundation and is therefore of a gentle and thoughtful nature. '

The Magistrate smiled. 'You know it's amazing how many of your clients are members of our great organisation. You are doing a wonderful job in recruiting them and converting them away from the evils of violence.

I find the defendant not guilty. You are free to leave.'

'No that's not right,' the victim said, leaping up from his seat in the court. 'I've never had a fit in my life.'

'With respect sir, haven't you read the defendant's criminal records? the Prosecution solicitor questioned. 'He is a known villain with dozens of crimes like ABH, GBH, wounding, affray, etc.'

'No sorry. Much too busy to read all that past history stuff. Besides his probation officer says he is better. So that's an end to it. Case dismissed.'

'But...' The victim started to say.

'Anymore from you and I'll have to send you down for contempt. By the way that's a nasty dent you've got in your head.'

'Yes, I think you'll find it's the exact match to the size of his boot.'

Gurney was amazed. It appeared to be an open and shut case. But the tables had been turned and it was obviously a miscarriage of justice.

But he reminded himself that he had to report the facts, not his interpretation.


As Gurney was scribbling his thoughts down, back in the reception area, he noticed that the thuggish guy was talking conspiratorially to his solicitor and saw a thick envelope changing hands.

The thug left court with a smile, no longer wearing the tree hugger's badge.

'Interesting! Perhaps there's more to this than meets the eye. Something to investigate, perhaps?


The court reconvened and the next defendant arrived along with a man carrying a stainless steel catering flask and a small hamper.

The court officials took their places and the chief Magistrate looked at the defendant in the dock and the man who was standing by his side.

'Mr Grime, where is your Solicitor?' he asked.

'Sorry your judgeship I'm not in to prostitutes,' Grime replied, looking puzzled.

The Magistrate looked over the top of his glasses, perplexed. 'Prostitutes!'

'Yes. They're the only solicitors I know,' the defendant answered, innocently.

'Don't be flippant, with me. We are not talking about ladies of the street. We are talking about your legal representatives. Where are they?' the Magistrate demanded.

'Oh! Why didn't you say. Yes, I've brought my barista.'

'The word is Barrister and where pray are they?'

'Here your worship. I'm his barista,' the man holding the catering flask announced. 'Would you like your coffee now or later?'

'Is this some sort of joke?' The Magistrate looked at the Justice clerk who shrugged his shoulders. 'Mr Grime you cannot be serious about having a mere coffee maker here to defend you.'

'Do you mind your Lordship. I am a fully qualified and certified barista,' the coffee champion pointed out. 'I've got my credentials here, if you want to see them?' he said, digging into his back pocket.

'Clear the court. You are in serious contempt. I fine you £300 for your disgraceful behaviour.'

'I was told I had to bring a ...'

'Clerk get this man some legal aid. Clear the court. Adjourned for lunch,' the chief Magistrate ordered.

Gurney couldn't contain himself any longer and burst out laughing.

'Members of the press. Please show respect to the court. Otherwise I will send you down for contempt too.'

Gurney stifled another chuckle and quickly left the courtroom.

'What the hell do I write in this report for Chrissake,' he wondered, but duly scribbled some notes down.

*Serial Flasher Guilty*

*Serial Flasher John Horatio Stibbins has pleaded guilty to exposing himself to school girls and has asked for four other offences to be taken in to account.*

*Magistrates have asked for a psychiatric report before sentencing.*

*A good Samaritan act mistaken for violent affray.*

*Today a member of the Tree huggers was found not guilty of violent affray. A career thug has been acquitted of kicking a man in the head because he claims to have been stamping on a cigarette butt to save him from further injury, whilst the other was having a fit.*

*Magistrate's heavy workload prevents him from reading previous case papers.*

*Coffee costa lot for Mr Grime,*

*Charged with cycling on the pavement while intoxicated. Mr Grime brought the court into contempt as his legal team consisted of a fully qualified barista rather than a barrister.*

*The magistrate took exception to the insult to the court and fined him £300. He is yet to plead on his original charges and having upset the magistrate he is unlikely to get away with a light fine.*

If that was the morning session. Roll on this afternoon.'

# CHAPTER 11

'The black dog was in front of me. Its eyes a demonic red,' the lorry driver explained.

'A black dog?' the prosecutor repeated, cynically.

'Yes. It was staring at me. Its eyes seemed to penetrate my very soul.' He said dramatically. 'I was hypnotised by it. I couldn't look away. All the time I was getting closer to it. It was getting bigger and bigger.'

The lorry driver banged on the top of the wooden dock to emphasise his point causing Gurney to 'jump'.

The afternoon session had started with a case of dangerous driving involving a lorry crash which immediately captured Gurney's undivided attention.

It was the cause of the tailback that he had encountered when he, Iris and Mother-In-Law were returning from Swansea in the now scrapped Metro.

'It was drooling a green slime through its open mouth,' the driver continued. 'My headlights reflected off its sharp fangs.'

'Really?' the prosecutor remarked sceptically.

'And then suddenly it changed shape. It became a little toddler with long blonde hair.'

'Your worship. Do we have to listen to this fantasy?' asked the prosecutor.

'Yes, it's a good story. Even if it isn't true. Carry on.'

'I braked as hard as I could and tried to steer around

her but the lorry jack-knifed and it ran off the road and into a ditch.'

'And then?'

'I was shitting myself, if you'll pardon the expression. Fortunately the bushes slowed me down before I hit the tree,' the lorry driver said, all in a rush.

'Well the later part of your story is well photographed. However, the cause is debateable.'

'I'd heard about the black dog on this part of the motorway before,' the driver volunteered, 'But I thought it was a load of rubbish. But now I've seen it for myself.'

'So did you hit this...this mythical creature?' the Magistrate asked.

'No sir. When I went back to see if I'd hit anything, there was nothing to be found.'

'And a subsequent search by the rescue services failed to find anything either,' the prosecutor added, dismissively.

Gurney frantically scribbled the lorry driver's statement until he got cramp in his hand. 'Oh shit, that hurts,' he said shaking his hand to ease the muscle spasm. Unfortunately his gestures attracted the attention of the Chief Magistrate.

'Members of the press are you trying to signal the defendant?' he demanded. 'If you are, you are in contempt.'

'No, Sir. I've got cramp in my hand,' Gurney replied, hoarsely.

'You are a distraction to the court. Either desist or leave.'

'I...I'd like to stay Sir, if I may Sir,' Gurney pleaded.

'I shall keep my eye on you and if there is any other interruption you will be ejected. Is that understood?'

'Yes Sir, thank you Sir,' Gurney grovelled.

'Carry on with the case,' the Magistrate instructed the prosecutor.

'A black dog!' the prosecutor repeated, slowly, emphasising his words.

'Yes sir. I wonder if it was one that was killed along there sometime in the past and it's the dog's ghost that's haunting the motorway?'

'I think we've heard enough of this fictional story. I put it to you that you fell asleep at the wheel.' The prosecutor, suggested.

'No sir.'

'Or perhaps you were using your mobile?'

'No. Check the records if you like,' the lorry driver suggested.

'It was surprising that your tachograph seemed to have somehow got damaged and was unreadable,' the prosecutor revealed.

'Well that was the crash that did that,' the driver explained.

'Although your dashboard was virtually undamaged!'

'Yes, that's right.'

'So we can't tell how long you'd been driving for?' the Magistrate asked.

'No sir. I don't know how it happened. It might have been the black dog coming into the cab and chewing it while I was unconscious,' the driver desperately grasped for an explanation.

'I suggest to you that there was no black dog. And you simply fell asleep at the wheel,' the solicitor for the prosecution proposed.

'No I was awake, honest.'

'No further questions your Worship.

'Mr Dee?'

'Nothing further.'

'Right, I think we've all seen through your, frankly, unbelievable story and through your own incompetence. I fine you £1,000 and put six points on your licence.'

'Six points! But that means that I've topped the number of points I can have on my licence and I've lost my livelihood.'

'Blame it on the black dog, not me,' the Magistrate said, smirking at his own wit, as he stood.

In the public gallery a petite woman smiled at the verdict. 'Nice to witness the successful outcome of the fruits of our labours,' she thought.

As they funnelled out of the courtroom, the woman forced her way in front of Gurney as he was trying to catch up with the disgruntled lorry driver.

At first he thought she was a child, due to her short stature, and was going to tell her off, until she turned and gave him a withering look.

Consequently, he had to chase after the man and eventually caught him up in the car park.

'Excuse me sir. My name is Gurney Leafmould. I'm from the local paper.'

The lorry driver ignored Gurney and strode off, clearly annoyed at the Magistrate's judgement.

'Sir could I just talk to you...about the black dog?'

'No you can't. Now bugger off.'

'Perhaps I can help you prove that there is actually a black dog and get your licence returned? I believe there have been a lot of crashes on that stretch of the motorway.'

The lorry driver stopped and looked around furtively. He put his face into Gurney's.

'Look sunshine. I suggest you keep your nose out of my business and leave the dog story alone.'

With that he turned on his heel and left a puzzled Gurney mouthing like a goldfish.

# CHAPTER 12

Gurney returned to the newspaper building and went to the sub editor's office. The veteran journalist looked up from scribbling over a printed page as he entered.

'Oh, hello Gurney. Back so soon? Well, how was your first day in court?'

'Strange Harry, very strange,' Gurney admitted.

'Grab a chair and let's talk. Did you want a cuppa?'

'No, I'm fine, thanks,' Gurney replied, having made multiple trips to the courtroom loo.

'Be a dear and pour me one, the newspaper man asked. 'There should still be tea in the pot.'

Gurney tested the temperature of a small teapot and poured some tea into a heavily stained mug.

'So why was it strange?' Harry asked.

Gurney duly gave the tea to Rolling before finally sitting down. 'There was this Flasher,' he said.

'Oh, Horatio! Doing his semaphore again was he?' Rolling asked.

'You know him?' Gurney quizzed.

'Yes. He's a regular. Psychiatric reports?'

'Yes.'

'Oh well, nothing's changed there then.'

'What an eye opener though!' Gurney said, collapsing into the chair.

'Don't be taken in with all the hard luck stories you'll

hear in court either,' the veteran newspaperman advised. 'Just remember, that the prisons are full of supposed innocent people...And people lie when giving evidence as well.'

'No they can't do that, they're under oath!' Gurney said, astounded at Harry's revelation.

'Oh don't be so naive. If they can get away with it by telling a lie, they will. It's only human nature after all.'

'But they swear on the bible,' Gurney persisted.

'Most people are atheists anyway and the bible is just another book, which means nothing to them.' Rolling explained.

'But if they don't have any moral conscience, then they can lie about anything.'

'And of course they do,' the newspaper man revealed.

'Oh that's terrible.' Gurney was astounded that the sacred principle of swearing on oath was considered to be an irrelevant gesture by some people.

'Welcome to the real world, sunshine,' the sub editor said, swigging some of his tea.

'Well it does seem that you need the right legal team batting for you,' Gurney declared.

'What do you mean?'

'There was one bloke who was obviously guilty but was found innocent because his lawyer told some 'cock and bull' story about protecting a man from a cigarette butt. When in reality, he was kicking seven shades of S H one T out of the victim.'

'I shouldn't worry about it. Don't forget. You're just there to report the facts, not to become Judge and Jury,' Harry reminded him.

'Yeah but this guy was obviously guilty. The CCTV footage was indisputable.'

'Clearly the Magistrates didn't think so, if he was found not guilty.'

'The solicitor gave the man a badge just before he went in to the court. Something to do with an organisation called tree huggers, I think,' Gurney persisted.

'Yes I've heard of similar instances of the old boys network and secret organisations.'

'I reckon it's one of those. There's definitely something strange going on with this tree hugger lark, with a verdict like that, the Magistrate is obviously a member.'

'Forget it Gurney. You've got a lot to learn,' the veteran newspaper man counselled.

'But I reckon there could be a scoop there, if I dug around,' Gurney persisted.

'Don't stick your nose in where it's not wanted.' Rolling warned. 'There are powerful forces out there, which you don't know anything about.'

'OK, if you say so,' Gurney said, resignedly.

'Anything else?'

'Then there was this lorry driver that crashed on the motorway.'

'Don't tell me, he swerved to miss a black dog which ran out in front of him?' Harry suggested.

'How did you know that?' Gurney said in surprise.

'Son, that's the lorry drivers' favourite excuse, when they fall asleep at the wheel.'

'Really?'

'The 'black dog story' is well known. Ask any of the authorities who deal with the chaos surrounding road traffic collisions,' the sub editor suggested.

'Oh,' Gurney shook his head in disbelief at this revelation of people's devious antics.

'It's never the drivers fault. They crash trying to avoid the 'dog', but it runs away, so no-one has actually ever seen one,' Harry continued.

'Right!'

'It's become a bit of a joke amongst the rescue services. The drivers never admit falling asleep. But strangely all the incidents happen at night.'

'Yes, you're right. This happened at night too. The driver was so convinced about it,' Gurney confirmed.

'Convinced or convincing - no it's all fiction. It's designed to help them keep their licence,' the sub editor informed him.

'OK. Well I suppose I ought to write up my report. How many column inches have I got?'

'That's a bedroom secret between you and your wife,' Harry joked.

Gurney blushed. 'I didn't mean...you know...that...I meant...'

'Yes I know. I was only pulling your leg. Let me have a look at your notebook.'

'It's only in rough at the moment,' Gurney confessed.

'That's OK, I can usually read all manner of handwriting,' the seasoned newspaper man said.

Gurney apprehensively handed his notebook to the sub editor.

'Blimey, I thought my handwriting was bad. What does this say?' the other asked studying Gurney's report.

*'Coffee costa lot for Mr Grime,'* Gurney read.

'So you've developed your own shorthand?'

'No, that's how I usually write,' Gurney admitted.

'In scribble!'

'Yes if you say so.'

'You'll have to read it to me,' Harry said, and handed back the notebook.

Gurney read the notes from the first case.

'Not newsworthy. Next!'

Gurney received the same responses to all his story lines.

'We won't go with any of your stories, but write them up anyway. Just be aware though, that the locals aren't up to reading tabloid headlines.'

Gurney's excitement leaked out of him, his ego crushed like a deflated balloon.

'Remember. Only the facts that were presented in court,' Harry reminded him.

'OK.'

'We don't want to be barred from the court,' Rolling reminded him.

'Right,' Gurney agreed, unenthusiastically.

As he made his way back to his desk Gurney couldn't get the 'black dog' story out of his head.

'Surely it must be true. The lorry driver was so convincing. Perhaps I ought to investigate further', he thought to himself. 'Yes, he would dig further into it,' he decided. Without telling anyone else what he was up to.

# CHAPTER 13

After it had been irritating him for a full minute, the editor finally decided to answer the phone and barked his name into the receiver.

'MOSS.'

'Do you know that's the third set of cones they've put out along the M50 and I haven't seen anyone working there.' Delores Eyes grumbled.

'Who is this?' the editor demanded.

'How soon you forget the pleasures of the past,' the old woman reminded him.

Then the 'penny dropped'. 'Oh hello Delores. How nice to hear from you again so soon,' the editor lied, putting his hand over the receiver and muttered. 'You evil bitch.'

'Don't you try to sweet talk me,' the old lady said, unaware of his disparaging comment.

'Yes I know those cones are a piggin nuisance but why are you telling me about them? I haven't got time to waste talking about trivia. I've got a...'

'I know. You've got a newspaper to run.'

'Exactly. So goodbye.'

Undeterred, Delores persisted, 'well if you ask me, someone should do something about it. It's scandalous.'

Moss sighed, 'I suggest you ring the Ministry of Transport or the Highways people. I'm sorry but I need to get on.'

'It slows everything down. It's a national disgrace. You should be doing something about it,' she dictated.

'I hardly think that it's likely to sell newspapers. I mean there are millions of cones scattered up and down all the motorways every day,' the editor said, clearly irritated. 'Is that all you're ringing me about?'

'In my view, it's very important. The country is grinding to a halt.'

'Yes, so you've said. Now look Delores, I've already got your son-in-law employment. What more do you want?'

'I want someone in power to sort out the scandalous situation with these cones,' she said vociferously.

'As much as I'm flattered by your faith in my abilities, there's not too much we can do about it. I'm sorry. I'm in the newspaper business, not the road business. Try Highways England,' the editor advocated.

'The least you could do is to ask the buggers who are putting out the cones why they're doing it,' she demanded, crossly. 'Ask them what they're up to... think of it as a public service. You call yourself a crusading newspaper. So crusade.'

'Look. I'm sorry to tell you but, we put away our suits of armour a long time ago,' he said, trying to remain calm.

'What the hell are you talking about, armour?' Delores Eyes puzzled.

'The newspaper doesn't have 'knights on horses', riding off to 'right the wrong' anymore. That's what I'm talking about. We simply don't have the staff,' Gordon Moss said exasperated.

'Well find somebody who can sort it. Or I make a call,' the old woman threatened.

'A call?' he queried.

'Yes. To the owner,' she stated, tweaking his Achilles heel again.

'Oh, for heavens sake. This is ridiculous.'

'I'm sure that's what the newspaper owner thought when he saw his 'decapitated' mini, don't you?'

'Well…If I must,' he capitulated. 'I'll send one of my reporters out and we'll see what we can find. We'll let you know.'

'Thank you. I knew you'd see sense,' Delores Eyes beamed at her victory.

'But this is the final time I'll do anything for you,' he warned.

'No, I don't agree. I think like any 'fairy', you can grant me at least three wishes.'

'Oh God! Don't say you've still got pictures of me in that fairy costume?' he queried, realising that she was alluding further blackmail.

'Of course. And you look so delightful,' she confirmed.

'It was a Christmas fancy dress party, for Chrissake.'

'But other people don't know that. Goodbye Gordon.'

The editor slammed down the receiver. 'Bitch!' he shouted. 'I could do without this hassle from my past.'

Angrily he stabbed the loud-speaker button on his phone and called the reporter's room.

'Reporters,' came back the response.

'Who's free? I've got a job for somebody.'

'Sorry boss they're all out. With the exception of Leafmould that is,' he corrected himself.

'Put him on,' the editor demanded.

'He's in the loo. Do you want me to get him to call you?'

'No. Tell him to get his sorry arse up here when he surfaces.'

'Surfaces is about right. Christ he spends more time in the bog than he does at his desk. We'll either have to move his desk into the toilet or give him a commode instead of a swivel chair.'

'Yes I know. He's got a 'urological condition'. Tell him. My office. Asap.'

'OK.'

The editor flipped the loud-speaker button off and slumped back heavily in his chair, angry at being ordered around by the spectre from his sensuous past.

A few moments later, and obviously having run up the stairs, a breathless Leafmould stood outside the editor's 'office'.

He quickly polished his toe caps on the back of each trouser leg and dusted the dandruff off his shoulders.

He knocked quietly on the side of the partition that made up the editor's ''pigpen'.

His knock went unheard, for there was no invitation to enter.

He knocked again with a little more force and waited. Still nothing.

Finally he decided to enter but collided with the editor's flabby stomach as he was making his way out.

'Didn't you hear me say come in?' he barked.

'Sorry sir. I didn't.'

'Whatever.'

Leafmould stood like a rabbit in the headlights, mesmerised by being in the presence of the great man. Finally he galvanised himself into action and followed the editor back in, already wrong footed by the incident.

'I haven't got time to faff around. What are you doing at the moment?'

'I...I'm finishing off yesterday's court report, sir.'

'How long will that take you?'

'Well about another two hours, I guess.'

'Make it an hour and get out to the M 50. I've had a call from your Mother-In-Law,' the editor informed Gurney.

'Oh! Has she broken down?'

'Unfortunately not. She's whining about cones on the motorway. I want to know what's happening with the motorway work around this coned off area and why no-one appears to be working there. Do you understand?' Gordon Moss asked.

'Yes Sir, I think so.' Gurney confirmed.

'Your Mother-In-Law, pain-in-the-ass, reckons they keep putting out cones and don't do any work before they move them again. Get out there and give me a short article, so I can get her off my back,' the editor directed.

Leafmould was overawed by being given a personal mission by the editor himself. He hoped that the roaring in his ears and wobbling room, generated by the nearness of this 'deity' would soon subside.

'Well go on then. What are you hanging about for?' the editor demanded.

'N...nothing. Thank you Mr Moss, sir. I'm on to it. Right away.'

Gurney hurtled down the stairs to his desk and completed his court report.

Consequently, his hurried and much précised court report, helped at least one person go through the judicial system without being publically castigated for his bad behaviour.

His report of Stubbins, rather than Stibbins, the local librarian, meant that his misdemeanour was safe from public disclosure until his next court appearance for 'flashing'.

Leafmould's inability to spell the surname correctly, meant that Stibbins was able to deny previous reports of the court appearance and maintain his job. Consequently, he was still exposing but not yet exposed.

# CHAPTER 14

As he wrote up his report, his gaze was drawn to the 'black dog' lorry driver's name and address that he'd written down in his notebook.

'Now that accident was on the M50 too, perhaps I can kill two birds with one visit,' he thought. 'I could go and have a look at the crash site. It can't be too far away from where we had our prang either?'

'The editor gave me an hour, so I've got time,' he thought, checking his watch. 'Yes, another fifteen minutes.'

He studied the details in notebook again.

'I wonder. If I call the lorry driver now, he might have calmed down and will speak to me...surely if these 'black dog' incidents are happening all over the country, there's got to be something behind it? It can't just be a well-known, 'get out of jail free' excuse that's being perpetuated nationally, can it?'

Gurney used several internet address sites until he found the lorry driver's telephone number and decided to call him.

The phone rang out for some time before it was eventually answered.

'Yes?' came the blunt response.

'I...are you Mr Stone. Mike Stone who appeared in court recently?'

'What if I am? I don't take cold calls. Now piss off.'

'Don't hang up, please. I'm the journalist from court the other day and I'd...'

'I told you to keep your nose out of my business, didn't I?'

'Well yes. But I actually believe your story about the 'black dog', and I'd like to help.'

'Help? Help yourself more like.'

'No, if we can identify something going on, we can...'

'Spread more lies in your newspaper and make me look like even more like a friggin fool,' the driver retorted.

'No I promise. If you could tell me again what happened and exactly where, I could start investigating from there.'

'Why do you want to help me? What's in it for you?' Mike Stone asked suspiciously.

'Well I'm new at this job and I want to show the boss what I can do.'

'I'm not so sure I want to help a 'creep ass' then.'

'Look. If I can discover some circumstances which support your version, you might even be able to overturn the judgement and get your licence back.'

'I suppose anything's worth a try,' the lorry driver agreed.

'Thanks. You won't regret it.' Gurney encouraged. 'Now, just before you crashed, what can you remember?'

'Let me think now... It was dark, obviously. There are no lights on that bit of the motorway. The traffic was light...Umm.'

'The weather?'

'Dry and still as far as I can recall.'

'Did you see anything as you approached the place where you crashed?'

'I vaguely remember seeing some vehicles on the hard shoulder... in a coned off area.'

'Do you know what type of vehicles they were?'

'I don't know. I didn't take that much notice. Road repair vehicles, I suppose. No, come to think of it, there was a tanker type vehicle there. An on-site refuelling bowser I presume.'

'When did you see the black dog?'

'I think it was just before the bowser. There were several foggy patches and at first I thought it was a fox or badger in the road. Well I don't stop for them, they're legitimate roadkill targets.'

'Oh how awful!' Gurney paled at the thought of the wanton slaughter.

'No it ain't. It's the law of the jungle. Food for the crows and magpies.'

'Oh dear,' Gurney's sensitivities made him feel queasy.

'Well it's too dangerous to suddenly brake anyway. Trying to avoid them might even end up causing an accident,' the driver continued.

'Yes of course,' Gurney agreed. Although, the lorry driver clearly didn't realise the irony of his words.

'As I said, there was some fog and then the black dog with his scary red eyes appeared.'

'What did you do?' Gurney asked, trying to imagine the scene.

'I kept straight on but eased up a bit. I started braking, nothing too hard.'

'Tyres weren't locked and smoking?'

'No. But then the dog changed. It got bigger and bigger and then suddenly, as god is my witness, it changed to a little toddler. That was when I locked everything up and ended up going off the road. I remember feeling a bit light headed.'

'Perhaps that was the shock?' Gurney suggested.

'Suppose it could have been,' the driver agreed.

'What happened then?'

'I was knocked unconscious but came round just as another lorry arrived.'

'Were you badly hurt?'

'No. I had a muzzy head as though I'd been having a session.'

'And had you?' Gurney probed, feeling brave.

'Don't be so daft. I value my licence too much.' Then the lorry driver remembered his current predicament. 'I used to value it, I should say,' he said miserably.

'Yes of course, the additional points on your licence,' Gurney said unhelpfully.

'So how does this all help me?' the driver asked.

'I'm not sure. I...I'll do some investigations and get back to you,' Gurney informed him.

'When?'

'I can't say. Sorry.'

'The accident investigators couldn't find anything. So why do you think you can?' the driver queried.

'I don't know, but I'm going to try,' Gurney promised.

'Well that was a bloody waste of time telling you all about that then, wasn't it?' the lorry driver said angrily.

'No...no, that has been really helpful,' Gurney said, trying to sound confident. But in truth, he wasn't sure what he would do with the information either.

'I'll be in touch.'

He quickly hung up and headed out for the M50, wondering what he'd find, if anything.

# CHAPTER 15

Gurney drove to the site of the lorry driver's crash on the motorway, apprehensive about what he was likely find.

He'd established that the crash site was near the junction 2 slip road exit which led to a road bridge spanning the busy motorway.

It was midday as he pulled on to the hard shoulder, his sudden manoeuvre attracting a blaring horn from the surprised driver behind him, as he slowed.

Nervously he brought his van to a halt, his vehicle rocking from the wall of displaced air, as cars and huge juggernauts thundered by just a few feet away.

He had bought the 1960s Ford Thames van as a stop gap, until the insurance was sorted out on the multivehicle accident involving his metro.

He put his hazard warning lights on, checked his rear view mirror, to find a gap in the traffic and quickly stepped out.

He ran to the front of his vehicle in the faint hope that if anything careered off the motorway, it would hit the van first and not him.

He wasn't sure what he was looking for, because it was now several months since the lorry driver's accident.

Perhaps he might find some paw prints or black fur on the fence, that might indicate evidence that the 'black dog' had been in the area, he really didn't know.

Gurney was just stooping down and examining a piece of fencing as he heard a car pull up behind his.

Quickly he stood up and his heart skipped a beat, as he saw a police patrol car, with its flashing blue lights, on the hard shoulder.

'Oh god, now I'm in for it.'

A stern looking policeman, wearing a high visibility jacket, approached him.

'Have we got a problem sir?' the policeman asked.

'Err no...no not really,' Gurney mumbled.

'You weren't going to use the hard shoulder as a toilet were you?'

'No officer, I was looking for something. You see I'm a journalist,' he said, grabbing the ID badge, from the lanyard around his neck.

'You're what?' the policeman shouted over the noise of the traffic. 'I think you'd better come and sit in our car,' he said, leading Gurney to the back of the patrol car and opening the rear passenger door.

'Sit in there please sir, he said, indicating the back seat. 'Mind your head.'

Gurney stepped in and the policeman closed the door and got into the front passenger seat.

'Has your car broken down?'

'No, I ...'

'You realise you are committing an offence by stopping there?

'Sorry I...'

'What were you doing then?

'Well I...'

'You could have got off the motorway, it's only two hundred yards to the slip road.'

'Yes, sorry but...'

'We'd better have some details.' The policeman pulled out his notebook. 'Name?'

Gurney struggled to speak, mouth fear dried. 'Umm…Leafmould. Gurney Leafmould.'

'Leafmould? You got to be joking. What sort of name is that?'

'Yes, it's my name,' Gurney confirmed.

'If you're lying, we'll soon find out your true identity,' the policeman informed him firmly.

'Honest,' Gurney said, starting to panic.

The police driver confirmed it. 'Yes, the van is registered to an Iris Leafmould, but he's on the insurance.'

'Thanks. But what a strange name!'

'I suppose it is,' Gurney agreed, feeling more confident.' People often say that. But I've lived with it all my life, so I don't take notice anymore.'

'Where does it come from?' the policeman queried.

Gurney had researched the history of the family name whilst waiting for a job. His nervousness now turned to verbal diarrhoea.

'The Leafmoulds' were an ancient tribe, who gathered fallen leaves to help grow food to feed the family. They found the technique of turning leaf mould into a fertiliser, which improved the crop.'

'Really?'

'Yes. And in those days, as one's name tended to reflect one's occupation, like people who made gaiters became known as the Gait family. My family were therefore known as the Leafmoulds.'

'Interesting. Now about you stopping on the….'

But Gurney was now into his story.

'Their food grew extremely well, much to the envy of

all their neighbours, who pleaded for them to tell how they were doing it. But rather than pass on the secret of their successful food production, the Leafmoulds decided to sell the leaf fertiliser instead. '

'Well good for them now…' the policeman tried again.

By now Gurney was in full throttle. 'So having identified the commercial aspects of the stuff, they set up a horticulturist business and made their living from supplying the best fertiliser in the country.'

'Mr Leafmould, we don't have time for…'

But Gurney was deaf to the policeman's intervention.

'The gardeners in the castles got to hear of it and soon the Leafmoulds were supplying leaf fertiliser to a succession of the ruling classes. The business thrived over the many centuries.'

'Yes well thank you for that comprehensive description. Now about you stopping…'

But Gurney was deeply into his story and again ignored the policeman.

'The family had also perfected the distillation of a very, very alcoholic spirit derived from the same tree leaves - different trees provided different flavours and so they had a wide range that appealed to many tastes.

Unfortunately the head of the house, who became the 'master spirit maker', became addicted to the leaf elixir, named very aptly, 'The spirit of the tree'.'

'Not a very original name that, was it?' the driver observed.

'Mr Leafmould. We've heard enough thank you. Now stop,' the other policeman demanded.

But Gurney's 'tape was running' and he continued blissfully unaware that the policeman was very irritated and stroking the 'pepper spray' container on his belt.

'He deserted the fertiliser business, which subsequently folded, and allowed the competition to take over their former Royal 'appointments'.

In his intoxicated state the 'spirit maker' would entertain the customers in the local ale houses, by pulling 'funny faces'. The high sugar content of the spirt had rotted his teeth, so he was able to contract and distort his toothless face into many strange shapes.'

'No stop,' the irritated policeman shouted.

'Just let him get on with it,' the police driver suggested, trying to calm his colleague. 'He'll finish in a minute I'm sure.'

Gurney continued anyway. 'While he was contorting his face, he would make strange groaning noises which, because of the shape of his mouth sounded like 'gurn'... His reputation spread far and wide and people would buy him drinks to get him to perform his facial gymnastics. Consequently, he became known at the 'gurnee' one.

Which, because of his new found reputation, he adopted the name for his family. This name was passed on from generation to generation - hence my name Gurney Leafmould.'

# CHAPTER 16

The policemen had listened with growing irritation to Gurney's long story about his family name and had now become officious.

'Yes, yes, very interesting. But what the hell are you doing risking your life stopping on the motorway, if your vehicle is OK?'

'I'm a journalist,' Gurney insisted.

'So you've said. But that doesn't give you the right to contravene traffic laws,' the policeman pointed out.

'I'm investigating for a court case,' Gurney advised them, proudly.

'An investigative journalist eh?' the police driver observed.

Gurney quite liked the description. 'An investigative journalist!' He ran the title around his mind. It sounded good. Much better than a court reporter.

'Yes. That's what I am,' he beamed. 'An invest - a - gate - tive - journalist,' he said, stumbling over the words. 'Yes one of those.'

'And you're investigating what?'

'The black dog.'

'The black dog! Oh that load of old tosh. You know it's a myth, right?' the policeman informed him.

'I'm not sure that it is.' Gurney said, feeling intellectually superior. 'I mean there might be some truth behind it.'

'The truth behind it is, that people fall asleep at the wheel or are too busy on their mobiles instead of concentrating on the road,' the policeman reposted. 'They make up excuses for their bad driving by blaming this mythical black dog.'

The police driver had been pushing buttons on his dashboard mounted computer and said. 'I see from our records that you are well known to us.'

Gurney was taken aback by the revelation. 'Known to you?' he queried.

'Public nuisance; Asbo from the utilities...ring a bell?'

'Yes, but that was when I was doing DIY. I had a few...err...a few challenges.'

'So I can see. Demolished your own house; set fire to an old ladies house.'

'But that's all in the past. I don't do DIY anymore. My wife has banned me from ever doing it again.'

'So you've had a career change and now you're causing us grief.'

'Well, no not really. I mean...'

The policemen's attention was suddenly drawn to a speeding car which zoomed past in the third lane.

'About a 100 mph, what do you reckon?' he said to his colleague.

'And the rest. Right Mr Leafmould, count yourself lucky this time. But don't let us find you doing this investigative stuff on the hard shoulder again. Right?'

'Right.'

'Out you get then. We've got a speed ace to stop.'

Gurney stepped out of the police car and within seconds it reversed back at speed and accelerated away narrowly missing his van as it pulled back on to the carriageway. Its two tone siren startled Gurney, as it cut its way back through the traffic.

Gurney had another quick look around on the hard shoulder but could see nothing apart from discarded chocolate wrappers and battered drinks cans, so he climbed back into his van and drove along the hard shoulder and up the 'slip road' on to the road bridge, where he parked and got out.

'Now where would a dog come from along here?' he wondered.

'From my vantage point here, I can see the crash site quite clearly. If I take a few photos, perhaps I can analyse them back at the office. I might be able to spot something.'

Whilst he was engrossed in taking the photos, he was unaware of the effect that his presence had on the speeding motorway traffic approaching the bridge.

The leading car of a group of motorists suddenly spotted Gurney with the camera in his hand and assumed it was a speed trap.

The driver lifted off the accelerator in the hope that the car would lose enough speed before it came within range of the camera.

Because of the absence of brake lights, the driver of the car behind, who was travelling much too close, didn't realise it was decelerating. Consequently, he failed to react to the slowing car with the inevitable consequence, and 'rear ended it'.

Although the collision was relatively low speed, it knocked off his own car's bumper, which, unfettered skipped and skidded along the motorway at a great rate of knots.

Cars tyres screeched as other drivers fought to avoid the errant bumper.

'God I'm glad I moved when I did,' Gurney thought. 'I could have been involved in that lot,' little realising that he had actually been the catalyst for it anyway.

As he bent down to take the photos through the railings of the bridge, he spotted a small electrical socket.

'Interesting! I wonder what gets plugged in to that?' he thought.

'Perhaps it's used for mobile speed cameras. It can't be one of those motion sensor cameras. They're permanently wired in, by the look of it.

Oh well, I don't suppose it's important.'

Little did he know, that he had just stumbled on a clue to identify the mystery of the legendary black dog.

'I'll just have a wander to see if there are any paw prints anywhere near here and then I ought to go and look at these cones,' he thought to himself. 'I think they're nearby.'

He couldn't see the two cars that had pulled up on the hard shoulder nearby as the driver's swopped insurance details.

The lady driver of the vintage Ford Prefect was being very 'unladylike' as she tongue lashed the young driver of the Vauxhall Zafira that had run into the back of her.

Satisfied that he had complied with his legal obligation, the Zafira driver dashed back to his car, glad to get away from the verbal barrage of oaths and insults from the grey haired old lady. So keen to get away too, that the old woman's hand gestures were lost on the fleeing driver.

# CHAPTER 17

Gurney found the idea of investigating the 'black dog' story much more exciting than his directive to check out the cone chaos, even though it had come from the editor himself.

Nevertheless, having found nothing else to support the black dog's presence, he left the bridge and set off to investigate Mother-In-Law's grouse about the cones.

He soon arrived at another road bridge crossing the motorway, where on the westbound carriageway he could see warning signs indicating 'road works ahead half mile'.

'Ah, this looks like it,' he thought. 'Presumably this is the start of the area where one lane has been coned off.'

He drove along the old road that ran parallel with the motorway and it wasn't long before he found the end of a line of stationary traffic.

He followed the queue of vehicles towards the front where he found the cause of the blockage.

The traffic was being diverted from two lanes into a single lane and then on to the hard shoulder.

Amidst all the cones signs and traffic chaos, there were no workers or any indication of work being undertaken.

Parking the van in a muddy layby, he took the opportunity to 'visit the bushes'. Having made himself more 'comfortable', he wandered along the lane overlooking the motorway, to see if he could see what was going on. There wasn't anything that he could see that was at all obvious.

He walked a few hundred yards parallel to the now slowly moving traffic and almost missed them.

For just as he was deciding that it was all of a waste of time, two white vans with flashing amber lights pulled up on the hard shoulder of the opposite, eastbound, carriageway.

Eight men, dressed in hi-visibility jackets and trousers disgorged from the vehicles and immediately started revealing previously covered road signs to indicate road narrowing.

With military precision, cones that had been blocking the westbound carriageway were repositioned on to the hard shoulder but cones on the eastbound hard shoulder were now moved to restrict the width of the carriageway.

Leafmould watched with interest.

'Somebody will get a bollocking for that,' he thought. 'They'd obviously put the cones out on the wrong carriageway earlier.'

Slowly the westbound traffic started moving again, in spite of a few minor 'shunts', that were left stranded on the hard shoulder.

Within thirty minutes the transition was completed and the 'cone movers' duly jumped back into their vans and moved off leaving the traffic on the eastbound carriageway grinding to a halt.

'How bizarre,' Gurney thought. 'I wonder if I can identify the contractor from their vehicle signwriting,' he said to himself, screwing is eyes up.

'What's that written on the side of the van? 'Highway Maintenance! That doesn't give much away. Perhaps I could track them down by their registration numbers? he wondered.

No good,' he said, peering at the disappearing vehicles. 'They're almost unreadable. The number plates appear to be covered with some reddish coloured mud.'

Leafmould recorded the curious goings on in his note book and added the timings as an afterthought.

'I suppose I ought to wait and see if anybody else is going to turn up to start work now,' he thought. 'No, sod it! I've already been here two hours, it's getting late. I'll come back tomorrow and see what they're up to.

Although, I suppose I ought to call the editor to let him know, that at least I'm here.'

He took his phone from his pocket and soon realised the battery was flat.

'Damn! I haven't got my power lead with me either. Oh well, I'll have to ring him later. I hope he isn't waiting for me to call. Anyway, there's nothing really to report,' he thought, seeking to ease his conscience.

# CHAPTER 18

After his fruitless vigil on the motorway, Gurney returned home to be greeted by a smiling Iris at the front door.

'Well what do you think? she asked, as he stepped into the hallway.

'What do I think of what?' he asked puzzled.

Then Gurney spotted the new addition to the house. 'What's that on the wall?' he demanded.

'It's an aerial picture of our old house, before you demolished it. Mother found it somewhere. Nice isn't it?'

'How come it's hanging up? There wasn't a picture there before!'

'Oh that. I put a rawlplug in the wall and hung it myself.'

'How?'

'I used your tools.'

'You had better not damaged them,' Gurney said, possessively.

'I was surprised how easy it was to do, considering all the fuss and mess that you usually make.'

'Yes, whatever.' Gurney was about to tell her that it was beginner's luck, but decided he was too tired to get in to an argument.

'Anyway, how did it go?' Iris asked enthusiastically.

'How did what go?' he wondered, tired from his day.

'Your day! Anything exciting happen in court?' she probed.

'I haven't been to court today.' Gurney informed her. 'I've been watching motorway mayhem and traffic cones.'

'You've been doing what? Have you been sacked?' she asked anxiously.

'No. I'm still working for the newspaper. Remember I told you about the black dog incident?'

'Yes, the lorry crash. And you thought we'd got caught in the tailback.' Iris confirmed.

'Well, the editor called me in and told me your mother had been bending his ear about the constant roadworks on the M50.' Gurney explained.

'Mother! What's she up to now?' Iris pondered.

'Yes, your mother. Anyway he sent me to find out what was happening.'

'But what's that got to do with the black dog?'

'Well, while I was out there, I investigated the scene of the lorry crash as well. I tell you, it's a nightmare on that motorway.'

'What do you mean?'

'In the brief time that I was there, there was an accident. I was lucky not to have been involved. But, fortunately, the police had earlier told me to get off the motorway.'

'The police! Oh Gurney. Now what have you been up to?' Iris said despairingly.

'Nothing. I was just looking for evidence about the black dog, that's all.'

'On the busy motorway!'

'Yes, it's flipping dangerous. Anyway, they got me off the motorway just in time.'

'Did you find anything?'

'No. The police reckoned I wouldn't either. They said the black dog was all a myth. But they did recognise me as an investigative journalist,' he said, proudly.

'So what's this got to do with mother?'

'Oh yes. Apparently she told the editor that every time she's gone through those roadworks, she hasn't seen anybody working on them. So the editor gave me a special job to investigate.'

'And?'

'Well all I saw was some contractors putting cones out on one side of the motorway and taking them in on the other side. They didn't do any work, but just cleared off.'

'But isn't that how they split the work, anyway?' Iris suggested.

'What do you mean?'

'They have a specialist team of cone 'putters outers' and another team of construction specialists,' Iris informed him.

'Might be, can't say,' he countered. 'But I waited for somebody else to come along and do work, but no-one turned up.'

'What are you going to tell the editor?' she probed.

'Nothing,' Gurney said, hanging his coat up.

'Are you sure? I gather he's a bit of a tyrant.' Iris reminded him.

'Well there's nothing really to report so I've decided that as I'm going back tomorrow, I might have something to tell him then.'

'Be it on your own head,' Iris warned.

'So long as your mother doesn't wind him up again, it should be alright.'

'What about reporting on the court cases?' Iris quizzed.

'The editor wants me to sort this out first. So he's the one 'calling the tunes'. In any case, the sub editor is censoring my reports and they haven't published anything I've written so far.'

There was a knock on the door. Iris went and answered it.

'Mother!' Are you alright? You look very pale.'

'Thank goodness you're in.' the old lady said. 'I've been involved in an accident.'

'Oh my God! Where is your car?' Iris asked, realising her car wasn't on the drive.

'Some idiot drove into the back of me on the motorway,' the old woman informed her.

'Not your lovely Ford Prefect? Is the car badly damaged?'

'No, fortunately. I was in the front. The maniac ran into the back of me and knocked his own bumper off.'

Gurney's ears pricked up. 'It must have been the same accident he had witnessed,' he thought

'There was some pillock with a speed camera on a bridge and I slowed down, but the car behind me didn't,' the old lady continued.

Gurney's heart skipped a beat. He thought the car in his view finder had looked familiar.

'Gurney you were out that way, weren't you? Did you see anything?

'Well I... The accident I saw was... umm probably further away.'

'How do you know? I didn't say where it happened,' Delores Eyes asked suspiciously.

I...err was out there because of your complaint to the editor about the cones.'

'Oh, he took me seriously at last, did he?'

'Yes. I was tasked to report on it.'

'Although if he sent you, he obviously didn't think it was that important,' the old lady said, disparagingly.

Gurney bit his tongue to contain his anger. He knew from previous 'sparing bouts' with his Mother-In-Law that he would be at the losing end if he said anything.

'But there were no cones where my accident occurred,' the old woman said, suspiciously.

'Don't worry about it. It's a long story Mother. Come on and sit down. You need hot sweet tea to help with your shock.

Gurney, take Mother in to the lounge.'

'I know where the lounge is, thank you.' The old woman said. 'I'm perfectly capable of walking there myself,' she said, shrugging off Gurney's helping hand.

Nevertheless, Gurney followed her into the lounge and sat with her in tense silence, until Iris joined them.

'Here you are. A nice cuppa,' Iris said, putting the tray on to a small occasional table.

'Do you mind if I ask you about these cones, that you've been complaining about?' Gurney asked, tentatively.

'No. So long as you can help to get rid of them.'

'Are they the ones on the east or the westbound carriageway?'

'The what bound?'

'He means what side of the motorway were they on? Were they on the side when you're going to your friend's house or coming back?'

'Why didn't he say that in the first place. Confusing me with points of the compass, indeed.'

'Well?' Gurney probed, annoyed that Iris had interrupted his interview.

'Both sides. It happens on both sides.'

'So that's the ones with the 50 mile per hour speed limit and the average speed cameras?'

'Average what cameras?' the old woman queried.

'The average speed cameras. They take a photo of you at the start of the roadworks and one at the end, and if you do that distance quicker than it's expecting, it will give you a speeding fine.'

'I don't know about that. I slow down when I come to the camera and speed up after.'

'Oh!' Gurney reacted to her lack of understanding.

'What do you mean Oh? I haven't been fined up til now.'

'Well perhaps you've been lucky. I gather some camera boxes, don't actually have working cameras in them,' Gurney informed her.

'Gurney, don't worry Mother with all this. You can see she's had a terrible ordeal. By the way Mother, Gurney is back out there again tomorrow. Hopefully he'll get to the reason for the roadworks and you won't have the problem for too much longer.'

'If he's involved with it, I doubt that will happen in my lifetime.'

'Mother!'

# CHAPTER 19

Prior to leaving the following morning to continue his 'cone' investigations, Gurney was rummaging in his wardrobe.

'What are you doing in there?' Iris questioned.

'I'm looking for my old, full length, black leather coat. Ah, here it is,' he said, retrieving it from the far reaches of the wardrobe.

'What do you want to put that ancient thing on for?' she demanded.

'Well, if I'm going to act like a detective, I need to dress like one,' he said, admiring himself in the mirror.

'You look more like Herr Flick from 'Allo 'Allo, than a detective.'

'Thanks for the vote of confidence,' he said, leaving the bedroom.

'Well you didn't wear it yesterday. So why today?' Iris continued.

'Because I want to get into character,' he said, petulantly.

'Well, you're certainly a character that's for sure,' she laughed. 'Be careful near those motorways. We don't want any more accidents,' she added.

Gurney Leafmould drove back to the same spot where he'd parked the previous day. As he arrived, he saw the same eight workmen jumping back into their vans.

'They've moved cones to the westbound carriageway again.' Gurney said to himself. 'What the heck is going on? I can't see any evidence of work being done on the eastbound carriageway overnight.

Right, I've got my sandwiches. I'm in for the long haul,' he thought. 'I'll stay here all night, if I have to.'

Soon the new width restrictions took effect on the morning rush hour traffic. As it slowly manoeuvred through the roadworks, it slowed to a crawl.

To relieve the boredom, whilst waiting for the anticipated roadworks to start, Gurney did the crossword puzzle in the paper and ate his sandwiches.

The warm cosiness inside his motor and the hum of the slow moving traffic enveloped him in a cotton wool cocoon and sent him off to sleep.


It was the pain in his neck and the need to relive himself that eventually woke him.

'Ooh,' he yawned. 'I must have dozed off.'

Slowly he fought through the soporific layers to full consciousness, but as he did so, he accidentally sounded the horn as he pushed himself upright.

The sudden noise made him 'jump', 'Shit! What the hell!'

His involuntary reaction caused him to head-butt the sun visor. 'Ouch, that hurt!'

He looked in the rear view mirror at his reflection.

'Oh God, I've got a dent in my cheek from the window surround. What's even more embarrassing, I've dribbled down my chin.'

He massaged his aching neck, trying to ease the stiffness. 'Must get some fresh air,' he said stepping out of the van.

Outside on the motorway, the westbound traffic was now travelling at normal speed, whereas the cones were now back on the eastbound carriageway again.

'Damn. I've missed the construction work again. I've got to stay awake so I can see what's going on,' he goaded himself, desperately trying to clear his head and become the detective, he'd intended to be.

To try to remain vigilant, he paced up and down the short section of the layby, stopping several times to relieve himself.

While he was thus engaged, the two white vans and eight brightly clothed individuals arrived and started moving the cones yet again.

'I don't believe that somebody did work on the motorway while I was having a piddle,' he said to himself.

He was annoyed at not being able to categorically say that nothing or no-one had done anything before the cones had moved again.

'The only thing to do is to have words with these guys to see what they're up to,' he concluded. 'I'll just have to nip down the embankment and shout across to them. Pity they're on the far side of the other carriageway.'

In order to get to the edge of the motorway he had to scale a barbed wire fence and cross a small field.

Making sure that there were no animals in the field, he cocked his leg over the wire and carefully pushed it away from his crotch.

Unfortunately, his coat snagged on the wire and as he tried to unhook himself it slipped out of his grasp causing the barbs to stick into the back of his upper thigh.

'Ooooh, that hurt,' he muttered, 'Still it could have been much worse.' he admitted. 'Perhaps this coat wasn't the best choice to wear after all.'

Finally after untangling himself from the barbed wire, he crossed the field towards the edge of the motorway, all the while keeping a lookout for any cows.

Finally, he came to a small three bar wooden fence bordering the motorway embankment.

Gingerly he climbed on to the lower rail of the fence and inadvertently stepped on the tails of his long coat as he transferred his weight on to the other side, which prevented him from moving any further.

Thus trapped, as he attempted to release himself, he lost his balance and fell over the fence landing in a heap.

Embarrassed at his fall, he quickly picked himself up, hoping no-one had seen.

Now he could see that the motorway lay in a cutting, down a steep embankment, thirty feet beneath his feet.

He wondered at the wisdom of descending, but decided he wouldn't be close enough to talk to the men, if he didn't.

Decision made, he walked to the top of the slope and started walking down sideways, like a snowboarder and feeling confident, he slithered down the first ten feet before losing his footing and falling painfully on his backside.

Now lying on his back, his full length leather coat acted like a sledge, and he hurtled, feet first, out of control, down the remaining twenty feet.

His plight went unnoticed by the 'cone shifters' on the other side of the motorway.

But Gurney was very conscious of the broken down car on the hard shoulder that he was hurtling towards.

Frantically he tried to slow his rapid descent and alter his trajectory. But try as he might, the collision was inevitable. He slammed feet first into the passenger side door panel, buckling the whole door inwards and smashing the glass.

'Ouch, that hurt,' he groaned.

Gurney was winded by the impact and was brushing off the glass fragments and slowly picking himself up when the car owner appeared.

'What the bleedin' hell. Look at my car.' the motorist said, inspecting the damage.

'Sorry, I...I slipped,' Gurney said, testing his limbs to make sure he hadn't broken anything.

'You bleeding idiot, 'the driver screamed and immediately seized Gurney by the throat. 'What the hell do you think you're doing, sliding down the embankment like that? Look what you've done,' he said, thrusting Gurney's head to look at the damaged door.

'I...I slipped,' Gurney managed to utter as the driver tightened his grip.

'I ought to rip your bleedin' head off. You twat. Look at my new car. It's ruined.'

'Sorry. I slipped.' Gurney repeated. 'It was an accident. I appreciate that you're emotionally upset by the damage. But I can't breathe,' Gurney gasped, struggling to escape.

'I ought to squeeze the bleedin life out of you, you friggin idiot.'

Gurney was starting to lose consciousness and in a desperate attempt to escape, he kneed his assailant in the groin.

The other immediately let go and doubled up in pain.

Gurney lost no time and ran away from the maniacal motorist who now further incensed by the painful blow to his nether regions, immediately chased after him.

As Gurney rapidly clambered his way back up the embankment, he caught a quick glimpse of the two white vans disappearing off in to the distance.

'Blast,' he thought, 'missed them again.'

The motorist was gaining on him and in desperation Gurney surprised himself by 'handing off' the chasing driver, pushing him in the face, like a rugby forward racing for the try line.

He recalled the lecturer saying that 'In-the-field' reporting was dangerous, 'and how!' Gurney mentally concurred.

Eventually, the fear of having one's head ripped off generated more adrenaline than that of the angry motorist.

And Gurney vaulted the fences easily. Fear gave him the extra height needed to prevent himself being emasculated on the barbed wire and he made it back to his van, quickly locking himself in.

In frantic haste he dug the keys out of his pocket and started the engine, only to stall it as his foot slipped off the clutch.

The angry motorist was just about to reach the van, as Gurney restarted it and 'gunned' the engine.

As it shot off from the muddy layby, the spinning wheels eventually gripped, but not before anointing his pursuer in a shower of mud.

Gurney looked in his rear view mirror, relieved to have escaped.

# CHAPTER 20

As he accelerated away from the mud soaked motorist, Gurney felt upset. He wasn't sure whether it was the shock of slamming into the car or the threat by the maniacal motorist.

But he had to admit that this journalism 'lark' wasn't going the way he'd dreamed.

'What have I achieved so far,' he asked himself, reviewing his journalistic progress. 'None of my articles have gone into the paper.

I'm no further forward with this 'cone conundrum' and everybody thinks I'm wasting my time looking for the black dog.

Oh this is hopeless! Perhaps journalism isn't my thing after all,' he conceded.

'I'd better go back to the office and tell the editor that I've found nothing. He'll have my 'guts for garters' though. Worse still, Mother-In-Law won't let me live this down either,' he thought pessimistically.

As he pulled up at a junction with the main road, coming towards him were two white vans.

'Oh, I wonder if they are the ones from the motorway?' he said, excitedly.

Overcoming his initial surprise, as the last one passed him, he was able to see the number plate was covered in reddish mud. On its side were the words 'Highway

Maintenance'. And inside he caught a glimpse of several people wearing high visibility clothing.

Gurney bit his knuckle with excitement. 'Oh my god! It's them, it's them,' he shouted excitedly. 'The heavens are smiling down on me after all,' he beamed. 'A break at last!

If I follow these two, I'll find out who they're working for and hopefully I can find out what they're up to.'

His heart hammered with excitement. Butterflies filled his stomach. His bladder reminded him of its large contents and its small capacity, but nevertheless, he immediately started following them.

The vans didn't drive on any logical route, which puzzled Gurney.

'They're either drunk or they've got a faulty Sat Nav. If I didn't know better, I'd say they are trying to shake me off because they keep doubling back on themselves.

I'll keep a sensible distance behind them and allow other cars to go in front, just in case they've spotted me,' he decided.

The excitement of the chase and the hour spent continually peering through the fly blown windscreen, was making him more and more uncomfortable.

'Not now,' he groaned, 'Not now!' His 'urine sac', however, reminded him of its urgent need to be emptied.

'I shall have to do something about this,' he thought, 'or my journalistic ambitions will be limited to the close proximity of the nearest loo.

But now I'm really on to something, I don't want to stop…Oh sod it,' he groaned.

The convoy of vans were coming into the outskirts of the city and he felt sure that they were close to where they would garage.

Suddenly two other white transit vans joined the convoy in front of him.

'Oh hello, what's going on here?' he puzzled.

The vans came to a roundabout and went off in four different directions.

'What the hell,' Gurney was taken completely by surprise at the unexpected tactic. 'Now which do I follow? What would I do if I wanted to lose somebody? Double bluff? I'll try straight on. Let's see where that takes us.'

Gurney manoeuvred across to the second exit on the roundabout but had lost sight of the van by the time he was able to proceed.

All the while, the call of nature was getting louder and more pressing.

'I don't believe it, I just don't believe it,' he ranted to the lifeless corpses on the windscreen.

'Perhaps I ought to get a bag fitted so I don't have to keep stopping.' The searing pain in his abdomen made him cry out.

'Shit,' he shouted, leaning forward to relieve his discomfort, 'I'm going to lose them.'

Gurney switched his attention to a desperate search for a 'convenient' spot.

'Bugger. There go my hopes of getting to the bottom of this. The editor will have to wait a bit longer, I'm afraid. But I've got more pressing matters to deal with right now,' he said holding himself.

Spotting a small copse by the side of a high chain-link fence, he screeched to a halt. The steering wheel twisting violently in his hand as the front tyre hit the kerb.

'Oh this will have to do,' he declared in pain.

The screech of tyres, blaring horn and tirade of abuse from behind indicated that the driver following was not practised in mind reading.

Yanking his seatbelt off, Gurney threw open his door, collecting a cyclist as he did so.

'Sorry mate. Urgent business,' he said, stepping over the spread-eagled figure in the road and ran bent double into the copse.

# Chapter 21

However, as he disappeared into the bushes, his stooped figure triggered off a movement detector linked to a security camera.

Unheard by the frustrated journalist, alarm sirens immediately sounded in the security room of the building surrounded by the high chain link fence.

The gentle whine of a focusing lens was unheard by Gurney as he relieved himself.

A shudder and a gush of breath emphasised his relief. Bizarrely, as he felt the pain ebbing, he thought of the children's joke, '*If a cabbage is a vegetable, what's a pea? A relief.*' He smiled at the recollection.

'What is it, Jenkins?' George Beach, the on-duty Security Manager shouted from a nearby toilet.

'I'm just checking,' the Security Inspector replied.

'That couldn't have come at a more inconvenient time', the Security Manager shouted. 'I just got me trousers around me ankles.'

'At least you was in the right place for reacting to the shock of it,' Jenkins quipped, his eyes scanning the bank of television monitors in front of him.

'This better not be another false alarm,' the manager said, making his way into the control room, pulling up his trousers en route.

'No, I don't think so. Somebody just ran down the side of the fence crouched over. I couldn't see if he was carrying anything,' he added.

'This one's for real then, I reckon. 'George Beach said, also frantically scanning the monitors to spot anything.

'You going to call Hereford or shall I?' Jenkins asked.

'The SAS will be right pissed off if we get it wrong again. They weren't happy when we called them the last time and neither was that courting couple they interrupted.'

'Our own lads are already on their way,' Jenkins advised. 'There they are now.' He pointed to the TV monitor, showing a group of blue uniformed men trotting alongside the wire fence.

Gurney's relief was short-lived as he tugged on his jammed zip.

The policemen spread out quietly around him, their Uzzi sub-machine-guns pointing menacingly in his direction.

Suddenly aware of their presence and self-conscious of pulling at his disobedient fastener, Gurney's mouth rapidly filled with cotton wool.

'H...h..cllo,' he muttered. His usual, and confident rapport with members of the constabulary, was now compromised by his state of semi-undress.

Mindful of how his actions could be misinterpreted and thinking about the middle-aged flashers he witnessed in court, he felt it necessary to quickly explain.

'It's not what you think,' he intended to say, but his words came out as an incomprehensible jumble, as he mouthed wildly.

'Put your hands above your head,' the nearest Policeman directed. 'And turn around.' His command was reinforced by the shifting of the gun into his shoulder.

Leafmould obeyed dumbly, pivoting on the spot, his errant zip still undone.

'On the ground,' the voice commanded behind him. 'Spread yourself on the ground.' The booted foot in the small of his back pre-empted any protest.

Gurney fell face first, into a puddle of still warm liquid.

He felt inquisitive hands searching his body.

'Anything?' he heard another voice demand.

'No. Nothing,' the other responded.' Looks like we've just got a pervert,' the voice added. 'Search the area anyway, just in case he stashed something before we got here.'

'Bravo 2 from Base,' he heard the policeman's radio call. 'Status report,' the radio demanded.

The policeman responded with an update confirming a false alarm. 'No fence breach. Suspect pervert. We'll take the character to the local police station and get them to sort him out.'

'Roger. Base standing by.'

'No weapons, Sarge. But I've got a few bottles the guy could have been using,'

'OK you. On your feet.' The polished toe cap of a size nine boot in the ribs, reinforced the order.

Gurney Leafmould struggled to his feet, his clothes muddy and his face wet from its encounter with the puddle.

'Right, you. You're going to the nick...and for Christ's sake do up your trousers, you bleedin 'purvey,' the sergeant commanded.

Still unable to get a coherent noise out of his fear dried mouth, Leafmould decided to keep quiet and do as he was told.

The policeman held his arm and led him back along the fence towards the road.

As the group of men turned the corner of the compound, Gurney shifted his shame faced gaze from the floor, to see where he was being led.

Then he saw them, two white vans with reddish mud obliterating the number plates. The vans were parked inside the compound. He had found them.

A broad grin spread across his face.

Unable to contain his excitement, he forgot about his current status and shouted, 'Yes, I'm in with a chance after all.'

Unfortunately for him, punching the air in self-congratulations was not the thing to do at that particular moment.

The policeman who had been leading Gurney by the arm assumed he was attempting to break free.

Worse still, when Gurney doubled up in response to a painful urological spasm, the policeman assumed he was going for a concealed weapon.

As his sub-machine-gun was slung over his shoulder, the nearest weapon available to the policeman was his staff.

The baton left his pocket at the speed that would have impressed a Wild West gunfighter and accurately impacted behind Gurney's left ear, attracting instant unconsciousness to the journalist.

The distant sound of voices slowly became distinguishable as Gurney Leafmould returned to consciousness. The lump on his head throbbed.

'Don't try that again,' the voice threatened. 'We're highly trained to spot that sort of terrorist trick.'

Gurney spat the dirt from his mouth. Indignation had replaced fear. His courage was fired by pain,' I'm no terrorist,' he spat. 'I'm a reporter with a weak bladder.'

'Never heard of it,' the Sergeant barked.

'Never heard of what?' Gurney replied, standing slowly and gingerly touching his sore head.

'Weak bladder.' came the response, 'I suppose it's one of those underground magazines?'

'It's not a magazine! It's a medical condition you moron. If you don't watch out you'll be starring in the Urbanite as a result of your police brutality and curbing the freedom of the press.'

The prospect of another story to enhance his journalistic career and dazzle his editor with his frontline reporting, triggered his imagination and shot an adrenalin missile to his troublesome organ.

The sudden surge caused him to groan and kneel down.

On regaining consciousness again, he realised that he was being loaded into the back of a police van. Bumps, now on both sides of his head were giving him a balanced headache.

Through the rushing waves of audible comprehension, he could hear the voice that had caused him the headache...'I warned him,' the voice explained. 'How was I to know he wasn't a terrorist?'

'We'll soon sort this out at the station!' the sergeant declared.

The rear doors slammed shut and the van accelerated away from the high fenced compound. Gurney was aware of an armed and uniformed figure sitting beside him, watching his every move.

'How was he going to explain this to the editor?' he wondered.

# CHAPTER 22

Foreman Cyril Barnacre had witnessed the police activities with Gurney through a small swastika shaped scratch in the whitewash of the toilet window.

The thick dust laden spider's webs, in the old fashioned gents toilet were evidence of the cleaner's interpretation of his duties, 'only to clean up to shoulder height.'

Unfortunately the cleaner's diminutive stature meant that only the bottom four feet of the painted walls were ever wiped down, resulting in an interesting colour scheme of magnolia, grime and gossamer cobwebs.

After a morning on the motorway Cyril was ready for his dinner and joined the others in the rest room.

'You missed a bit of excitement out there,' Cyril announced, as he lowered his fifteen stone frame into the standard crown office 'chairs restroom'.

He dug into the bag by his side and pulled out a newspaper. He enveloped his upper torso in the expansive broadsheet.

'Security lads just caught a flasher. Gave him a bit of stick... and treated him to a bit of truncheon meat and carted him off to the nick. Typical flasher; black full length leather coat, big beak.'

'Black leather coat! That's odd. I wonder if it's the same guy we saw earlier on the M50. He was acting a bit strange then – wasn't he?' volunteered Frank Sully, who had been thumbing through the pages of an ancient copy of 'What Car.'

Having caught the headlines Cyril put down his newspaper and covered his huge thighs with it as he rummaged through his old shopping bag, the handle of which had been mended with string and bound with adhesive tape. He was never known to throw anything away, if it could be repaired.

Out from the bowels of the bag, he retrieved a battered flask and an equally battered sandwich tin.

'Yeah, now you come to mention it, I've seen him on a few occasions. He drives a bluebird blue Ford Thames van.

Somebody's put windows in the sides of it. It's a non-standard configuration for that year and model,' Frank chipped in, screwing up the grease stained paper, that had held his fish and chip dinner.

'Should we mention something to security?' he added, using his tongue to dig into the caverns of his ill-maintained molars. 'I wonder if he was the one tailing us? Perhaps we ought to move the vans undercover in to the secure garage,' he added.

'Yes, we're starting to get a bit sloppy in our security procedures,' Cyril reminded them.

'You don't reckon he's a Russian agent do you?' Frank suggested

'After the Geoffery Prime thing, no. They all stayed well away after that. Mind you, I wouldn't put it past the CIA to try something. We ought to mention it to Beach, though,' Cyril concurred, through a spray of wholemeal.

'Anyone coming out for a constitutional?' enquired Frank – now attacking his teeth with a matchstick.

'Not me mate, I've got to do the pools coupon to get it to the agent before knocking off time.' Dean Splot replied.

'I suppose you'll be stuck into your crossword as usual Cyril?' Frank suggested.

'Yes. Have you got the special instructions?' Cyril asked.

'Yes of course. In the envelope, as usual. I'll see you later.'

With that Frank Sully 33 year old, father of two villainous offspring left the old wooden hut and headed for his usual constitutional meander through his Aladdin's cave - the motor car scrap yard - via the local park.

As he left the main gate, Frank waved to the uniformed security guard sitting in his fibreglass security booth; which always reminded him of a portaloo with windows; it's occupants were therefore well located, he'd decided, since they caught him taking a can of paint home for resale.

His plea that as a government funded organisation, he had paid for it through his income tax, fell on deaf ears. 'You can't call that stealing,' he'd pleaded. 'Come on have a heart.'

They did and they took the paint off him and let him off with a verbal warning.

He didn't hear any more about the incident or the tin of paint, except that he noticed one of the security guards had recently painted his garage door in a familiar colour.

The lunchtime traffic thundered past Frank but he was unaware of it, as he scanned the ground ahead looking for dropped coins.

He had developed a sixth sense for finding things and had made a 'small fortune' during his dinner time walks.

Slowly he made his way into the park gardens, the usual departmental envelope in the pocket of his khaki overall.

# CHAPTER 23

At the police station Gurney was not taken to the custody sergeant or charged with anything, but taken directly into an interview room.

The room contained a desk, four chairs and was equipped with a recording machine and video cameras. On one wall there was a large gallery window.

Gurney was feeling sorry for himself. The hiatus of the day ending with this incarceration had been too much for his frail spirit.

However, the long wait was punctuated by a young police surgeon who checked Gurney's lumps and bumps and then shortly after, by a large grey-haired police sergeant who invited Gurney to a small side room to give a sample of breath.

Finally a middle-aged, pock-faced, pot-bellied plainclothes detective came to interrogate him.

'Hello Mr Leafmould, I'm DS Constable. I've come to talk to you about what you've been up to and this underground magazine 'weak bladder', he announced.

'Look,' Gurney said, speaking slowly as if he were explaining to a child. 'I am a journalist. I have a medical condition, which causes me to urinate a lot especially when I get excited or stressed...Please call my editor. He will explain....just telephone this number,' Gurney said, handing him a business card. 'He will confirm my story.....please....'

The detective took the card, studied it for a second and then left the room.

Two hours, six cups of tea and ten visits to the toilet later, Gurney was still in the interview room, staring blankly at the floor when the pot-bellied detective sergeant waddled back.

'OK Jennings,' he said to the young constable, who had been keeping Gurney company, 'You can go and have a cuppa, I'll be with you in a minute.'

The PCSO stood up and left, closing the door quietly behind him.

'I've established with this person you call your editor,' the detective said, trying to sound officious, 'that there is a person matching your description, who is employed by that newspaper.

I won't repeat what else he said,' the policeman added.

'Thank god. Now do you believe my story?' Gurney said, relieved.

'Suffice to say, that if this incident appears in any way in your newspapers, we will be pressing charges for indecent exposure, resisting arrest and trying to pervert the course of justice....you understand...sir? ' the policeman asked.

'What do you mean? No I don't understand, I've told you what happened,' Gurney blurted.

'Come now sir. We're not that naive are we? I don't have to spell it out do I? the policemen said, patiently.

'You...you wouldn't dare!' stuttered Gurney, 'You mean... No you wouldn't dare! This is blackmail!'

'No sir, I wouldn't say that. I would say you have made a minor indiscretion, for which we have decided to give you the benefit of the doubt...so long as you recognise the sensitivity that we are treating you with... now do you understand?'

Gurney held his head in his hands. The roller coaster of emotions had drained him totally.

First there had been the excitement of trailing the vans, then the disappointment of losing them: then the fear of the run-in with the gun totting police; then seeing the vans inside the compound; then being rendered unconscious by two blows to the head by lignum vitae batons and then this! This threat of blackmail if he published anything.

His head felt as if it were going to explode.

'*Investigative journalism is tough.*' the lecturer's voice played in his mind.

Behind the one way glass, George Beach smiled. 'I think we have him Inspector Clueless,' he said, to the uniformed policeman by his side. 'I don't think Mr Gurney James Leafmould will cause us any more problems, do you?'

'Well, if you tell me what he is sticking his nose into, I can give you a considered opinion,' the officer replied. 'I've always felt uncomfortable around state secrets. A lot of nasty things go on behind the blanket of the official secrets act. Sooner or later these things always come back to bite us. East Germany's Eric Honeker could have verified to that.'

'Don't worry about our friend out there. We will ensure that he won't be investigating or reporting on anything other than the colour of the roses at the local flower show....' the security manager added.

'Listen I don't want any sudden disappearances on my patch. We've already had more than our share of press coverage around here due to Leafmould's previous antics,' the Inspector said.

Back in the interview room Gurney stood up wearily, too tired to think. He felt defeated. His story would never be seen. Reluctantly, he resigned himself to being legally gagged.

'That's very intelligent of you sir,' the detective patronised. 'Now if you hurry along you'll get to your van before we book you for parking it in a manner likely to cause an obstruction...'

# CHAPTER 24

George Beach returned from Chelster police station and stormed into the restroom.

'Right Cyril, I want an explanation before I get hold of your boss. Why didn't you park your vans out of sight in the secure garage? Now we've got a bleeding journalist sniffing around.'

'Yes, sorry George. The lads were dying for their lunch and Frank's chips were getting cold.'

'So you compromise the security of the department for his sodding chips,' George fumed.

'An army marches on its stomach George. Although in your case, Redcaps march on everybody else's backs don't they?'

'Let's not get personal Cyril. Let's put our former Regimental loyalties behind us. We're all in the same team now. I've got to send my boss a report. What shall I say?'

'Say what you like George. You're paid more than me.'

'It looks like you all need to be re-trained in escape and evasion for a start.'

'We were careful. We did all that we were trained to do. The guy just got lucky, even after the 'star burst' at the roundabout with the other two decoys,' Cyril explained.

'Clearly not careful enough though. When Cabbage gets to hear of this, she'll go ballistic. You know what she's like?' the security man reminded him.

'I'll have nothing said against her, the foreman said defensively. She might be tough, but she's fair.'

'I'm going to recommend that the M50 project is closed too.'

'You can recommend away,' Cyril advised. 'But if she doesn't want to close it, you'll soon know about it.'

'It won't be my shout. That's up to my gaffer, John Ripple.' George Beach argued. 'They can battle it out at their level.'

'Anyway, Frank has parked the vans in the secure area now and we're not due to go out again today.' Cyril advised. 'So we'll carry on with the schedule until we're told to stop.'

'Closing the door after the horse has bolted' isn't a good way to run our business,' Beach advocated.

'George, you keep to your 'cloak and dagger' stuff and leave us to get on with doing the real work. Now if you've finished, it's my home time,' the Leading Disruption Officer shouted angrily, putting on his coat.

George Beach turned on his heel and went back to his own office to write his report.


Before going home though, Cyril sent an email to alert Eunice to the situation before anybody else could give her a 'kicking'.

She had explained that no matter what the problem was, she wanted to know first-hand, rather than being 'sandbagged' at a meeting over a problem that she didn't know about.

Although she was a 'self-confessed tyrant', men who used their fists to convince the merit of their views, 'warmed' to her.

She couldn't do anything wrong in their eyes, especially if it meant their own managers were discredited or demeaned. Most working men held her in awe, either as a domineering mother or as an 'anti-hero'.

However, Eunice Cabbage was an angry person; a six foot six amazon, imprisoned in a diminutive five foot frame. She was angry at having to over-compensate for her size, in order to be taken seriously.

She was angry with her growth genes.

Angry at her parents, for not investing in some form of hormone growth treatment.

She was angry with always having to be angry.

She carried her anger like a scythe, lashing out at anyone who dared question her ways.

She had a brusque no nonsense manner and didn't suffer fools gladly.

Many who disagreed with her views were subjected to a severe tongue lashing.

She was a workaholic and expected the same effort from her managers. Nine to five did not exist in her working life. Instead, her hours were dictated by an 'until the job was done' psyche.

She lived in an old mill in the beautiful Cotswolds, the local stream still turning the old mill wheel.

Exaggerated claims from her roadmen reckoned that Managers who failed to do her bidding, were strapped on the mill wheel and 'water boarded' – a sort of land based 'keel hauling'.

Eunice Cabbage had been made a Level 3 Senior Manager on a sideways promotion having been originally recruited as a catering manager, but reorganisations within the territory had placed her in charge of the Roadworks section.

She was both loved and feared by her 400 strong workforce.

Loved only as a General can be, men had started punch-ups to defend her name.

And feared because of the vehemence of her wrath, if something went wrong.

She had never actually carried out her threat to make eunuchs of those who upset her. But few doubted that she would, and wield the knife herself.

Her colleagues knew that to cross her meant trouble.

# Chapter 25

Gurney took a few days off on sick leave to get over the trauma of the incident at the compound.

On his return to the newspaper offices, he was summoned to the editor's 'pigpen'.

In fear and trembling he made his way up to the top floor.

Standing in front of the entrance to the pigpen, he knocked loudly on the partition this time.

'Come in, sit down and shut up,' the editor directed, gruffly.

Gurney entered and sat in a hard chair facing him.

'Leafmould, I don't like receiving calls from the constabulary about my staff.'

'No sir, sorry sir.'

'I said be quiet.'

'Yes sir.'

'What the hell have you been up to?'

'The cones...'

'I said be quiet.'

'Yes sir, not another word sir.'

'You are a representative of this paper, and what you have done undermines the integrity of our standing within the community.'

'Sorry sir.'

'What were you doing to get arrested?'

'Scoop sir.'

A scoop! Ha. Apart from knowing that they're used for ladling out ice cream, you wouldn't know a scoop if it came up and bit you.'

'The cones...'

'Stop talking about those bloody cones. I suppose this is all your Mother-In- Law's doing?'

'No sir. I think the cones are being placed by a government department.'

'You think! You think. I think the world will end in a war. But I don't know. Facts boy. You need facts to back it up.'

'Yes sir. I have facts.'

'Such as?'

Gurney went on to explain to the editor how he had monitored the cones being put out and moved around, without any work being done.

He conveniently omitted the incident when he'd been assaulted by the irate motorist following his tumble down the embankment.

'And then I was able to follow the vans that had been moving the cones, which subsequently led me to finding them in the government compound.'

He again conveniently skipped the events following on from the urgent toilet stop.

'They're probably only contractors fiddling their contract,' the editor said, dismissively. 'There's unlikely to be anything newsworthy there.'

'But...'

'Speak when you're spoken to.'

'Yes sir.'

'On the other hand, if these contractors are fiddling their contract, that might be worth a story I suppose. I'll get one of my senior journalists to dig around and see what they can uncover.'

Gurney's face fell. His hard work was going to be usurped.

'Well perhaps you've vindicated yourself after all,' the editor continued. 'The owner will be very pleased, IF we can get a scoop out of this.'

Oh!' Gurney retorted, feeling totally deflated that HIS story was going to be commandeered. 'I thought as I knew the background, that I could...follow it up,' he tentatively suggested.

'Dream on Leafmould. You're still wet behind the ears.'

'But I want to be an invest-a-gate-tive journalist,' Gurney confessed.

'You! An investigative journalist? Why you can't even say it, let alone be one. You must be joking,' the editor sneered.

'But I tracked the vans and it was me that made the link,' Gurney reminded the editor.

'Yes but look what happened. All you had to do was follow them and you end up getting arrested and compromising, not only yourself, but the newspaper too.'

'But...'

'Just count yourself lucky that you've still got a job,' the editor said harshly. 'Now get back to court, before I change my mind and show you the door.'

'Thank you but...'

'No more buts Leafmould. Good day and no more cock ups, hear me?'

'Yes sir.'

Gurney left the office, dragging his fallen ego behind him.

# CHAPTER 26

Gurney rang home in a sulk.

'Hello, the Leafmould residence,' Iris announced.

'Iris, I'm fed up,' Gurney blurted.

'Gurney, what's the matter now, you sound awful?' she said concerned.

'They're going to use somebody else to investigate the strange goings on with the cones on the motorway,' he said, dolefully.

'Who's they?'

'The editor.'

'Well can you blame them, after getting yourself arrested?' Iris reasoned.

'I suppose not,' Gurney admitted.

'Are you sure you're alright?' she probed.

'Yes, I suppose so.'

"I'm concerned about your health Gurney,' she confessed. 'Especially after being beaten by the police.'

'No, honest. My head's OK. I'm just peed off that my work is going to be taken over by somebody else, after I literally suffered to get the story,' Gurney explained.

'I can understand why you're disappointed,' Iris said, sympathetically. 'Let's talk about it tonight.'

'Yeah, OK. Anyway I've got to go and do some reporting at the Magistrate's court now. See you.'

'Yeah, see you later,' Iris said, concerned that he'd even made the call.

'What's the matter with the whinger now?' Delores Eyes asked, after eavesdropping on the conversation.

'The editor has taken Gurney off the case of the cones,' she informed her mother.

'Well I hope whoever takes it on will sort it out quickly. You can guarantee that every time I go to Mary's I get stuck in the traffic,' she griped.

'I don't think it's fair. Gurney suffered to get that story,' Iris added, firmly. 'Can't you do something about it mother?'

'No, I've already called in a few favours to get him the job, as it is.'

'But if he gets depressed again, he'll be around my feet. And you know what that means?'

'Yes, you'll be cramping my love life again, by coming to my house moping. Oh, OK. But I'm not sure I can swing it again.'

'Thank you mother,' Iris said, trying to give her mother a hug.

The old lady sidled away from her and rang Gordon Moss.

'Moss.'

'Gordon!'

'Oh not you again?'

'Yes, I'm sorry to bother you again so soon. But I'm having a crisis of conscience.'

'A crisis of confidence, about what?' the editor asked suspiciously.

'About withholding information concerning the newspaper owner's cuckolder,' the old woman revealed.

'I knew you wouldn't be able to keep your trap shut,' Moss declared, exasperated.

'I think that's a little harsh to say to an old friend.'

'Friends don't blackmail each other,' the editor said coldly.

'This isn't blackmail. Just an old friend asking for help,' the old lady said sweetly.

'Go on. What is it this time?'

'I understand you've removed my son in...' the family association stuck in her throat, 'my daughter's husband, from pursuing the cone problem.'

'Now you're going too far. Don't you start telling me how to run my paper,' the editor screeched down the phone.

'Of course I wouldn't dream of interfering with the running of your paper, I just wanted to get the facts right for when I meet your boss,' she informed him.

'Meet my boss?' the editor queried.

'Yes, didn't I tell you? I've been invited to his cocktail party,' she lied.

'I don't know anything about a cocktail party,' the editor said, alarmed at not being invited to the mythical party.

'Well perhaps you've already fallen from grace then,' she added, 'rubbing the salt' into his damaged ego.

'OK. I can take a hint. I'll put him back on the case. But that's it, no more favours,' he said firmly.

'Thank you,' she beamed and quickly hung up.


The editor called Gurney back to his office.

'Look Leafmould, I've changed my mind. Perhaps for the sake of continuity it might be better if you carried on investigating the cones mystery.'

'Oh, thank you, thank you so much sir,' Gurney beamed, attempting to shake the reluctant editor's hand.

'Leafmould, if you get yourself into any more trouble, you're on your own. Do you understand? You're nothing to do with this paper. However, if you manage to get sufficient evidence to prove something strange is going on, I will personally support you to the hilt,' Gordon Moss said sincerely.

'Yes sir, thank you sir,' Gurney was so happy he nearly genuflected his delight.

'And if there is something in it, I'll take most of the credit too,' the editor thought.

'Now you're going to have to be professional about this. Have you given it any thought?' Moss persisted.

'Yes, I...'

'OK. How are you going to go about it?' the editor probed.

'I...I wondered, if I... applied for a job there, I would be best placed to uncover what is going on... A sort of whistle-blower,' Gurney revealed, which was actually the first thought that came into his head.

'Yes, that's one way of tackling it I suppose,' the editor agreed. 'Of course, if you do get a job there, your pay from this newspaper will cease,' he informed Gurney.

'Oh, why?'

'They'll know something's afoot if you're being paid by us as well,' the editor clarified.

'Oh yes, of course. I hadn't thought of that,' Gurney admitted.

'In the meantime, you'll carry on reporting at the courts until such time as you get a job with them. By the way who are they?' Gordon Moss asked.

'I believe it's something to do with the Ministry of Defence. I spotted the letters MOD on some of the buildings near the fence, before I was assaulted by the police.'

'Right off you go... and Leafmould, tell your Mother-In-Law the good news. Tell her also, the fairy has granted her third and final wish.'

'Yes sir, whatever that means.'

'She'll know,'

'Thank you sir. You won't regret it.'

'I already am,' the editor thought.

# CHAPTER 27

John Ripple opened the well recycled brown official envelope.

Like all mail in the department, the envelopes were multi-used, with a list of previous 'duty reference' addresses crossed out and the new address added.

The envelope was secured with a plain gummed label and stamped 'In Strictest Confidence' in red.

The contents caused him some concern. It was a printed report from his security manager at Elmley.

A handwritten post-it note had been stuck to the top and read:- '*JR, you might be interested in the attached. GB*'

## Security Report

**Security Incident:** Possible *breach of security.*

**Details:** *A journalist, named Gurney Leafmould had been tailing the local traffic unit back to their base and spotted vehicles in the compound because they were not parked in the secure garages.*

*He was apprehended by onsite security and searched but nothing was found. He made two attempts to escape but was subdued by baton both times.*

*He was then arrested and handed over to the local police where he was interviewed in my presence.*

*He claims to be working on directions from his*

*editor to discover why cones were being positioned on M50. Note: Kept mentioning 'weak bladder.'*

***Resolution:*** *Released with a caution and gave an undertaking not to publish anything. Seemed adequately traumatised by the threat of being named as a 'flasher'.*

***Recommendation:*** *No further action against Leafmould; Monitor output from paper; Suggest to Road traffic division that cone scheme should be abandoned in this area; Refresher training for Road teams in escape and evasion.*

***Report Author:*** *George Beach,* ***Location:*** *Elmley:*

'I don't agree with you Beach. I think Mr Gurney Leafmould needs to be further investigated and perhaps psychologically 'disrupted',' Ripple decided.

'And I'm not sure how Eunice Cabbage will view your suggestion to shut down her scheme either.'

John Ripple, head of Security, a retired member of Her Majesty's constabulary, picked up his phone and dialled '0'. He listened to the ringing tone until the telephonist answered.

'Get me Chelster police HQ, please,' he instructed.

'I'll call you back sir,' the telephonist advised him.

'Why the hell do we have such an antiquated phone system, when we use all the latest technology elsewhere,' he muttered, shaking his head.

He busied himself setting up a file for this new investigation. Capturing and recording everything was his hallmark of thoroughness and also assisted his failing memory.

John's former police career had seen him in various postings around the UK and British protectorates.

He had never been static long enough to strike up a serious relationship with any women, although he'd had a few 'flings' in a few places. Consequently, he remained a bachelor.

He had been on the Falklands in 1982 when the islands were invaded, and had obviously impressed someone for creating mayhem for the invading Argentinians.

His subterfuge had included taking down road signs and swapping names of communities, even changing some maps to confuse the enemy.

Prior to the main British force arriving, he had been contacted by a small group of heavily armed, balaclava wearing soldiers who wanted intelligence about the island and more importantly about the invaders.

He was able to go about his normal duties and provide information for them because the occupiers wanted to maintain an atmosphere of normality to the inhabitants.

Although he was unable to categorically confirm it, he thought one of the group of British soldiers was Carrington Jones.

But due to the regime of secrecy and anonymity in the clandestine world of the special forces, he was unlikely ever to find out for sure.

Nevertheless, at the end of the conflict he was approached by some 'civilian' defence bods who suggested he contacted them when he returned to London with the chance of a possible job opportunity. He had been in the organisation ever since.

The telephone rang, 'Ripple!' he answered.

'Your call to Chelster police Station, sir,' the telephonist announced.

'Yes, thank you.'

'Chelster police how may I help?' the distant operator asked.

'Extension 212, Special Branch please,' he requested.

'Putting you through.'

The phone was answered almost immediately.

'Constable, special branch,' the speaker answered.

Brian Constable had been plagued with unfunny witticisms about his name since joining the force many years previously.

Constable Constable got fed up with the leg pulling and feigned laughter, but only when Senior Officers chose to repeat the obvious clash of names.

Therefore when the opportunity of promotion came along, he was very happy to eventually become a Detective Sergeant.

'Brian! John Ripple here. I believe you've been dealing with something we might be interested in?'

'Hi John. We have?'

Yes! A local journalist by the name of Leafmould apparently has been sniffing around our compound.'

'Oh yes. I remember. Odd fellow,' the Detective recalled.

'Got any background on the guy? Has he got a record or anything we should know about?' Ripple probed.

'Yes! I've been in touch with the local nick and they've got volumes of records on him.'

'Really!, tell me more,' Ripple said, preparing to take notes.

'Yes, he's got an ASBO on him,' Constable informed him.

'Surely, that's no big deal.' Ripple suggested. 'What's he been anti-social about?'

'He keeps wrecking the local utilities infrastructure.'

'Oh dear. Is he some sort of protester then?' Ripple probed.

'No, just somebody with ideas above his abilities. He got labelled the DIYer from hell,' the detective explained.

'So nothing subversive then? Nothing serious?' Ripple summarized.

'No. Not that we've found. Do you have access to the PNC, the Police National Computer?'

'Not currently, no.'

'His history is pretty well documented on there.'

'So have you established anything else about why he was sniffing around our compound?'

'Yes. He works for a local paper and was investigating something about continual roadworks on the motorway.'

'Yes, I've got George Beach's security report here.' Ripple advised the detective. 'But should we be worried?'

'No, I don't think so,' the policeman said. 'He appears to be a bit of a drip if you ask me.'

'That could be a ruse, of course,' Ripple suggested.

'He's a flipping good actor if he is.'

'I see George has mentioned something about 'weak bladder' in his report,' Ripple observed.

'Yes. I thought he might. Leafmould kept muttering about it when he was brought him in.'

'Does that mean anything to you?'

'No, apart from a medical condition.'

'OK, we'll deal with it from here. But if you get any more intel, you know where to find me. Tell you what, if I get down to your 'neck of the woods, we'll go for a pint OK?'

'Sounds good. Cheers.'

Ripple replaced the receiver and made a careful note of the conversation, noting date and time.

'Weak bladder! Weak bladder. I wonder what the hell that's all about?' he mused. 'I wonder if it's one of those exposure websites.

I guess I ought to get down to Gloucestershire to see if we are 'exposed'.'

# CHAPTER 28

Carrington Jones, or CJ as he liked to be called, smiled as his car radio announced the results of Eunice's team's latest efforts.

'*Drivers are advised of a five mile tail back on the clockwise direction of the M25 motorway between junctions 6 and 16.*'

An ex-army intelligence officer with the Special forces, Carrington Jones had been invited to leave the services following a scandal over foreign currency dealings.

The 'old boy's' network had seen to it that he was quickly absorbed into a branch of the Civil Service, where his background could be fully utilized.

CJ soon saw the stream of traffic in front of him slowing. Red brake lights semaphored the forming tailback along the line of traffic.

Then, as a body, the whole section of traffic slowed to a crawl and nearly all stopped, although a brief skidding sound, smashing glass and a cloud of steam indicated that at least one driver had not been driving with 100% concentration, but had now also stopped.

'Another slight delay for the commuters,' he thought.

The performance figures should be good this month.

He reached into the box behind his seat and retrieved

a magnetic 'amber rotating beacon' – a yellow flashing light, which, having wound the window down, he placed on the roof of his car.

He plugged the curly black power lead into the cigar socket of the Range Rover and switched the beacon on. Deftly he flicked down the passenger sun visor, which displayed a 'Motorway Incident Manager' sign and swung on to the hard shoulder.

The white Range Rover purred past the stationary traffic, its yellow flashing beacon announcing its authority.

His special odometer indicated that the tailback was now over 6 miles long and getting longer by the minute.

'The weed killing operation must be undertaken on the motorway. It is an essential part of motorway maintenance,' he'd insisted. 'The timing of the application of the chemicals is critical too.'

Unfortunately for the motorists trapped in the huge jam, according to his edict, the critical times just happened to occur during the morning rush hour, when the percentage air to carbon monoxide and lead level ratios are correct. 'This ensures complete emulsification,' he had lied.

The motorway maintenance managers hated the sight and sound of Carrington Jones and his Roads manager Eunice Cabbage. For together, they were the architects behind all the weird road schemes in which the motorway managers became reluctant participants.

Consequently, they, not CJ's department got the 'stick' for the subsequent delays from all motoring organisations, irate motorists and transport firms.

CJ could see the signs that announced the two lane closure 400 yards ahead. Soon the three lane jam became two lanes and finally came down to one single lane.

Drivers fought to leapfrog each other in the orderly queuing system and switched lanes only when the cones forced them to move over.

Pushing their way into a polite queue of conforming drivers became a catalyst for road rage incidents from mild mannered motorists. The intruders, cutting in to the disciplined single lane, generated a cacophony of blaring horns and flashing headlights.

Tempers flared, expletives exchanged. 'Punch ups' were only avoided because no-one wanted to lose their hard won place in the queue.

Ahead in the distance CJ could see the cloud of spray that indicated that weed killing was proceeding as planned.

'*The chemicals in the weed killer will combine with the vehicle exhaust fumes and rainwater to corrode the metal central reservation barrier.*' he was assured by the Ministry's chemists.

'*This will mean replacement of the Armco metalwork in six months' time, thus perpetuating the road cones on this section of the motorway for at least another eighteen months.*'

He had quietly lobbied parliament to scupper the programme to change the metal central reservation to continuous concrete barriers, citing significant cost implications.

Fortunately the chair of the select committee was a major shareholder in the firm that made the metal barriers.

With a feeling of great satisfaction CJ switched off the beacon and slipped out of the motorway chaos through a 'maintenance vehicles only' exit and headed back to his office in the city.

Although the majority of the cities rush hour traffic was still battling its way through the traffic cones on the M25, there were sufficient buses and taxis on the city's roads to encourage CJ to switch on his other queue beating technology.

Pulling out from behind a slow moving bus, he hit the switch for the 250 decimal siren and the concealed blue lights mounted in the front and rear panels of his car.

The sudden noise caused the driver of the large red bus to glance guiltily at his speedometer and instinctively put on his brakes.

Carrington Jones sailed by, smiling at hearing the sound of screeching brakes and breaking of glass, as a taxi made an impression in the back of the bus.

Ahead, the traffic lights were red and against him, the traffic already stationary as he screamed past.

He reached for the traffic light override switch on the dashboard, which operated a special radio transmitter.

The traffic lights of the opposing traffic flow, instantly turned to red, missing out the normal amber sequence.

Several cars shunted each other as leading drivers, fearful of getting caught by the traffic light cameras, jammed on their brakes.

The road junction was therefore clear as Carrington Jones sailed over.

As he cleared the junction, he remotely reset the lights with his 'override button' and noticed that all lights had turned to green.

Mayhem ensued as all eight lines of traffic met together in the centre of the crossroads.

He made a mental note to add the incident to his report. Things were looking up.

The siren's wail bounced off the high rise buildings as he screamed through the city.

He noted with pleasure, the various streets closed off for no apparent reason and holes dug and abandoned in the middle of roads and left coned off.

Everywhere there was evidence of his road manager's brilliance. He was particularly proud of her efforts in persuading the city to reduce the workable width and capacity of its arterial roads by putting in exclusive cycle, bus and taxi lanes.

And the department's suggestion of a congestion charge and installation of pollution areas were pure genius, he felt.

CJ was proud of the departments toll of disruption which they'd imposed on the city.

His successful lobbying of the bureaucrats and environmentalists to adopt their 'crazy' schemes had been easier than he'd expected. Just like the children's story of the Kings new clothes, he'd persuaded them that only fools would fail to see the obvious advantages.

# CHAPTER 29

Finally, CJ arrived at his office and parked his car in the underground car park.

He made his way up the concrete steps to emerge by the side of the security turnstile, flashing his pass at the doorman.

'Morning Mr CJ.'

'Good Morning,' CJ beamed.

The security guard waved him through, releasing the inner security latch remotely. The solenoid clicked audibly, inviting Carrington Jones to push the turnstile.

CJ made his way onto the first floor, passing the ornate coat of arms bolted to the wall. Its motto *'Chaos res est' (Chaos is our Business)* reflecting the aims of the secretive organisation - the Ministry of Disruption.

Whereas the original war time office had been a small, almost cupboard like room, the department had mushroomed over the years and now occupied several floors in Whitehall.

Each operational area contained a supporting clerical section, which in turn was supported by a catering section – freshly brewed tea being always available.

All employees were positively vetted, a process that searched in to family background and in true civil service tradition usually took years to complete. Fortunately the low turnover in staff ensured the 'vetters' were not overwhelmed. However, when additional or replacement staff was needed, recruitment from family relatives was positively encouraged.

CJ continued his journey through a labyrinth of corridors, until he reached his large office.

Within a few seconds of sitting down at his desk, a cup of tea arrived in his special 'Nigel Mansell' mug.

'Thank you Matilda,' he said, acknowledging the old lady who had brought it.

'My pleasure,' she said, going back to her tea trolley.

Deep in the bowels of the building a National Coordination Centre monitored the effects of all Ministry projects underway nationwide.

Here, headset clad operatives received intelligence of Disruption activities and plotted their locations by positioning various shaped symbols on a huge table map of the UK.

The tables, still in use since the organisation was founded during the Second World War, indicated the varied effects of operations being conducted all over the country.

Always apprehensive of the possibility of power failures and hacking attacks, the organisation had decided that tokens moved around a large table was fundamentally more resilient and secure; although it recognised that it was inefficient, time consuming, labour intensive and restrictive. But it was safe.

The plotting table, lit by high intensity lighting, was surrounded on four sides by a darkened glass fronted observation gallery, which overlooked the huge map.

Managerial discussions and plans were formulated in the gallery, without disturbing the cathedral like atmosphere of the plotting room.

CJ switched on his monitor screen.

'I'm glad I persuaded them that this was more efficient than running down to the gallery every few minutes,' he thought. 'They were obviously swayed by my argument that the CCTV monitor screens were 'safe' when run through direct cables.'

As the screen 'came to life', he adjusted a joystick on his desk, which controlled his remote camera monitoring the plotting table, three floors below.

Refocussing the lens, he zoomed in to the area of the M25 that he'd driven through earlier and was pleased to see the traffic tailback had now reached 10 miles.

CJ felt extremely smug as he slouched back in his chair and drank his tea, the first of twenty that he would consume during the day.

Although, in another part of the building, things weren't quite as calm.

Before heading off to the Cotswolds, John Ripple had been summoned to see the Head of Road Disruption, Eunice Cabbage.

"This is simply not good enough,' she exploded. 'How dare you interfere in my road schemes?'

'I...err...'

'One of my staff has reported to me that you are planning to close down their work on the M50.'

'Well, that's actually not...'

'You have no authority to dictate to my staff, what they will and won't do.'

'That's not...'

'Your man, what's his name at Elmley'

'George, George Beach.'

'Yes him. He is bullying my staff.'

'That's actually not the…'

'I'm going to report you to CJ for overstepping your responsibilities and affecting my remit.'

'If you'd let me…'

'D will be hopping mad. If she finds out.'

'Your staff compromised the security of…'

'I won't have a word said against them, do you hear?'

'If you won't let me explain…'

'If anybody needs to get a bollocking, I'll deal with it.'

'Glad to hear it.'

'Now get out,' she ordered.

He backed out of the office, eager not to turn his back on her. She had a reputation of throwing things at receding backs.

'Which, I suppose is better than at receding hairlines,' he mused.

Thankfully John Ripple felt the hardness of the door handle in the small of his back, he turned and stepped out in to the corridor. Closing the door quietly, he collapsed, mentally exhausted, against the outside partitioned wall.

He closed his eyes and slowly shook his head in disbelief at the irrational tirade of abuse that he had just endured.

# CHAPTER 30

Gurney had spent the morning in the Magistrates court, listening to whinging motorists, claiming faulty technology was the cause of them being recorded doing 50mph in a 30mph zone.

So he decided to go to the nearby park gardens to think of something to liven up his court report, hoping the beautiful profusion of flowers would trigger some literary prose.

As he was gazing at the colourful array, he noticed a man acting strangely. The person was wearing a long khaki overall, which was unusual in itself.

As the man walked through the park, he stopped and looked around furtively then moved on a few paces as if admiring the flower border.

Gurney was aware of the sinister people that parks sometimes attract. He had first-hand knowledge based on several court cases, that he'd recently attended. So immediately he was on his guard and ready to 'leg it', if the man approached him.

As the stranger came closer, Gurney lost direct sight of him and curious to see what he was up to, he moved to peer through a gap in a hedge.

The person continued his furtive perambulations until he reached a sunken garden, where he took out an envelope from his pocket and making sure he wasn't being observed, bent down and 'fiddled' around on the ground in front of him.

Checking again that he wasn't being watched, he stood up and walked out of the park without a backward glance.

Gurney was puzzled. 'How odd,' he thought. 'I wonder what he's up to? maybe drugs or something. Perhaps he's stealing plants, although he didn't appear to have anything in his hand when he left.'

Gurney's public spirited curiosity got the better of him and after the other had gone, he wandered over to the sunken garden himself.

He couldn't see anything obvious, which would connect the man to the strange behaviour.

Set in the midst of a colourful display of daffodils and narcissi, the small garden was adorned with a two foot high stone statue of an unattractive mermaid.

'I'm sure he had an envelope in his hand when he knelt down, but nothing when he stood up. Unless he's a magician, it's got to be here somewhere,' Gurney mused.

Just then a park warden approached him.

'Excuse me sir. Can I ask what you're doing?'

'Umm...well nothing really. Just, admiring the flowers.'

'I see sir. Could I ask you to move away from this spot? Only one of my colleagues ashes are sprinkled here and some people have been umm...taking the soil because...they think...it's special fertiliser,' he lied.

'Oh I'm terribly sorry,' Gurney said, suddenly feeling guilty. 'I don't want to...and I'm no gardener...the wife you know.' Sorry. I'll go and umm...' he muttered apologetically, walking away backwards.

'That's OK sir. You weren't to know.'

Embarrassed by his innocent venture, Gurney left the park heading back towards the court house.

'Oh perhaps that's what the guy was doing. Paying his respects. It figures. He was wearing a park keepers type overall,' Gurney convinced himself.

As he walked along the edge of the park though, he spotted the Park warden bending over.

'How nice,' Gurney thought, 'paying his respects too. His colleague must have been well liked,' he concluded.

Then, as he crossed the road, he noted that the Park warden was standing and pocketing an envelope.

'That looks like the same sort of envelope that the other man had in his hand earlier.

'Strange! I didn't see anything on the ground when I was over there. I wonder whats going on?' he pondered.

Gurney stopped and watched the warden leave the park. When he reached a small white van he took off his hat and coat before driving off.

'I think I need to investigate this. There's more to this than meets the eye,' Gurney decided.

# CHAPTER 31

The following day Gurney went back to the park and returned to the place where all the mysterious activity had taken place.

As he knelt down to examine the flower border, his pen fell out of his pocket and bounced off the top off the Mermaid's statue.

'Bugger!' he muttered. 'Hang on, that sounded wrong. It's not stone.' Picking up his pen, he tapped the Mermaid's head with it.

'It's not solid, it's a hollow casting,' he decided.

As he examined it further, he spotted a crack at the base of the statue, by the tail. As he touched it, the tail turned ninety degrees.

'Oh that's novel, it's even got a moveable tail.'

As he was about to straighten it up, he realised that the statue was now loose on its base. 'Oh dear, I think I've broken it!'

However, as he checked to see what damage he'd done, he pushed the head, which swivelled at his touch.

'This is very strange,' he thought. Gently he returned the head to its original position and pushed the chest instead. This time, the whole statue moved backwards.

'Crikey, it's hinged at the back and the tail must be a catch to lock it.'

'Why would you have something like this in a park? '

Gingerly he pushed it further back, to examine the void inside and then stopped with a sudden thought.

'Oh God! What if it's where they keep the blokes ashes!...Perhaps it's a sort of urn!' he gasped, in horror.

Quickly he righted the statue and moved the tail back to its original locking position, unconsciously wiping his hands on his trousers.

Satisfied that the park keeper was nowhere around, he made his way to the bench where he'd sat the previous day.

'Let's think this through,' he said to himself. 'Perhaps that bloke wrote a letter to his dead colleague and posted it with his ashes.

Perhaps the park warden is like the tooth fairy and helps people to believe in some sort of psychic link with the departed by taking the letter.

Yeah I've heard of these things...what do they call them? Dead letter box (DLB). Yes that's it! Dead letter boxes.'

Pleased with his own explanation, he left the park and went home. Iris was just preparing a light lunch as he arrived.

'Hi!'

'Hi!' Been in court again today?' she asked.

'Not yet. Have you heard of a 'dead letter box'?'

'Yes. Why do you ask? Was it something that came up in one of your court cases?'

'No. It's something I stumbled across in the park.'

Gurney gave her an account of the dead park warden's ashes, the letter, the statue and his theory about the grieving man.

'Very interesting theory,' she agreed. 'But there are many uses of the 'dead letter boxes'. During the cold war, spies used them for passing on secrets,' Iris informed him.

'No. You've been watching too many spy movies,' Gurney derided.

'When I worked for HMRC, we came across all manner of tax evasion methods. The 'dead letter box' was one method that we used for paying off our informants,' she told him.

'Oh! That's interesting. I wonder what's going on in the park then?'

'Be careful. You might end up biting off more than you bargained for. There are some powerful 'players' out there,' she warned.

'I'll bear that in mind. This might be the start of a major scoop, he beamed.

# CHAPTER 32

Gurney had eventually persuaded a very reluctant Iris to help him investigate his suspicions, concerning the 'dead letter box'.

'Just think. If I can get a scoop on this, and something about the cones story, I shall be world famous.'

'You already are,' she said, thinking of the YouTube coverage of their house, literally falling down around their ears, as she rescued him.

'Yeah OK, but this is different. I can get my own back on the paparazzi who made my life hell after my unfortunate incident with our house.

'Unfortunate! That's a bit of an understatement. Undermining the foundations!' Iris retorted.

'Anyway, I thought we'd agreed not to talk about it anymore. It's all 'water under the bridge' now, isn't?' he reminded her.

'If you say so!' Iris added unconvincingly, still suffering flashbacks of her collapsing house.

'You mentioning the cones, I forgot to tell you. Mother says thanks.'

'Your mother, thanking me. That's a first. What did I do?'

'The cones on the M50.'

'What about them?'

'All gone. She has no delays anymore visiting Mary.'

'So I can do something right then? I'd better record this, her thanking me. I doubt that it will ever happen again.'

'Pity you won't get a story out of it though,' Iris added.

'I wasn't, anyway. I was persuaded to keep quiet or become known as a flasher.'

He had been 'staking out' the 'dead letter box for a week, in between court cases, and Iris had been bringing him food and drink throughout the day, but there had been no repeat of the envelope exchange.

'Well unless anything happens today, I think you should pack it in,' Iris informed him firmly. 'I've got better things to do with my time.'

Nevertheless, she stayed with him for several hours reading newspapers and playing games on his 'tablet' but still nothing happened.

'Right, that's it. This is a waste of time,' Iris declared, starting to pack their things up in her recycled bag.

'Hang on. Over there. Look,' he pointed. 'A man in a khaki overall. He's back. I told you I wasn't imagining it.'

They watched as the character slowly made his furtive approach to the mermaid.

And, as before, the envelope from his pocket duly disappeared as he knelt down. Having deposited it, he quickly left without a backward glance.

'Right! Keep an eye open for a white van and a bloke with a green hat and coat,' Gurney instructed Iris.

'Why? Where are you going?' Iris demanded.

'I'm going to see what he's left, before the park warden comes. I still reckon I'm right about that bloke writing to his dead friend,' Gurney said, smugly.'

'And what if the warden comes?'

'Let me know, of course.'

'How?'

'I don't know. I'm sure you'll think of something.'

Quickly Gurney rushed over to the statue and could see the head was pointing in a different direction from when he'd seen it before.

Making sure no-one was approaching, he knelt down, moved the tail of the Mermaid and as expected the body moved. Gently he pushed the torso and found the envelope inside the statue.

With great excitement, he removed it and examined it, expecting the 'depositor' to have addressed it to his former deceased colleague. But there was no name on it. The envelope was sealed but completely blank.

'Oh that's disappointing,' he said to himself. 'Now how do I prove my theory? I suppose I could open it and put it in a different envelope. Nobody would know.'

Just at that moment, Iris let out an ear shattering whistle. Gurney turned to see the white van parking nearby and the park warden arriving.

In a panic, Gurney crawled away on all fours, with the letter still in his hand. Keeping as low as possible, he made it back to Iris, but the warden had seen him and hurried over to the statue.

Immediately he could see the statue was open and the expected contents were missing. He knew that Gurney must have taken the letter.

# CHAPTER 33

The park warden moved fast, but not fast enough to catch Gurney and Iris, who had run to their van in a panic.

'Why did you have to be so stupid and take that envelope? You idiot.' Iris breathlessly berated Gurney. 'Now you've disturbed the hornet's nest, you've exposed us to great danger from unknown and probably ruthless people.'

After a reluctant start, the van's engine finally fired up and Gurney planted his foot on the accelerator. They zoomed off in a cloud of exhaust fumes, quickly disappearing into the traffic.

The Warden ran back to his own van and made a desperate call on his encrypted radio.

'Base from DO88,' he panted.

'*Go ahead DO88,*' came the response.

'Base. Code one. DLB compromised. Contents stolen. In pursuit of Blue Ford Thames van. Assisted guidance required.'

The reply came back instantly.

'*Code One acknowledged. Scanning CCTV screens.*'

The warden screeched out of his parking place and was immediately brought to a halt, as a large articulated vehicle started backing into the loading bay of a nearby superstore.

Straightway he was back on his radio. 'Have we got an operative in an artic here?' he demanded.

*'Negative. You are the only departmental vehicle in the area.'*

'Sod it,' he cursed. 'Just keep scanning the screens. Can you despatch all available mobiles to join me?'

*'Roger. Wilco.'*

Impatiently the warden waited for the huge lorry to shunt back and forth and park up, eventually leaving the road clear.

The warden drove off in the direction from where he thought the blue van had gone. But after an hour of fruitless searching, he called it off.

'Base, what happened to the CCTV coverage?' he demanded.

*'Unfortunately we had a planned mains outage exercise running at the same time. It took out the cameras as well as some of the traffic lights.'*

'Damn!'

*'We think we might have one shot of your target, before the cameras went down. The team are analysing the shot to try and decipher the vehicle registration number. As soon as they've done that, I'll let you know the address.'*

'Roger. You need to inform the depositor of his lost message. He will need to re-site the DLB, now it's been compromised.'

*Roger that. Base listening out.*

# CHAPTER 34

Gurney and Iris had successfully evaded attempts to catch them and had returned home.

'They'll track us down because the warden has seen the van.' Gurney observed. 'Where should we park it?' Gurney asked an ashen faced Iris.

'W…We need to park it in the garage, out of sight,' she stammered.

Gurney drove to the front of the detached garage, as Iris opened the 'up and over' door.

He drove in, extricated himself out of the van and quickly closed the garage door.

They approached their house cautiously, scanning the road to make sure they hadn't been followed.

Iris unlocked the front door and they stepped in. With a final check, she looked around before closing and bolting the door.

'What have you done Gurney?' she bellowed.

'I…I didn't have time to put it back,' he said, nervously.

'Whoever it belongs to, is after us now. You stupid fool.'

'I'm sorry.'

'So now you've got it, what are you going to do with it?' she demanded.

'We could always sneak it back,' Gurney said meekly.

'Oh don't be so stupid. They will have the place staked out by now and anyway, they will probably have removed the statue as well. You and your stupid ideas! I should have known,' Iris said, sitting heavily on to a kitchen chair.

'Shall I open it to see if I'm right about the letter to his dead mate?' Gurney proposed.

'I don't believe you got us into this mess, just to prove your idiotic theory?' Iris was beside herself. 'You stupid, stupid moron. Well you might just as well, I suppose. It can't get any worse.'

Gingerly, Gurney slipped his finger under the flap of the envelope and ripped it open. Inside was a single folded sheet of A4 paper. It was blank.

Gurney turned it over to see if there was anything on the back.

'It's blank,' he announced, looking questioningly at her. 'Why would anybody put a blank piece of paper in an envelope in a place like that?' he queried. 'And why all the secrecy?' he puzzled.

'Perhaps they wanted to catch you in the act,' Iris suggested. 'Perhaps it was just a test, after they spotted you the last time? Oh I don't know.'

'Yes, you're right it could be a test. Although, when I was a kid, when we pretended to be spies, we wrote letters in invisible ink.' Gurney volunteered.

'Spies!' ...Iris thought for a moment. 'You might be right. If its cloak and dagger stuff, It might need special treatment to reveal the contents.'

'But who would do that?'

'Who knows. The Government! Russians! Foreign agents!' she suggested.

157

'Foreign agents!' Gurney repeated, recalling all the horror stories he'd seen about tortures conducted by James Bond's enemies.

'Oh dear. If that's the case, I think we are in big trouble,' Iris observed critically.

'On the other hand…perhaps the bloke got confused and put the wrong sheet of paper in the envelope,' Gurney suggested unconvincingly, attempting to add some levity into the situation.

'You're clutching at straws.'

'No I'm not. Why I've even forgotten to put a card in and sent an empty envelope,' he confessed.

'Yes I know, she concurred. 'It was Mother's birthday card. 'No! I reckon this is serious stuff.'

'Why would anybody deliberately put an apparently blank piece of paper in an envelope though?' Gurney pondered.

'In case idiots like you stumbled upon the letter and would think it was a blank piece of paper.'

'That's another fine mess I've got us into,' Gurney said, flippantly.

'This is no time to be making stupid remarks,' she scolded. 'Save your senseless breath and go and get some fish and chips for tea while I think what we should do.'

In a huff, Gurney threw the blank piece of paper on the table and went to the front door. He unbolted it and cautiously opened it a chink to see if anyone was loitering outside. Satisfied no-one was watching, he stormed out of the house.

As she laid the table with plates, cutlery and condiments, ready for his return, Iris wracked her brains to work out how they could detach themselves from yet another one of Gurney's bright ideas.

'And I thought he couldn't possibly get into any trouble being a journalist. How wrong was I?' she berated herself.

# CHAPTER 35

Gurney duly arrived back home with the fish and chips.

'We can save the washing up if we eat them from the paper and use our fingers,' Gurney announced.

'Over my dead body! We'll use plates and cutlery, thank you. You really have some disgusting habits.' Iris replied, looking at him disdainfully.

She duly transferred the fish and chips onto the plates and binned the paper.

'I can see by the quantity of the chips, that those two nice young people served you again. What's their names?' Iris asked.

'Do you mean Rose and Alex? Yes, I think they've taken a shine to me.' Gurney suggested.

'More like they feel sorry for you,' Iris proposed unkindly.

'They never put enough salt and vinegar on at the shop though, do they?' Gurney said, anointing his plateful with lashings more.

'Look what you're doing with that vinegar,' Iris chided.

Gurney gave her a sour look. 'Now look what you made me do. I've splashed that letter,' he said, through a mouthful of chips.

'And don't talk with your mouth full.' Iris scolded. 'You really can be a pig sometimes.

'It doesn't matter, it's blank anyway,' he announced.

'For heaven's sake be more careful.'

They ate the rest of their meal in silence, but as they were clearing away, Gurney picked up the blank sheet of paper and became animated.

'Hey Iris. Look at this. See where the spots of vinegar have splashed on the paper. You can see some letters.'

'Let me have a look?' she demanded. 'Well, well, well. Who would have thought it? Using an alkaline based ink.'

'I suppose they wouldn't expect you to have a bottle of vinegar in your pocket, if you stumbled over the message though would they? Let's sprinkle some more over it and see what it says.'

'Hold it over the plate,' she ordered. 'I don't want you to spill any more on my table cloth.'

Gurney did as he was instructed, whilst Iris closely supervised.

'See I told you it was government stuff,' she reminded him. 'Look, its MOD headed paper. That's the Ministry of Defence,' she assumed, incorrectly.

Eventually the sheet revealed all of the message following its soaking with vinegar.

'Yeah alright, so you guessed correctly. But the rest is in code by the look of it,' he pointed out.

'Double security measures.'

'Here, you're good at puzzles. Why don't you try to decode it?'

'Don't be so silly. If it's a secret document it will be encrypted. Although *MOD* is in plain English and so is '*For DO88*',' Iris conceded.

'Perhaps because, to all intents and purposes, it's a blank piece of paper, they might have used a simple code too.' Gurney suggested.

'Mmm, you might be right,' Iris said, studying the vinegar soaked document. 'Now let's see, if we invert the alphabet what have we got?'

She wrote down the alphabet A to Z and underneath Z to A.

A B C D E F G H I J K L M N O P Q R S T U V W X Y Z

Z Y X W V U T S R Q P O N M L K J I H G F E D C B A

'I don't believe it,' she said, as she methodically went through the message and scribbled down a series of letters.

They have used a simple code that even a child could decipher. Perhaps it's one of the children's activities where they hide things. A bit like Geocaching? '

As she finished decoding the message she read it out.

MOD

FOR DO88

Most Secret - Eyes Only

Collect vehicle serial number 'Tanker 23'

Place vehicle M50 marker post. A123.1

Set charges to ignite at 0430hrs.

ENDS

'Oh my God!' Gurney blurted. 'This isn't a children's game! This is a sabotage message. What have we stumbled on to?'

'That's it! No more messing around,' Iris said, firmly. 'We've got to go to the police and hand this in.'

'Yes, I think you're right.'

'On the other hand. The people who left the message will know that we've opened it and they will know, that we know what the message says.'

'But we could pretend we haven't cracked the code,' Gurney suggested, grasping at straws.

'No, on second thoughts, perhaps we should just get rid of it and forget all about it,' Iris reasoned.

'Forget all about it!' Gurney exclaimed. 'What if this is part of a terrorist plot? We ought to tell somebody about it.'

'And the park warden saw me as well as you,' Iris added, starting to feel the panic rising.

'He saw our van as well!' Gurney declared.

'We're going to be hunted down and tortured,' Iris said, fearfully. 'These are probably highly classified state secrets.'

'Yeah but hang on. Why would they be putting state secrets in a 'dead letter box'?' Gurney asked.

'It gets worse. We've stumbled on a terrorist ring. We need to go to the police,' said Iris panicking.

'Iris are you alright? You've gone a funny colour. Iris! Oh god, she's passed out.'

# CHAPTER 36

*'DO88 from control.'*

*'Go ahead. Over.'*

*'Owner of vehicle identified. Security will take over operations now. Await further orders and new location of DLB. Over.'*

*'Roger. Over and out.'*

Iris had slowly recovered from the shock of being thrust into an unwanted 'adventure' and went about her domestic duties to help take her mind of the trauma.

As she was putting the empty milk bottles on the doorstep, she spotted suspicious activity in the street, which set her pulse racing again.

Bravely, she encouraged herself to walk up the short garden path to her front gate and see what was going on.

There were several unmarked white vans in the normally quiet road.

A group of men who had been standing in a huddle, started walking away when they spotted her.

Iris rushed back into the house.

'Gurney! They've come,' she said, leaning against the door as if to prevent anyone from entering. 'They're here.'

'Come! Who's here?' Gurney asked, puzzled.

'The letter. I think it's them.'

'Oh my God! What shall we do? What shall we do?' he panicked.

'Have you destroyed it?'

'No. I was holding on to it for evidence.'

'Evidence! For whose benefit? If they find it here, they'll know we know.'

Just then, through the pebbled glass, they could see a person in a high visibility vest approaching the front door.

'Quick let's go out the back door. Just as well we parked the van in that old lock up garage,' Gurney said, grabbing his coat.

As they made their way silently to the back door, the fluorescent jacket wearer knocked firmly on the front door.

'Hello inside. Gas board.' The man shouted. 'We're investigating a strong smell of gas. Please open the door.'

'I couldn't smell anything,' Iris said. 'It's a trick to get us to open the door.'

'As soon as we do, they'll jump us. If we keep quiet perhaps they'll think there's no-one in,' Gurney suggested.

'They'll break in anyway.'

'Oh my god. What to do, what to do?' he flustered. 'I know, I'll put them off the scent and burn the envelope and a blank piece of paper in the sink to make them think we've got rid of the note. Perhaps that will stall them for a bit.'

'I'm not so sure they'll be fooled that easily,' Iris counselled.

'Pick up the letter and let's go,' Gurney directed.

Iris duly put it in to her hand bag.

The knocking continued. 'Hello in there. You're in real danger. Please open the door,' the man insisted.

'Hang about. What if there really is a gas leak?' Iris suggested.

'I hadn't thought of that. No, it's a ruse. It's them alright. I'm going to do it.'

Gurney lit the paper and dropped it in the sink. As they stepped out into the back garden and quietly closed the back door, the smoke alarm went off.

'You and you bright ideas,' Iris cursed.

# CHAPTER 37

CJ zoomed his plotting table camera to view an area displaying a red flag.

He quickly rang the gallery supervisor.

'What's the 'red flag for?' he quizzed.

'It's a 'code one'. Somebody has stolen the contents of a 'dead letter box' and currently they've evaded capture.'

'We on to it?' he asked firmly.

'Yes. We're running the analysis on the data at the moment. It will only be a matter of time before we get them.'

'OK, keep me updated,' he directed.

As he hung up, CJ knew that if 'datamining' was underway, they would almost certainly track down the individuals.

Carrington Jones immediately called Security and spoke to John Ripple, head of the unit.

'John, I see we have a 'code one' on at the moment.'

'Yes. The contents of a DLB has been stolen. We're on to them. Helicopter and sniper on standby. It won't be long before we get them.'

'Good. I knew you'd have your finger on the pulse.'

'Oh, while I'm on to you CJ, I've got a Security report from my manager at Elmley about a recent incident. I think it's significant. There is a similarity in the names.

'What do you mean?

'Well the one at Elmley was involving a journalist called Leafmould following our road teams back to base and it appears the code one might be the same individual, except he has a female accomplice this time, possibly his wife.'

'Right, let me know the moment you've got them. Don't like the sound of a journalist sniffing around.'

'Don't worry, we have the technology to help them forget.'

'So long as they haven't already passed their findings on to other people.'

'Let's hope not,' Ripple added.

'Keep me in the loop,' CJ instructed.

'Yes will do. Mr Leafmould is very much on our radar now,' the security chief confirmed.

'But first you've got to find him,' Carrington Jones observed.

'I'm confident; it's just a matter of time, the other said optimistically.

'Nice to hear. Usual monitoring, after you've sorted him out with his memory?'

'Yes. We'll have so many bugs in place, he won't to be able to fart without us knowing.'

'Good man.'

# CHAPTER 38

As they stepped out of the back door into the garden, Iris suddenly stopped and grabbed Gurney's arm. 'What's that funny smell?'

'I can't smell anything.'

'Of course you can't. I forgot you've got no sense of smell. Gurney there is definitely a smell of gas out here. What have you done?' Iris accused.

'Nothing.' Gurney said defensively. 'Don't blame me.'

'Nothing! Are you sure?' she probed.

'Well the only thing I can think is, I put that stake in the ground the other day to support your roses. Come to think of it, it was difficult to get it in,' Gurney recalled.

'Oh Gurney!'

'Well how was I supposed to know there was a gas pipe under there?' he pleaded.

'Oh, I give up.' Iris shook her head in disbelief. Even preventing him using his tools was not enough to prevent him continuing to cause chaos.

'So we don't need to leave after all,' Gurney said, walking back towards the back door.

'Yes we do,' Iris insisted.

'Why?' he puzzled.

'Because it doesn't explain who that group of people were in the white vans. They might be using the gas man as a cover.'

'And they might also be contractors ready to dig up the road,' Gurney said logically.

'Ssssh, there's somebody coming along the alley.'

'They've come to get us. Quick, behind the shed,' Gurney whispered pushing Iris roughly into the small gap between their neighbour's fence and the wall of the shed.

They held their breath as the handle of the back gate rattled as someone turned it. The hinges squeaked as the gate opened.

'Damn, I forgot to bolt it,' Gurney whispered.

'God yes. The leak is definitely here,' a voice said.

A face and then a Hi-visibility jacket came into view. The word 'GAS' was printed in white, on the back.

Iris and Gurney breathed a sigh of relief. However, they were now trapped. Either they had to show their faces and explain why they were hiding behind the shed or stay there until the gas leak had been repaired.

Iris took the initiative. Squeezing out from her cramped hiding place, she cleared her throat and said. 'Yes Gurney, I agree. We do need to do something with the fence. Oh hello, are you from the gas board?'

'Yes Mrs. I knocked on your front door but got no reply, obviously you were out here. I'm investigating a report of a smell of gas...and I think it's coming from your garden.'

'Oh, yes, now you come to say, there is a slight odour. Don't you think Gurney?'

Gurney, who had been unsure of her tactics had still been hiding behind the shed also slid out.

'Yes, you're right. Definitely. Well if you don't want us to let you into the house, we've got an urgent appointment,' he said, pushing Iris towards the gate.

'Yes sorry.'

'By the way I think your smoke alarm was going off earlier,' the gas man said.

'Yes, it's faulty, I keep meaning to change it one of these days. Thanks.'

With that they scurried past a bewildered gas engineer and drove off in Iris' car.

'Now where to?' Iris asked.

'Just drive. We need to think.'


Meanwhile the security team had called John Ripple.

'We are at the address given, but it looks like a building site.

There is no sign of anybody living here. The neighbours say that the couple haven't lived here since the husband demolished the house. Developers have bought the place and are building flats here.'

'Damn. They obviously haven't informed the DVLA of their change of address then. Check on the name. There can't be too many Leafmoulds around.'

'OK. I'll stand my team down from here then.'

'Yes and check on any other addresses he might have gone to. His parents, her parents, siblings, friends. You know the score.'

'Roger.'

# CHAPTER 39

Iris and Gurney had been driving around aimlessly for some time, both lost in their own thoughts and fears.

Gurney broke the silence. 'Oh, I forgot to tell you that I've actually applied for a job with the MOD.'

'The MOD! But you've already got a job. Mother called in a lot of favours to get you that job at the Urbanite.'

'Yes, and she hasn't let me forget it either,' he added.

'I thought you wanted to be an investigative journalist too? That was the last fad you came up with,' Iris reminded him.

'Yes that's right...but it's...'

'It's what, for heaven's sake? What crazy ideas have you got going on in that echo chamber, that you call a head now?'

'I shall still be working for the paper, but I hope to become a whistleblower,' he proudly informed her.

'A whistleblower! What a referee?'

'No, it's all part of becoming an invest-a-gate-tive journalist,' he explained.

'As usual, you've lost me,' Iris confessed.

'The cone shifters work for the MOD.'

'Yes, so you've told me. But I thought they'd warned you off from any further involvement? Besides which, the cones have now been cleared away.'

'Yes, I know but there's something strange going on there and I want to find out the extent of it.'

'And I thought you couldn't get into any mischief being a reporter. How wrong was I?' Iris cringed at the thought of future chaos.

'If they've warned me off, that means they must be hiding stuff,' Gurney concluded.

'And you, Gurney Leafmould can go in there and find the reason?' Iris said cynically.

'Yes, I need to get inside their organisation to observe what's going on and then I can become a whistle-blower and get my scoop,' he said enthusiastically.

'Heaven help us! In any case, with your arrest record you're not likely to stand a chance of getting the job anyway,' Iris suggested, trying to ground his ambitions.

'No probably not, but I'm giving it a try anyway,' Gurney said optimistically

'So is this letter from the dead letter box all part of the supposed conspiracy?' Iris queried.

'Yes, I think so. But I'm not sure.' Gurney confirmed. 'Do you think we could stop?'

'Why?'

'I'm dying for a wee,' he said jiggling.

'We're close to Mother's house. I'm sure she wouldn't mind so long as you put the seat down, after you've been.' Iris proposed. 'Perhaps she can help us decide what to do about the letter too?'

'I don't want that old trout getting her nose into my business. Let's keep it between ourselves. But if you don't hurry up, I shall wet myself.'

'If you do, you'll have to pay for the seats to be cleaned,' Iris said firmly.

They drove towards the old lady's house unaware that, on the way, her car had been clocked by an Automatic Number Plate Recognition (ANPR) camera recording her number plate and broadcasting her location to the MOD.

As they turned into the drive, Gurney had a mild panic attack, as he recalled the disastrous episode that had occurred here previously resulting in sending him 'over the top'.

Painfully he recalled the nightmarish episode.

Iris had drugged him to sedate him; he'd accidentally locked himself out trying to disentangle himself from a vicious cat; he had almost frozen to death in soaking wet pyjamas and created a catalogue of damage, whilst attempting to get back in....and then the armed police had arrived.

The stress of his recall, didn't help his polyuria and set him jiggling uncomfortably.

'Oh Mother's boyfriend is here.' Iris said, parking her car next to a large Harley Davidson motorbike. 'I haven't seen him since he drove us away from that farm blaze last year.'

'Don't remind me,' Gurney groaned, holding himself. The nightmare rushed back at him. Iris being ko'd by that awful farmhand, the electrical overload, the fire, Mother-In-Laws rescue from the cesspit. And worse of all, saying goodbye to his kindred spirit the farmer, Sam.

She had helped him regain his self-confidence and feel worthy again. But now he was pitched back in another stressful situation.

Iris knocked on the front door. 'Mother it's only us,' she called.

'Come on, hurry up, you old trout,' Gurney jiggled, 'or I shall have to water your garden.'

Eventually Mrs Eyes could be seen shuffling along the hallway adjusting her clothes.

As she opened the door, Mrs Eyes said 'I didn't like the term you used. Us implies he's with you,' and she glared at the wriggling Gurney.

'He wants to use your toilet. It's a bit urgent.'

'Can't an old woman have some privacy? Well, you'd better come in, I suppose,' she said, begrudgingly. 'Make sure you aim properly and put the seat down afterwards,' she shouted at the fleeing Gurney.

'Thanks Mother. We need to speak to you anyway. We've got a problem. A BIG problem.'

'Well just living with him is a big enough problem. I'll put the kettle on. Is it him again?'

'Yes. He's really dropped us in the mire this time and I don't know what to do.'

Iris relayed the story of Gurney finding the DLB, taking the letter and them subsequently deciphering the hidden coded message.

'We don't know what we've found, but it's headed MOD, so we assume it's some sort of military thing.'

'Have you got the letter?' the old lady asked keenly.

'Yes.' Iris dug around in her handbag and gave the letter to her mother.

'That's strange for a start.'

'What's that?'

'Well it might be nothing, but I thought the 'O' of the MOD was always printed in lowercase,' the old woman pointed out.

'Does that make any difference?'

'No. But it could be that the letter isn't genuine.

'Or perhaps somebody just wrote it down wrong?'

'Yes, that's probably it. Perhaps it's a training exercise?' Delores Eyes suggested.

'Training exercise!'

'Yes, when I was nursing, we used to do work with the Ministry of Defence on mass casualty training exercises' the old woman informed her.

'It could be I suppose. But who would set fire to a tanker on a motorway?'

'That might be just a spoof message, to see if the information is passed through the organisation correctly,' Mrs Eyes suggested.

'What do you mean?' Iris puzzled.

'Surely you've heard the message that got an army defeated?'

'No!'

'The General sent a message -'Send reinforcements, we're going to advance. But it was received as 'Send three and four pence, we're going to a dance,' the old woman explained.

'Perhaps you're right. It is simply a training exercise,' Iris agreed, feeling brighter about the alternative suggestion.

'Although it does sound more like a plot from a movie, doesn't it? You sure they aren't filming around there?'

'Yes. Positive. So what should we do?' Iris implored.

'Well, you seem to stagger from one disaster to another with that idiot of a husband of yours.'

'Don't remind me.'

'I suppose it might be genuine. Are you sure they are hunting for you now?'

'Yes, I think so. But we haven't seen anybody though..'

'Well if they are. I don't want them staking my place out again. Jimmy and I have only just got my garden back to a reasonable state, after your husband got up to his tricks the last time.'

Gurney rushed into the room. 'It sounds like there's a helicopter hovering overhead. They're on to us,' he said, breathlessly.

'Helicopter! Are you sure you two aren't over dramatising this?' the old woman said calmly.

But before either of them could answer, the sound of several vehicles skidding to a halt in the drive and running feet was sufficient evidence to confirm their worst nightmare. They were being hunted.

# CHAPTER 40

'Quickly, out the back door, while I go and delay them,' the old woman said, being unusually helpful.

'They will know we're here though. My car is parked on the drive.'

'Don't worry about that. Now go,' she urged.

While Iris and Gurney ran out of the back door, the old lady waddled to the front door and yanked it open.

A large number of people wearing black balaclavas and weighed down by vests festooned with various military hardware were just about to take up prone positions in her flower borders.

'Oh no you don't,' she shouted, 'What the bleedin' hell are you doing on my property?' she demanded.

'We are in search of two fugitives. For your own safety, please get out of our way.

'On who's authority?'

'The MOD.'

'I can assure that there are no fugitives in my house,' she said authoritatively.

'We have reason to believe you are lying,' the leader shouted.

'How dare you accuse me of lying,' Mrs Eyes hackles rose. 'Now get off my property before I call the police.'

Ignoring the old lady's comments the group slowly

edged towards the house, guns raised, fingers hovering over triggers. 'Stand aside please,' the leader repeated.

Playing for time, Delores Eyes decided on a different tact and engaged the leader in conversation instead. 'So who are you looking for?' she asked.

'The owner of that car, Mrs Iris Leafmould and her husband,' the leader informed her.

'Well she isn't in there,' the old woman replied, hoping she was being truthful and that Iris and Gurney had fled.

'We'll be the judge of that,' the leader said, still cautiously approaching the doorway.

While Mrs Eyes had been speaking to the assault group, Iris and Gurney had left the house through the backdoor and was ducking and diving through the small orchard trying to keep out of the view of the helicopter.

However, desperate to get away, they had to break cover and were immediately spotted by the helicopter observer, who relayed the message to the assault group leader.

The leader held his earpiece to hear the incoming report. 'OK guys. The helicopter has just reported movement from the back of the house. Two targets running up the hill into the countryside.

We need to go through your house Madam,' the leader said firmly.

'Over my dead body,' she said, stubbornly standing in the doorway and crossing her arms in defiance.

'Sorry Mam,' the leader said, rushing forward intending to move her aside.

'Don't you touch that lady,' came a booming voice from behind her.

The leader looked up to see the doorway was now filled with a giant of a man wearing a black leather motorcycle jacket.

'Sorry sir. We need to go through the house to get to the fugitives. So please step out of the way,' he ordered.

'You heard what the lady said. No,' the man mountain replied.

'I warn you. If you do not move that I will have to Taser you,' the leader said, removing his Taser gun from his belt.

'And I warn you, that if you Taser me, I shall get very angry. I don't turn green like the hulk, but I can become very destructive. And for your information, for some reason, Tasers don't work on me.'

At this stage of the impasse, the old woman joined the man mountain in the doorway and said, 'It's alright Jimmy, my love. I don't want to see you hurting them. Let them pass.'

'Are you sure?' he asked, putting his massive hand on her shoulder.

'Yes. They have a job to do.'

She then addressed the armed group, 'but you're not running through my house in those dirty boots. Please take them off and carry them. I think that's a reasonable request don't you?'

'OK guys, do as she says,' the leader said, reluctantly agreeing.

The group of men duly unlaced their boots and satisfied that they had complied, Delores Eyes gave her boyfriend permission to let them pass.

In the meantime a sniper had 'fast roped' down from the helicopter and was in hot pursuit of the two fugitives.

# CHAPTER 41

The figure in the camouflage anorak suddenly appeared, the overhang of roots crumbling under his combat boots, sending a cloud of fine red soil down into the cutting.

He held his SA80 rifle tightly across his chest as he repositioned himself ready for the 10 foot drop into the ancient sunken salt road.

He had missed his quarry by minutes but he knew his fitness would quickly make up the distance.

He studied the footprints briefly and continued his silent, relentless pursuit. Leaving little visible evidence of his own presence, he could soon make out the figures of his frantic targets.

Spurred on by fear, however, Iris and Gurney were making good progress over the deeply rutted path.

Their shoes slithered over the hidden rocks at the bottom of the muddy brown puddles, each step soaking their clothes, the damp material slapping around their legs, chaffing their tired shins.

The pursuer knew the track would soon be sloping down to the road and they would reach comparative safety. He needed to act fast.

Quickly leaping out of the sunken lane he chose a high point. The beech tree would provide a firm platform for him to lean into.

He methodically threaded himself into the rifle sling, tensed and relaxed his muscles as his big hand supported the heavy barrel.

He took a deep breath to oxygenate his lungs, calming his breathing and clearing his vision. His right hand automatically prepared for stopping his prey, safety catch off, his finger gently resting on the trigger. The sight picture moved up and down the figure of the woman; the head, back, legs and the back again.

Exhaling, and with the rifle rock steady. He applied slight pressure to the trigger and heard a satisfying 'hiss' from the silenced weapon which announced the special missile was on its way.

Satisfied he'd found his target, he paused fractionally before he went through the same routine again to prepare for the second shot, this time for the man.

In his peripheral vision, he could see that the woman had stopped running, in response to the stinging pain in her back.

Gurney saw Iris pause and halted his own run to query the reason for her stopping.

The knees of the woman started buckling as her brain tried to understand what had happened.

She fell. And as her knees hit the ground, Gurney suddenly understood. His eyes turned back to look for the unseen pursuer.

At the same time, the second missile hit him, going in under his armpit. He yelped at the sudden pain and held his side.

However, it didn't take long before his astonished expression disappeared and was replaced by a blank look, his eyes rolling as the drug surged through his system.

Like a headless chicken his brain demanded one final act of escape. His legs obeyed for two steps before the paralysis set in.

He fell onto his back, one final spasmodic move of his feet and he lay still.

The hooded figure quickly leapt back into the bridleway, the years of training flexing his body as he dropped. He barely stopped as he ran towards the fallen figures.

His fingers sought the PTT button on his radio giving three quick presses. The response was immediate.

Two long clicks sounded in his earpiece. They would know he had been successful and his personal tracker would show them the exact coordinates to send a vehicle to lift the unconscious figures.

# CHAPTER 42

Gurney and Iris were taken to a secret MOD interrogation centre to recover from the effects of the tranquiliser darts.

They were placed into separate rooms and woken at different times by staggered injections of an antidote and truth drug.

John Ripple had travelled down to conduct the interviews. Iris was the first to be woken.

'Hello Mrs Leafmould, how are you feeling now?' Ripple asked, sympathetically.

'Mmm... what... happened? Where... am... I?' Iris asked, her speech slurred.

'You were running somewhere and fell over. You've suffered from mild concussion. Do you remember where you were?'

'I...we were... running away. They were hunting us.'

'Who were they?'

'We don't know.'

'Good response,' John Ripple thought. 'We are not compromised. They have no idea with whom they are dealing.'

'Why did you have a letter in your handbag headed MOD?'

'Gurney found it in a park in Chelster. A man came before he could put it back. Gurney thought it was a letter to a dead colleague. But we found it was a letter containing instructions to blow up a tanker.'

'I expect that was very disturbing,' Ripple said kindly. 'What did you think the letter was for?'

'We thought it might be a training letter for the Ministry of Defence.'

'Yes you're correct. That's' what it was,' he lied. 'So, nothing to worry about.'

'Nothing to worry about,' Iris repeated, dreamily.

'Now I expect you still feel a bit woozy at the moment after your fall, so we'll give you something for that and when you wake up you'll be as right as rain.'

'Th…Thank you.'

Iris was duly sedated and the security man moved to Gurney's room.

The same drugs cocktail was given to Gurney to bring him round.

Gurney slowly regained consciousness and Ripple asked the same series of questions.

'Why did your wife have a letter in her handbag headed MOD?'

'I… found it… in a mermaid… in a Chelster park,' Gurney said, his speech also slow and stilted from the medication.

'Why were you in the park?'

'I was admiring the flowers.'

'Were you watching for somebody?'

'Yes, there was a man in a khaki overall that looked suspicious. I wondered what he was doing.'

'What did you see?' Ripple continued.

'The man left an envelope inside the mermaid,' Gurney relayed.

'Which you took?'

'Yes.'

'Why were you following the vans from the motorway?' Ripple probed.

'They were doing suspicious things with the cones.'

'Who do you think those people work for?'

'I think they work for the MOD, the Ministry of Defence.' Gurney relayed.

'Are you a spy?' the security man demanded.

'No I am a journalist with a weak bladder.'

'Is that the name of a subversive magazine?

'No.'

'Is weak bladder associated with leaks?'

'Yes, of course, in a manner of speaking.' Gurney explained dreamily.

'Ah, ha,' Ripple thought. 'He is a subversive after all.' Not realising that Gurney was subconsciously referring to his urinary problems.

'Now I expect you still feel a bit nauseous at the moment, so we'll give you something for that and when you wake up you'll feel fine.' John Ripple assured him quietly.

'Thank you.'

Gurney was given the same sedation as Iris.


Later, John Ripple rang CJ and relayed the whole story to him about capture and questioning.

'Do you think that's it?' CJ asked. 'Just the two of them or do you think they might have mentioned the message to someone else?'

'They fled to her Mother's house, so it might be prudent to deal with that possibility too.'

'Yes, good idea,' CJ confirmed. 'And this stuff you've given them, will it erase their memory anyway?

'Yes, Phenloramide is very targeted. It attacks specific parts of the brain's storage area. So the idea is that it will only be mermaids and messages that disappear from their memories.'

'Is there anything else we need to consider?' CJ asked.

'No, I don't think we need to do anything else,' Ripple advised. 'Just continue to monitor them, that's all. Yes. Surveillance is ongoing anyway.'

'Has that mermaid DLB been moved?' CJ queried.

'Yes.'

'Good job too. That was crazy, putting it in so public a place,' Carrington Jones observed.

'Yes I agree. I've spoken to the team and they've seen the errors of their ways. Although Eunice Cabbage was not pleased that I did so,' the security man added.

'Don't worry about Eu. I'll smooth the waters. My little lamb is like putty in my hands,' CJ boasted.

'Little lamb! I'd call her many things, but a little lamb wouldn't be one of them,' Ripple thought.


As expected, the memory selective drug Phenloramide, a cutting edge technology devised by Professor Barber of the MO Disruption research laboratories, had eradicated Gurney's and Iris's memory of the clandestine events surrounding the dead letter box.

Mother-in-law and Jimmy had received a nocturnal visit by a specialist team. Their memories of Iris and Gurney's visit and that of the armed response team were also eradicated.

The old lady put the gap in her memory down to old age.

Iris's car was taken back to their home and was waiting for them on their release.

# CHAPTER 43

The memory erasing drugs had not been as clinically precise as the MO Disruption scientists had hoped and the side effect had left a vagueness in Iris and Gurney's memories about other things in their lives.

'Where are you going all dressed up like that?' Iris asked.

'I've just had a reminder on my phone, that I've got a job interview at the MoD today,' Gurney explained.

'An interview!'

'I had forgotten,' he confessed. 'But I think I might have told you about it?'

'Did you? I can't remember,' Iris said racking her brains. 'But you've already got a job at the Urbanite.'

'Yes I know,' Gurney said, trying to understand the conundrum.

'So what happens about your journalist job?' Iris asked.

'I'm not totally clear. Was I going to give it up?'

'Search me. It's your job.'

'Yeah well, it's only an interview,' Gurney added.

'For what?' she probed.

'I'm not really sure,' Gurney said, racking his brains. 'A job I suppose.'

'Yes, that's usually why you go for a job interview,' Iris said cynically.

'Was it something to do with investigations?' he wondered.

In the MoD! What are you going to investigate for heaven's sake? The number of soldiers wearing boots?' Iris asked disparagingly.

'No need to be like that. Oh, what the heck was it?' Gurney pondered.

'Pass,' Iris shrugged. 'But you're already working for the Urbanite newspaper,' she reminded him again. 'So why another job?'

'Was I going to go undercover to investigate something?' Gurney suddenly recalled.

'Were you?' Iris queried.' It's no good asking me.'

'Oh, you're no help,' he replied, frustrated at her lack of interest.

'Well, there's no point in going, if you don't know why you're going there,' Iris suggested, sensibly.

'Was it something to do with strange goings on the road network?' he mused.

'You're making this up,' Iris said firmly. 'There is no interview is there? You're doing DIY stuff again aren't you? If you are, that's it. The end of us,' Iris informed him.

'No. Honest. It's nothing like that…Least, I don't think so.' Gurney said vaguely.

'So what is it then?' she demanded.

'I'm not sure. But do you remember when we got stuck in that traffic jam on the M50?'

'You mean the one in which you nearly got us killed?'

'Iris, don't exaggerate. It wasn't as bad as that.'

'It was a pretty close thing then,' she insisted.

'And your Mother had been complaining about the cones on that bit of the motorway for ages?' Gurney relayed, starting to get some clarity of thought.

'Yes. She's always complaining about something. But it's usually about you.' Iris confirmed.

'And there was something to do with vans in the 'government' compound too,' Gurney recalled, digging deep into his memory. 'But I'm not sure if I wasn't imagining that.'

'I expect so. It's probably one of your Walter Mitty stories,' Iris belittled his recollection.

'That's it! I've got it! he said, suddenly clearer in his mind. 'Cones and the government! I reckoned there was a story behind it, so I was going to investigate and get myself a scoop,' he beamed.

'That's just it isn't it. IF there's a story! But you're not sure?'

'Well no. Not at the moment,' he confessed, unnerved by her interrogation.

'So how are you going to go undercover? Wear camouflage paint?' Iris mocked.

'No. I remember now. That's right,' he said smiling at the recollection, 'I'm applying for this job with the MoD. That's why the interview is at Elmley Farm. And apparently I've already got through the paper sift.' Gurney looked at her in smug satisfaction.

'They've obviously not caught up with your criminal records yet then,' Iris jibed.

'Why are you so horrible to me?' Gurney pouted. 'When I'm trying to do something for us?'

'I'm not being horrible. Just realistic,' Iris clarified.

'Thanks for the vote of confidence. Anyway, how do I look?' Gurney straightened his tie and ran his fingers through his hair.

Iris scrutinised her husband's appearance as he rotated on the spot in a mock floor show.

'Here, what have you got down the side of your trousers?' she asked, studying some white marks.

'Where?' he asked, following her gaze.

'There, look,' she said, pointing above his trouser pocket. 'It's a white line. It's above both side pockets.'

'Oh that! Yes. I…I mistook the toothpaste squeezer for the deodorant and squirted toothpaste under my armpits.'

'You did what?'

'I was thinking about the interview and without looking I grabbed the wrong container out of the bathroom cabinet. I thought I had wiped it all off,' Gurney said, twisting around to see the stains.

'You didn't do very well then. Turn round here,' she said, rubbing a damp cloth over the white marks. 'How the heck are you going to become an investigative journalist If you can't even recognise toothpaste from deodorant?' she demanded.

'The worse bit of my mix up is getting the taste of deodorant off my toothbrush,' he admitted.

'Oh, you're hopeless,' Iris said, shaking her head in disbelief at his stupidity.

'I shall be OK. You wait and see. I'll be incognito. 'Wish me luck,' he croaked.

'You'll need it,' she said, as he closed the door behind him.

# CHAPTER 44

So here he was, about to undertake another step on his journalistic career. Nervously he checked his phone for the tenth time to make sure he was in the right place at the right time.

The interview was to be held in a modernistic building at Elmley which reminded him of the circular lines of a colossal grounded flying saucer.

Nearly everything that the memory manipulation drugs had sought to erase had come back to him now; the cones, the vans, the incident with the police and the possible scoop.

However, there was still a fog in his head about something else, which niggled him and about which he couldn't 'put his finger'.

But Gurney was buoyed up by recalling that he had persuaded his editor about the big story waiting to be revealed, although unbeknown to him, Mother-In-Law's help and her long memory had ensured that he was the man to do it.

Initially the editor had not been convinced, but then he decided that if things went wrong Gurney was dispensable anyway and he could still deny all knowledge of Gurney's activities.

On the other hand, if Gurney was right, then the editor would bask in his reflected glory.

The newspaper owner was surprised that the editor had actually been thinking 'out of the box' and welcomed the suggestion of probing into a 'state secret'.

He liked the sound of having an 'Investigative Unit' in his newspaper kingdom; something that would make him politically powerful.

Gurney arrived on time for the interview at the office block that the locals had called 'the Yorkshire pudding', because of its circular shape, high rise sides and sloping central roof.

After being signed in and 'badged up', he was escorted to the interview room by a young lady who looked like a shorter version of Janet Street-Porter.

'Hello, you must be Gurney Leafmould?' she asked, extending her hand.

'Yes that's me,' Gurney forced a nervous grin and completed the handshake.

'My name is Pollen. I'm a People's Services consultant,' she informed him.

'Pleased to meet you,' Gurney replied, 'Sorry! I didn't get what you did.'

'People's Services consultant! We used to be called Human Resources.'

'Yes of course,' he lied, feigning understanding.

'Leafmould, now that's an unusual name,' she observed.

'Yes I've been explaining about my surname name all of my life.'

'I have great sympathy. For I too have to make defences for my name.'

'Oh?'

'Yes. You see, my parents were, shall we say, 'hippies in the sixties'; flower power people free love and all that.

When my mother was lying on the grass after I was… mmm…conceived, flowers from her floral headband fell on to her belly … Anyway they thought it was a good omen, so they decided to call me Pollen. Furthermore it worked well because our surname is Flower. Well it was the sixties after all and I'm sure the hashish helped convince them of their psychedelic decision.

'Oh how embarrassing. Sorry I didn't mean to be rude. It's a…a pretty name.'

'Now I've got used to it, it's not too bad. So I've lived with the name Pollen Flower for twenty six years. But you can call me Polly'

'Polly. Yes I like that too.' Gurney confirmed.

'But my brother Dan wasn't so lucky. ' Pollen continued.

'Dan's quite an ordinary name.'

'Yes but his full name is Dandelion Flower.'

'Oh, that's not so good. Same reason as yourself?' Gurney asked.

'Yes. Except it was my fault. I blew a dandelion clock and the seeds fell on Mum's bump when she was pregnant with him and she decided that it was a good sibling omen.' Pollen explained.

'And I though my family were strange,' Gurney thought.

'Anyway here we are,' Pollen said and opened a door into a small interview room.

She introduced Gurney to the two people already in the pastel coloured room, sitting in casual chairs.

'This is a relaxed atmosphere, so please make yourself comfortable wherever you'd like to sit. I sometimes take up a yoga position on the floor.' Pollen informed him.

Gurney wondered what sort of 'laid back 'organisation he was getting in to, it was a world away from anything he'd experienced whilst working at the Artificial Insemination centre or the Urbanite.

The interview was conducted by three people, one of whom was Pollen, an Operations manager named Ken Burbidge and a disinterested Human Resources spinster lady, Sally Grey. Gurney estimated her to be about 55 years old and who clearly had had her 'nose pushed out of joint' by the gushing consultant, Pollen.

'Thank you for coming today.' Pollen breezed. 'The interview will be a competence based discussion. There are no right or wrong answers. We all look at life from different perspectives so we won't be judging you on correct answers,'the consultant explained.

'We are looking for you to give us examples on key areas of the post for which you have applied. Do you understand?' the consultant asked.

'Yes I think so,' Gurney replied, nervously, wiping his sweating palms in the groin area of his trousers and giving, Miss Grey palpitations.

Gurney so desperately wanted the job so that his journalistic career would take off, and to prove to the editor and the rest of the world, that he wasn't the useless idiot that he'd been labelled.

'Your application form says your previous occupation was...?' The Operations manager asked pointedly, leaving the ball in Gurney's court.

Gurney cleared his throat for the interrogation that he knew he must pass. 'Umm. I was a...a labourer at an Artificial Insemination Centre.'

'And what was the cause of you leaving that employment?' the Operations manager demanded.

'I'm sorry Mr Burbidge, but under EU Human Rights employment laws you are not allowed to ask that question,' the consultant interjected.

'What!' the manager exploded. 'Can't ask why he left? Why ever not?'

'Because his former life's experiences have no bearing on his future.'

'Of course they do. If he is unreliable I don't want to waste my time managing the man every day.

I have a department to run and targets to achieve, let alone having to make reports, give warnings before I can sack him and then find a replacement.'

'You're rather getting ahead of yourself. He hasn't got the job yet,' she reminded him.

'Unfortunately, since we have been using your recruiting firm's services, we have had a series of disasters in recruiting a stable work force,' the spinster lady bleated.

'I've spent no end of time interviewing for the same post, because your company has undermined our recruiting standards,' the Operations Manager added.

All the while the three were arguing, Gurney sat in amazement but finally worked up enough courage to speak.

'I...I don't mind saying,' he volunteered.

'You mustn't feel pressurised to say anything,' the consultant added, quickly.

'No. It's OK. It was a health issue. I had complications from having my big toe nails removed. I needed a long convalescence and when I returned, I couldn't comply with Health and Safety requirements to wear toetectors, so I was sacked.'

'Well, thank you for your openness,' Pollen schmoozed. 'That really is most heartening in this day and age.' She duly put a tick on Gurney's application form.

He noted her action and felt a surge of positivity.

'Now, as this is a competence based interview and we are looking for people with creative imagination, can you give me an example of an idea that you had which you were able to successfully implement?' the Operations Manager asked.

Gurney thought for a few moments while he recalled several of his bright ideas but discounted many.

'Don't rush. Take your time,' the consultant encouraged quietly.

The Operations Manager looked at his watch in frustration, only to be tutted at by Pollen.

'There is no pressure,' she repeated firmly.

'I...I brought an old 19th century farm's bathroom facilities into the 21st century,' he said, finally. Conveniently omitting that the end result was a blaze that destroyed most of the farm buildings.

'That must have been an amazing project. Did you do the work yourself?'

'Yes,' he said, squirming slightly at his less than honest reply. In reality, Sam the farmer had done the majority of the practical work.

'So you're obviously a person who can think and implement. That's excellent. A practical person?' Pollen summarised.

'Yes.' Awkwardly he recalled his Mother-In-Law's translation of that practical ability. *Practically everything he did went wrong.*

'You realise that if you are successful in your application, following a background check, you will have to sign the official secrets act and be expected to attend various training schools?'

'Yes. I would expect to be trained to do my job properly,' Gurney confirmed starting to feel as if he'd already got the job.

'Well are there any questions that you'd like to ask us?' Pollen asked.

'Yes. What does the job entail?' he asked, hoping to get a jump-start on his journalistic investigations.

The Operations Manager looked at the other two and said officiously, 'I'm afraid until you have been background checked and signed the official secrets act, we are not at liberty to discuss your role in the organisation.

If however you wish to withdraw your application, now is the time to do so before a considerable amount of work is undertaken.'

'No, no. That's fine,' Gurney backtracked quickly. I'll await all those things. Just curious to see what I've let myself in for, that's all.'

'Defence of the realm and for Queen and country is all you need to know at this stage,' the Operations Manager added gruffly.

'Well if you have no further questions, I'll show you out, the consultant said happily.

Gurney shook their hands in turn and attracted a, '*I think you needn't worry*' smile from Pollen; a gruff, bone crushing handshake from the Operations Manager and finally a limp 'wet fish' handshake from the Human Resources spinster.

Back at the entrance Pollen took his visitor's ID badge from him and said, 'Thank you for your interest. We will be in touch shortly.'

'Well, I think that went well,' Gurney thought as he walked across the car park. 'That's the first step in uncovering all your secrets. Hopefully.'

# CHAPTER 45

Gurney was buzzing when he got home. Iris greeted him at the door, keen to hear how he'd got on.

'Why are you holding your hand behind your back. Don't say you've hurt yourself?' she demanded.

'No. I've bought these for you my angel,' Gurney said sweetly, producing a bunch of flowers.

'What have you been up to? she asked suspiciously. You never bring me flowers.'

'I haven't been up to anything,' he replied defensively. 'But ask me how the interview went?'

'Well! Don't keep me in suspense. How did it go?' she demanded.

'I'm more or less already employed,' he beamed. 'They said they'd make their decision today and offer me a job subject to a security check. So I need to start planning how I'm going to do this.'

'To do what precisely?' she queried.

'Become a whistle-blower,' Gurney reminded her, disappointed that she'd already forgotten about his journalistic intentions.

'What if there's nothing to blow a whistle about?' Iris observed critically.

'Oh!... Well I hadn't thought of that,' Gurney's cup of euphoria sprang a leak at her cold evaluation.

'Well, I suppose at least you'll have a job,' his wife added.

'Yes but it's not the job I want. It's the intelligence about the goings on that I'm after. Anyway, I said I'd let the editor know how it went,' he said, feeling deflated by her reality check.

Gurney rang the editor, but constantly got engaged tone so after the tenth attempt he decided to go to the newspaper offices in person.

Eventually, after waiting impatiently for two hours, the editor gave him 'five minutes'.

'Yes?' the editor barked, without looking up from the copy he was editing.

'I've come to tell you about the job interview at the MoD. I think I've got it,' he gushed, smiling.

'Good. When do you start?' the editor looked up briefly.

'They've got to do a security check on me first and then they'll let me know.'

'Are you likely to pass that with your history?' the newspaper man asked, pointedly.

'Well I hope so…I don't think they'll find anything to stop me,' Gurney said innocently.

'Yeah, right,' the editor thought sceptically. 'It'll be a miracle if you get in with your track record.'

'I'm very confident the jobs mine,' Gurney repeated, relishing the moment.

'OK. Let me know if you get it and we'll go from there. But in the meantime get back to the court. There's a heavy schedule of cases for you to report,' the editor grounded Gurney's euphoria.

It wasn't exactly the positive response that Gurney was anticipating. In his mind he was expecting the editor to shake his hand and congratulate him for his enterprise. 'Perhaps when I get the job, he'll be more excited for me?' he thought, as he left the editors office.

Gurney logged in to his terminal and began looking at the cases going to Magistrates court. He was surprised to see the name 'Eyes' on the list.

'Surely there's not too many people with that surname,' he said to himself, looking for the charge.'

'Oh here it is; driving too slowly in a manner likely to cause an obstruction. What's this second charge? Obstructing a police officer in the course of his duty. That's got to be the Mother-In-Law. She doesn't know when to stop. How I'll enjoy reporting that,' he smirked.

Just then his mobile rang.

'Mr Leafmould is that you?' the caller enquired.

'Yes. Who's calling?'

It's me, Pollen. Pollen Flower from the MoD.'

'Oh hello again,' Gurney felt a surge of excitement when he realised who the caller was.

Mr Leafmould, may I call you Gurney?' Pollen asked.

'Yes, that's fine. That's my name after all,' he tittered nervously.

'Oh good. I find it much more friendly using first names. You can call me Polly if you like.'

'Thank you...Polly.'

'Well Gurney further to your interview this morning.'

'Yes,' Gurney's stomach churned, he crossed fingers and toes.

'And subject to security checks. We'd like to offer you the job. Congratulations.'

'Blimey, that's a bit quick. I wasn't expecting to hear from you so soon.'

'Well, the reason we are able to quickly offer you the post, is because of a new initiative; my initiative actually,' she guffawed. 'We are introducing my initiative called 'fast fill' into the MoD.

We aim to get all vacant posts filled within weeks rather than months. Sometimes, in the past, it has even taken years to fill them. Some, so called essential, posts have even remained empty.'

'Really?' Gurney said, his mind elsewhere.

'Our belief, well mine actually, is that if there's a need for a post to exist, somebody needs to be filling it.'

'When will the security check occur?' Gurney asked. 'I hear that can take up to a year.'

'Oh no. Not these days. By doing away with the backlog, these checks are within the 'fast fill' project as well. As a matter of fact, yours is already underway even as we speak.'

'Heavens!' Gurney was impressed by the efficiency of the organisation.

'You might like to warn your referees, if you haven't already done so,' she counselled.

'Yes, I'll get on to that straight away,' Gurney confirmed.

'Furthermore, to help with the process, I shall be your personal mentor throughout your employment at the MoD,' Pollen informed him.

'Oh that's brilliant. I shall look forward to having some sessions with you,' Gurney said, without realising the innuendo.

'Oh really?' the contractor giggled. 'It's Personnel Services I offer, NOT personal services.'

'Oh, I'm dreadfully sorry. I didn't mean to...to imply that we...' Gurney flustered.

'Don't worry. It happens all the time. It was a lot easier when we were called Human Resources. At least there was no misunderstanding with Human Resources. I look forward to working with you,' she concluded.

'Me too,' he said. Gurney was now on 'cloud nine'.

# CHAPTER 46

Even as Gurney and Pollen were finishing their conversation, two investigators were already knocking on Delores Eyes door.

As she opened the door she glared at the two men in front of her. 'Yes. What do you want?' she demanded. 'If you're selling anything you can clear off straight away,' she said, looking from one to the other.

The investigators, former military intelligence interrogators, were taken aback by the harsh greeting from this seemingly, genteel grandmotherly figure.

Immediately they were wrong footed and nervously thrust their ID badges at the old woman.

'We're here for our appointment to talk to you about...' the lead investigator checked his paperwork, 'Mr Gurney Leafmould. I presume you are Mrs Eyes?'

'Yes, and I don't know why you want to spend time discussing that useless waste of space.'

'As we explained on the phone, he has applied for a civil service job and as you are one of his referees, we need to talk to you about him.'

'The ungrateful swine. I've only just got him a job at the local newspaper. So why does he want to change already?' she demanded.

'I don't know why. We're here because we've been instructed to undertake a check, that's all,' the lead investigator replied.

'See, that's what you get for being helpful,' Mrs Eyes feigned hurt. 'I called in a few favours and leaned over backwards for the sake of my daughter and you have it thrown back in your face,' she raged.

'Sorry about your feelings, but he needs to be fully vetted before an invitation for employment can be confirmed,' the other investigator added.

Why?' the old woman demanded.

'We PV everybody for ... the... ah Government,' the lead investigator added.

'PV! If it stands for Per-Verted, you've definitely got the right person in that idiot. Well you'd better come in I suppose. I don't want the neighbours knowing my business. Take your shoes off and leave them there,' she demanded, pointing at the outside door step.

'Sorry. I'm not happy about that. These are new calf leather shoes,' the deputy investigator said. 'What if they get stolen?'

'Stolen! Stolen! What sort of neighbourhood do you think I live in?' Delores Eyes screeched.

Embarrassed by the 'put-down', they duly removed their shoes.

The deputy suddenly remembered that he was wearing a holey sock.

Self-consciously, he tried to hide it and slid his right foot over the hole that exposed his left big toe nail.

But he was not quick enough to hide the offending sock from Mrs Eyes, who immediately tutted, making him feel even worse.

'Thank you for sparing your time to see us,' the lead investigator said. 'You have a lovely house.'

But even that scene setting statement, sent Mrs Eyes off in a rant.

'Well it is now. But no thanks to that useless 'waste of space' of a son-in-law of mine.

'You mean, Mr Leafmould?' the deputy asked naively, preparing to write her response in his notebook.

'Yes. Him. I can't even bear to speak his name.'

'Well if you feel comfortable calling him, 'Him', that's OK with us,' the lead investigator explained quietly, already getting the feeling that he wouldn't be recommending the confirmation of a job offer.

'Would it be possible to sit down somewhere, perhaps in the lounge?' the deputy investigator asked, looking around.

'Most certainly not,' the old woman reposted. 'I can give you five minutes of my time, that's all.'

'Oh, OK!' the lead investigator accepted, feeling uneasy at the curfew on her time. 'Now what can you tell us about Mr Leafmould?'

'Where do you want me to start?' Mrs Eyes asked. 'When he tried to blow me up in the bathroom or his burglary of my house? Perhaps wrecking my house or how he tried to murder me in a cesspit in Devon? Not to mention that he demolished his own house and razed a 19th century farm to the ground,' she ranted.

'Oh, I see. Quite a character then,' the deputy said, and immediately regretted uttering his thoughts, as the old lady froze him with a 'Medusa stare'.

'The man is a maniac and should be locked up for everybody's sake,' she continued. 'Did you know, he even got a hospital closed down by causing a flood of… excrement. Why even the thought of it makes me feel ill.'

'Take your time. We have all day,' the investigator encouraged, scribbling down her comments.

'Well you might have all day but I don't,' the old woman informed them. 'I have a dinner date with my friend Jimmy.'

'Does Jimmy know Mr Leafmould?' the lead investigator probed.

'Why do you want to know?' she asked, suspiciously.

'Well we try to pick up information from other people, just to cross check that we have the full story.

'Are you accusing me of lying?' the old woman's hackles rose.

'No, no good heavens no. It's nothing like that,' the lead explained. 'It's like building up a jigsaw puzzle. For instance, we spoke to one man's employers and they painted the picture of a sober, very useful employee but when we checked with his friends, he was quite the opposite. He made homemade wine, was drunk all the time and was a social pariah.'

'Home made wine! That's how 'he' demolished his house,' Delores Eyes informed them.

'Really! Did the still blow up?' the deputy asked, naively.

'You don't use a still to make wine,' the lead investigator corrected his colleague. 'Stills are used for distilling spirits.'

'Well he came pretty close to being a spirit himself. Had it not been for the courage of his wife, my daughter, who foolishly risked her life to save him from the collapsing house. Stupid girl.' Delores Eyes informed them.

'Now I believe the Tactical Arms group were called out to deal with a 'situation' here, too,' the lead said, checking his notes.

'Yes, that was all down to him,' she explained dismissively.

'At the time he accused you of... drugging and incarcerating him, I believe,' the lead investigator added.

'Yes he would, wouldn't he?' the old woman confirmed. 'The man's a maniac and should be locked away.'

'Yes, so you've said,' the deputy acknowledged.

'Anyway, you've had enough of my time.' Delores said, moving to the door. 'You'll have to leave now.'

'But...what about his accusation of you drugging and incarcerating him?'

'Don't believe everything you hear from that mad man,' she advocated. 'I'm sorry, but I've wasted enough of my time talking about him.'

'You say this Jimmy knows of him and his disastrous ways?'

'Yes,' Mrs Eyes confirmed.

'Would you give me his details please, so we can have a chat to him as well?'

'No. I don't want you intruding into our affairs. Not that I'm having an affair,' she said quickly, colouring up. 'Out you go.'

Mrs Eyes shepherded them to the door and closed it while they were putting on their shoes, unfortunately trapping the lead investigator's fingers in the door jamb as she did so.

His scream was strangely effeminate, as he hopped around with one shoe on, sucking his throbbing fingers.

He then stood on a sharp stone in his stocking foot which simply added to his vocalised pain.

Thus 'wrong footed', in more ways than one, the experienced investigators left without doing the thorough cross checking investigation that they would normally do. But they'd decided, the outcome was obvious.

# CHAPTER 47

A few days later Gurney was shown into a small interview room by Pollen Flower. He was beside himself with excitement. All the signs were good that he'd got the job. 'Please take a seat,' she invited.

'Thank you,' Gurney said but thought, 'she's being a bit terse, not like the other day when she was very friendly.'

'Thank you for coming back today,' said Pollen looking at the papers in front of her.

'My pleasure. I'm keen to start,' Gurney confirmed.

'Well, I'm sorry to say, that as a result of your background checks, I have to inform you that you were considered unsuitable for working for the Ministry of Defence.'

Gurney's heart sank like a stone. 'Oh damn! Unsuitable!' he repeated. 'Can I appeal?' he questioned.

'No. The decision can't be overturned,' Pollen advised him firmly.

'But you...at the interview and the phone call sounded so...so positive,' his saddened face telegraphed his disappointment.

'Yes, well I'm sorry, but you were unsuccessful and that's it. But it was nice to meet you.' Pollen stood and offered her hand. Gurney did likewise and they shook.

'If you'd like to wait here, somebody else will show you out. Thanks for your interest and good luck in the future,' she said tersely.

Gurney sat back down and cursed his luck.

'What was the point of bringing me back here and wasting my time, just to tell me that I'd been unsuccessful. Why couldn't they have sent me a letter or even just phoned me,' he fumed.

'More importantly, how was he going to explain this major setback to the editor. So much for my plans of being an investigative journalist,' he thought, miserably.

'It's over before it's begun. That's the story of my life. Nothing's changed, I'm still a miserable failure.'

He waited another ten minutes trying to think of what he could do, when the door opened and a tall man wearing a navy coloured jacket stood in the doorway.

'Mr Leafmould?'

'Yes.'

'Would you like to follow me please?' the man invited.

Gurney stood and followed the man, whom he assumed was a security guard. But instead of going back the way that he'd entered the complex, they went in the opposite direction.

'The rejects exit,' Gurney concluded.

Gurney, head down, followed the man along a series of anonymous windowless corridors, all painted in soulless magnolia, and all lit by fluorescent strip lights.

After what seemed an age they came to a door with a warning notice 'Authorised Access only'.

Above the door was a CCTV camera and by the side a push button key pad.

The man swiftly keyed in a number and Gurney heard the solenoid operate to unlock the door.

The man pushed open the door and stepped inside. He waited for Gurney to enter and closed the door behind them.

They had entered a large cupboard like room, which was about six feet square. It was empty.

Gurney felt tense. He was in a locked cupboard with a man he didn't know. He backed into the door and felt around for a door knob. There wasn't one.

The man reached into his inside pocket.

Gurney's mouth dried. Was he going to be kidnapped or killed?' his heart rate increased.

But the man only retrieved what looked like a small credit card out of his pocket.

Gurney gave an audible sigh of relief.

The man swiped the card at an unseen detector in the wall opposite and a door in the far end slid sideways.

'How did you do that?' Gurney asked, surprised.

'Electronics,' came the brief response.

The man stepped out of the room and Gurney followed, intrigued by the experience. As they walked through into another corridor, the door automatically slid shut behind them.

'Obviously a secret exit from the complex,' Gurney thought.

After walking along another series of anonymous corridors, they arrived at a teak panelled door. The man opened it and revealed a similarly equipped meeting room to the one they'd just left.

Gurney wondered whether they'd just gone around in a big circle, following the circular design of the 'Yorkshire Pudding'.

'Please take a seat, Mr Leafmould.'

'Thank you.'

'My name is Noone. Peter Noone. I gather the Ministry of Defence have considered you as unsuitable for their operations.'

'Yes, I'm sorry to say,' Gurney shrugged.

'However, we have identified that you have special skills that we would like to use.'

'Really!' Gurney said, flabbergasted at the others statement.

'Yes, the background check has identified your … shall we say, natural attributes.'

'Natural attributes!'

'I believe you've created a bit of chaos during your lifetime,' Peter Noone alluded.

'What do you mean?' Gurney asked defensively, his ego already bruised by his earlier job rejection.

'Your ASBO, barring you from all DIY shops. Seems to speak volumes.'

'Yes but I've given all that up. I'm now chaos free.'

'Really? Furthermore, a comment from one of your referees, has confirmed the genuine nature of your achievements.'

'No honestly, I'm better now,' Gurney pleaded.

'We believe that your core skills are just what we are looking for.'

'You are?' Gurney said in amazement.

'Well before we go any further, you must realise that you are being offered a unique opportunity to serve your country.'

'Serve my country?' Gurney repeated dumbly.

'You might like to say something other than just repeating me.'

'What! Are you offering me a job?'

'That's the general idea, yes,' the man confirmed.

'Really?'

'Yes. Now let's stop this silly dialogue.'

'Well I'm just gobsmacked that you think I am going to be of use. All my life I have been told I'm a walking disaster. I have little self-confidence as a result,' Gurney said, emotionally.

'I can understand that.'

'But I'm confused. If you're not the Ministry of Defence, who are you?'

'You're going to have to sign the official secrets act before I reveal anything else. Are you willing to do that?'

'Well, yes. I…I suppose so,' Gurney said, suspiciously.

'Suppose so, was not the answer I was looking for. A bit more positivity might be better,' Noone explained.

'Why yes. Yes of course.'

Gurney was over the moon to be getting in to the heart of an organisation he didn't even know existed, whatever that organisation was.

'Here you are. Please sign this document. This means you can NEVER reveal anything you hear, see or become involved with. Do you understand?'

Gurney put his left hand in his lap and crossed all his fingers. In his mind, this childhood trick meant that he was exempted from the solemn promise he was signing.

He felt uncomfortable, for he was basically an honest person. However if he followed the 'letter of the law' this could scupper his aim of reporting any findings.

'You realise you will now be subject to random security checks from time to time. And you won't know when you're being observed.'

'Oh! OK,' Gurney gulped.

'Right. Now you've signed that, I can inform you that you are being recruited into a secret organisation called the Ministry of Disruption.'

'The what?

'The Ministry of Disruption. As far as the world is concerned it doesn't exist. It is a state secret. So secret that even the Prime Minister doesn't know it exists.'

'Wow,' Gurney thought all his Christmases had come at once. This really would make him a world famous investigative journalist.

'Your rank will be a D2A.'

'I have a rank?'

'Yes, standard Civil Service arrangement.'

'I've never had a rank before,' he admitted. Not knowing what it meant anyway.

'Once you start on the training scheme you will be a DO-in-training.'

'A DO! What's that?'

'Sorry, I tend to forget newcomers don't know the jargon. A DO is a Disruption Operative.'

'What like those guys putting out the cones?' Gurney hazarded a guess, the penny at last dropping. The vans didn't belong to the Ministry of Defence as he'd originally assumed. They belonged to the Ministry of Disruption and they shared the same compound.

'So you know about those do you? No they are usually D2Bs with a foreman in charge. He's an LDO or Leading Disruption Operative.'

'I can see I have a lot to learn.'

'Well your starting point will be the induction course, so that you will understand the reasons for the organisation and the secrecy surrounding it.'

'OK. Thank you. I will do my best to...to serve my country.'

'Congratulations and welcome aboard.' They shook hands. Gurney beamed. He was on track after all.

# CHAPTER 48

As they returned to the meeting room Gurney admired the elegant design of the internal fitting of the massive 'Yorkshire pudding' complex.

'Wow, this is smart. It's like you've got your own shopping mall. It's so spacious,' he said looking around.

'Yes, they allowed various franchises in to populate the area known as 'the street'. It's got different types of shops and a hairdressers too,' the manager, added. 'Including a very modern café.'

'That was a nice cup of coffee we had from there,' Gurney agreed.

'It's a pretty good working environment all round, if you pardon the pun,' Peter Noone joked.

'Pun?' Gurney puzzled.

'Yes the building's design! Being circular and an all-round environment,' Noone clarified.

'Oh yes...all round, of course,' Gurney forced a chuckle.

Gurney beamed. He was going to like working here.

'Right. Now we need to do some domestic stuff,' the manager informed him.

'Domestic stuff?' Gurney puzzled. 'What like laundry, bed making?....'

'Not that sort of domestic. Like taking your photograph, finger prints and a DNA sample.

'DNA!'

'Yes, in case we need to identify your body.'

'My body?' Gurney looked at the other in horror.

'Yes, it's nothing to worry about. We haven't had to use it on many operative's bodies,' Noone assured him.

'Oh, I'm glad about that,' Gurney said sceptically. He was now starting to panic. 'What the hell had he let himself in for, where he might only be identified by his DNA?'

Having been given his photo ID badge, Gurney was shown into a small well decorated room. Six examination type chairs were arranged to face a large wall mounted 72" LED television.

On each chair seat was a notebook and pen. There was no-one else in the room apart from Gurney and his new Manager.

'Please feel free to take any notes for questions. However, you will not be allowed to take them away with you. So please memorise them and run them through the shredder before you leave, ' the manager instructed.

'Also ensure that you do not display your ID badge outside this building. If you are spotted, that could mean instant dismissal.'

'Blimey that's a bit draconian isn't it?' Gurney observed.

'You will appreciate the reasons after this short documentary about the Second World War. I'm afraid it's in black and white.'

'OK,' Gurney said, wondering what the Second World War had to do with his new job.

Peter Noone pushed the button on the remote and

the screen filled with an image of lines of small ships and boats in a choppy sea close to shore.

Crewmen were helping soldiers to climb into the boats. While long lines of others queued, waist deep in the rough sea, patiently waiting for their turn to be taken on board.

A plummy Pathe News style voice filled the room with a voice-over.

*'The hurriedly organised armada of 800 little ships has pulled off a dramatic evacuation of 350,000 allied soldiers from the beaches of Dunkirk.*

*Under heavy fire and strafing by Stuka bombers, the brave crews of ordinary people undertook an extraordinary mission risking their lives to rescue 'our boys' from the gates of hell.*

*Following their repatriation, Prime Minister Winston Churchill has put all the military services on a high state of alert. For it was feared that the 'Hun' will chase our brave soldiers across the English Channel.*

*After the unfortunate retreat from the hell that was Dunkirk, members of the Home Guard have been called upon to defend the British Isles, while our heroic soldiers are still regrouping and rearming.*

The pictures changed to show a motley assortment of Home Guard volunteers running around on exercise.

*'At the same time, a secret initiative was launched to recruit volunteers from the 'Home Guard' to go underground at the first signs of an invasion. '*

The pictures showed volunteers descending in to Royal Observer Corp underground bunkers and closing the trap doors.

*'Their role; to fight a guerrilla war, disrupting the enemy whenever and wherever they felt would cause the most disruption.'*

Scenes of explosions and demolished bridges filled the screen.

*The teams were formed in a cell like organisational structure, so that in case of capture and interrogation, no-one would have sufficient knowledge to compromise the whole organisation or know the vastness of its operations.*

A war time sign appeared, 'Careless talk costs lives.'

*This was further strengthened by the creed, the code of silence, to which all members were called upon to sign, with a death penalty if they reneged on the promise.'*

Gurney went weak at the knees. 'How was he going to get around that?'

*'Fortunately Hitler failed to follow up after Dunkirk, but the British underground organisation that was put in place then, still continues to this day.'*

Gurney's mind filled with images of centenarians still hiding in bunkers, wearing khaki uniforms and sporting tin hats, clutching old Lee-Enfield rifles.

*'No-one knows when the next war will erupt, so we need to be in a constant state of readiness and be prepared for the unexpected.'*

The video ended on that gloomy note.

Gurney felt depressed by what he had seen, and felt ill at ease. What had he got himself involved in?

'How do they maintain a state of readiness?' he asked. 'Do they play war games on places like Salisbury plain?'

'No, that would be the job of the Armed Services. They are part of the Ministry of Defence. We are not armed. At least not at the moment,' Noone replied.

Gurney relaxed slightly. He wasn't going to be shot at or asked to kill people after all.

'So we need to be more subtle,' the manager continued. 'However, we do undertake regular training exercises. But ours are undertaken covertly.'

'What do you mean covertly'?' asked Gurney, puzzled.

'Let me answer your question with a question.

'OK,' Gurney said, apprehensively.

'What would you do if you saw something going on that was causing a problem?'

'Such as?'

'A herd of cows blocking the road.'

Gurney shifted uncomfortably in his chair and coloured up trying desperately to think of an answer that would appease his inquisitor. He made a mental note not to ask any more questions.

'I... I...err would probably...intervene to stop the cows causing the problem,' he answered tentatively.

'Precisely,' the other replied.

Gurney beamed. He had somehow dredged up the right answer.

'But if you didn't know that there was anything causing the problem...then what would you do?'

Like a rabbit in the headlights, Gurney froze.

'Let me help you,' the manager proposed, seeing Gurney's confusion. 'If you don't know that there is anything causing it, you wouldn't know that you needed to do anything to rectify it would you?'

'I wouldn't?' Gurney said, confused.

'No. And that's exactly what we do. We cause untraceable problems.'

'Untraceable problems!' Gurney repeated, dumbly. And then the penny dropped.

Gurney thought back to the reason that he was there in the first place; His pursuit of the cone movers.

'Like putting cones on the motorway when there's...'

'...no work going on. Precisely,' the manager said completing Gurney's sentence.

'Yes!' Gurney mentally punched the air in success. The confirmation of his suspicions made him feel euphoric.

'The vans were nothing to do with the Ministry of Defence at all. They belonged to the Ministry of Disruption,' he clarified in his mind.

'There WAS something going on, after all. Now all he had to do was to find out more and report it, somehow...without being caught and endangering his life.'

222

# Chapter 49

After the induction course, Gurney booked his ID badge back in with the security desk and was shown out through a concealed exit, at the back of the 'Yorkshire pudding'.

Quickly he made his way through the security gatehouse, to the bus stop to catch a shuttle bus back to his car at the nearby 'park and ride'.

He now understood why he had been told to park there. It was one of the precautionary measures to protect this clandestine organisation.

'I've done it,' he beamed. 'I've just joined a secret organisation. That's the next step on the road to my journalistic career.'

He did a little jig at the bus stop, having first checked that no-one was watching.

But the 'fence' cameras had picked up his 'strange' St Vitus dance, much to the amusement of the security team monitoring the screens.

'Here, look at this bloke dancing,' Phil Jenkins pointed out. 'It's a bit early to be on the bottle isn't it?'

'It takes all sorts. Hang about, his face is familiar,' George Beach said, gazing at the screen. 'Zoom in a bit.'

Jenkins did as requested and the image grew larger.

'Well I'll be buggered. It's that journalist bloke, Leafmould. I thought we'd warned him off. What's he

PAUL GAIT

doing sniffing around here, I wonder?' the security manager added.

'Catching a bus,' the other volunteered, unhelpfully.

'Where did he come from?' the manager demanded.

'I don't know. I've only just clocked him.'

'I hope for his sake, he isn't up to anything.'

'Here's the bus now. Yes, he's getting on it.'

'We'll have to be extra vigilant, in case he comes back though.'

Gurney took the bus back to his car and drove home in a happy frame of mind, bursting to tell Iris the good news, but was surprised to find a large white van parked outside his house.

Working inside his house, were two men, with fully equipped tool belts festooned around their waists. Both wore navy polo shirts with the name, 'Networks' embroidered on them.

'Excuse me. What are you doing?' Gurney demanded.

'Installing you a new secure telephone system,' the tall, long haired individual informed him.

'I didn't order a new phone.'

'It's a requirement of your new job, sir,' the long haired one informed him.

'New job?'

'Yes, your new job.'

'My new job! Blimey that was quick. I've only just been told that I've got it. '

'Well, we have to be on top of everything. Pontification causes problems,' the engineer pointed out.

'How much is this going to cost me?' Gurney asked, feeling peeved about picking up a bill for something he hadn't even ordered.

'No charge, Company provided,' the other said, scooping up scraps of wire.

'Oh, that's OK then.' Gurney said, relieved by the others assurance. 'What about the broadband?'

'Yes, and you've got a new one of those as well. High speed, 120 meg. You also have a secure email system too. Ditch the old one.' The engineer directed. 'We don't want you to cause a Hilary Clinton problem and find your stuff on Wiki Leaks now, do we?'

'Surely they wouldn't bother to hack me?' Gurney queried.

'They'll hack anyone. And the trouble is, you won't know you've been hacked either.'

'Yes vigilance at all times,' the other engineer added. 'Remember. You have a special job now and 'walls have ears', lf you know what I mean,' he said, touching the side of his nose conspiratorially.

'Well, yes, I think so. What did my wife say about your visit'?'

'She wasn't in.

'So, how did you get in...?'

'Let ourselves in of course. Our keys open any door. You haven't got any secrets that you need to hide from us, have you?'

'Well no... Of course not,' Gurney replied, wondering where he'd left his newspaper ID badge.

'Anyway, we're finished here now.' The men said collecting up their tools. 'Cheerio. Don't forget you're part of the team now. 'Mum's the word'.'

Gurney watched the van drive off, wondering what he'd let himself in for. He had an awful feeling that he'd wandered into something way beyond his depth.

He shook himself out of his inaction and went indoors. 'Must ring the editor to let him know I've got the job and my theory was spot on.'

He picked up the new phone and dialled the editor's direct line and then just as it started ringing, he replaced the receiver.

'Walls have ears. Mum's the word,' he thought recalling the engineer's words. 'What if my phone's tapped.' He looked at the handset suspiciously. 'What if they've bugged the whole house?'

He looked up at the ceiling to see if there were any additional boxes installed,

but could see nothing.

'What have 1 done? Our privacy isn't private anymore. It sounds like big brother will be watching and listening to us from now on. Oh my god. What will Iris say?' he groaned.

# CHAPTER 50

The editor picked up the receiver 'Yes,' he barked.

'It's me,' Gurney whispered.

'If this is one of those cold calls, you can go and f... yourself....'

'Boss, it's me,' Gurney interrupted.

'What? You'll have to speak up. I can barely hear you.'

'It's Gurney Leafmould. Now can you hear me?' Gurney said increasing the volume of his voice.

'I thought we'd agreed you'd come in and see me. What are you doing pratting around on the phone?'

'I'm being followed and my home phone is tapped. So I've come to a phone box to call you.'

'Followed! Phone tapped! You sure this isn't one of your fantasies?'

'No, it's true, honest. I'm now part of an organisation that I can't tell you about because I've signed the Official Secrets act.'

'Well if you can't tell me anything, what's the point of you being there?'

'I'm working on it. But we'll have to find a secure way that can't be traced back to me. I need to keep a low profile.'

'So who are you then? Double 'O' six and three quarters?' the editor asked, cynically.

'No…it's… they even got my DNA in case they have to identify my remains.'

'Your what?'

'It's all a bit scary really. So if I suddenly disappear, you'll know they've got me.'

'Yes well, you've made your bed and you'll have to lie in it. Have you found out anything yet?' the editor demanded.

'Yes. I've confirmed my theory that there is an organisation behind the traffic disruption. But it's still early days to report anything yet.'

Gurney nervously peered out through a small gap in between 'business cards' advertising escort services.

'I must go,' he dropped his voice. 'A man is standing nearby and keeps looking in my direction. I think I have been tailed.'

And repeating the warning he'd been given, he said dramatically, 'Beware, 'walls have ears'. Goodbye. I'll call again soon.'

"Walls have ears'! Have you been drinking? What the hell am I going to tell the owner?' the editor bawled.

But by this time Gurney had hung up and was striding away from the phone box.

As he left the kiosk, a thickset man wearing a black jacket went straight in there.

'God! I wonder if they had that phone tapped too?' Gurney thought.

Shortly after, the man emerged and looked around to see where Gurney was. Having spotted him he started to follow him.

As Gurney turned a corner, behind a row of shops, the man followed suit and was now clearly tailing him.

Gurney increased his pace, but the man was still on his trail and catching up.

Gurney went into a few large shops to try to lose his 'tail' but the man was still there and as he emerged from one shop, the man started gesturing to him.

Gurney was now almost running as he dodged down an alleyway, only to find a lorry blocking his exit.

'Damn it.'

The man appeared at the entrance of the alley and came towards him. Gurney was trapped. He didn't know what to do. Should he hit the man or just run past him.

He decided against the former, as he detested violence, and might get hurt himself.

Instead, he decided to try to walk nonchalantly past the man on the right hand side of the lane.

But as he changed direction, so did the man.

Gurney crossed to the other side of the lane. The man changed too.

Perhaps he was going to stab him with a poisoned needle or kidnap and torture him.

'I've only just started my new job and already I'm a target on somebody's hit list,' he wailed.

As they were getting closer together, the man pulled his hand out of his pocket. Something glinted in his fist.

Gurney's heart almost beat itself out of his chest. He was panting in fear.

The man brought his hand forward at chest height and stepped in front of Gurney.

'Oh my god, he's going to stab me,' Gurney thought.

He could see the other was talking to him, but Gurney couldn't hear anything. He was deafened by his increased blood pressure roaring in his ears. His legs refused to move. He was 'fear frozen' to the spot.

Gurney was wondering how women could scream so easily, when they needed to, because he didn't know how to, but desperately wanted to.

The anxiety built up to a hysterical level in his mind.

At any moment he was going to be stabbed. He could imagine the knife piercing his flesh, puncturing his heart. There would be blood and...

He forced himself from eye contact with the man to look at the knife, hoping to work out a way to avoid the blade. But somehow it had changed.

The man was not holding a knife, but some keys. A bunch of keys.

Then at last he heard the man's voice.

'I said. Are these your keys? I bloody hope so. I'm knackered chasing after you,' the man said, breathlessly. 'You're bloody lucky that I've still got them. I was going to bin them, if I hadn't caught you now.'

'My keys! My keys!' Gurney laughed nervously. 'Only my keys. Oh thank God for that. I thought you were going to...trying to...Oh thank,. Thank you so much.'

The man gave Gurney the bunch of keys, turned and walked away, muttering, 'that's the last time I do anybody a bleedin favour.'

Not normally a solo drinker, Gurney went to the nearest pub and ordered a whisky to calm his frayed nerves.

# CHAPTER 51

'Leafmould working for us! How the hell did that happen?' CJ exploded.

'It appears we have a procedural problem,' Ripple said, awkwardly.

'A procedural problem! Jesus, that's a bit of an understatement.'

'Yes. Operations recruited him without our knowledge. But my guys spotted him nearby and crosschecked the records.'

'How far has he got? What's the damage?'

'We're trying to evaluate that now,' Ripple added.

'Evaluate, be buggered. I need something more than that,' CJ demanded.

'Well we know he's been through his induction course,' Ripple revealed.

'So the 'cats out of the bag'. Right! I want action and I want it now. A permanent solution too. No more pussyfooting around with memory drugs.'

'Yes I appreciate that, but it appears that Leafmould is still a member of the press. So we need to be careful on our actions.' Ripple counselled. 'We think he's an investigative reporter, out to make a name for himself.'

Ripple didn't want to admit that he'd had his suspicions about Leafmould's intentions and mentally kicked himself for not realising that Weak Bladder was a code for...Leaks. 'Wiki Leaks', perhaps.

'So what?' CJ probed.

'So he can't just suddenly disappear,' Ripple explained.

'Why not? we've done it before.'

'Parliament would be up in arms if it came out that we'd interfered with the 'freedom of the press'. The last thing we want is for a select committee to be investigating us again,' Ripple cautioned.

'If we can't make him disappear, what's your suggestion then?' CJ quizzed.

'We continue to train him.'

'We what? Are you out of your mind?' CJ shouted.

'Recruit him and drip feed him with information, but only the stuff we want him to publish.'

'Information about what, precisely? CJ demanded.

'Misinformation! False news. We tell him mythical things that never happen. He publishes it in the papers and on social media. The public are misinformed and cause chaos of their own making. And he becomes discredited.'

'False news! Such as?'

'Simple road traffic reports. Start a rumour that a particular route is being closed for roadworks or an accident. People find their own way around alternative routes and congest them as well.'

'We're already doing that,' CJ berated,' as part of normal operations.'

'Oh! I didn't realise ....other than that, I can't think of any other way of getting around the situation,' Ripple confessed. 'I understand that he's due to do his foundation course soon and then he'll know the full scale of the Ministry's disruption portfolio.'

'Damn! Can't we stop him?' Carrington Jones thumped the desk.

'How about if we wait?' Ripple suggested.

'Wait! So he can spill the beans on all of our secrets. Are you mad?'

'No. I was just thinking…knowing what a walking disaster he is, I think it's just a matter of time before he cocks up himself and we will be able to control him. If you know what I mean?' Ripple alluded.

'I can't believe we're even having this conversation,' CJ shouted. 'It was your team that PV'd him in the first place.'

'No, it wasn't,' Ripple said defensively. 'It was the Ministry of Defence's people. We just intercepted their report and Peter Noone decided that all the list of disruptive things that Leafmould had done by himself, seemed to make him a perfect recruit for us.'

'How come he missed the fact that he was still working for a newspaper?'

'We're restricted to the knowledge we can use. We can't cross-check records between departments.'

'Why ever not?' CJ demanded.

'It's EU Human Rights regulation, apparently.' Ripple advised him.

'Jesus!' CJ stood up and looked out of the window in frustration.

'We're prevented from compiling a comprehensive report based on records held by other departments,' the security chief explained. 'That is, according to their Human Resources contractors.'

'Bullshit! This is serious stuff. The whole of the Ministry of Disruption is compromised by some stupid assed rules not of our making! Have your team checked out this Human Resources firm?' Carrington Jones questioned.

'Well…no…not really.'

'Why ever not?'

Well they were brought in by the Ministry of Defence Human Resources people. And we believe they're on their 'preferred suppliers' list.'

'Preferred Suppliers list?'

'Firms that have been approved to work for the company.'

'And who creates the 'preferred suppliers' list?' CJ asked, pointedly.

'Oh shit! It's their Human Resources department,' Ripple realised. 'We've been shafted!'

'Haven't we just. So how are you going to get us out of this mess, Ripple?'

'We need to discredit them somehow. But how?'

'Can we 'kill two birds with…'

'One stone?'

'Yes, I know the phrase,' CJ said, irritated by the other's interruption. 'I was thinking of perhaps sacrificing Leafmould by feeding him some misinformation about this Human Resources mob. What do you think?'

'I think it's a great idea,' Ripple agreed, relieved he had been offered a glimpse of salvation.

'We'll wait until he's done his training first though.' CJ agreed. 'As you say knowing his calamitous reputation, he might well make a 'rod for his own back' and we'll get away with it that way.'

'Yes, good idea,' Ripple agreed, grateful that CJ was thinking on similar lines.

'You can only hope he does, otherwise you're going to be looking for a new job,' CJ added vehemently.

# CHAPTER 52

'I can't believe they're sending you to the MOD training school so soon,' Iris said, leaning in to the driver's window.

'Well as my boss, told me, 'there's no point recruiting you and not getting the most out of you,' Gurney told her.

'Goodbye Gurney, call me when you get there,' Iris instructed.

'Yes, I will', he said, pulling away.

He drove his old 'bluebird blue' Ford van up the M5 and M6 motorways, admiring the large number of sites, where the MO Disruption's 50 mph fixed speed limits were in operation.

'Marvellous,' he thought. 'They are now just accepted as part of everyday motoring. Nobody would know that the roadworks are, purely 'cosmetic delay making' activities.'

He came off the M6 and navigated the Staffordshire country lanes via Minshall to the training school at Yawnfield near Granite.

'Ah, this must be it,' he said, pulling up next to a sign announcing '*Trespassers will be shot. Patrolled by Guard dogs.*'

'Blimey, that's a bit scary. What the hell have I let myself in for?'

The central training school buildings were on the site of a former Second World War American army base.

The MOD student's dormitories were located in the same ancient 'H' shaped wooden huts that were originally used for billeting the American troops.

This particular location had been selected because of the normally poor weather conditions, which were experienced in the area. Most of the time it was cloudy and overcast, which dissuaded Nazi bombers from jettisoning their unused bombs, after pounding the Liverpool dockyards.

All the buildings were single storey structures, with the exception of one tall brick complex situated in the centre of the camp. This rounded corrugated asbestos roofed construction served a dual purpose of canteen and a part time cinema.

The large cinema was an essential element of camp life both then and now, for there was little else adjoining the camp, except an estate of red brick lecturers' houses.

As he turned on to the private drive, he could see a line of cars in front of him.

'I hope this isn't going to take long, I'm dying for a pee,' he muttered to himself.

But the line of traffic took almost an hour to reach the security barrier, where two uniformed people were inspecting paperwork and the inside of the cars. By this time Gurney was 'bursting'.

'Hello sir, paperwork please,' the guard demanded.

Gurney handed him the course 'call up' paperwork from the passenger seat, his hand shaking. His discomfort was now blocking out any polite conversation so he was only able to give monosyllabic replies.

'Are you OK sir,' the guard asked, concerned, peering at Gurney's reddening face.

'Yes, medical condition, need wee. Have toilet, can use?' he squeaked.

'Fraid not sir. The one in the blockhouse here is for our use only. We have to be very careful. Anybody could plant anything in there.'

'As if anybody would want to make a political statement by blowing up a security hut in the middle of nowhere,' Gurney thought. 'The only thing that was likely to be planted, would be a large turd.'

'That would compromise our security,' the guard continued. 'We won't take long. Now let me see.' The guard looked at Gurney's paperwork. 'That's a very unusual name. Where does that come from? Is it English?'

Of all the times that Gurney didn't want to discuss the origins of his name, this was one.

'No, sorry. Bladder,' Gurney muttered, through gritted teeth.

'OK, be like that,' the guard said, taking umbrage. 'But you don't appear on this list. Just a second there's another one in the office.'

The guard deliberately took another five minutes before he re-emerged, by which time Gurney was doubled over in pain.

'Yes, you're on my list. I'll have your mobile please. Collect it when you leave.'

Gurney handed over his mobile, which he'd already switched off.

'Drive straight up the road and it's the first car park on the right. I'll just lift the barrier and let you through.'

The barrier had just started lifting as Gurney shot through underneath, snapping off his radio aerial.

'Mad bastard,' the Guard shouted, as Gurney exceeded the 10 mile per hour speed limit.' Some people are so impatient. I can see we're going to have trouble with him.'

Gurney hurriedly parked in the *'registration only'* car park and ran, bent doubled, towards the buildings following the *'registration'* signs.

He leapt up the small flight of steps, ignoring the beautifully manicured flower borders both sides and quickly sought out the appropriate room, emerging five minutes later, very relieved.

Now that he had regained control of his mind and restored clear vision, he looked around his surroundings.

He had entered a large reception area where there were a lot of people milling around several desks.

He spotted a large overhead notice directed at arriving students to;

*REGISTER at table 'A' to obtain an ID badge (with lanyard);*

*OBTAIN ACCOMMODATION at table 'B' for dormitory room allocation and to sign for a key, ('lost keys are chargeable)*

*BOOK COURSE at table 'C' .*

Having conducted his business at table's A & B, Gurney made his way to Table C.

'Good morning...err,' the young lady seated opposite said, staring at his newly received ID badge, 'Mr Leafmould, may I call you Gurney?'

'Yes of course.'

'What course are you on?' she asked.

'To be honest I'm not sure.' Gurney confessed. 'Can I

look at your list just to jog my memory,' he asked. 'I had to rush in and I've left the papers in the car.'

'Yes of course. But it's a very long list.'

Gurney studied the very comprehensive list of courses on the sheet.

'Another information gathering opportunity for his article,' he thought.

He had already been informed that the department was very keen to over-train their operatives, but was amazed at the number of courses on offer.

**Disruption Courses:-**

***Driving*** – *How to slow Motorway traffic down (the unseen stoppage)*
*Multiple pileup and low speed shunt driving (for maximum disruption)*

***Road Works*** - *Maximum disruption – Precise timing*

***Road Congestion*** - *Managing congestion to maximise disruption (Basic)*
*Managing congestion to maximise disruption (Intermediate)*
*Managing congestion to maximise disruption (Advanced)*
*False reporting to Radio Road Reporters – Part 1*
*False reporting to Radio Road Reporters – Part 2*
*Tweeting false congestion*
*Police Car look alike driving course (at 65mph )*
*Police Car look alike – Parking for maximum disruption*

*Wide Loads – planning 1- most disruptive route*
*Dark Canine implementation A*
*Dark Canine implementation B*
*Dark Canine disruption planning*

**Weather** - *Creating Fog*
*Gritting with instant snow*
*False weather road data*

**Airport** - *Flight       disruption       (Mechanical*
*- Aeroplanes)*
*Flight disruption (Mechanical – Baggage*
*mechanism)*
*Flight disruption (Electrical & Electronic*
*– basic)*
*Flight disruption (Industrial relations)*

**Supermarket** - *Checkout chaos A (queue disruption*
*inc. cheque & no card)*
*Checkout chaos B (inc. too many*
*items in 5 items only)*
*Too many items in the bagging area*
*(mechanical adjustments)*
*Aisle blockage planning*

**Advanced Management Course**
*Arranging large sporting events in*
*areas where transport infrastructure is*
*inadequate (or made to be temporarily*
*inadequate)*

**Disruption Operative**
*Basic A*
*Basic B*
*General*
*Line Management*

*Measures*        *Disruptive Index (D.I.'s) for Line*
                  *Managers*

*Appraisements*   *Handling un-success*

'Good heavens! So many courses! I didn't realise you did so many,' he said handing the list back.

'Yes. We cater for all situations. We are the central training school after all.'

'I think I'm on the 'Disruption Operative, Basic A' course,' Gurney decided.

The course administrator checked her list and spotted his name. 'Yes you're correct. OK, the course starts at 2:00 pm in hut 24.

You will need to leave your luggage in your room and get some lunch before classes start. The canteen is adjoining the cinema,' she explained. 'Welcome and I hope you enjoy your training course experience.'

'Thank you. I intend to,' he beamed, heading for the canteen. 'Actually I am a bit peckish, so I could do with a bite to eat and a cuppa.'

# CHAPTER 53

Gurney followed the signs to the canteens. Canteen 1 displayed a notice indicating it was closed, but canteen 2 had a line of people walking into it, so he followed suit.

The canteen reminded Gurney of the pictures he'd seen of factory canteens of the fifties and sixties, from the BBC radio lunchtime programme, 'Workers Playtime'.

It was a tall hangar like space, with badly fitting rusty metal framed windows, set high in the side walls.

The un-plastered brickwork walls had originally been painted magnolia, but years of lack of maintenance had allowed it to peel off in sections, exposing the 'naked' bricks beneath. Due to the poor upkeep, he later learnt that diners often received an unwanted paint flake supplement on their food.

The lighting was provided by a number of large glass globe lamp shades hanging in clusters from the high ceiling. Underneath were rows of round formica topped tables with tubular metal legs accompanied by chairs with hard wooden seats.

As he queued for his food, Gurney could see the washing up area in the kitchen, where glum faced, heavily tattooed staff, noisily handled mountains of plates and bowls. Unusually they were washing them by hand, rather than machine.

He subsequently found out that they were inmates from the nearby open prison, working on the 'getting back to the community' phase of their sentence.

After putting a plate of over-cooked slimy spaghetti topped with a covering of brown 'stuff', allegedly bolognaise, on his tray, he picked up a small glass bowl of jelly, which had a thin veneer of custard resting on the top.

He helped himself to a mug of 'stewed' tea from a stainless steel urn and made his way back to find an empty table. He passed several which showed signs of careless diners until he found a less 'mucky' one.

The new intake of students were scattered around the canteen, sitting self-consciously by themselves. Comradery would come in the bar later.

As Gurney tucked in to his meal, he was suddenly aware of movement around the high window sills.

He couldn't believe his eyes. It was cats. Tens of cats. Mangy looking, feral cats.

They had squeezed through the badly fitting windows and were now prowling around the hall looking for food scraps.

Then he spotted the signs on the walls; 'DO NOT FEED THE CATS.'

The sight of the mangy animals parading around the inside of the canteen, curtailed Gurney's limited interest in his unappetising food and he decided to leave it and go to the dormitory instead.

He was on his way to the exit when a loud authoritarian voice directed. 'TAKE YOUR TRAY BACK TO THE HATCH. What do you think this is, the bleedin Ritz?'

The noise of cutlery on plates suddenly stopped, as did the hubbub of conversation as people looked around to see who was being castigated. The diners stared at Gurney, shamed-faced he returned to his table, picked his tray up and carried it to the hatch.

The journey seemed a long trudge, through a sea of relieved faces, happy to see that he was the culprit and they had escaped any admonishment.

Gurney scraped his uneaten food in to an overflowing waste food bin and put the empty plate on a stack of others.

He stored the now empty tray on top of a precarious pile of others, and hoping not to initiate a noisy avalanche, he rushed out.


Gurney made his way back to the carpark and found a note under the windscreen wiper of his van. As he read it, an officious man dressed in traffic warden's clothes approached him.

'This your car?'

'Yes.'

'Can't you read?'

'Yes, why?'

'What does that notice say?'

Gurney turned to where the man was pointing and read the notice out aloud. '*Registration Only carpark.*'

'Precisely. So why is your car still parked here?'

'After registration I went for a meal. I haven't eaten since breakfast at 6:30am.'

'Is that registration?' the warden probed.

'Well no. Strictly speaking, no.' Gurney agreed. 'But...'

'I shall be reporting you to the Principal. Now move it.'

'I'm sorry if I overstayed my allowance, but there doesn't seem to be a problem. There are about 50 other spaces available,' Gurney pointed out, looking around a half empty carpark.

'Yes, because other people follow the rules. Now move it.'

'How about, move it please?' Gurney said, annoyed at the others rudeness.

'Is this your first course?'

'Yes.'

'Well it could be your last, if you don't move, now,' the officious warden threatened. 'And don't forget, after you've unloaded your car, leave it in the student's parking area designated for your hut. We will be checking on the windscreen stickers.'

'Windscreen sticker?' Gurney queried.

'Yes you were given it when you registered earlier,' the warden informed him.

'Oh, it's in the envelope is it?'

'Yes and I suggest you get it out and stick it on.'

'I'll do it when I park,' Gurney said bravely, seeking to antagonise the warden.

'See that you do.'

Gurney decided that to continue the argument would be futile and drove off.

'Well if the organisation is run by car park attendants, then the world would soon grind to a halt, trussed up with officialdom and red tape,' he ranted.

# CHAPTER 54

Gurney followed the signs for the student accommodation. Fearful of falling foul of any other regulations; he faithfully adhered to the 10mph speed limit.

'Surely they're not putting us up in these old wooden huts are they?' he wondered. 'Well, there doesn't appear to be anything else. So it must be right.'

There was a plethora of small wooden fingerposts showing directions to various accommodation blocks.

'Now where am I going?' he wondered, studying the envelope he'd been given at reception.

'Room AA 12B. Right, well there's blocks A, B, C... crikey! I'm going to be the furthest away from the centre of the site, I reckon.'

After a confusing ten minute drive, circumnavigating all the feeder roads leading to the wooden dormitories, he eventually found the one that he was looking for. But soon discovered, that the road ended fifty yards short of hut AA.

To his further annoyance he found that the designated carpark for the hut, was already full.

'That's brilliant. So where do I park then? he wondered. 'Oh sod it, I'm not going to drive round the site looking for another space. I'll park here,' he said, parking half on the grass verge and half on the adjoining footpath.

However, recalling the officious warning from the car park 'Fuhrer', he dug out the vehicle sticker and stuck it to his windscreen.

'At least, he can't have me for illegal parking, because I am in the right carpark,' he thought, rechecking the carpark sign *'Parking for Hut AA only'*.

He grabbed his bags out of the back of the van and went to the entrance of his hut.

As he opened the door, the smell of floor polish overwhelmed his senses, making his eyes water.

Stepping in, he could see that the floor was covered in highly polished brown linoleum.

In an alcove, near the door, he noticed a floor buffer, obviously used by the proud cleaner, to maintain his pride and joy in a highly polished state.

In front of him, a one person wide corridor, ran the full length of the hut. Either side were the dormitories.

Dormitory doors were laid out in a strange configuration. Leading into each room there was a V' shape entrance. One door was positioned at 45 degrees to the corridor with the adjoining room door sloping the other way.

The pair of rooms had the same number but were marked 'A' and 'B'.

Gurney wandered along the corridor and found his dorm'.

Putting his suitcase down, he retrieved the Yale key from his pocket, unlocked the door and stepped into a claustrophobically small room.

'God, this is tiny,' he muttered. 'I ain't going to be able to 'swing too many cats' in here.'

The room was 6 foot by 8 foot. Just long enough for a bed and wide enough to walk down along the side of it.

He latterly concluded, that they had divided one
12 x 8 foot room into two 6 x 8 rooms by installing a
plaster board stud partition down the middle.

The room was painted in magnolia and frugally
furnished with an iron frame bed, complete with a soft
mattress covered with sheets and blankets; a small
bedside table, a chair, with a mirror fitted on the stud
partition wall and tall narrow wardrobe.

He dumped his suitcase on the bed and was intending
to load the wardrobe with its contents, when he spotted
the woodworm holes in it.

'Perhaps not. I think I'll keep it in the suitcase,' he
concluded.

As he looked around the room, he suddenly realised
there was a vital facility missing. 'Oh bugger, it's not
ensuite either. That'll be a nuisance getting out for my
several nocturnal visits. Sod, I wonder where the toilets
are?'

He put his door on the 'latch', turned right along the
corridor and immediately found them, for adjoining his
dorm' was a room containing a line of toilet cubicles,
opposite which were a line of wash basins.

The communal 'bathroom' area also housed two
showers with 'stick to the body' plastic curtains.

'Oh, that's going to be great, trying to sleep next
door to that lot,' he thought. 'Bang goes my lay in.'

He glanced at his watch. 'I'm going to be late for my
first class, if I'm not careful. I'm not sure how many
miles I'm going to have to walk to find it.'

Making sure he had the key in his pocket, he closed
the door and studied the map of the large sprawling
campus to try and find his way to hut 24 and the
training course.

# CHAPTER 55

Eventually, Gurney arrived at hut 24, spot on 2 o'clock, after getting lost several times enroute.

The shabby lecture room was already full of students sitting in rows of small tables. He estimated there were about twenty on the course.

Hot and sweaty from his exertions, he self-consciously took his place at the one vacant table in the front row.

Several people acknowledged him, while others were too focussed on reading newspapers.

After a quarter of an hour, Gurney had cooled down enough and restored his confidence to ask the person next to him, whether he was in the right class.

'Is this Disruption Operative Basic A?'

'Yes mate.'

'I was told it started at two.'

'Yes that's right. This your first time here?'

'Yes.'

'Well the lecturers are never on time. They can be anything up to half an hour late. After lunch break they can be even later because they normally have a 'liquid lunch' in the bar. So there's always a strong smell of peppermints in the afternoon.

They usually arrive with some corny gags too that they've picked up from the other lecturers.'

At that moment, the door opened and in came a bearded, bespectacled, hippie looking type, with long untamed shoulder length hair. He wore a sports jacket, with leather pads which had been sewn on at the elbows and cuffs. Underneath the jacket, an open necked white shirt, a pair of faded denims and open toed leather sandals over white ankle socks completed the ensemble.

'Good afternoon gentlemen,' and spotting a lone female at the back of the room he added, 'Sorry, and lady.'

'I'm not a lady. I am not married to aristocracy and I don't want any sexist platitudes, thank you,' the woman responded, vehemently.

'Glad that's out in the open,' the lecturer said in surprise. 'What shall we call you then? And before anybody comes up with any disparaging remarks, I have another solution. Let's all write our names on the cards that you will find on your tables,' he quickly suggested.

'My name is John Jeffries,' he informed them, lifting a name holder displaying his name on to his desk. 'This is one I prepared earlier.'

He looked around the room as the students each found their cards. 'Please write on the front and back of the folded white card. I'll pass round some marking pens, so write in large letters, please.'

'Why the back of the card?' Gurney puzzled. 'I know my name.'

'It's so that people behind you know your name, too,' the lecturer advised him.

Gurney coloured up. 'Of course.'

I expect you've already experienced the bureaucracy and slow pace of life here?'

The class chorused a frustrated, 'yes.'

'It's all done deliberately. It's to give you the exposure to life style disruption. And as the Principal constantly reminds me - You have to practise what you teach.'

At that moment, there was a knock on the door and before the lecturer could say anything, it opened.

The parking attendant that Gurney had received a lecture from earlier was standing in the doorway. He had obviously been rushing around, for he was red faced

'Beg your pardon Mr Jefferies, but one of your students has illegally parked.'

'Oh dear! A heinous crime indeed,' the lecturer mocked. 'Who's going to be fed to the lions?'

'The attendant quickly checked his clipboard. 'Leafmould,' he blurted.

The class all simultaneously breathed a sigh of relief, followed by a mocking 'Tut tut.'

However, Gurney's heart sank, his mouth dried. 'I'm going to be slung out before I've even had a chance to discover any secrets,' he thought.

'I parked in the right carpark,' he retorted. 'My sticker is on the windscreen. So what did I do wrong?'

'Oh it's you again is it? I might have guessed. You parked on the grass,' the attendant shouted.

'Shame,' the class mocked.

'Well the carpark was full,' Gurney explained.

'Then you should have gone to the overflow carpark,' the warden berated.

'I didn't know there was an overflow carpark. How was I supposed to know?'

'I suggest you two go and resolve this outside, so I can get on with my lecture,' John Jefferies suggested.

'That's the second time I've had to deal with him. You watch him carefully Mr Jefferies. He's trouble if you ask me.'

'Well, it's unlikely that I will. But thank you for your observations. Off you go then Mr Leafmould. You're only going to miss some domestic stuff. The others will fill you in later.'

Gurney left the classroom with the carpark attendant, strutting along in front of him.

# CHAPTER 56

After being closely supervised by the warden to ensure he removed his illegally parked vehicle, Gurney eventually found the overflow carpark and parked his van.

Irritated by the intrusion to the start of his course, Gurney quickly made his way around the labyrinth of roads and paths back to the classroom, arriving all hot and bothered. However on his arrival, he found his classmates were just returning from a tea break.

'Did I miss anything?'

'No. After you went we just filled in a few forms, introduced ourselves and spoke about our hobbies. Then the lecturer decided in was our turn to have a tea break.'

'So early?' Gurney said, surprised.

'Yes, it's because there are so many classes and the tea room over here is very small. We had to go at our allotted time. So no, you didn't miss anything,' the other student advised him.

'Oh good.'

'Oh apart from a laugh about the feminist. Have you spotted her name?'

'No!'

'Quick before she comes back.'

Gurney looked at the name card on her desk. 'Chardonnay!'

'Yes. The guys think it's because she 'whines' a lot.'

'What?' Gurney looked puzzled.

'Chardonnay wine…whines a lot,' the other joked.

'Judging by her size then, she should be called Keg, not Chardonnay. She must be 18st stone, if she's a pound,' Gurney added, unkindly.

'I wouldn't like to get the wrong side of her though. Watch out, she's coming.' They both resumed their seats as Chardonnay waddled in, followed by the Lecturer.

'Right, people. I need to emphasise to you, about the importance of security and keeping quiet about the secrets of the organisation,' John Jefferies said quietly.

'I won't say that we have a big brother organisation overseeing everybody, but let's say that employees who are considered to be a danger to the integrity of the organisation, cease to become one, if you get my drift. So I hope none of you will ever find out.'

Gurney shuffled uncomfortably as the lecturer seemed to be addressing him specifically. 'Did he know my intentions?' he wondered.

'You might already have spotted some of the Second World War security notices, scattered around the place. The one I particularly like is 'walls have ears'.

Let that be your mantra. Watch what you're saying, when non organisation people are around. Be aware also that modern listening devices can be secreted in some very small places too. Some televisions connected to the internet are also a listening source.

You might have wondered why there are some Dad's army photos displayed on many of our walls, here.

Just remember that they were the brave souls who were the founder members of what our organisation has evolved into today.

Don't let them down. OK with that, everybody?'

Silence was the stern reply.

'I'll take that as a yes then!

Gurney, you missed out on telling us about yourself, what do you like doing in your spare time?'

'Caravanning.'

'You do what?'

'Caravanning! Yes I go caravanning. I've only just started, to be honest.'

'Oh you're one of those brainless idiots that block up the roads then,' the lecturer observed.

'Well it's not too dissimilar to our job is it?' Gurney reposted. 'Slowing the traffic down.'

'Yes, but that's quite different. You can't compare the two.'

'How's it different?' Gurney asked bravely.

'Well. The Ministry's activities are all meticulously planned and...'

'Surely the odd bit of caravan tailback still helps though?'

'You're missing the point. Disruption is a science.' The lecturer became animated. 'It is a coordinated series of actions designed to facilitate maximum chaos.'

'Yes. I understand that. But...'

'But your random caravan chaos is uncoordinated. It could be dangerous under the wrong circumstances. You could create unresolvable gridlock. The country could grind to a halt,' the lecturer elaborated.

'Yes, but that's what we do anyway, isn't it?'

'Hello. Is there anybody in there?' Jefferies said, unkindly tapping Gurney's head with his knuckled hand. 'The master plan is controlled and coordinated. Imagine if you get a line of caravans travelling slowly along a main road.'

'Yes, but caravans do. They are restricted to 50mph on main roads and 60mph on dual carriageways and motorways,' Gurney explained rationally. 'We didn't make up the law. I assumed it was done by one of the MO Disruption departments to add to the general chaos.'

'No. It was the Ministry of Transport. I hope you have declared this as an extraneous activity, likely to impact on your duties?'

'No! Why?'

'The technical instructions are perfectly clear. It's a conflict of interest. You could be subverting the department's integrity. If the press got hold of it, they'd go to town.'

Gurney's conscience made him feel uncomfortable. After all, he could be the one writing the press report.

'Well, each to their own,' the lecturer said, looking at his wrist watch. 'Right. Well as its nearly finishing time and you've all had a long day, I suggest we finish early tonight.

I expect you'll all want to go for a beer later on. No hangovers in the morning please. We start getting into the processes and procedures tomorrow. It can be quite heavy going. Not good if you're suffering from alcoholic poisoning'.

The class broke up, thankful for an early finish.

# CHAPTER 57

Gurney soon found out how thin the dorm walls were when he returned to have a quick nap. The comings and goings of people in and out of the toilets next door, seemed to create endless noise.

Eventually he gave up, and leaving the door on the latch, went to the washroom for a quick wash himself.

He was feeling very self-conscious about his ablutions when several other students came in to use the washroom, but he particularly felt uncomfortable when a short, pot-bellied student waddled in for a shower.

The man was naked with the exception of a towel wrapped around his large waist, the material exaggerating the hemispherical contours of his enormous beer gut. Had he been a woman, the size of his stomach would indicate a full term pregnancy and a set of twins would be due for immediate delivery.

Gurney was further embarrassed when the man then whipped off his towel, exposing his 'bits' and thick rug of body hair, before going behind the curtains.

Painfully shy, Gurney was very self-conscious of his immature 'weedy' body. He had hated school changing rooms and communal showers and risked the wrath of his sport's teacher by never venturing into the large filthy bath, after playing rugby.

He could never understand why people wanted to expose their naked bodies to perfect strangers. It was bad enough when Iris caught him naked coming out of the bathroom, just after they'd got married.

They had married late in life and by then had developed their own standards of modesty. It was not a very sensuous marriage, he had to admit, but they got by, usually with the help of a darkened room.

Having already been subjected to the unwelcome view of the man's bloated body, he hurried his own ablutions to ensure that he'd leave before the man came out of the shower.

Behind him, someone in the communal toilet was making loud noises and greater smells. He left quickly, gagging from the smell of last night's curry.

'Oh, I hate communal,' he muttered.

After changing his clothes and forgoing the 'pleasure' of an evening meal in the canteen. Gurney meandered his way through the site to where he thought the club was situated.

Several of his class were already in there, including Chardonnay, whom he recognised,.

'Hi,' she greeted, spreading herself along the bar.

'Hi. Have you been waiting long to be served?'

'No, not long. Trouble is, there's only one barman and he's trying to serve fifty people.'

'Pity we can't nip behind there and help ourselves,' Gurney suggested.

'Yeah. That would be a good idea. Did you have a meal tonight?' she asked.

'No. I didn't fancy it.'

'Just as well. It was gross,' she revealed

'Why are there so many cats in there?' Gurney screwed his face up at the recollection of the mangy animals.

'They breed under the huts and no-one has taken the initiative to spey them,' Chardonnay informed him.

'Why ever not?'

'Because of the cat lovers in the offices, I believe.'

'They put me off eating anything in that canteen,' Gurney confessed.

'The answer is to just go for stuff sealed in packets, especially at breakfast time' Chardonnay suggested.

'Why particularly at breakfast?'

'The cats sniff around all night and you can't be sure what they've been up to on the food. At least if it's sealed, you stand a good chance of avoiding food poisoning,' she counselled.

'That's a good idea. I might try that,' he agreed.

'Is that right that you go caravanning?

'Yes.'

'I can't imagine why anybody would drive slowly hundreds of miles, then take several more hours setting up camp?'

'For fun of course.'

'Fun! Why not just drive there and simply walk into a hotel? You can do the same trip in half the time,' Chardonnay observed.

'Yeah, but in a caravan you're out in the countryside away from the crowds and pollution, breathing fresh air. It's great.'

'What about the smell from cow muck?' 'God I couldn't deal with that.

'It's only the smell of the countryside, you soon get used to it.'

'Anyway, what do you do for water and electricity?'

'They're all usually on site. Although, occasionally, you have to rely on a generator to charge your battery.'

'I can't see the point of cramming yourself into those small tin cans.'

'They're actually nice and roomy. Anyway we always put up an awning.'

'Well that's only a tent stuck on the side.'

'Yeah but awnings double the space.

'No. You won't catch me in one of things anyway,' Chardonnay said firmly.

Gurney looked at her bulk and decided it probably wasn't a good idea to mention her size.

'We've got all the mod cons inside too,' he continued. 'No need to slum it.'

'Why not stay at home then?' she persisted.

'It's different. You should try it sometime. A glass of wine in the open air. Wonderful!' he gushed.

'And there's the swarms of insects too.' Chardonnay shuddered at the thought.

'Insect spray kills them off. No problem.'

'I suppose you've been caravanning for years?'

'No, just the once, he confessed. 'But I quite liked it.'

'You big bullshitter,' Chardonnay disparaged. 'There was me thinking you knew what you were talking about.'

'Well, I'm learning. Anyway, this barman is taking his time,' Gurney said, desperately trying to change the subject.

'When we eventually get served, do you fancy a game of darts?' she asked.

'Yeah, OK. Where do we get them from?'

'I've brought some a couple of sets. You can use my second best set,' she offered.

'Thanks.' Gurney was saved from having to explain that he was hopeless at darts, by the barman's arrival.

'Six pints please,' she demanded.

'Six pints? Blimey, you're a big drinker,' Gurney observed.

'No, that's three each.'

'No, I'm not a regular drinker and besides, I haven't had anything to eat. I couldn't possibly manage that many.'

'When you're with me, you'll soon learn.'

'Why don't we just have one? Then we can go back when our glasses are empty?'

'What and wait another hour to get served?'

Gurney, lost the argument.

# CHAPTER 58

So, clutching three pints each they carefully made their way to the dart board.

'What do you want to play 501, 301 or 'around the clock'?' she asked putting her beer down effortlessly.

'I'm actually a bit rusty,' Gurney confessed, spilling the contents of two pints on to the table. 'Sorry, hand slipped.'

Eventually, having seen Gurney's pathetic attempts to hit what he said he was aiming at, they decided on a game of 501 so that he didn't have to start on a double.

After a few three dart 180's by Chardonnay, Gurney admitted, 'You're pretty good at this aren't you?

'Yeah well I should be. I play in a darts team,' she informed him, smiling.

Finally, having played several games, where Gurney continued to show his inadequacy and had made multiple trips to the loo, they packed it in.

'You're hopeless,' she said, frustrated by his inept playing.

And what was worse, he was becoming more and more dangerous with his 'alcoholically enhanced' random throwing.

'I used to be vvvery good,' he slurred. 'I don't seem to be able to get my eye in tonight.'

'I've run out of beer, she said looking at her empty glasses. 'I'll go and get some more.'

'Not for me,' he giggled,' I...I...think I've had sufficient.'

'Have you ever played split the carrot?' she asked.

'No. Whaz that?' Gurney queried, looking puzzled.

'The idea is, I throw a dart between your feet and you've got to be brave and not move them.'

'I can do that. I can be brave.'

'Stand up then.'

'Like this?' Gurney swayed uncontrollably, as he stood.

'Open your legs a bit more and I'll throw the dart at the gap between your feet and you've not to move, OK?

'OK.' Gurney held on to a table to steady himself.

Chardonnay threw the dart which landed bang in the middle of the gap in between Gurney's feet, level with his instep.

'See, it's that easy. Right, now it's your turn Gurney,' she said, handing him a dart.

'Are you sure? I'm not that good. And I think I'm a little bit... a little bit tipsy.'

'You'll be OK. Just stand a bit closer,' she coached.

'Like this?' he swayed.

'Yes. That's good. Now concentrate, hard.'

'OK, here goes.'

Gurney made exaggerated throwing movements, bringing his arm back and forward several times and closed one eye.

Finally he threw the dart. Unfortunately, he missed, the floor and instead hit the top of Chardonnay's left foot.

'Shit! How can you miss the floor? It's the biggest thing here,' she moaned.

'Oh God. I'm so sorry,' Gurney giggled.

'You could sound as though you meant it,' she moaned.

'Tee hee, you look so funny. Shall I pull it out?'

'No. It's OK. I'll pull it out myself thanks.' Chardonnay said quickly, grabbing the dart. 'It's only a pin prick, and I can't feel a thing. The alcohol helps to dull the pain.'

Unfortunately, as she pulled the dart out, she discovered that he'd hit a vital target, the anterior tibial artery on the top of her foot. And blood started pumping out through her sock.

'Oh my god,' she said, seeing her life blood pooling on the floor.'

Gurney shook himself out of his guilt and yelled. 'First aider. Have we got a first aider here?'

Chardonnay fainted into Gurney's arms, as the barman arrived.

'What happened?'

'A dart landed in her foot. And when she pulled it out...'

'Right, we just need a bit of digital pressure and that should staunch it. I need to put some rubber gloves on first though.'

'By the time you've done that, she'll have bled to death,' Gurney bleated.

'Do you want to risk me getting aids?'

Gurney let go of the casualty, who slithered to the floor.

'Has she got aids?' he asked, backing away from her.

'Not necessarily. But she might have,' the barman called, vaulting the bar.

'Within 30 seconds, he was back, wearing purple rubber gloves and pushing his thumb onto the top of Chardonnay's foot. The blood flow stopped instantly.

'Will she need a transplant?' Gurney asked, gazing at her bloody foot.

'I think you mean a transfusion; No, of course not. It looks worse than it is.'

'If she does, I'll donate,' Gurney said, rolling up his sleeve.

'That won't be necessary. If you want to be helpful, can you call the medical centre from the phone behind the bar?' he asked.

'What number?'

'All the nines. It connects with the emergency team on site.'

Gurney commanded all his senses and swayed towards the bar. After attempting to leap the bar unsuccessfully as the barman had done, he found the entrance and staggered to the phone.

'What was that number again?' he shouted.

'Nine, Nine, Nine.'

'OK, I've got it,' Gurney tried to focus on the numbers on the phone. After the third wrong number, he managed it.

'Come to the bar, a woman is bleeding to death and I'm so sorry it was me what did it,' he whined.

Within five minutes, the team were there. After peeling off her bloody sock, they could see the small puncture wound, which had now stopped bleeding. They put on a small plaster and mopped up the blood.

'Oh, what happened?' Chardonnay said, coming round.

'You fainted that's all. You'll be OK in a minute. Have you had a recent tetanus injection?' the first aider asked.

'Yes.'

'In that case you won't need to go to hospital.'

'What about all that blood she's lost?' Gurney wondered.

'It's nothing.'

'It might be nothing to you, but she might have an empty toe with no blood in it,' Gurney slurred.

'I could do with a drink to get over the shock,' Chardonnay said, slowly standing.

'Yes, I'll buy it. I owe you one,' Gurney said, rummaging unsuccessfully in his pocket.

'You've both had enough for tonight,' the bar man suggested, 'I think you ought to go back to your rooms now.'

'Yes I think I'd like to go to bed now,' Gurney confessed, holding on to the table again.

'You're a crap darts player,' Chardonnay berated.

'I told you I wasn't any good.'

'Good! You nearly killed me,' she said, dramatically.

'I'm sorry. How can I make it up to you? Can I help you to walk back to your dorm, just in case you pass out again?'

'You can help me hobble back, but no funny stuff. Right?'

Slowly they staggered their way out of the club and started making their way along the poorly lit paths.

'Right! Where... bouts ... your room?' Gurney slurred.

'Block A.'

But thaz miles away from mine,' Gurney pointed out.

'Well, that'll serve you right for stabbing me, you tosser.'

'Why don't they put all the people on the same course in the same block?' Gurney puzzled.

'Because of the end of course do's. They'd wreck the place.'

'I see,' Gurney agreed, although he didn't know what an 'end of course do' was, but he was due to find out, and how.

He suddenly stopped.

'I thought you were supposed to be taking me back to my room,' she said, wondering why he'd stopped.

'Sorry but my legs have gone all funny. I don't think I can make it.'

'Alright, I'll take you to yours,' she said reluctantly. 'Where is it?'

'I think it's AA something or other,' Gurney giggled, drunkenly. 'Why do they call you Chardonnay?'

'Because that's my name, plonker.'

'It's a funny name. Why Chardonnay?'

'My mother's favourite tipple.'

'Oh!'

At which point, he fell flat on his face.

'Oh Gurney. Fat lot of help you are as an escort. OK, up you come.'

Chardonnay duly lifted Gurney on to her shoulders and carried him back to his dormitory in a fireman's lift.

'When they eventually arrived at block AA, Chardonnay took him off her shoulder and leant him against the wall. 'Where's your key?' she asked.

'Issh in here somewhere,' he said, digging into his pocket.

Finally, he found it and she half carried him along the corridor and unlocked his room.

'Here you are, bed,' she said, sitting him on the hard mattress. 'You can undress yourself.'

'Than...you. So..sorr..ee. Dart,' he muttered and fell back on to his pillow completely out of it.

'Goodnight Gurney. See you in the morning,' she said. 'I think I'll just have a memento of tonight though,' she added, retrieving her mobile from her pocket.

Carefully she framed the sleeping Gurney and took a photo of him before leaving.

By which time, Gurney was snoring, loudly.

# CHAPTER 59

Gurney woke with a major hangover. His mouth felt like it was full of feathers and his head as if someone had dragged his brain out through his eye socket.

'Oh God... my head!' he groaned.

Slowly he sat up and massaged his aching temples. 'God I feel awful. Must have some air, it's so hot and stuffy in here,' he muttered.

'What's the time?' he said, trying to focus on the face of his watch.

After several failed attempts, his vision finally cleared. 'Damn, it's five to nine. I've overslept. Classes start at nine.'

Not even the noisy early morning ablutions of the other students had woken him. But as all of the occupants had made their way to breakfast or classes, the block was deathly quiet.

Forcing himself to get out of bed he swung his legs to the floor. 'Oh, I feel terrible,' he groaned.

As a semblance of conscious thought resurfaced, he realised he was still wearing the clothes he'd worn the previous night.

Quickly he struggled out of his coat and discarded his wrinkled shirt. He ransacked his suitcase to find a clean one and fought the carefully ironed sleeves to slide his arms inside.

'Come on,' he cursed. 'Why does that always happen when you're in a rush?'

Eventually his success was marred by the fact that he'd missed a button hole as he'd fastened it.

He caught sight of the lopsided shirt in the mirror as he stood to put his jacket on. 'Oh, Sod, it'll have to stay,' he grumbled.

He wrestled his way into his jacket and made for the door.

His shaky hand fumbled with the door catch. Still alcoholically uncoordinated as he opened the door, his foot was in the way and it banged his big toe.

'Ouch!' His head throbbed in sympathy.

Clutching his wash bag, he stepped in to the deserted corridor. Leaning heavily against the wall, he limped into the adjoining toilets.

As he cautiously bent down to turn on the cold tap, he caught sight of himself in the wash basin mirror. A pair of bloodshot eyes and a very sorrowful looking Gurney glared back at him.

Desperate to get to class, he splashed cold water over his face to wake himself from his lethargy. The freezing water causing him to take a sharp intake of breath as hit his throbbing forehead.

He reached for his toothbrush in order to freshen his breath to eradicate the bottom of the bird cage taste he had in his mouth.

After several failed attempts, eventually his shaking hands allowed him to retain a line of toothpaste on his brush. But the intrusion of the foreign body in his mouth caused him to gag as he scrubbed his teeth, fortunately he managed to fight the nausea that threatened to overwhelm him.

His ablutions finally completed, he staggered his way back towards his room, only to hear his bedroom door click shut, just before he got there.

'Oh shit! And the key was on the bedside table,' he cursed. 'Now what am I going to do with this wash bag?'

Perplexed by having to make another decision, he leant heavily against the wall hoping for a flash of inspiration. 'I can't leave it out in the corridor. I'll just have to take it with me.'

Finally, he headed for the exit and ricocheted off the walls as he made his way along the narrow corridor, gulping in the fresh air as he got outside.

He quickly abandoned any ideas of running to make up for lost time as the cranial pain and blurred vision reminded him of his delicate state.

It took him 20 minutes to get to class and as he opened the door, he could hear the lecturer in full flight.

'Oh nice of you to join us Mr Leafmould. Hangover?'

'Yes. Sorry I'm late. I…'

'Don't worry, you haven't missed much. Try to make sure it doesn't happen again though.'

'Yes…sir.'

'I'm not a knight of the realm, like Chardonnay was saying yesterday, I've not been lucky enough to get on the New Year's honours list yet. Call me John.'

'OK… John'

'Do you want to go and get a black coffee before you join the class?'

'No I think I'll be alright.'

'Incidentally, nice floral purse you've got there.'

'My door slammed before I could put it back in the room' Gurney informed him.

'With the key inside?' the lecturer said knowingly.

'Yes.'

'You'll need to buy another one from reception, at lunchtime then.'

'Buy! But I haven't lost it,' Gurney pleaded.

'No, but that way, you'll return the spare key and get your money back,' John advised him of the official process.

Gurney nodded and instantly regretted making the gesture, because of his delicate 'condition'.

'OK, now where was I? Oh yes. Laid in large drainage pipes deep underneath several large cities is a secret transport system for the MO Disruption called the Super transit MOD subterranean Monorail or STMSTM for short.

The purpose of the STMSTM is to enable MO Disruption people to get around whilst the city is choked by disrupted traffic. This is essential to be able to manage, monitor and measure road disruption.

The tunnels were drilled and pipes installed by contractors who were told that it was part of a major drainage and water transfer scheme.

Final commissioning was done by MO Disruption staff, who laid the rails and did all the various testing.

The specialist STMSTM teams were recruited from ex Network Rail engineering groups, solid and dependable types, who could be relied upon to keep a secret.

As the system was being built, all the stores, equipment and building components were delivered to the shaft entrances by the normal road network prior to be lowered underground.

Public notices, associated with the STMSTM

roadwork shafts, were designed to perpetuate the water drainage scheme story.

The temporary traffic lights, an essential ingredient to the mix of disruption, were programmed to slow the traffic even further and were positioned by MO Disruption operatives.

'Yes, I've been caught up in a couple of those schemes,' Gurney advised. 'So that's what was causing it!'

MO Disruption surveyors selected the appropriate above ground sites to maximise road chaos. This usually involved closing off half of a main feeder road into a city.

Roadworks were moved to different sites following the laying of each section of underground pipes. This also helped to thwart any motorists getting used to alternative 'get round' routes.

Any questions?'

'So it's like a secret tube network?'

'The very same. Right, I can see that most of you are looking a bit hung over this morning, especially 'Mrs' Leafmould. So we'll have an early coffee break.'

Chardonnay limped to the front of the classroom and slapped Gurney on the back of the head.

'Alright Gurney?' she beamed

'Oh don't do that,' he groaned. I've got a blinder. Haven't got a headache pill have you?'

'Never get headaches,' she replied.

'How's your foot?' he countered.

'Painful,' Chardonnay admitted.

'I'm so sorry. I did tell you that I was no good.'

'Yeah I suppose it was my own fault. I should have listened.'

'Have you got a hangover too?' he asked.

'No, I'm used to drinking up to eight pints during a darts competition. So it doesn't affect me.'

'Did I miss anything important this morning?' Gurney asked concerned.

'No. Not really. Anyway it's all revision for me.'

'Revision?'

'Yeah. I've worked for the firm for five years, and they thought I could do with some official training to formalise it,' she told him.

'So you know all about this stuff then?'

'Yes, pretty much,' Chardonnay confirmed.

'That's great. I can probably get some inside information from her,' Gurney thought, 'rather than waiting to do a whole lot of courses.'

'Come on, I'm dying for a coffee and by the looks of you, you already have.'

# CHAPTER 60

After the early coffee break, the class duly returned to the classroom to find the lecturer already there.

'Thanks for being punctual. We have a busy day ahead of us. Today we're going to go to the little town of Granite to make some disruption.' John Jefferies announced. 'This will be your first practical, and it will be assessed.

The course groaned.

'We're going mid-morning, so that we are in place in our various roles to frustrate local office workers.

As many of you might know, there is usually a flood of office workers rushing to the supermarket during their lunch hour to do family shopping. It's apparently the only available time they can fit it in.'

'Sir, I mean... John. Pardon my ignorance, but why are we doing it?'

'We are going back to basics, to understand what frustrates people so that, you appreciate the science behind frustration and hence how we can target our disruption.'

'I was never any good at science,' Gurney volunteered. 'I could never do the maths behind it. So I'm lost even before we start.'

'Perhaps this will help you. This is the scientific formula behind creating disruption; It's called The

Frustration Index.' And he put up a slide on the interactive whiteboard:-

*Frustration Index*

*Frustration Index (FI) = Personal Targets (PT) + Barrier To Success (BTS)*

*FI's are in the range between 0 to 10*

*Where 0 equals no frustration; 10 is maximum. (maximum FI's often have police involvement)*

*PT's range between 0 to 5 (where 0 is min and 5 is max)*

*BTS's range between 0 to 5 (where 0 is min and 5 is max)*

'Let me explain what I mean.

A person's need to do something is their 'Personal Target' and circumstances that get in the way are a 'Barrier To Success'; A combination of these factors become a measure of Frustration.'

The lecturer looked around the room at a sea of confused faces.

'OK, I see that I've lost you already. Let me give you a few examples.

*Example 1:*

*(Urgent Personal Target (PT)); Need medicine for sick child = 5*

*(Small Barrier To Success (BTS)) can't find parking space = 1*

$FI = PT + BTS$

$FI = 5 + 1$

$FI = 6$

*Example 2:*

*(Non-urgent PT) Need toothpaste = 1*

*(Big BTS) Stopped by Security, falsely accused of shoplifting = 4.*

$FI = PT + BTS$

$FI = 1 + 4$

$FI = 5$

'Personal Targets and Barriers To Success have now been given a British Standard Institute (BSI) value. These are documented is a series of reference volumes,' the lecturer advised.

'Now we've got a value, how does it actually manifest itself?' He put another slide up.

*Frustration is evidenced in various ways:-*

  *a. Increased blood pressure; use of bad language; tears of frustration; emotional breakdown; aggression*

  *b. It can be short or long term.*
    *i. Short term is acceptable to the Ministry*
    *ii. Long term or lasting frustration is our aim.*

  *c. The 'Knock On Effect'(KOE)*

*All Frustrating Incidents will have a 'Knock On Effect' or KOE, which continue after the initial incident. This can sometimes be more disruptive than the initial incident.*

'Sorry John, I don't understand,' Gurney admitted.

'OK, here is a practical example.

The expected 'Knock On Effect' of today's exercise is that the frustrated office person will return to work moaning about not being able to do all their shopping, because of the delays they've experienced. Incidentally, those are the delays that you will be creating.

By endlessly going on about their experiences (caused by your disruption techniques), this will then annoy their work colleagues, who are not at all interested and are trying to focus on their job.

This in turn will create disharmony in the office and the organisation becomes unstable and in the worse cases, the feud causes it to implode.'

'Wow, that's incredible. Who'd have thought that could happen,' Gurney observed.

'But that's not the end of it. The KOE continues outside the office, including angry office workers creating road rage incidents,' the lecturer continued.

'On returning home, still fuming at the supermarket fiasco and fuelled by the disharmony at work, the office person then upsets the family, who berate the parent for not getting their promised treat. This ends in a big family row.

The kids go to bed crying and hungry, the husband or wife, goes down the pub, gets drunk and causes a punch-up and ends up in jail.'

'Just by getting frustrated in the Supermarket! Well I never,' Gurney winced as he slapped his forehead in amazement.

'Ouch!' Overcoming his fleeting pain, he asked. 'What happens to the frustrated supermarket shopper?'

'Don't know! Probably pours themselves a cuppa and watches EastEnders in peace.'

'That's the perfect storm... in a teacup,' the lecturer joked.

'I must write that down,' Gurney thought. 'Wow, how far reaching is this MO Disruption stuff?'

# CHAPTER 61

'So here is our plan of campaign for disrupting the Supermarket,' the lecturer began.' We will arrive 'en mass' and...'

'Considering the organisations need for secrecy, what if we're spotted?' Gurney interrupted.

'We don't wear uniforms, so to all intents and purposes, we will just be normal members of the public arriving on a coach, but getting in their way,' the lecturer explained.

'However, you will all be wearing special electronic trackers that will record your activities, which will enable us to review how each of you did during the exercise.

We will interrogate the devices and analyse the data when we resume back in class this afternoon.'

'You mean we'll be wearing some sort of GPS?' Gurney asked.

'Something more sophisticated than that. This gizmo will record conversations as well as picking up the level of frustration that you create,' John Jefferies explained.

'What about a camera?'

'Yes, you'll all be wearing small buttonhole cameras too.

I want Gurney and Chardonnay to partner up, as Mr and Mrs and in deference to your poor state of health Gurney, you will have a pram to push.'

'So long as there's no baby in it,' Gurney pleaded.

'For authenticity, there is a sound alike baby in it, I'm afraid.'

'Oh, I couldn't put up with a crying baby in my current delicate state,' Gurney whinged.

'Perhaps you'll think of the implications with regard to your job, the next time you over-indulge.

Anyway, you and Chardonnay will be playing a pivotal role. The pram is filled with data recorders, receivers and transmitters to collect data from everybody's electronic devices.

It's very expensive stuff, so don't lose it. Any questions?'

Everyone was trying to second guess what they were actually going to be doing.

'One word of caution. There will be people who take your attempts to frustrate them in their stride. These are likely to be calm, rational people; Tai Chi or Yoga exponents.

Don't get dragged into frustration yourself. If your actions fail to frustrate, move to somebody or something else.'

'Can't we just park a broken down car on the approach to a roundabout?' Gurney suggested, not relishing the exercise at all.

'Yes we can of course. But can anybody tell me why you wouldn't want to do that in this instance?'

'It would be ineffective as a training session, if we didn't know the human frustration factor it creates.'

'Precisely! Well done Chardonnay. Gurney, you will learn a lot from her.'

'I sincerely hope so,' Gurney thought. 'I've got a report to write at the weekend and I need to capture as much as possible before I forget. Hopefully the editor will be impressed with the list of revelations that I've found out so far.'

'Here is a list of tactics for you to choose. You might like to work in pairs.'

The lecturer pulled up a slide on the interactive board again.

*Tactics include:-*

- *Wearing pyjamas; (Security Team usually involved - causes disruption)*
- *Damaged Barcode (use of sandpaper)*
- *Arguments about wrong advertised price on two for one offers;*
- *Wheelchairs or pushchairs in aisles;*
- *Two shopping trolleys parked opposite each other in the aisles;*
- *Dropping a bottle of something effectively closing an aisle;*
- *Creating conflict by having the last of a special offer;*
- *Spending time sorting through the best before dates; (blocking shelves)*
- *Moving 'deserted' trolleys while their owner is looking for another item.*

Gurney, you and Chardonnay will take every opportunity to block the car park entrance as you wheel your charge around.'

'OK, no problem,' Chardonnay confirmed.

Remember, timing is important to maximise the effect. Blend in, make it seem as normal as possible. So, no outlandish costumes.

I want some of you to 'make up' and act slowly like old people though. This usually winds up the office shoppers because *'the retired people could do their shopping anytime. Why in a lunchtime when I'm in a rush?'*

Right. Go and get your surveillance equipment fitted and then quickly get on to the coach.

We will review the results in the afternoon. Let's see who can make the biggest frustration factor.

'Anyway, enough of the theory, let's get out there and do it.'

Gurney held the door open for Chardonnay.

'You can cut that out for a start. I can open doors myself. I'm not a bleeding weakling. Male chauvinist, Sexist pig. And by the way, don't expect me to play the mother stereotype that pushes baby. Got it?'

Gurney said nothing, but got it.

# CHAPTER 62

The 50 seater coach pulled in to the supermarket car park, going the wrong way up the one way traffic system. Exiting motorists had to pull over to avoid the large obstacle. Very soon, the carpark was filled with the sound of irate motorists leaning on their car horns.

Gurney felt ill at ease as they made their way through the cacophony of noise and avenue of shaking fists.

'I don't like this,' he whispered to Chardonnay.' I don't like conflict.'

'You'll soon get used to it, doing this job,' she counselled.

Eventually, the coach got to the supermarket entrance and disgorged its strange cargo of shoppers.

Gurney and Chardonnay made their way to the back of the coach and took out the old fashioned collapsible pram. They extended the fold down handle and switched on the electronics, as they had been shown.

Much to Gurney's annoyance, and a painful reminder of his delicate condition, it was fitted with a programme emulating the sounds of a 'wailing' baby.

The programme generated a random cry at various volumes. Unfortunately for Gurney, the output couldn't be turned off without switching off the whole electronics package.

The pram was also fitted with small electric motors that moved the cover, to simulate the wailing baby moving its feet.

Meanwhile, the other members of the class had switched on their electronic devices and made their way into the supermarket.

Entering via the exits, rather than the entrance, they caused chaos as they barged their trolleys into the store.

Very soon they were causing mayhem in the aisles too, just as the first batch of harassed office workers arrived.

The coach driver, too, was part of the exercise, so leaving his vehicle blocking the roadway he had gone for a coffee.

Gurney and Chardonnay walked around the parking areas of the supermarket, so say trying to placate the crying baby and causing a tailback of arriving cars, trying to find somewhere to park.

Inside, the MO Disruption class were creating various elements of mayhem that they'd selected from the classroom list.

Two 'old people' were blocking a busy bread aisle with two trolleys pushed opposite each other.

Someone dropped a bottle of olive oil near the exit, which smashed and effected a closure.

Others surrounded the takeaway food section preventing office workers from getting to it.

Several students blocked up the self-service checkouts.

Two of them went to the 'five items only' checkout and argued with each other that a six pack should not go through it.

Someone put items on the moving belt and then went

off to get something else, effectively blocking out that checkout.

Outside, Gurney and Chardonnay were still slowly wending their way around the car park attracting a lot of verbal tirades of abuse from shoppers who had been delayed by their noisy perambulations.

'I don't like this,' Gurney admitted. 'I need a wee, and then let's go for a coffee.'

'What do we do with the pram?' Chardonnay asked.

'I suppose we could leave it outside.'

'Not with all the electronics in there. It might get 'nicked'.'

'We'll just have to take it inside with us then, wailing baby and all.'

After Gurney's visit they made their way in to the café, but in the confines of the corridor, the volume of the distraught electronic child seemed to increase.

People were staring at them as they arrived in the café.

Gurney found a table and with the sobbing 'baby' beside him, waited for Chardonnay to buy the coffee and cakes and subsequently join him.

They ate and drank without speaking, as conversation was impossible with the electronic child screeching his lungs out.

Office workers intending to lunch there, were quickly dissuaded and joined the queue to try and get some ready-made sandwiches.

Eventually, Gurney and Chardonnay were ejected by security staff after they'd finished their coffee.

They moved outside near the exit and Chardonnay left Gurney alone while she went to use the toilet.

Gurney was feeling very self-conscious as the crying child attracted critical comments from frustrated shoppers leaving the supermarket.

'You should do something about that child, it's obviously in pain,' said a woman.

'It needs its nappy changing,' a grandmother figure pointed out.

'Is it ill or is it just teething?' queried a young mother with a child in a sling.

'Social services have been called,' a security guard informed him.

Gurney wished he could switch the baby off, so decided to 'leg it' instead, to get away from the critical comments.

In his haste, he failed to negotiate the trailing leash of a dog tied to a post.

The pram wheels passed over the lead, but the startled dog panicked and attempted to run off, effectively putting a trip wire in Gurney's way.

He duly tripped over the lead and fell. In order to save himself from a 'face plant', he let go of his charge.

Unrestrained, the baby carriage shot off down a service road into the path of a reversing lorry.

Unsighted, the driver continued reversing until he felt a bump. Immediately he stopped to examine the cause and was horrified to see the pram jammed underneath his vehicle. He duly passed out with shock.

Fortunately, the collision had at least stopped the electronic baby's wailing.

Chardonnay came back to see a frightened Gurney staring wide eyed at the accident site. She followed his gaze.

'What have you done you pillock?' she demanded.

'I tripped. All the electronics stuff is destroyed.'

'Oh, crickey. You cocked up big this time.'

'We need to let them know that there was no baby in there,' Gurney said apprehensively.

'Yes, eventually,' Chardonnay said, conspiratorially. 'Remember we have to create disruption for as long as we can.'

'Yes, I know but...'

But Gurney was thinking that they'd sack him now and send him home. His dreams of the scoop were disappearing in the crushed debris of the pram.

One of the employees, helping to supervise unloading of the lorry alerted management and shortly after the emergency services were on the scene and the supermarket was closed.

A screen was put around the lorry and all customers were ushered away.

Chardonnay eventually explained that the child had 'gone with its Grandparents' and reclaimed the mangled pram.

When they were eventually able to leave the supermarket, the students returned to the classroom as planned.

'Hope you all had a good opportunity to cause some real chaos, before the store closed,' the course lecturer said. 'It certainly looked like you frustrated a considerable number of shoppers.

Unfortunately, we won't be reviewing your individual performance data because Gurney got the electronics package crushed by a lorry.

This in itself caused a critical category incident, which closed the supermarket for the afternoon, as everybody thought a baby had been run over.

So, Gurney, you're forgiven for costing the department thousands of pounds, and are to be congratulated for creating mayhem and major disruption out of the incident.'

Think yourself lucky that you aren't going to be charged for the lost equipment.' John Jefferies added critically.

Gurney was 'gobsmacked'. He felt sure that he would be held to account and sent home.

'Congratulations to Chardonnay for her quick thinking, in keeping the incident going for as long as possible.'

Chardonnay blushed at the compliment.

'OK, I think you've had enough excitement for today.' John Jefferies, suggested. 'Class dismissed. And Gurney!'

'Yes?'

'Don't be late tomorrow, otherwise I'll start thinking you don't want to be here.'

'No John, I won't.'

# CHAPTER 63

Before going back to his room, Gurney decided to call home.

'Hello Iris. It's me. How are you?'

'Nice of you call,' she said, sarcastically.

'Sorry, I couldn't call you before. I had to hand my mobile to security when I arrived on site. There are no mobile masts within 5 miles of here apparently. Anyway, as it was, I had to switch off the phone 10 miles away so we couldn't be tracked.'

'A likely story.'

'No, it's true. I'm calling you from a phone box onsite. There is a line of six of them that we can use, but there's always a queue.'

'I cursed you last night,' she moaned.

'Why, what did I do?' Gurney wondered.

'I thought I was going to be murdered in my bed.'

'Oh heavens, why?'

'The coat rack that you put up fell off in the middle of the night with a loud bang. It gave me such a fright.'

'Sorry. I didn't have the proper wall plugs when I put it up.'

'No, well that's typical of all the bodged jobs you do.'

'That's not fair.'

'And I've had enough of those plastic pots you keep putting under the leaking radiators.' Iris said, extremely exasperated.

'I keep telling you. It was only a temporary fix, but you've taken my tools away from me. It only needed the glands tightening.'

'So you've been saying for the last six months. Well you needn't bother. I've got a plumber to fix it.'

'Oh no. You haven't wasted money, on a plumber have you?'

'Yes I have, and he wasn't very impressed with your plumbing at all.'

'He'd say that, because he's toting for business,' Gurney said, defensively. 'You haven't taken his offer to do anything else have you?'

'I'm very tempted. He was very polite and seemed to know his business.'

'Iris, I could sort it out at the weekend, if you let me use my tools.'

'No, I don't want you touching anything anymore. The house is reasonably tidy without your muddles and messes around. Incidentally, how is the course?' Iris finally asked.

'Oh it's very good. I'm learning a lot.'

'Any major disasters?'

'No,' Gurney said, conveniently putting the crushed pram at the back of his mind. 'Why would there be?'

'Well that's unusual for you. You and disasters normally come together.'

'Give me some credit. Anyway I've got to go. There's somebody waiting to use the phone. I'll see you Friday afternoon.'

'OK.'

'Bye.'

Gurney hung up. 'Why does she do that? Undermining my self-confidence? It wasn't my fault Chardonnay forced me to drink three pints, I did tell her.

And getting me to throw a dart at her was pure masochism.

And the supermarket thing. It was her turn to be looking after the pram, not mine. It wasn't my fault that the dog tripped me over and the lorry ran over the pram.'

Gurney had lied to Iris, for there was no queue so he picked up the phone again and rang the editor's direct line.

After a few rings the editor answered.

In the surveillance booth, housed in a nearby hut, a red light flashed up on the operator's console.

'Aye up! We've got a bogey. Somebody is making a call to an unauthorised number. Quick! Get security to booth three.'

'Roger,' his colleague said, dialling the number.

'Yes,' the editor bawled, obviously distracted from, something he was doing.

'Boss, it's me.'

'Me! Who the bleedin hell is me?'

'Gurney, Gurney Leafmould sir.'

'Oh yes. How are things?'

'Very good. I'm getting some real meaty stuff up here. I'll give you a full report when I've finished the course.'

'Good. The owner is very excited about your possible investigation. He's keen to promote the paper as a champion of the people. Make sure no-one else beats you to your exclusive.'

'No, okay.'

'How are you recording it?'

'Saving it on a memory stick.'

'Is that recording and video as well?'

'No, just written.'

'Pity! Recording and video stuff is more powerful and undeniable, when it's played back. See what you can do.'

'OK.' Gurney wondered how he could smuggle stuff in through security. He felt sure the cleaners checked the student's bags, when they 'cleaned' the rooms.

'Where are you keeping it?'

'I...I haven't actually started it yet. I plan to do it at the weekend and store it in a secret hiding place. As a new recruit, I think I'm under surveillance all the time.'

'In that case you'd better go. Keep in touch,' the editor instructed and rang off.


Security's phone rang for five minutes before being answered.

'Where the hell have you been? Oh, don't bother to explain with some lame excuse. Get your ass to the phone boxes. Booth three, they've rung an unauthorised number. Arrest them immediately.'


As Gurney made his way back to his room he was nearly being knocked over by two security people, running towards the phone booths.

An unfortunate person, who had gone in after Gurney's departure, was dragged unceremoniously out of booth three, handcuffed and led off for interrogation.

# CHAPTER 64

Clutching his floral wash bag, Gurney went back to his room with his £5 duplicate key, that he'd 'purchased' from a grumpy receptionist.

'You make sure you bring it back, otherwise it will go on your record,' she warned.

Relieved that the key worked, he let himself in his room, keen to have a rest before going out later.

As he pushed the door open, he found a brown A4 official looking envelope on the floor.

'Oh dear, whats this? Are they kicking me out?' he wondered, nervously ripping open the envelope.

'Oh my god!' What the hell?'

Inside was a photo of him lying on the bed naked. Nearby was a bra and pair of frilly knickers. The woman photographer had included her shapely bare thigh in the shot.

Printed across the picture were the words '*We can keep a secret off the internet, but only if you can.*'

The threat was obvious. Someone had found out that he was a journalist. If he published anything about anything, he would be exposed, literally.

'This is blackmail…I've been rumbled. Now what do I do? Is there any point in me staying here now, if I can't use anything?' he wondered.

He studied the picture again.

'The worse part about this is, if I was involved in an orgy, I don't even remember if I enjoyed it,' he thought.

'Hang on, that's' not my body. I wish I had pecs like that,' he said, stripping off his shirt and studying his pale hairless chest in the mirror.

'I've been photo shopped. Oh my god! What happens next?'

Unable to get the photo out of his mind, he went for a walk around the site, hoping that he would get some inspiration about what he should do...but nothing came. Instead he decided to go and watch TV in one of the television lounges to try and take his mind off the events of the day.

None of the dormitories had TVs in them. Instead, four television lounges for BBC 1 & 2, ITV 1 & 2 had been set up in the central administration block.

In each lounge a large old fashioned TV was tuned into one of the main four channels. The control knobs had been removed to prevent students 'channel flicking'.

However, this didn't prevent some people smuggling in a spare knob and changing channels anyway.

On the hour or the half hour as programmes ended and began, there was a regular footfall between rooms.

Hence an evening's viewing might also consist of a series of hikes between all four rooms.

After sitting in front of several un-interesting programmes, he made his way to the canteen and helped himself to some hot chocolate.

He sat by himself, lost in his own misery, totally oblivious of the feral cats circling around him, like hyenas, waiting for a crumb of something.

Consequently, Gurney went to bed that evening alcohol free, and spent the night tossing and turning from the nightmares about the photograph being published on the internet.

Exhausted by his sleep interrupted night, he got up early the following morning and went to the canteen for breakfast.

Heeding the warnings about the cat's nocturnal adventures, he forced himself to open a packet of Weetabix and downed a stewed cup of tea before getting a newspaper from the onsite newsagents.

He left early for the lecture room and was pleased to find that he was first in class to arrive. He tried desperately to concentrate on reading his paper, but failed.

Eventually, all the other students appeared and acknowledged him. He was gutted however when they 'pulled his leg' about the supermarket incident.

'I wouldn't apply for a babysitter's licence, if I was you.'

'That's no way to treat a fretful baby.'

'Have you got deep pockets, that's your bonus down the pan.'

'Creep ass, who's teacher's pet then?'

Chardonnay was last to arrive and made a beeline for his desk.

'What happened to you last night? I had the beers lined up for you and in the end had to drink them myself.'

'Oh, I didn't fancy any more booze. I watched telly and went to bed early.'

'You big girl's blouse! Well, how about coming to the pictures tonight and going for a beer later.'

Gurney's stomach churned at the word 'pictures. 'OK, but no darts.'

'Too true. My foot's still sore from you missing the floor.'

At which stage the lecturer arrived.

# CHAPTER 65

'Good morning course persons. Hopefully there's nothing there to offend anybody with that greeting,' John Jefferies said, looking at Chardonnay for a reaction.

She didn't disappoint and looked daggers at him.

'Before we get into the days business, which some of you might find a little heavy going, I have a little joke for you.'

*'Once upon a time there were three balloons; Mummy balloon, Daddy balloon and baby balloon.*

*They'd had a busy day playing in the park and went to bed early, quite exhausted.*

*But during the night baby balloon became frightened as a thunderstorm crashed and flashed around and he wanted to get in bed with his sleeping parents. But no matter what he tried he couldn't squeeze in, so he let some air out of Daddy balloon, but still he couldn't squeeze in to the bed. So he did the same to Mummy balloon but there was still insufficient room for him. Finally he let some air out of himself and was able to squeeze in and go to sleep with them.*

*In the morning however, on discovering what baby balloon had done, his father was furious. And told him off. 'You've let me down. You've let your mother down and worst of all you've let yourself down,' he berated.'*

The class groaned.

'Well certainly during yesterday's practical you didn't let the department down. Sorry about the awful link with the joke,' he apologised. 'But you all did as required and caused a bit of local disruption at the supermarket, although Gurney went above and beyond the remit and caused a major disruption incident.

So today, we're going to look at the 'bigger picture'. The Ministry of Disruption's portfolio of chaos includes all means of transport i.e. road; rail; air; sea; as well as communication chaos of mobile & landline phone systems and of course 'snail' and email.

Now hopefully having had a good night's sleep, you won't doze off during the next session which covers Measures.'

Somebody muttered 'Boring.'

'Why do we need measures? Anybody?' the lecturer asked.

Silence.

'OK. Let me help you. Some geek came up with the expression, *If you can't measure it, you can't manage it.*' So we need to manage our disruption carefully.

You saw yesterday the examples of the Frustration Index. Where you learnt about the values assigned to Personal Targets and Barriers To Success and KOE.

Anybody remember what KOE stands for?'

'Knock On Effect.'

'Well done Chardonnay, I can see you've been listening.

So the KOE of your exercise at the supermarket yesterday, caused the police to deal with two pub fights and three domestics last night.'

'Now each functional grouping, road; rail; air; sea, etc. has a head of department responsible for a measureable count of chaos.

John put a slide on to the interactive whiteboard.

Their performance is measure by the following:-'

### Disruptive Indices (D.I.)

*D.I's are a measure of disruption associated with an area of infrastructure within the section of responsibility.*

*E.g. Road delays per mile; Length of traffic jam per road. etc.*

*Average speed of traffic in towns;*

*Average speed of traffic on motorways.*


**Accountability meetings** *are held with Line Managers to ensure that* **Disruptive Indices (D.I.)** *are achieved.*

*Managers consistently failing in their disruptive targets are given sideways moves into other state run companies.*


'Still with me? Nobody dozed off yet?' he asked, looking around the room. 'Why is that important to get rid of failing managers, do you think?' Jefferies probed.

'It shows that they are not capable of producing disruption if the need arose,' Chardonnay said.

'Good. Full marks again Chardonnay.'

Chardonnay grimaced at the compliment, feeling she'd been ingratiated again.

'This is the bit which should interest you, as your pay could well be reflected by what you do.'

*Disruption Operatives (D.O.s) are clandestine members of the organisation recruited for their <u>devious</u> natures; often sourced from retired members of the constabulary or armed services.*

'How many of you consider yourselves to be devious?'
Silence.
'Somebody must have thought you fitted the criteria, otherwise you wouldn't be here.'

*D.O.s are usually singletons and work in isolation so that if he/she is detected or defects; he/she could not implicate anybody else in the organisation.*
*D.O.'s orders usually come through 'dead' letterboxes in true spy tradition – usually hidden in bushes. always carefully camouflaged and at ground level.'*

'Also, usually well visited by inquisitive male dogs,' the lecturer added. 'Indeed, the use of felt tip pens was banned after it was discovered that some orders weren't carried out due to a dousing by a dog.'
'OK. You've all done very well to stick with me. Lunch time then folks,' the lecturer announced to a relieved audience.

'Dead Letter Boxes. That rings a bell,' Gurney thought, racking his brains. 'Now why do I know about them?'

# CHAPTER 66

Gurney and Chardonnay carried their lunch trays to an empty table.

'I'm concerned,' Gurney said, sitting down.

'About?' Chardonnay asked, already shovelling a mouthful of steak and kidney pie into her mouth.

'Blackmail.'

'What. Doing it? or being a victim of it?' she asked, nonchalantly, chewing on a tough piece of meat.

'Victim,' he whispered, looking around to see if anyone was watching them.

'In that case, you need is to report it,' she advised, pulling a half chewed piece of gristle out of her mouth. 'I'm not sure about this steak. If I didn't know better, I'd say it tastes more like cat.'

'I can't report it,' Gurney said conspiratorially, disgusted by her open mouth eating habit.

'Why not?' she queried, spraying pie crumbs across the table.

'Gurney looked around to see if anyone was within earshot. 'I think it's the department that's doing it,' he revealed, quietly.

'How do you come to that conclusion?' she said, scooping up a fork full of peas and dropping half of them down her front.

'This is very awkward. I...er...'

'Go on, you can tell me. We're friends after all, aren't we?' she suggested belching.

'Well ...errr... Somebody has photo shopped a picture of me in an embarrassing pose.'

'Sounds interesting. Can I have a look?' Chardonnay asked, enthusiastically.

'No.'

'Well sorry. I can't help you then,' she said.

'Oh... OK. But remember it's not me,' he added quickly.

'Is it that bad then?'

'Well, no not really. Did you carry me back to my dorm the other night?'

'Yes. You were paralytic and it was the only way to make sure you got in safely.'

'Did we? I mean... You know... ' he blushed.

'Did we what?' she asked, suspiciously.

'You know. Do it?...stuff.'

'If you mean, getting intimate. Good heavens no,' she refuted.

'Well that's a relief,' he admitted.

'What are you insinuating, that you wouldn't want to do it with me?'

'No. I would. No, I didn't mean that. Umm...' he squirmed.

'Stop digging yourself into a hole and just show me the photo.'

'Okay,' he capitulated.

Gurney took the photo out of his jacket pocket and looked around before he removed it from the envelope. Reluctantly, he handed it to Chardonnay.

'Wow, that's a fine body you have,' she beamed, studying the photograph closely.

'It's not mine,' he insisted. 'As I said, I've been photo shopped. But where they got the original picture of me from, I have no idea.'

'If I were you, I'd claim that body as your own,' she advised, still gazing at the photo.

'I haven't got hairs on my chest, my pecs don't exist. I have moobs... and as to that thing... '

'Stop there sunshine. Don't run yourself down anymore. Perhaps somebody has a fantasy about you?' she suggested.

'Yeah but look at the message on it. I think the security people have done it to warn me off.'

'Warn you off! Why would they want to do that?' she asked, puzzled.

'Because of the job that I did previously.'

'Which was?'

'I was a journalist,' Gurney revealed.

'Oh I see.' Chardonnay said. 'Yes, they are a bit nervous about having reporters around. Remember the logo... ?'

'Yes I know. 'Walls have ears',' he repeated unenthusiastically.

'The trouble is, we live in a world where everybody is out to make a point, without realizing the implications of exposing secrets,' she pointed out.

'What do you mean?'

'Secrets are secret for a good reason.' Chardonnay said firmly, holding him with a fixed stare. 'We should accept that fact for the good of our health.'

'Yes but that's how dictators start. Subjugating the masses,' Gurney argued.

'Oh I think you've been reading too many tabloids. Just remember, you have joined a secret organisation.

Don't forget, it needs to be kept that way, for the good of the country. Can I keep the photo?' she said lightening the tone of the conversation.

'No of course not,' he said, snatching it back from her and returning it to his jacket pocket.

'Misery! Anyway, It's time to go back,' she advised, picking up her tray.

'But I still don't know what to do,' Gurney exclaimed.

'If you want my advice, just do as the message says,' Chardonnay said firmly, fixing him with a matronly stare.

# CHAPTER 67

The class reassembled and John Jefferies arrived shortly after.

'I appreciate you had a bit of heavy morning and I'm afraid the afternoon is likely to be similar, so let's start off with a joke shall we?

*A little girl came home from school and said to her mother, 'Mummy, today in school I was punished for something that I didn't do.'*

*The mother exclaimed, 'But that's terrible! I'm going to have a talk with your teacher about this … by the way, what was it that you didn't do?'*

*The little girl replied, 'My homework.'*

The course groaned.

'Sorry about that, but the quality of the jokes in the staffroom is a bit poor at the moment.

Anyway back to it. This morning we talked about Disruption Operatives, so we're now going to have a look at what they do.'

He put up a slide on the interactive whiteboard.

***Disruption Operatives (DOs)** cover a wide range of **Disruptive Practices (DPs)**.*

*D.P.'s are methods used to create 'disruption'.*

*E.g. Coned off motorway lanes; Lorry fires; broken down cars; leaves on the line; broken down airport luggage belts etc.*

*One indicator of the successes of Disruptive Practices in the roads section is that during last year, motorists, on average, spent at least 32 hours stuck in traffic jams.*

'Your Disruptive Practice exercise yesterday at the Supermarket was scheduled to be a minor DP, which turned major. Didn't it Gurney?

Gurney became embarrassed at the reminder, looking down at his notes, trying desperately not to show his discomfort.

The lecturer continued, 'now we move on to using human nature to help us do our job.'

The lecturer put up a slide which brought a sharp intake of breath from the class.

### Child Manipulation

'I want to emphasise that there is no physical contact here. We are merely utilising the natural mischievous nature of children, by providing them with the opportunities and the wherewithal to get into mischief.'

'How does that work? Surely they are not employed by the department and they certainly wouldn't be able to keep a secret,' Gurney observed bravely.

'No, you're right. They don't, but we capitalise on their youthful inquisitiveness. Consider youngsters who come across a hole in fencing, bordering a railway line for instance. What would they do?'

'Go through it,' Gurney volunteered.

'That's right, they'd obviously want to explore,' the lecturer continued.

'How would they make the hole?'

'We'd make it for them. One would mysteriously appear, overnight.'

'Devious! But what about British Transport Police would they be in on it?'

'No. The DO setting it up would have to make sure they weren't caught by the BTP.'

'I don't understand. What's the point of it, just going through a hole in a fence?' Gurney wondered. 'Surely it's very dangerous.'

'Yes you're right it could be potentially dangerous, but we deploy watchers to ensure they can't get hurt and intervene if necessary. We maintain strict Health and Safety standards to ensure no-one gets hurt during this sort of operation.'

'Oh. Well I suppose that's alright then,' Gurney said relaxing.

'Let me ask you then what would you expect the children to do if they found convenient sized pieces of debris just lying around the track?'

'They'd probably jam them into rail track points,' Chardonnay suggested. 'But the trackside electronics would flag up the malfunction.'

'Precisely. They'd be detected. But that action would disrupt intercity routes until the debris was cleared.' the lecturer explained. Likewise, what would they do if they found a discarded catapult and a convenient pile of small stones?'

'Shoot stones at each other?' Gurney volunteered.

'How about signal shooting?' Jefferies suggested.

'Oh of course!'

'The statisticians calculated that 'child manipulation' was guaranteed to lose Network Rail at least 20 hours

of daily scheduled running time, across the country.
And this DP has formed the basis of one of the
measurement criteria for a Disruptive Index (DI).'

'Something as simple as that?'

'Yes. It is a well-documented fact that the highest DIs
occur during School holidays.

'Bored kids, I suppose?'

'Yes, but it drops to a low over the Christmas school
holidays, when kids are more likely to be playing with
their presents, prior to boredom setting in again in
January. Then the amount of mischief and hence the
Disruptive Indices increases again. '

'Who'd have thought of that?' Gurney wondered,
imagining his scandalous headlines, if he ever got to
write his scoop.

*'Government dangerously manipulates our kids'.*

'Gurney, I'm impressed with your interest. Any more
Questions?'

'If only you knew my reasons,' Gurney thought. 'Yes,
that's all very well giving them the opportunities, but
how do we control it?'

'The truth is we don't. It is so random and unpredictable,
that we just keep an eye on the chaos and adjust our
'hole cutting' accordingly.'

'Right!'

'Anyway, moving on.' The lecturer flicked on the
next slide.

### Research and Development (R & D)

*The department has R & D offices for inventing
technical disruption solutions. Their inventions are top*

*secret but as an example they have invented - Shopping Trolleys with a 'mind of their own' i.e. non spherical wheel bearings which cause trolleys to be difficult to steer?'.*

'Why supermarket trolleys?'

'They were chosen because the stores provide a large, relatively safe environment to create this low level of disruption, similar in scale to our recent supermarket exercise.

The class muttered their approval of such a simple idea.

The lecturer put up a new slide.

'Right this is our last for the day and it's a message I will repeat endlessly.'

### Secrecy

*Keeping secrets are vital - walls have ears; Careless talk costs lives.*

*Thorough positive vetting is not always 100% in identifying 'moles';*

*The code of silence - is key to our future effectiveness.*

'I don't want to frighten you, but it is believed that operatives, who are unable to keep the code of silence and talk carelessly, disappear from the payroll.'

Gurney tightened his butt cheeks as his bowels reacted to the obvious veiled threat. 'Perhaps he didn't have a story after all.' he thought. 'Perhaps he should let sleeping dogs lie. If the Ministry had been in existence since the 1940's who was he to expose it now?'

The lecturer's voice broke into his thoughts.

'When asked where you work, just say, '*I work for the government*'. It might get some knowing looks, but normally, you'll find the conversation topic is dropped.'

'I've used the story of working for a paper clip manufacturer previously. People soon lose interest in discussing your job when you talk about manufacturing and distributing paper clips,' one of the students explained.

Again the murmur from the class.

'I've been telling people that for five years and no-one believes me,' Chardonnay added. 'They think I work on the buildings.'

'Anyway, it's been a hard session. Thank you for your attention. That's it for today. See you tomorrow,' the lecturer announced.

As they made their way to the door, Gurney playfully pushed in front of Chardonnay expecting to get some earache about his manners, but it didn't come.

'How come you know so much about these measures then?' Gurney wondered.

'I used to be a manager, and got demoted because I kept missing my DI's.'

'Now I understand,' Gurney thought. 'There's more to her than meets the eye.'

# CHAPTER 68

Gurney met Chardonnay in the reception area just outside the cinema.

'I was going to buy you a ticket, but I figured out that you'd have been annoyed at my chauvinistic generosity, so I didn't,' he explained.

'Bum! I wouldn't have minded that. Now I've got to queue up,' she sighed.

After queuing for ten minutes, Chardonnay re-joined him.

'Did you ever think of changing your name?'

'No, why?'

'Well, you're really not a Chardonnay are you?'

'Do you have to keep going on about my name? If I was sensitive about it you'd be on the floor by now with a bloody nose.'

'Sorry, just curious, that's all.'

'It was my mother's hope that I'd turn into a girly girl. As you can see, it never happened. I was a disappointment from the moment I started feeding,' she explained uncharacteristically softly.

'Why?'

'I was sucking all the goodness out of her,' she volunteered.

Gurney had a mental image of a deflating balloon as she suckled from her mother.

'So I went on to a bottle and ballooned even more,' Chardonnay continued. 'Anyway, you can talk, with a name like yours.'

'Yes you're right. None of us choose our names do we? But we're stuck with having to defend our parent's choices all our life,' Gurney concurred.

'The queue's moving, come on,' she urged him.

'What are we going to see anyway?'

'The Sound of Music.'

'Really! I suppose it will waste sometime,' he observed.

They filtered into the cinema after giving a security guard their tickets at the door. Fortunately the seats weren't numbered, which was just as well because they couldn't see much in the gloom.

They planted themselves in two worn-out seats, Chardonnay's bulk overflowing her space and invading Gurney's.

'Bit tight isn't?' he uttered.

'Cosy,' she added, enjoying his nearness.

Gurney was confused by the messages Chardonnay was giving him. Was she flirting with him? Should he make a move?

In order to address his rising hormones, he decided to take his mind of things and talk about the organisation.

'Can you explain what Ranks are all about in the MOD?' he asked.

'Ranks! Well that's a bit of a strange topic to talk about. It's easy. It's just like the army I suppose. It's all about knowing where you sit in the pecking order.'

'OK but how does it work?'

'As you've probably gathered by now it's all based on the letter 'D' for Disruption.'

'Go on.'

'Well like James Bond where 'M' is the head of the organisation, 'D' is our big boss.'

'Right. So is it based on salaries then?'

'Salaries and skill levels yes. For instance a D2B is a labourer, the next skill level is a D2A and obviously we are DOs - Disruption Operatives.

'What about Managers?'

'Oh they tend to cascade from the top down. For instance the next in line to D is her deputy, DD or double D as he's sometimes known.'

'Sounds like the size of a big ladies bra,' Gurney chuckled, instantly regretting it as Chardonnay's elbow dug into his ribs.

'Anyway, the films starting now, so no more talk about ranks,' she ordered.


When the film ended, they went to the bar and after waiting the customary 30 minutes to be served, they took two pints each back to a table.

'You say you've worked for the department for how long?' Gurney asked.

'Five years,' she replied.

'And during that time you must have heard of the story of the Black Dog. '

Chardonnay looked at him suspiciously. 'Why do you ask?

'I'd heard that it was an excuse that lorry drivers use if they'd had a crash. But I think the department might have a hand in it somehow.'

'What grade are you?' she queried.

'DO in T.'

'A Disruption Operative in Training, mmm. What level of security clearance have you got?' she probed.

'Why do you ask?'

'Because there are certain things that cannot be discussed unless you have the appropriate security clearance,' she explained.

'What level do I need?'

'Level four.'

'Oh...I've got level three,' Gurney lied. 'What's the difference?'

'One...'

'It doesn't take a mathematical genius to work that out. Yes I appreciate that.'

'What I was going on to say, was ONE hell of a difference in security terms,' she confirmed.

'Oh! So you can't tell me?'

'No, sorry.' She then pointed to the pen Gurney had been given when he joined the MOD and put her finger to her lips in a 'don't say anything' action.

Deftly, she plucked it out of Gurney's top pocket and laid it down on the table and led Gurney away to the other side of the room.

'What was all the stuff about taking the pen out of my pocket?'

'Keep your voice down. It's bugged,' she said quietly.

'You mean, that they can hear everything I've been saying?'

'Yes and writing.'

'Writing!'

'Yes, the pen is fitted with miniature gyros and it can work out what you're writing and transmit that back to control.'

'Oh my god. Well if it can translate my writing, it does better than I can. Half the time, I can't even read my own writing.'

'Had you not wondered why the pen is so bulbous?'

'Well yes. Now you come to say.'

'How many times have you mislaid it?'

'Scores of times, but it suddenly reappears on my desk. I assumed it was the cleaners returning it.'

'No. There is a dedicated team that go round and reunite owners with their pens. This ensures the department has also got access to your non computing communications at all times,' Chardonnay informed him.

'Wow. What will they think of next?'

'Your ID card.'

'This one?' Gurney asked, touching the badge suspended from the lanyard around his neck.

'Yes. Do you know why you have to wear it all the time?'

'Security of course. So they can quickly identify strangers in the building.'

'Partly right, but it's also a tracker.'

'A what?'

'It's a tracker, so they know where you are all the time.'

'So do they know we're together at this moment?' Gurney said, furtively looking around for a CCTV camera.

'No. When you get to the next level of security, you become a trusted member and they drop the security scrutiny.'

'So you don't have...'

'No pen and just an ordinary ID badge. That's right,' she confirmed. 'Anyway going back to your earlier observation. For security reasons, I can't tell you anything about the 'Dark Canine' project.'

'The what project?' he puzzled.

'The Dark Canine.'

Gurney looked at her, confused.

'What did you say you had suspicions about?' Chardonnay prompted.

'You mean the Black Dog?'

'Yes. And another word for dark is?'

'Black.'

'And for dog?'

'Canine. Oh my god! There really is a black dog. It isn't just a myth!'

Gurney had forgotten that he'd promised the lorry driver to track down the mythical black dog. But now he had stumbled on to something.

'Well, I'm only informing you because I know you'll soon be having your security status increased to four when you get promoted.

'So what is the Project?' Gurney asked his companion.

'I can't tell you anything. However, I can confirm whether your guesses are correct or not,' she whispered.

'So it is an MO Disruption tactic after all?'

A nod from Chardonnay.

Gurney beamed. 'Does the department breed and train hundreds of black labradors all around the country?'

The other replied by shaking her head.

'Are the dogs real?'

Again the shake of the head.

'So if they're there, but not real...are they some sort of K9 electronic robotic dog?'

The shake of the head again.

'Well, unless it's some sort of projected image then...'

The other nodded.

Over the next hour, through a series of questions, nods and shakes of the Chardonnay's head, Gurney discovered that the black dog was in fact a hologram fired into clouds of anaesthetic gas.

She further confirmed that all the incidents occurred on windless, still, dry nights, on dark unlit motorways, near a slip road with a nearby bridge over the motorway.

And that a bowser filled with the gas is parked on the hard shoulder and pipes are strategically placed over a few hundred yards to create several banks of 'fog' on to which the images are projected.

The high power laser that creates the hologram is located on a slip road bridge and plugged into a special socket, which Gurney had inadvertently stumbled on to.

He recalled his recce looking for paw prints at the site of the lorry driver's crash. He realised now that he had been on a fool's errand. There was no dog to find.

All the accidents had been an elaborate part of the Ministry's meticulous road disruption regime.

Gurney also wondered why anaesthetic gas was used and informed by nods and shakes, that the gas prevented the driver from being hurt too much, in the ensuing accident.

The first bank of gas was intended to start relaxation of the foot on the accelerator, hence slowing the lorry. It also helped with distorting coherent thought and compounded the images in the mind of the driver.

As soon as the road traffic collision occurred, the MO Disruption operatives quickly recovered all the equipment and departed the scene.

A trained paramedic operative was left on site, to ensure the driver received appropriate medical attention, having already alerted the emergency services.

'I should have guessed,' thought Gurney. 'But how do I report that? And in any case who would believe me?'

Then he recalled the photo blackmail threat. 'Would he even have the courage to try anyway?

'My round,' he said, suddenly downing his pint.

'I thought you weren't drinking much,' Chardonnay said, surprised by his invitation.

'This helps me more than you know,' he admitted.

Just at that moment a security guard came over to their table.

'Mr Leafmould, I believe this is your pen?' the guard said, handing it back to Gurney.

Gurney looked at Chardonnay in disbelief. She just smiled.

# CHAPTER 69

'Right, today you will take an exam,' the lecturer, announced the following day.

The course groaned.

'If you pass, you'll be put into the next pay band. If you fail, you'll be given one more chance and then if unsuccessful again, it's the highway…and not the tarmac sort either.'

'What do we have to do?' Gurney asked.

'You have to demonstrate flexible and creative thinking on the spur of the moment. Identifying, implementing and measuring disruption of your own making.'

'Sorry, I don't understand,' Gurney continued. 'How? Where?'

'If you'd allow me to finish the introduction, you'll soon find out,' the lecturer said sharply.

'Sorry,' Gurney apologised.

'You will conduct the exercise 'on site' in teams of two. But anything to do with the infrastructure of the training school is strictly out of bounds.'

'What, no fire alarms or floods?' someone asked.

'No. If you do, you'll be sent home immediately.'

'How long have we got?' another asked.

'Three hours, up until lunch and then we'll review the results after.'

'Only three hours?'

'Yes, that's bags of time.' John Jefferies informed them. 'The team who creates the most disruption, will win the course cup and have their name put on the wall of fame. And your scheme might even be adopted nationally.'

'Big deal,' one of the students muttered.

'It is, if you want to get on in later years,' the lecturer advised. 'As I say, you'll be working in pairs. Select a partner and be back here at 2.00 PM having completed a scheme. I want to see a set of disruption measures and a brief report. Questions?'

The class was stunned into silence.

'Right off you go,' the lecturer ordered.

Chardonnay grabbed Gurney. 'You and me, OK?'

'Yes fine.'

'What shall we do? Got any ideas?' she asked.

'How about on the Internet spreading false news?' Gurney suggested.

'No, too vague.' Chardonnay rejected it. 'How would you measure it anyway?'

'Pretending we've got a serious disease that's contagious?'

'Dhur! For what purpose? Come on. Think.'

'Cut off the electric and crash the server.'

'No. He said it can't be infrastructure,' Chardonnay, reminded him.

'Set fire to the building?'

'Don't be daft.'

'Ring up the media and say they've found a way to make gold here,' he said, throwing in random thoughts.

'No, they don't want to advertise that this place exists,' Chardonnay reminded him.

'What do you know about birds?' Gurney asked out of the blue.

'Diddly squat,' she said, rapidly losing interest.

'I read in the paper the other day about a load of bird watchers who gathered to watch a special bird, rarely seen here. There must have been hundreds of them all with their binoculars,' he informed her.

'And?'

'What about if we put a false spotting of an even rarer bird on Facebook, websites and Twitter feeds?' Gurney proposed.

'Go on.'

'Potentially, that will attract an even greater crowd,' he enthused.

'OK, but how will that cause disruption?' she puzzled.

'If we say the bird is located where the carriageway is narrow.'

'Yes, go on.'

'And the road is a vital 'feeder road' to something important.'

'With you so far,' she agreed.

'The twitchers will park all over the shop and cause road congestion.'

'Yes good idea,' she agreed. 'But where's a good place?'

'Let me think...How about...near Bristol airport?' he suggested.

'Bristol airport! Yeah, that's genius,' she said getting excited.

'And more importantly, it might even have a knock on effect to flights as well as the roads. Two birds with one stone...if you pardon the pun.'

'Why?' she wondered.

'Because, the aircrews will get stuck in the traffic jams, too,' he suggested.

'Genius,' Chardonnay beamed. 'Do you know any rare birds though?'

'I don't, but I expect Uncle Google will. Here we are,' Gurney said, using the lecturer's computer and tapped in rare UK bird sightings. 'How about the Blue Rock Thrush.'

'Sounds good to me. Let's do it,' Chardonnay agreed enthusiastically.

Over the next hour, they investigated satellite images of the roads near the airport and identified an exact location which suited the criteria of narrow road and limited parking opportunities.

They used Highways England data to measure the volume of traffic and recorded various CCTV images.

Satisfied they'd sufficient data, they duly posted the sighting of the 'Blue Rock Thrush' on various internet sites, to claim where the rare bird had been spotted.

The effect was almost immediate. It was as if people were travelling around in cars just waiting for an announcement; A sort of, fast response twitcher unit to go to a sighting.

Within fifteen minutes of posting it, the narrow roadside was becoming a 'pinch point' and the traffic started backing up. Soon the congested traffic was trailing back several miles to the motorway exits.

'I've just heard a report of the queues on the local radio website. It's on their traffic news. Furthermore, they've also mentioned the rarity of the bird, so that's generated even more traffic,' Gurney informed her.

The pair monitored the situation getting more and more excited as the chaos was evidenced on the motorway data and on the roadside cameras.

'How long have we got to write the report?'

'Thirty minutes. I'll do it,' he volunteered. 'I'm quite good at this sort of thing,' Gurney stopped himself from 'crowing' about his Journalistic qualifications.

He completed the report over lunch in the canteen, complementing the words with a random pattern of small yoghurt stains.

After lunch they were first back, feeling smug about their scheme. The other students returned to the lecture room at the prescribed time looking glum.

'Right people, how have we all got on?' John Jefferies asked, looking around at the sea of faces.

The class responded with mixed replies - 'we didn't have enough time'; 'can we have another hour?'; 'Our scheme didn't work as we'd hoped.'

'Well there is one scheme that has worked extremely well.' He informed the class. 'At least I assume it's one of our teams. Who is responsible for gridlock around Bristol and Weston?'

'Yes John. It was Gurney and I,' Chardonnay said, proudly.

'Well pray tell us what you did to create such an impressive level of disruption.'

'Rare birds,' Chardonnay informed them.

'Yes rare birds and fanatical bird watchers,' Gurney piped in.

The pair explained their scheme to an envious class. They presented the road congestion reports and aeroplane cancellation data and even showed some time elapsed video from the motorway cameras.

'Just one question. How is the traffic going to return to normal?' the lecturer probed. 'There must always been an exit plan, to restore things to the norm.'

'As soon as the twitchers realised they'd 'missed' the sighting, they all started leaving,' Gurney advised. 'Even then, it was taking a long time for the traffic to move again and it continues even as we speak.'

'Well can anybody beat that?' the lecturer asked the class.

Everybody else, with the exception of a euphoric Gurney and Chardonnay, looked down to hide their disappointment of an unsuccessful scheme.

'I don't think there is any question of who are the winners of the Trophy.'

The lecturer concluded, 'Well done Gurney and Chardonnay. You can celebrate your incredible achievement, in style, tonight.'

# CHAPTER 70

'Come on Gurney, the 'end of course do' is traditional. We'll have a great time, it's good fun,' Chardonnay said, attempting to persuade a reluctant Gurney to join them on a night out to celebrate the end of the course.

'No, it's not my thing,' he declined.

'We'll be able to let our hair down, after all that stodgy crap they've been feeding us all week.

We won't be doing much in class on Friday morning anyway. Just reading newspapers, going for a coffee break and sharing a few jokes,' she added.

'Yeah, but I've got to drive home on Friday,' he explained, trying to think of acceptable excuses.

'And so have most of us,' Chardonnay replied.

Gurney felt pressured to accept and having run out of excuses, he reluctantly agreed.

'OK, but I'm not going to be drinking much,' he declared.

'No, of course not,' Chardonnay said, with a knowing smile.

'Oh OK, I hope I won't' regret it.'

'No, you won't. Good man. We're going on a minibus to a Night Club in Stafford. It'll be great.'

They were duly collected by a minibus outside the security gate.

And as they boarded, the smell of deodorant and after shave was overpowering.

They danced all night, in between drinking competitions, which Gurney was persuaded to enter, his abstinence intentions forgotten.

Gurney did some 'dad dancing' with Chardonnay, who, in spite of her large frame, proved to be an excellent dancer.

They emerged in the early hours completely sozzled, but all indulged in the mandatory greasy kebab from a van parked outside.

Eventually, the minibus arrived to pick them up and they were driven back to the training school, stopping several times enroute for people to 'off-load' their excesses.

On arrival back at site, the noisy crowd disembarked from the minibus, only to be warned by the security guards to 'be quiet'.

As often happens to people who are 'alcoholically enhanced', their whispers were louder than normal speech and carried right across the site.

Slowly they meandered their way through the huts, accompanied by an anal wind orchestra, playing a miscellany of different tunes and punctuated by giggles.

Chardonnay suddenly grabbed hold of Gurney and gave him a rib crushing bear hug, that took his breath away, and then kissed him fully on the lips.

Gurney returned the kiss, only to be pushed away by her.

'That was nice Gurney. But that's all you're getting. Goodnight.'

Gurney was 'gutted' as she disappeared into the darkness. He wasn't expecting any passion at all, but Chardonnay's actions had stirred his primal urges.

'Wow, I think I'm in there,' he muttered, rubbing the back of his hand over his lips. 'She's alllll woman, thaz for sure.'

After a few minutes staring into the night, wondering whether to follow her or not, the effect of the alcohol became the decider and he reluctantly headed to his own dorm instead.

'Now where the hell ish my hut?' he wondered. 'Must be up here,' he decided and staggered off into the darkness.

'Whaz was my hut called? This mush be it,' he muttered, almost falling through the external door of the nearest hut.

Slowly he groped his way along the corridor and fished out his key. 'At least I remembered to bring it with me,' he said, putting it in the lock.

The key failed to turn. 'Whass the matter with my door? Why won't it unlock?' he said, to himself, shouldering it.

'You're in the wrong room, you prat. Now piss off.' a voice called from inside.

'Ssso sorry. The huts all look the same to me.'

Gurney swayed his way back out of the hut, bouncing off all the dorm doors as he did so.

After drunkenly trying several other huts and receiving abuse from the now woken occupants, he eventually remembered that his block was labelled 'AA'.

'Ah. Block AA. I should have remembered, Alcoholics Anomon on ymous. Here we are, home sweet home.'

However, when he tried to open the external hut door, it would only open a fraction, before hitting an obstruction.

He pushed harder and the blockage appeared to move. He put his shoulder into it and it opened wider but not quite wide enough to get in.

As he peered around the door, to his horror, a large eye blinked back and startled him.

Then, suddenly the door opened fully, and a large black and white cow ran out of the hut, almost bowling him over.

'Oh my God! What the hell? Sssomebody has herded a cow inside my hut.'

As he entered, he could see and smell that the poor cow had obviously been in there for some time, as the floor was 'swimming' in cow muck.

'Oh dearie me. The cleaner isn't going to be happy about thish. Their posh floor ish a sea of cow crap.'

As Gurney waded through the 'pancakes' on tiptoe, he was desperately trying to hang on to the beer and kebab, but the smell wasn't helping.

Half way to his room, he had an irrational thought.

'I ought to try to rescue that cow before it hurts itself,' he decided. 'The aminal should be easy to spot because it's vvery big.'

He turned around and retraced his steps carefully manoeuvring himself through the mucky minefield.

After staggering around the site for ten minutes, he eventually found the cow, contentedly chewing the cud.

'There's something strange with the cow. Now whazz is it? Oh god! Somebody has painted a white stripe around the poor thing. I must clean it off before the paint dries.'

Gurney found an outside tap and duly managed to catch the cow. Using his wet handkerchief, he started to wipe off the 'paint' around the cows middle.

'Sssteady Mrs Cow, 'he encouraged.

However, as the cold wet handkerchief was applied to its belly, the cow became restless and bolted from Gurney's grasp.

In its desperation to escape, it 'nudged' three parked cars and the collision set off the car alarms. The horn symphony woke all the occupants of all the surrounding huts.

Gurney pursued the now frantic cow, only to run into a security patrol.

'What the hell's going on here? they demanded. 'Cattle rustling are we?'

'There was thish cow and it was locked into our dorm,' he slurred, very unsteady on his feet.

'Oh yes! Are you sure it wasn't you that locked it in there?'

'Yes...I mean no... We just came back in the minibus, but sssomebody has painted a white stripe on the poor thing. I wazz just trying to clean it off when it ran off.'

'Well, clearly you're drunk or otherwise you'd have recognised that as belted Galloway cow.'

'A whated Galloway?'

'A belted Galloway. We use them on the site for keeping the grass down.'

'Izz a strange name. Isn't?'

'Guess why it's called a belted Galloway.'

'D'no.'

'Because it has a white strip around its middle,' the security guard explained calmly. 'Just like a belt.'

'Oh. I didn't know. I'm ssso terribly sssorry.'

'So what have you done to these vehicles?' the guard asked, turning his attention to the parked cars. 'Have you been vandalising them too?'

'No, twas the cow. It bumped into them as it wazz 'scaping.'

By now the shrill of the car alarms had been silenced by three owners, but their complaints to the security guards hadn't.

'There's a big dent in my front wing', one said; 'My mirror had been knocked off,' another complained. 'There's a big scratch in my paintwork', the third one moaned. 'Who's going to pay?' they chorused looking at Gurney.

'Sssue the cow. I didn't do it.'

'Right, let's have some names and we'll sort this out in the morning.'

'I suggest you make your way back to your hut, before you do anymore damage,' the security guard advised

After giving his name to the security guards and getting some threatened agro from the car owners. Gurney staggered his way back to his hut.

'I wazz only being kind to the cow,' he muttered.

As he got closer to the hut, the farmyard smell got the better of him and his efforts to keep the beer and kebab in his stomach failed.

Now feeling very poorly indeed, he ventured back into the hut, misplaced his foot in the manure minefield and slipped over, landing with a splosh, flat on his back in the sea of slurry.

'Oh my god, that hurt,' he said, picking himself up, only to slip again, this time falling face first. 'Oh shit, I'm covered in it. Now what am I going to do? I can't go in my room like this. I'll…just go and have a shower.'

He swayed along the corridor, leaving a brown smear along the whole length of the corridor wall, until he reached the showers. Pulling back the plastic curtain, he stepped into the shower tray and turned on the shower.

Standing fully clothed under the shower as the brown water pooled at his feet, he cursed himself for giving in to the night's adventure.

The shower had the effect of sobering him up slightly, so eventually when he got into his room, he remembered to undress and put his soaking wet clothes on the floor and was snoring loudly within a few minutes.

# CHAPTER 71

It seemed like he'd been in bed only a few moments, when he was woken by the cleaner noisily clearing up the mess in the corridor and cursing all 'bloody students to hell.'

'Oh my head,' Gurney groaned.

Slowly he dragged himself out of bed, feeling very much the worse for wear. He found a black bin liner in the bottom of his suitcase and put his soaking wet clothes in it. He used a clean towel to mop up the pool of brownish water from the floor, where his wet clothes had festered overnight.

He decided to forgo his ablutions, as he'd showered in the early hours. So having ransacked his case again, he dressed in his spare clothes.

Grasping suitcase and black bin liner in his hands he made his way slowly out of the hut, avoiding eye contact with the irate cleaner.

As he walked out into the fresh air, he realised what an awful smell still lingered in the hut.

Slowly he found his way to the overflow carpark, threw his suitcase and black bin liner into the back of his van and slammed the doors, instantly regretting the acoustic assault on his throbbing head.

Lethargically he wandered over to the classroom via a coffee machine and sat reviewing and regretting the evening and early hour's adventures.

Chardonnay arrived bright and breezy.

'Good time last night Gurney wasn't it?' she grinned.

'It was until I discovered a bleeding cow in my dorm,' he said, painfully recalling the incident.

'A what?'

'A cow!' he repeated.

'Oh, I haven't heard of that student prank being done for a long time now. Yes, now you come to say, I can smell it on you,' she said moving away.

Gurney relayed the other events as far as his sketchy memory could recall.

'Just as well it's the end of the course. Otherwise you'd be sent home, I should think,' Chardonnay suggested.

Gurney put his aching head in his hands.

'I'll get you coffee,' she volunteered and as she left, the lecturer arrived.

'Ah, there you are,' he said, addressing Gurney. 'The farmer is looking for somebody to paint some more of his cows,' he laughed.

'Very funny,' I don't think,' Gurney muttered.

'Well, I have to apologise for not including the topic of cow identification on the course,' the lecturer joked.

'How did you hear about it?' Gurney asked.

'It's the main topic of conversation in the staff room this morning. Even the principal is laughing,' John Jefferies explained.

'Great. Will anybody at home hear about it?' Gurney asked tentatively, hoping the matter wouldn't leave the school.

'Yes. It'll go in your course report. But don't worry about it. They won't throw you out. It's all part of the uniqueness, which the department likes to see in our people.'

Gurney wasn't reassured.

The day unfolded very much as Chardonnay had told him and after swapping telephone numbers, the course broke up, promising to see each other on the next one, perhaps.

Chardonnay gave him a big hug.

'Might see you on an exercise sometime Gurney,' she said touching his shoulder.

'Yes, look forward to it. But I doubt you'll even remember what I look like.' he said abjectly.

'Don't you be so sure, I've got a *photographic* memory.' she replied, smiling slyly.

'And I've got a photo and no memory,' he thought. 'But no darts, next time,' he added.

'No. No darts. Take care.'

Gurney offered his hand, instead she enveloped him in a bear hug.

'See you.'

'Yeah, bye.'

They both got in their cars and drove slowly down the drive, collecting their mobiles from security as they left.

Gurney had a lump in his throat as he joined the main road. He felt sad to be going home. Worse still he had to rethink his planned exposè of the MO Disruption. He'd felt part of the team and besides which, he didn't want to become one of the 'disappeared'.

# CHAPTER 72

Gurney drove home very carefully, fearing that if he was stopped, he would fail a road side breathalyser.

Finally, he arrived at his house, still feeling very delicate.

Iris, however, was in full rant mode as she greeted him at the door, still going on about the disasters with the coat rail falling off and his poor plumbing.

When she saw the black bin liner full of wet clothes, she went 'ballistic'.

'What the hell have you been up to? I thought you were on a training course, not mud wrestling in a farmer's field. Oh the smell is disgusting. If you think I'm going to put that in my washing machine and wash it you've got another think coming.'

Like a dementor in the Harry Potter stories, her nagging sucked the happiness out of him.

What a contrast. At the training school the course camaraderie had made him feel good. The successes he'd achieved with Chardonnay made him feel positive and worthy.

After a respectful period listening to Iris's trivia, he made his excuses and disappeared off into a bedroom.

He looked around for anything that could conceivably be a hidden camera. Satisfied that he wasn't being spied upon, he wrote down some notes.

Recalling Chardonnay's warning about the abilities of the MO Disruption's pen to transmit his written word, he used a cheap biro and recorded the scope of MO Disruptions activities, and the Dark Canine Project.

'Perhaps I ought to tell the lorry driver that he hadn't imagined the black dog; that it did actually exist,' Gurney thought. 'But how would I explain it, without compromising the Ministry's work? No, perhaps I'll leave it for the time being.'

He hid his notes and the photo in the bottom of the first aid box. 'Nobody will think of looking in there,' he decided

'They will be ready for me, IF I produce an article for the editor,' he thought. 'On the other hand, do I want to do this anymore or am I 'playing with fire'? What if they publish that pornographic photo of me? How would I live that down?'


On Monday morning, Gurney made his way back to the MO Disruption section of the 'Yorkshire Pudding', and wondered whether the report from the training school had arrived.

However, as he walked in to the office Peter Noone gave him a friendly greeting with no hint of anything that would send him straight home again.

'Ah, Gurney, nice to see you're back. How was the course?'

'It was very... informative,' thank you,' Gurney replied and thought to himself, in more ways than one. 'But I couldn't believe how antiquated the whole place was, compared to these modern offices.'

'It's because it's a listed site. They're not allowed to modernise it. It has historical significance dating back to the Second World War.'

'I'll say it does.'

'Now you're back and a trained DO, I want you to do some research on the RARDMS figures,' the Manager requested.

'The what?'

'RARDMS.

'How do you spell that?'

'R A R D M S. Surely you covered that up there?'

'Well ...err...yes,' Gurney lied, wondering if they'd done it on the day he was late and suffering from his hangover.

'Can you put it on my desk by close of play today please? We need to provide them for head office ready for the Good Friday exercise.'

'Today!' Gurney felt the usual 'pressure prompt' from down below. 'Yes of course. What exercise would that be?' he asked.

'Sorry Gurney, I can't tell you. You haven't got the right level of security clearance yet for me to be able to brief you.'

'But I'm going to be looking at the data anyway,' Gurney thought. 'So what's the difference?'

Peter left the office for a meeting.

'Now where the hell do I start looking for RARDMS figures? If only I knew what it meant, that might be a help.'

While he was in the gents, he chanced to ask a fellow 'trough user'.

'Excuse me.'

The other shuffled away from him, apprehensively.

'Have you ever heard of RARDMS?' Gurney asked.

The other looked at Gurney strangely, thinking it was a 'chat up line.' No sorry mate.' Hoping his stream would dry up quickly.

'Only I've been asked to find some stats called RARDMS.'

'Oh Stats! Why don't you have a look in the telephone directory? You might find somebody in there who can help,' he blurted and relieved, quickly left.

'Thanks.' Gurney said, washing his hands. 'I suppose it's a starting point.'

# CHAPTER 73

When he returned to Peter Noone's empty office, Gurney looked around to see if he could find a directory and was relieved to spot a thick book labelled 'Internal Telephone directory'. He quickly flicked it open to find an index.

'I wonder if there's anything in here?' he said, turning the pages. He looked for an entry for Stats or Statistics. There was none.

He looked under 'RARDMS' again there was no entry.

'Damn, what could it be I wonder? Is it a code for something?' he wondered. How about a special department for code words in the business?'

He ran his finger down the index and spotted an entry. 'Ah, here it is,' he said, spotting an entry for 'Business Code Words'.

He dialled the number and after a few minutes his call was answered.

'Good morning, BCW, how may I help?'

'Hello there. Do you keep a list of the business's code words?'

'Yes, that's correct.'

'Can you tell me what RARDMS stands for?' Gurney asked.

'I'm sorry, you've got the wrong department. I only deal with TATs.'

'Pardon?'

'TATs. That stands for - TLCs And TLAs.'

'No, sorry. Still don't understand.'

'Two or Three Letter Codes and Two or Three letter Acronyms.'

'Right!' Gurney said, puzzled.

'You want the SAS department,' the woman informed him.

'Special Forces?' Gurney wondered.

'No! SAS covers Six and Seven Letter Codes and Acronyms.'

'What! Do you mean there's a different section that deals with six and seven letter codes?'

'Yes, of course.'

'Don't tell me, there's another section that deals with Four Letter Codes, right?' Gurney suggested sarcastically.

'Yes that's right. That's the FAFs team. They deal with Four and Five Letter Codes and Acronyms.'

'At least they've doubled up their responsibilities,' Gurney said, flippantly.

'Yes, of course, otherwise we would be overstaffed, and we wouldn't want that, would we?' the woman missed the irony.

'I think you've already reached that level,' Gurney thought.

'It's easy to remember the groupings. T's, F's and S's.'

'It is?'

'Yes of course, 'T's are Twos and Threes; 'F's are Fours and Fives and 'S's are Sixes and Sevens.'

'OK, got that, but what about ELC's and NLC's?'

'Now you're being silly...there are no Eight or Nine Letter Codes. The business decided that when you get to eight characters you might as well use the complete word instead,' the lady admonished.

'Don't tell me, that's another different department too.'

'Naturally! It's quite complex controlling all the business jargon,' she said, passionately.

Gurney was now quite intrigued by the obvious over resourcing. 'So do you have other departments dealing with *complete* words?'

'Yes. It all adds to the security and compartmentalisation of the business. *Complete* code words and hyphenated code words are tightly controlled,' she informed him, zealously.

'Even sentences perhaps?' Gurney tentatively suggested.

'Sentences are used for defining the various codes and that department too is always extremely busy.

As is the Project names team,' she continued. 'We have a list of new names that Project Managers are allocated when they start a new project,' she informed him keenly.

'It's a bit over bureaucratic though isn't it? I mean, vast departments just controlling company jargon? They're all non-jobs,' Gurney observed.

'Non jobs! Non jobs! I'll have you know, its a vital foundation of any large business.'

'Really? Gurney said sceptically.

'Yes, otherwise, you could get the board talking about different topics from misunderstandings of the various codes and jargon,' she said defensively, all in a rush.

'Surely misunderstandings don't happen that often do they? I mean, isn't this just overkill to have all those people keeping an eye on words?'

'They would be insulted by your ill-conceived suggestion that all they did was 'kept an eye' on the words,' the office worker rebuked. 'The reason we don't have problems is due to their focussed diligence,' she continued. 'They maintain the integrity of the business through their keen stewardship.'

'I'm not convinced,' Gurney muttered.

'Well judge for yourself then. Did you hear about the big company fiasco several years ago, where the board were asked to authorise a vast amount of money for a project?'

'Remind me.'

'Well somebody took advantage of the confusion of 'buzz words' that existed in the company and invented a mythical project with the same letters as an existing project and they duly filtered off millions of pounds in to their own PBA.'

'Sorry, PBA?' Gurney puzzled.

'Personal Bank Account,' she clarified.

'Really! No, I didn't hear about that. They must have kept it Mum.'

'MUM. Do you mean, Minimum Use Methodology?' the woman volunteered.

'No. They must have kept it under their hat,' Gurney added, to clarify what he meant.

'Do you mean, Held Awaiting Talks?' the woman suggested.

No I mean kept quiet. Like, no-one said anything,' Gurney said frustrated.

'Sorry, that's not in my section.'

'What's not in your section?'

'QUIET. That's an FLC. You'll need to talk to them about that. That's not one of mine. I only do TAT's.'

'What! I wasn't using a code. I was...Oh! Never mind,' Gurney said exasperated with the discussion. 'Where do I find the SAS team?'

'You'll find them on extension 247,' the woman explained.

'Thanks. Is that in another building?'

'No that's my colleague, who sits next to me. You'll find she's very helpful. Aren't you Sylv?'

'Helpful? Yes, just like you,' her colleague agreed.

'Can you hand her the phone then?'

'No, sorry. I must keep my phone line open for general enquiries and TAT's. Thanks for calling the BCW helpline.'

Frustrated at her 'helpfulness', Gurney hung up, rang extension 247 and spoke to Sylv.

'Hello, can you tell me what RARDMS stands for?'

'RARDMS? Yes it stands for Road And Rail Disruption Monitoring Statistics.'

'Thank goodness, sanity at last. Where do I get them from,' he asked expecting to get another bureaucratic run around.

'They are available to download from the MIS,' Sylv informed him.

'Sorry MIS?' Gurney repeated, puzzled.

'You'll have to ring my colleague who deals with TAT's for an explanation.'

'This is bureaucracy gone mad,' Gurney moaned. 'Can't you tell me?'

'No, sorry. It's not within my remit.'

He duly rang the original number again.

'Good morning, BCW, how may I help?'

'Can you tell me what MIS stands for...before I go mad,' Gurney demanded, trying to keep his temper in check.

'Yes. MIS is the Management Information System.'

'Where will I find it?'

'It's a computer system, accessible from your desk. You will need a password to access it though,' she informed him.

'So from where do I get a password?' Gurney asked, expecting another load of bureaucratic instructions and wasn't disappointed.

'You will need to fill in a form, get it authorised by your Manager and then submit it to Access Control. Is there anything further I can help you with?'

'No thanks,' Gurney said, exhausted by the long winded exchanges.

'Thanks for calling the BCW.'

Gurney shook his head in frustration. 'Talk about jobs for the boys.'

# CHAPTER 74

Eventually, after a frustrating day of filling in forms and getting his Manager to authorise his access request, Gurney submitted the form to Access Control.

He followed it up with a phone call.

'Access Control, Wendy speaking, how may I help?'

'Hi, I've just submitted a form for access to MIS, can you tell me how long it's likely to be?'

'Currently there is a backlog. We are estimating three months for new requests.'

'Three months! I need access today,' he demanded.

'Sorry. If you want to escalate it, you will need to complete an urgent request form and once submitted, you will need to get your manager to call my manager.'

'Oh this is crazy,' Gurney exploded, now completely frustrated by the 'red tape'. 'I'm supposed to put it on his desk today.'

'Sorry, forward planning often helps to avoid situations like this. Don't shoot the messenger for your bad planning,' the Access controller berated.

'Yes, but... OK where do I find this form?'

'It's on the MIS site.'

'But I don't have access to the MIS site. That's what I'm trying to get,' he ranted.

'Sorry, I must terminate this call now, as I have reached the time allowed for me to handle your call.

Goodbye. Thank you for calling Access Control. We're here to help.'

Gurney eventually found someone who would download the form for him, but would not run the report, because of his security profile.

Even so, with the 'Urgent request' form, it took until the end of the week to get access into the system.

It was not helpful either, when he had to get the 'un-helpfuldesk', as he called them, to reset his password three times because he'd mistyped his user ID.

Finally, on Friday he was able to successfully log on to the system only to be confronted by a bewildering array of RARDMS sub reports.

'I don't know which one he wants,' he said, mesmerised by the scores of options. 'I'll run a report for each of the twenty different versions and hope that there is one that he wants somewhere amongst them.'

However, when he went to collect the reports from the communal office printer, he was faced with a large mass of paperwork spread across the office floor, plus a group of irate office workers who were waiting to print off their own reports.

'Who the hell's been printing this lot off?' they asked each other.

In great embarrassment Gurney stepped forward and apologised.

'Sorry I didn't realise it would be such a large report,' he grovelled, lifting several reams of computer paper off the floor.

'You should have got the computer centre to print it off on their high speed printer. You'll need to get the office trolley and another box of paper too, as this one is now empty,' they berated.

Shame faced, Gurney took the mountain of reports and stacked them around Peter's desk. Having done so, he tracked down a replacement box of paper and returned to the printer and his irate colleagues.

'It's just a learning curve,' he thought. 'It's bound to get better, isn't it?'

# CHAPTER 75

Unfortunately the mountain of printouts that Gurney had obtained only had various bits of required data scattered throughout it. Consequently he and, an incensed, Peter Noone had worked late into the evening, to extract the correct information for the required RARDMS report. Stopping only for a MacDonald's takeaway they worked feverishly to meet their deadline.

'Why the hell did you have to decimate a rain forest, to print all that lot off? I never had this problem with your predecessor.'

'Sorry,' Gurney said, shame faced.

'Anyway, I thought you said you'd covered it on the course?' the manager queried.

'Yes...well...errr...it was different up there,' Gurney lied. 'It was only dummy data.'

'Peter Noone ran his eye over the spreadsheet précising the 'rainforest' figures. 'Well I think that's what we usually send,' the manager said. 'You might as well send it to CJ in London and hope he agrees.'

'Are you sure you want *me* to send it?' Gurney asked, hoping to be relieved of the task. 'I might get it wrong.'

'On the other hand, you might get it right,' the manager replied, whilst thinking, 'if he cocks it up, Gurney would also get the blame and he'd be blameless.'

Within a few minutes, CJ was looking at the newly arrived email with the spreadsheet attachment. 'At last, here's what we've been waiting for,' he declared.

Quickly he checked the summary and went to Eunice Cabbage's office and handed the printout to her.

'I think you'll like some of the new jargon in this report,' CJ beamed.

''Crop of Cones', that's brilliant.' Eunice Cabbage exclaimed 'Give the person a bonus. They've really come up with a great one,' she said, smiling. 'Who is it?'

'I see from the email, it's one of our new recruits, Leafmould,' CJ informed her.

'Isn't he the one we're closely monitoring?' Cabbage pondered.

'Yes, he's a character alright.' CJ observed. 'He appears to have built up quite a disruptive reputation already.'

'Apparently he won the DO course cup for creating major chaos on my patch,' she advised him.'

'Something to do with a rare bird sighting around Bristol airport, I seem to think,' CJ recalled.

'Yes, unwittingly, he helped improve my figures no end,' Cabbage added.

'I think he's going to be a great asset to the Ministry,' CJ observed.

'But I gather he was a journalist in his previous job,' Cabbage remarked.

'Yes, that's right, But don't worry about that. We have already put the 'frighteners on him. I don't think he will be publishing anything, even if he is still working for the newspaper,' CJ informed her.

'More reports coming in about our targeted disruption campaign,' Cabbage said gleefully, looking at her monitor screen.

'18 mile northbound traffic jam M6, Mam,' another voice announced.

The control room was electric, as additional data came in from across the country.

M25 at a standstill. A1(M) 4 miles and building.

As the national chaos was being carefully recorded and displayed on the plotting table, there was an air of excitement. People breathed a sigh of relief as months of meticulous planning was coming to fruition.

In the managers' offices champagne corks were being launched into the ceiling tiles and the sound of back-slapping could be heard.

'Well done everybody,' CJ announced over the control room tannoy.

CJ gave Eunice Cabbage a hug. 'Well done Eu, magnificent job as usual. I'll let D know.'

'Great team effort,' she agreed, responding to his embrace. 'The buffet has just been delivered for our usual campaign celebration party. I'll see you there,' she winked.

'Too true. I'll pop back to my office and call D. Save me some sandwiches.'

'CJ rang the familiar number and after a short period of ringing, the Head of the Ministry of Disruption answered.

'D. Who's calling?'

'D, Carrington Jones. Operation Bullseye complete, Mam.'

'Has it all gone as planned?' she queried.

'Yes Mam. All as planned, and more.'

'What did you employ this time?'

'Mainly a few 'dented' cars on the hard shoulder of some motorways.'

'Curiosity is a wonderful human foible to exploit, isn't it?' she observed.

'Yes, without exception everybody slows down and 'rubbernecks' to see what's going on. And we get 'instant tailback' and miles of traffic jams,' he added.

'What about the weather manipulation exercise?' D asked.

'Yes, we did use technical wizardry there by 'seeding' the clouds and using ultrasonic rain generation equipment. It worked like a dream.'

'Usual effect?'

'Yes from the random occurrences of torrential downpours, it created lots of spray, with the inevitable aquaplaning and multiple shunts,' he said enthusiastically.

'What about the media?'

'I've just heard that the National Radio stations have started special 'phone in' programmes for people stuck in traffic jams.'

'Quite like the old Dunkirk spirit,' the Chief of the organisation observed. 'That's the ticket.'

'We removed many cones from strategic places around the country, to demonstrate to the public that we wanted to ease their journeys.'

'The media need to have their ego stroked too. Anymore manipulation there?' D enquired.

'Yes. The newspaper article about the free flow of traffic was a good PR exercise, but nevertheless it still helped bring the road traffic in some areas to a complete grid lock.

'And the potholes?'

'Yes. We created a few additional ones, which led to large numbers of punctures requiring inside lane closures.'

'Good for you.'

'And the rail figures are good too?'

'Yes. Very pleased with the simultaneous cancellation of rail services due to engineering works!'

'How did you manage that?'

'A few D.O.s infiltrated the planning teams,' CJ informed her.

'Well, I'm very impressed.'

'Thank you Mam.'

'Please pass on my congratulations to your teams.'

'Yes I will. The exciting thing is, that's only the chaos of people going on holiday.'

'Yes of course,'

'Just like that reporter said, during the Falklands conflict. '*We counted them out…*' and we're going to count the chaos back in as they return home.'

'I am delighted to know we have such an effective organisation in place. Well done again.'

The Head of the Ministry hung up, as CJ dreamed of his trip to the palace.

# CHAPTER 76

Gurney was exhausted by the RARDMS episode and was glad to be dragging his weary body to the bus stop for the 'park and ride' trip back to his car, when he bumped into Pollen.

'Hello Gurney. Nice to see you. How are you?'

'Oh hello Polly. Nice to see you, too.'

'What brings you back here at this time of night?'

'Oh I got a job. '

'You got a job? Oh well done. Who are you working for?' Polly asked.

'Oh I got a job with... With...umm. '

'With whom sorry?'

'Oh, I'm not sure I'm allowed to say.' He hesitated, all the while desperately trying to get his tired brain to remember the cover story he'd been told to use.

It's OK, I've signed the official secrets act. So whatever you say, your secret is safe with me.'

'Well, OK. But you must promise not to say anything to anybody.'

'Of course. Cross my heart and hope to die,' she recited flippantly.

'Well after you told me that I didn't get the job because of my failed vetting...'

'Yes, I'm so sorry about that. I was actually 'told off' for giving you the initial impression that you'd already got the job.'

'What I couldn't understand was, if I hadn't got the job, why you couldn't tell me on the phone? Rather than wasting my time, our time, by calling me back to tell me,' Gurney wondered.

'I did think that too. Initially I refused to do it, but they reminded me that my contract was up for renewal, so....'Polly replied, awkwardly.

'Anyway, after you left, somebody came along and collected me. I thought they were going to show me out. But they didn't.'

'What do you mean?' she puzzled.

'The bloke turned out to be a manager of a secret organisation.'

'Secret organisation! Where?'

'In the Yorkshire Pudding.'

'In there? she said, pointing at the modern structure. Where?'

'There is a door that leads into another part of the complex. It's all secret.'

'What's the organisation called?' Polly persisted.

'Well I'm not sure I should tell you. I've probably said too much already,' Gurney said feeling uneasy.

'Oh! I'm sorry that you don't think you can trust me,' she sulked.

'No, it's not like that... I've been sworn to secrecy,' Gurney reassured her.

'As I said, your secret's safe with me.'

'Well, if I tell you, you mustn't tell anybody else, OK?' Gurney demanded, looking around.

'OK.'

'Actually, I'm surprised you don't know about it anyway, because the initials are the same,' he explained.

'The same as what?' she wondered.

'The MOD.'

'The MOD?' she repeated, thinking that Gurney had lost it.

'Yes. And I believe that it's funded from the same budget as your employer, the Ministry of Defence.'

'Really! she said playing along with his fanciful idea. 'That's interesting!'

'Yes, I thought so too. But it's all beyond me.'

'So what's its name?' she asked sceptically.

'The Ministry of Disruption,' Gurney whispered.

'The Ministry of what?'

'You'll have to keep your voice down?' Gurney warned her, looking around to make sure no-one else was in earshot.

'OK,' she agreed. Now reassessing her initial thoughts of Gurney's fantasy.

'The Ministry of Disruption!' Gurney whispered.

'Are you sure you're not confusing it with the Ministry of Defence?'

'No, it's a secret army. Guerrilla fighters,' he elaborated.

'Guerrilla fighters!' Polly repeated, and laughed.

'Sssh, you'll get me shot!'

Pollen whispered, 'You've got to be joking. Why would we want Guerrilla fighters? We aren't at war!'

'No, but it's just in case,' Gurney said, feeling uneasy about how much he was revealing.

'In case of?' she probed.

'In case we're invaded!'

'So are you a guerrilla fighter?' she asked sceptically.

'Well I suppose I am. In a way.'

Pollen smiled. 'Really? I can't see you as a Rambo figure.'

'Ah you see, that's just it. We're just ordinary people who you wouldn't suspect. We're training constantly.'

'What, playing war games?'

'In a way, yes. Anyway, I think I've told you enough,' Gurney said finally deciding to end the conversation.

'No, you can't leave me without telling me more about the organisation,' she pleaded, now fascinated by the possibility of a secret group.

'I don't know anything other than it's huge and covers the whole country. It reaches to the top, if you know what I mean!'

'So why the name, Disruption?' she continued.

'That's what we do. Disrupt,' Gurney explained.

'Disrupt! Disrupt what?'

'Everything. Our training creates chaos on a daily basis. And we're pretty good at it too.' Gurney boasted. It's all clandestine stuff.'

'Would I have been disrupted?' Polly probed.

'Stuck in a traffic jam?'

'Yes.'

'What do you reckon caused it?' he asked knowingly.

'Well, in this case it was a lorry fire.'

'How'd you think the lorry caught fire?' he questioned smugly.

'Brakes overheated, I expect.'

'Really! Coincidence that it happened on a busy motorway where it could cause maximum disruption though, wasn't it? Gurney suggested.

'You mean!!! '

'Yes. Disruption at its most sophisticated,' he observed.

'Then are you saying that all accidents. '

'Correction, road traffic collisions.'

'Yeah, whatever. Are you saying that they are all caused by you Disruption people too?' Pollen queried.

'No, not all. There are obviously bad drivers who do the job for us, through their own incompetence,' Gurney clarified. 'But the effect is still the same.'

'But you must be costing the country millions in lost appointments, late loads etc.'

'You seem to be missing the point. The country is much stronger. It is more resilient now,' said Gurney, recalling something from his induction.

'How do you figure that?' Pollen asked, cynically.

'The country continues to function in spite of all these delays. Us Brits always find a way of getting round problems. It's the Blitz spirit if you like,' Gurney added brightly.

'Oh my God!' Pollen exclaimed, as the full implications of what Gurney had told her hit home.

'Now you mustn't tell anybody about this. Promise?' he demanded.

Pollen crossed her fingers behind her back. 'Yes I promise.'

'Here's the bus. I have to go home to bed. I'm dead on my feet.' Gurney said clambering on to the bus and flashing his pass.

'Goodnight Gurney, thanks for the chat.'

'Don't forget, Mums the word,' Gurney croaked collapsing into the nearest seat.

# CHAPTER 77

Carrington Jones had been summoned to the large country mansion and was standing in front of the Minister of Defence, Angela Flower-Hardwoman, in her plush office.

Eunice Cabbage wanted desperately to go to the meeting, but D had decided, that as diplomacy was not one of Eunice's strengths, CJ would represent the department.

'Sit down Mr Carrington Jones.'

'Please call me CJ.'

'I hardly think that is appropriate in the present circumstances,' the Minister informed him tersely.

'Present circumstances?' CJ said, taken aback.

'You are here because your senior manager appears to be shy about coming to see me.'

'Really?' CJ feigned surprise, as he had already been briefed by D.

'So you're going to have to be the bearer of bad news. Mr Carrington Jones.'

'Oh?'

'Whom do you work for Mr Carrington Jones?'

'The government.'

'Who specifically in the government?'

'I'm sorry but I'm not at liberty to say,' he said firmly.

The Minister looked at the piece of paper in front of her.

'Let me jog your memory. Does the name, Ministry of Disruption ring any bells?'

CJ's facial spasm gave the game away.

'No,' he replied, recovering quickly. Ministry of what?'

'Don't play games with me. Your organisation has been in existence since the second world war and has been embezzling funding from the Ministry of Defence budget.

'Sorry, I don't understand what you mean,' CJ refuted.

'Don't play me for a fool,' she said standing and glaring at him. 'I know what's been going on. The leeching of the funds from the MoD budget will cease forthwith. I am going to present my findings to the forthcoming select committee. I expect they will close you down.'

'But Minister, you can't!' Carrington Jones asserted.

'What do you mean I can't? The Ministry of Defence is my responsibility.'

"Minister, it is a vital defensive organisation which needs to be funded.'

'Then find your own funding,' she suggested vehemently.

'It is a clandestine organisation and needs to be invisible to the world. Hence it is camouflaged under the MoD's budget.'

'No, it is a renegade, maverick organisation without government control and needs to be made accountable,' she countered.

'We have a proud unbroken record, since the second world war,' CJ said passionately.

'Well jolly good for you. But the truth of the matter is there are insufficient funds to support you. Do you know that we can't even afford to buy equipment for our front line troops, because your organisation has been embezzling the funds.'

'We're not embezzling it. We are doing the same as you. Defending our country,' CJ said, ardently.

'I want you to tell your boss that funding is at an end. And if the consequence of that is that your organisation goes, then that is down to your own incompetence. You can either do it quietly and no-one will know, or we can have an open debate in the full glare of the world's press,' she suggested, firmly.

'Our operational modus operandi has always been to be inconspicuous. Clandestine operations are essential. If you now make public our existence, our role is compromised,' CJ explained patiently. 'The enemy, whoever they may be in the future, will then be aware of our covert forces and will track them down and execute them.'

'Fool! Do you think that any military invasion force would not already be aware of such covert teams?' the minister reposted.

'You can't just demolish more than seventy years of military service at the stroke of a pen!' CJ said, becoming increasingly angry.

'Of course I can. We will use the title of 'Options for Change', downsizing the Armed forces, if you like, to save your embarrassment,' she suggested. 'No, this is a time of peace and the budget is better spent on peaceful things. Tell your organisation that the announcement will be made by the Chancellor at the next budget.

The maintenance of a secret army is an unnecessary drain on the resources of the state.

I am determined that the Ministry of Disruption WILL be disbanded,' she said firmly.

'Goodbye Mr Carrington Jones,' she directed, closing the file in front of her and putting it into her desk drawer.

Carrington Jones glared at her. He hesitated for a moment, but could see no further benefit in arguing. He turned on his heel and petulantly slammed the door as he left.

'Didn't go well then?' D said, as he stormed into her office later.

'Hardened bitch! She knows it all. We've been compromised by somebody. When I explained the necessity of the organisation, she wouldn't listen.

She is plugging the leak that is giving us our funding,' he informed her.

'Well, as you know, without funding, we're sunk.' D reminded him.

'She is insistent that the MO Disruption goes. She says the funding issue is to be announced by the Chancellor as part of the budget statement,' CJ added.

'OK, you know what to do,' D directed. 'We have been in this situation before with numerous politicians. Time to implement 'Operation Survive' again.'

'She will rue the day she crossed swords with us,' CJ said, dramatically.

# CHAPTER 78

Gurney feared the worst that his exploits at the training school had caught up with him when he was told to report to Carrington Jones' London office.

Apprehensively, he knocked on the door and waited to be invited in.

'Come.'

Gurney opened the door tentatively and stepped in to the plush office.

The huge carpeted room was dominated by a large conference table in the centre, around which were positioned six matching wooden conference chairs.

He was surprised to see another man sitting in a black leather chair alongside CJ. The man was not wearing shoes.

'Take a seat Gurney,' CJ directed. 'Allow me to introduce John Ripple, Head of Security.

Gurney's heart froze. Had he been rumbled?

'Pardon my state of undress Leafmould,' John Ripple said, 'only I've got gout and its bliss to discard my shoes.'

'Oh,' Gurney replied, not sure what to say.

'I expect you're wondering what this is all about?' CJ said, quietly.

'Yes sir.' The butterflies filling his stomach, took flight.

'I have read the report from the training school,' CJ said, putting down a piece of paper.

'Oh dear, have you?' The butterflies were now in Gurney's throat.

'Yes, and it makes for interesting reading,' the manager revealed.

'I don't know what to say,' Gurney said and hung his head. 'Was his secret out? Was this how he would disappear?' he wondered fearfully.

'I think you show the promise that we need in our organisation,' Carrington Jones said, smiling.

Gurney couldn't believe his ears. 'Sorry! I thought you said...'

'Yes. You appear to have a...uniqueness that we're looking for,' CJ confirmed.

'I do?' Gurney said in amazement.

'We would like you to undertake a very special mission,' CJ directed.

'Really? What sort of mission?' Gurney asked, excitedly.

'A clandestine mission,' the other revealed.

'Well, yes, of course, I'll do it. What do I have to do?'

'We'd like you to conduct a DIY job on the Minister of Defence's house,' he explained.

'DIY! Oh no. No sorry. I promised my wife, I'd never to do any more DIY jobs ever again.' Gurney panicked.

'Yes, I know all about that. So don't worry,' CJ assured him. 'Your wife will never know that you did it.'

'Furthermore, I am legally restrained. I have an ASBO preventing me,' Gurney said, desperately trying to think of an excuse to wriggle out of the proposed mission.

And as for the ASBO, we'll sort out the legal side for you,' Ripple advised him.

'I feel honoured that you have selected me. But umm… but isn't there anybody else who could do it?' Gurney suggested, nervously.

'No. We believe you're the best man for the job. Are you refusing to do it and thereby failing to serve your country?' CJ asked, critically.

'No… it's just that…'

'Good. That's sorted then. Here are all the details,' CJ handed him a file of paperwork.

Gurney tentatively took the file and flicked open the cover.

'What if I haven't got the skills to do it?' he countered.

'You have. I've checked your file.'

Finally accepting that he wasn't going to be able to wriggle out of it,' he asked. 'What is the job anyway?'

'We have intercepted a request from the Minister of Defence to a local firm for the installation of a gas fire. She wants it fitted in one of her ten bedrooms,' CJ informed him.

'Ten bedrooms!'

'Yes, it's an old mansion house,' Ripple added.

'Well, I have done several gas jobs before and I know how to do it. Only my past results have been a bit… 'Gurney confessed.

'You mustn't burden yourself with your past, umm… failures. ' CJ soothed.

'But I'm not CORGI registered either.'

'That's OK. It's a government job. Not required.' CJ dismissed.

'But…'

'You are a different person now. Aren't you Gurney?

Look at all your successes winning the top student cup at the training school.' Ripple encouraged.

'Well yes...yes I suppose I am.' Gurney thought for a moment and finally said, 'OK. When do you want me to do it?'

'Immediately. The stores and tools are already in the van, which bears the livery of the firm she is expecting.

The vehicle is fitted with false number plates, so you don't need to do anything other than drive there and fit the gas fire.'

'OK. I can do it. I will do it,' Gurney said, positively, pumping himself up.

'Oh, there is another important job to do, while you're there.' Ripple added.

'Yes?'

'Keep your eyes open for some files or paperwork referring to our organisation, the Ministry of Disruption.'

'Our organisation!' Gurney wondered.

'Yes. It appears that we have a mole in our team who has been leaking information about us.' CJ explained.

Immediately his bus stop conversation with Pollen came into Gurney's thoughts. 'Surely she wouldn't be telling tales, would she?' he thought. 'I mean, she's signed the official secrets act and she promised.'

'The Minister is threatening to expose us and close us down.' CJ informed him. 'We must get our hands on whatever evidence she has.'

'Evidence. Yes,' Gurney repeated. Wondering how he was going to find it, let alone retrieve it.

'At ALL costs. Do you understand?' Carrington Jones said firmly. 'At ALL costs.'

Gurney gulped, 'Yes. At all costs,' he confirmed. 'OK. For Queen and Country, I'll do it,' Gurney heard himself say.

'Good man. Oh by the way. There is no need to take your paint brush,' Ripple added.

'Paint brush?' Gurney wondered.

'There are no cows to paint,' said CJ laughing.

Gurney grimaced at the bovine reference, but left the room with a spring in his step. He had been selected to do a vital job. They had chosen him out of all the other DOs who they could have picked. His confidence soared.

'Are you sure we've done the right thing?' Ripple asked. 'I mean the man is a walking disaster.'

'Yes I know and that's why I think he's the right man for the job. The arrogant bitch deserves his type of disastrous DIY expertise. With any amount of luck he'll blow it all up,' CJ suggested. 'She's already warned us against using any dirty tricks to retrieve the evidence against us.'

'What about security?'

'He will have fake ID documents, so should be able to get round the former SBS soldiers guarding her.'

'Mind you, if he blows himself up, that will be another thorn out of our side.'

'Yes, you're right. But how did she get the information in the first place? I thought we were watertight.'

'I'm not sure that it wasn't Mr Leafmould himself. He's been seen talking with that Human Resources contractor in the MoD.'

'Contractor?'

'The one who interviewed him before he joined us.'

'If that's the case, our bug pen has obviously failed to catch him in the act.'

'Even so, I think we ought to back him up with somebody else.'

'I've got just the right person in mind. I'll make the arrangements,' Ripple said.

# CHAPTER 79

Gurney was nervous. He had been parked in front of the huge black wrought iron mansion gates for five minutes. He crossed his legs to help relieve the additional pressure from his 'condition'.

He had never impersonated anyone before and was desperately trying to ensure that he had his cover story straight in his head.

He controlled his shaking hands long enough to push the intercom buzzer on the pillar at the side of the drive, and anxiously waited for a reply.

After a few moments, a tinny voice crackled over the speaker. 'Yes?'

Gurney cleared his throat. 'I have come to fit the gas fire for the Minister.'

He heard the CCTV camera on the large brick pillar buzz, as it zoomed in on him.

'ID badge,' the voice demanded.

Gurney took the false ID badge from his pile of paperwork and held it up towards the camera.

After a few seconds the gates swung open. He pocketed the badge and drove the falsely liveried vehicle into the grounds of the estate.

Carefully he steered the van round the long, sweeping, tree lined drive, towards the impressive Cotswold stone building.

As he arrived at the beautiful oak panelled front door, a large man, wearing a military type sweater, with an earpiece planted in his ear, gesticulated for him to drive around the back of the property instead.

The man followed the vehicle to the back door, where Gurney parked in a bay marked 'visitors'.

As he got out, the guard stood by his side and ordered him to put his hands on the roof of the van.

Gurney was subjected to a thorough body search, checking everywhere, especially his pockets.

'Can I see your ID please?' the guard demanded.

Gurney nervously took the false badge out of his jacket pocket and offered it to the man, who kept eye contact with him all the time, as if trying to read his mind.

The security man studied the badge and photo carefully, examining it to check for any signs of tampering.

'Can I see what's in the back of the van please?'

'Yes, of course. It's only the stores and my tool bag. The advice note for the job is on the passenger seat.'

The security guard took out a small hand held device and scanned Gurney's bag.

'Whats that for?' Gurney asked.

'I'm checking for electronic listening devices. The Minister would be most upset if she found that you had been planting anything in her house,' the man growled. 'The newspapers will try all manner of dirty tricks.'

'I don't know anything about that sort of thing. I've just come to fit a gas fire. That's all,' Gurney said, tensely.

Satisfied that Gurney was a non-threat, the guard shepherded him into the large, old fashioned kitchen, where a chubby faced housekeeper was sitting talking to a uniformed chef.

'Gwen, this man has come to fit a gas fire. Do you know anything about it?'

'Yes Andy, leave him with me.'

'No, my orders are to stay with him.'

'OK, please yourself. Come this way young man,' she said, addressing Gurney.

The housekeeper showed him around the house and indicated where the fire was to be fitted, eventually leaving him with the security guard, who shadowed his every move.

Gurney planned the job meticulously and decided that the easiest route for the pipes was running them outside and around the building from the supply in the kitchen to chosen bedroom.

However, mindful of his previous errors, before he started, Gurney sought out the housekeeper.

'I'm going to run the pipes outside. It will make the job a lot faster,' he informed her.

'You're going to have to think again. The building is Grade 2 listed,' she advised him. 'You can't spoil the beauty of the house with ugly pipes.'

'Well if I take them through all the rooms, it's going to be a long job.'

'That's OK. It's taxpayer's money anyway,' she informed him coldly.

'Oh!' Gurney was taken aback by her cavalier attitude to the cost. 'OK, let me have a rethink,' he pondered. 'I might be able to hide the piping behind the tall wainscoting, which skirts all the rooms.'

'Yes, that sounds like a better idea. But make sure

you don't damage the paintwork. Otherwise the Minister will have your 'guts for garters'.'

'No, I'll be careful,' Gurney reassured her.

The housekeeper left him to re-plan the job, while the security guard looked on.

Shadowed by the guard, Gurney went back to the van and got a chisel. Returning to the house, he carefully prised the wainscoting off along part of his intended route and was relieved to see that there was indeed, a sizeable void behind it for the pipes.

'Bingo,' he said gleefully, 'that'll do nicely.'

As he started getting the tools and stores out of the van, he felt very apprehensive about what he was about to do. He had never done a DIY job for anybody other than the family before. The spectre of failed jobs ate away at his self-confidence.

'Come on Gurney, you can do this, you can do this,' he encouraged, psyching himself up.

As the pipe run took shape and there had been no disasters, he started to feel more and more confident.

The 'doubt demons' were being laid to rest and his self-confidence was coming back. He was really starting to enjoy getting back into DIY. Above all, using top quality tools made the job so much easier. Simple things, like sharp drill bits made boring holes a joy.

He worked diligently throughout the day, unhindered, and at 5 o'clock decided it was time to quit, while he was ahead.

'I've banished a few DIY ghosts,' he said to himself as he proudly looked at his workmanship on the partly completed job.

Pleased with himself, Gurney was taken to the housekeeper by the guard.

'OK. I've finished for tonight. I've tidied up and left everything safe. I'll be back tomorrow to line the chimney, finish the pipe run, fit the fire and connect the gas.'

'Very well, but don't you be late tomorrow I've got a banquet to prepare,' the housekeeper told him.

'No I won't. I'll be here bright and early,' Gurney confirmed.

As he drove away from the mansion, he was on 'cloud nine'.

# CHAPTER 80

Gurney drove back to garage the van and telephoned CJ.

CJ answered almost before it rang.

'Carrington Jones,' he announced.

'CJ, it's me, Gurney.'

'Hello Gurney, how did it go?'

'Great. The jobs coming on a treat. I'm nearly half way through.'

'Good. Have you found her records concerning our organisation yet?' CJ probed.

'Nothing yet I'm sorry. It's going to be very difficult because I have a security guard with me watching my every move. But I've done some great pipework and the joints are…'

'Yes well, that's not important at the moment,' CJ interrupted.

Gurney felt deflated at the put down. He was itching to discuss the DIY challenges that he'd overcome and the great discovery of the void behind the wainscoting.

'Anything else going on there?' CJ enquired.

'No, no I don't think so. Only, I think the Minister has a gym in the room next to where I'm working, because there was a lot of grunting, groaning and heavy breathing going on intermittently during the day.'

Carrington Jones' ears pricked up. 'Was there anybody else in the room?'

'I couldn't see inside. I just heard it, that's all.'

'Pity.' Carrington Jones drummed his fingers on the desk.

'Now I come to think of it, there was a bloke going backwards and forwards to that room. Actually, I think the guard said he was her Private Secretary.'

'Private Secretary eh? Now that would be interesting if there was some shenanigans going on. See if you can get anything on tape.'

'I haven't got a recorder.'

'Yes you have. It's inside your meter.'

'I didn't realise that there was one in there. Are you sure?'

'Yes, positive,' CJ confirmed. 'It's a standard configuration that we always use.'

'They ran an electronic scanner over my kit to make sure I wasn't leaving any bugs and they didn't find it,' Gurney explained.

No, because they'll expect some electronics in it anyway,' CJ informed him.

'So they won't suspect anything?'

'Don't worry. They won't detect the recorder, I can assure you,' CJ reiterated.

'Well, they didn't find it yesterday,' Gurney agreed. 'But I wished you'd told me.'

'Why? You'd have worried about getting caught, wouldn't you,' CJ suggested. 'It was better for you not to know.'

'I suppose you're right,' Gurney agreed.

'Don't worry. We've got away with using it before, CJ reassured him. 'The opportunity might arise for you to use it. Just be vigilant.'

'Yes OK.'

'You're doing a good job. The department is pleased with you,' CJ exaggerated.

Gurney grinned. He was unused to praise.

# CHAPTER 81

On his way to the mansion the following day, Gurney felt good.

Not only had he received praise from CJ for a job well done, but here he was, on the threshold of his scoop. Exposing a secret organisation, uncovering interdepartmental subterfuge and as a bonus, reporting on a possible scandal involving a Minister. It was pretty earth shattering news, in any ones book.

The only niggle in the back of his mind was the threat of being, literally exposed, with that photo-shopped porn picture, on the internet.

He was in a quandary and didn't know what to do - would he have the courage to write the report?

As he arrived at the mansion, the gates opened without him having to request entry. The security guard was having a cuppa and didn't even bother to 'pat him down' or scan his gear. He didn't even bother to shadow Gurney, obviously satisfied that he was bona fide.

This gave Gurney the opportunity to nose around as he was completing the pipe run.

As he opened a cupboard door near where he was working, he came across a box containing some A4 clip files labelled 'Ministry of Disruption'.

'Magic! This really is my lucky day,' he beamed. 'This must be what CJ was talking about.

Oh my god, what's this by the box? Black leather harnesses and handcuffs! I suppose it must be part of the security team's gear,' Gurney thought to himself.

He closed the cupboard without disturbing anything. 'How the hell am I going to smuggle that stuff out without being caught,' he wondered.

Deep in thought, he continued completing the pipe run and refixing the wainscoting as he went.

'Just one more piece to refix,' he encouraged himself. But the timber was reluctant to fit into its former position with the pipe in place.

'Damn! Why is it always the last bit that plays up? I'm going to have to put extra nails in to hold it flat.'

Finally he nailed it back in place, making sure he didn't mark the paintwork.

'Right, that's that done. Now to fit the liner down the chimney.'

Gurney went back to his van and retrieved the three section extendable aluminium ladder from the roof rack. He shouldered it and carried it to the side of the building where he'd established that the bedroom chimney emerged.

Carefully he extended to ladder to its full height and leant it against the side of the chimney stack.

'God, that's a long way up there,' he thought. 'Come on Gurney, you can do this,' he encouraged himself.

Nervously he climbed the ladder, carrying the stainless steel liner coiled over his shoulder.

As he reached the windows of the room, that he thought was the Minister's gym, he could see that it was not a gym at all, but just a large old fashioned office. All the walls of the room were bedecked with floor to ceiling bookshelves, in the centre of the room a large antique desk with orderly piles of paperwork, sat next to a red ministerial briefcase. A black leather high backed chair was tucked neatly into the knee hole of the desk.

He paused in mid-climb to catch his breath and as he looked into the room he could see the Minister and her Private Secretary were romping around the room in a sex game.

The groans he had assumed were from gymnastic exertions were in fact created by a carnal activity.

The Private Secretary was naked, on all fours and wearing one of the harnesses Gurney had found earlier in the cupboard and the Minister was nude, riding on his back and whipping him.

Gurney nearly fell off the ladder in shock, mesmerised by their antics. Fortunately, they were so engrossed in their game that they failed to see him ogling at them.

'Pity I haven't got a camera with me.' Gurney thought. 'CJ would love to see this action.'

However, focussing on the job in hand, reluctantly he dragged himself away from the peep show and duly installed the liner.

He crept back down the ladder without being spotted, stopping only briefly to ensure he had not been imagining it.

He wasn't disappointed, for the pair were still at it, but had changed roles; the jockey was now the horse and vice versa.

Leaving the ladder in situ, he quickly returned to the bedroom where his tools were. Retrieving his special meter, he recorded the carnal noises coming from the adjoining room.

With his mind in a whirl, he quietly fitted the liner to the gas fire and secured it into the fireplace then went back downstairs.

Fearing discovery if he took another peep into the room, Gurney retrieved his ladder and returned it to his van.

He made his way into the kitchen and turned the gas on.

'Right now to see if all my hard work has been successful,' he thought, jogging happily back upstairs into the bedroom.

He checked for leaks around the fire and satisfied it was OK, he 'fired it up' with no problems.

Next door, the noises had ceased and satisfied with his work, he fetched the housekeeper and showed her the completed installation.

'Is there a smell of gas in here?' she asked.

'Sorry, I don't have a sense of smell. But that will probably be where I flushed the air out of the pipes before I lit it. You have to do that otherwise, you could end up with an explosion,' he informed her.

'Very well. I'll let the Minister know that you've finished. She will probably start using this room now there's some heat in here.'

'Well they were certainly making their own heat next door,' he thought.

'I've put most of my tools in the van already, but I just need to check in the cupboard to see if the joints are OK,' Gurney informed her, hoping to make off with the files that CJ was so desperate for him to retrieve.

'OK. Well, you go ahead. I've got work to do,' the housekeeper said.

Gurney waited until she'd gone and quietly opened the cupboard door. Unfortunately, just as he was reaching for the folders, a flushed faced Private Secretary came out of the adjoining room and came towards the cupboard.

He was carrying the black leather harness that he had been wearing earlier.

'What the devil are you doing in there,' he demanded, quickly hiding the harness behind his back.

'I...I'm just checking for leaks. I've been fitting the gas fire.'

'Well I suggest you jolly well hurry up. I've got a lot to do and I need to get something out of there.'

'Oh, I've finished now, thanks.' Gurney cursed his luck. This would have been the icing on the cake to have a successful installation AND take the reports back to CJ.

But it was not to be. The Private Secretary had thwarted his plans.

He had mixed feelings as he drove back to the garage. He had succeeded with the gas fire and exorcised his DIY demons, but had failed with the most important aspect of his task - getting the files. CJ wasn't going to be happy.

# CHAPTER 82

Gurney parked his van back in the MO Disruption car park and left it with mixed feelings. He'd enjoyed getting 'on the tools' again, and realised how hurtful the DIY ban was on his well-being.

On the other hand, he had failed in getting the vital documents that would save the MO Disruption.

The reality of it was that if the department disappeared, his scoop would go too.

At least he had seen the files and he could tell CJ about the sex game. However, the recording of some grunting noises could be anything done by anyone not attributable to a naked Minister during sexual 'horseplay'.

He entered at CJ's invitation to his knock, in his temporary satellite office.

'Ah, Leafmould. You're back.'

'Yes I've done the job.'

'And tested it?'

'Yes it worked well, thanks.'

'And there were no problems?'

'No.' Gurney read into this question that CJ was expecting him to have made a hash of things so he became quite defensive. 'Should there have been?'

'No, no of course not,' Carrington Jones lied.

'Well, as you reminded me, I'm a different person now,' Gurney said bravely.

'The important thing is, did you get the documents?'

'No. I was just about to retrieve them, but her personal secretary nearly caught me. Sorry,' Gurney grovelled.

'Damn!' CJ banged the desk.

'At least we know they're there,' Gurney suggested trying to find a positive out of the situation.

'That's all very well, but how do we retrieve them now? Carrington Jones asked, not expecting a reply. 'She is threatening to use them shortly.'

'Sorry. I don't know what to say,' Gurney grovelled.

'What about your suspicions about her sexual antics?'

'Oh yes,' Gurney said, delighted to be the bearer of, at least, some good news. 'I saw them in a sex game.'

'A sex game!'

'The Minister was riding naked on the back of her Private Secretary,' he recounted.

'Great,' Carrington Jones rubbed his hands together. 'Any video of it?'

'No, sorry I didn't have a camera,' Gurney confessed.

'What about on your phone?'

'Oh, I didn't think of that. But I do have something you might like to listen to though.'

'You've got something?' CJ smiled.

'Yes. I recorded them doing it.' Gurney pressed a button on his modified meter, but nothing emanated from the device.

Carrington Jones picked it up and studied it carefully. 'There's nothing recorded on here,' he said, disappointed.

'There was something on there. Honest. I played it earlier to make sure,' Gurney said, checking the meter as if CJ had failed to operate it properly.

'Then you've deleted it, you great blithering idiot,' CJ berated.

'Sorry. But they were saying things.'

'Such as?'

'About showing you up, as a leech on the Ministry of Defence budget and exposing the organisation to the worlds' press. Then they were at it again.'

'For heaven's sake, Leafmould.'

'Sorry.'

'Damn. You'll just have to go back and get the documents. That's all.'

'But I've finished the job,' Gurney pleaded.

'Well you'll just have to tell them it's a follow up inspection or something like that,' CJ said sternly.

'I believe they were having a meeting with somebody tonight to discuss budgets,' Gurney volunteered.

'Then it might be too late.' CJ thumped the desk in frustration. 'Oh go and write a report about it. It might be your last,' the manager said, exasperated at Gurney's failure.

'You mean you're going to get rid of me?'

'No. More likely she's going to get rid of all of us. I can't believe you had your hands on the files as well as evidence to bring her down and you even blew that,' CJ castigated.

'Sorry,' Gurney grovelled and left completely deflated. 'At least I did a good job on the gas fire,' he thought.

# CHAPTER 83

Shortly after Gurney had left the office, an animated John Ripple rushed in, holding a small recorder.

'We've just intercepted a call to the gas firm we've infiltrated. Listen to this.' John Ripple pressed the play button on the recorder.

*'I want you to urgently send your man back. There is a strong smell of gas in the room where he installed the gas fire. I already told him about this, but he ignored me.'*

'Perhaps Mr Leafmould has gone back to his disastrous ways after all,' CJ said. 'Right, let's get him back there straight away. He might have the opportunity, this time, of getting his hands on those files before their meeting tonight after all.'

'He will need a hand,' Ripple suggested.

'Yes, send your DO in to give him some assistance. We can't afford to miss this opportunity. In the meantime, get Eunice to arrange for some road closures around the mansion to delay her guests.'

'Did you say she was going to the Select Committee next week?' Ripple asked.

'Yes and if the bitch presents that information, that's the end of us. Quick, get Leafmould.'

Gurney duly arrived, still crestfallen, expecting to be sacked.

'Right Leafmould. You have the chance to redeem yourself.'

'Redeem myself! How?'

'They are complaining of a strong smell of gas in the room where you installed the fire.'

'I told them it was nothing to worry about. It was where I purged the pipes to get rid of the air,' Gurney explained.

'Yeah well, whatever. They want you back there.'

'When?'

'Immediately. And make sure this time you get those files, CJ ordered. 'We are sending somebody to help you. They will meet you outside the gates.'

'What if I can't find them?'

'Use whatever means you can. Bring them back or destroy them. It is vital she can't use them. Do you understand?' CJ shouted angrily, the veins on his neck standing out like vines.

'Yes,' Gurney said meekly.

'And if you can get something to discredit the Minister, so much the better.'

'OK.'

'Don't come back without having it sorted. You are NOT to fail this time,' CJ ranted.

'No, I won't,' Gurney said, frantically wondering how he was going to do it.

On his way to his van, Gurney's mind was in overload. On the plus side, he had a chance to save the department and still get his journalistic scoop. But on the other side, he was peeved that CJ had rubbished his job.

'I did a good job and I'm very proud of that,' he muttered, trying to massage his battered ego.

He duly arrived in front of the mansion's entrance gates to find another similarly liveried van already there. The other vehicle flashed its lights and indicated that it would follow him in.

As Gurney moved forward the gates opened, without challenge.

He drove around to the usual 'tradesman's entrance'. The other van followed. 'I wonder who is going to be helping me? Some bolshie individual I expect.'

As he walked towards the other van, the driver's door opened, and out stepped Chardonnay.

'Chardonnay! What are you doing here?' Gurney gushed, looking very surprised.

'I understand you've got an important job to do,' she said, 'and you might need a hand.'

'Not really, but CJ insists on it…'

'Whatever! The 'A' team is back together,' she enthused, offering him a high five. 'We can do this. So what's the story?'

'I've fitted a new gas fire and ran in a pipe to supply it.'

'I didn't realise you were so talented,' she volunteered.

'Well, the office doesn't think so,' Gurney grumbled. 'I've been sent back to find the cause of a gas smell.'

'Yes, so I gather.'

'There isn't a leak. I told them. It was where I purged the pipe that's all,' Gurney whined.

'Apart from the cover story, I gather we've got to find some documents too?' Chardonnay clarified.

'Yes, that's right. I know where the file is and nearly had my hands on it but somebody came along at the wrong time,' Gurney explained.

'The job's as good as done,' Chardonnay encouraged. 'It's now down to us to save the department.'

'Yes, you're right. We can do this,' Gurney agreed, bolstered by having Chardonnay's enthusiasm to spur him on.

Together they sought out the housekeeper. She was in her favourite chair cup in hand and immediately berated Gurney.

'And about time too! We could have been poisoned with that gas pouring out of that fire.'

'No you couldn't. As I explained previously, the smell came from me clearing the pipes of air. It just lingered, that's all.'

'Has she come because you have no sense of smell?' the housekeeper enquired, looking at Chardonnay suspiciously. 'Who would think of sending a gas fitter with no sense of smell? I ask you?'

'He's a good fitter Mrs,' Chardonnay, interjected.

'So good, that they've even sent somebody else to sort it out,' the housekeeper sneered.

'No Mam, quite the opposite, I've come to learn from Mr Leafmould. I'm the apprentice,' Chardonnay said.' I'm sure he won't mind me telling you that he lost his sense of smell rescuing a family pet from a house fire,' she lied. 'Flames burnt all his nose hairs.'

Gurney looked at Chardonnay, impressed with her 'off the cuff' story.

'Bit old to be an apprentice, I'd have thought,' the housekeeper observed. 'Anyway, we switched the gas off at the mains,' she informed them.

'OK thanks. Don't you worry. We'll soon have it sorted,' Chardonnay advised. 'Won't we Gurney?'

'Yes of course.'

'Just as well, because I have guests coming tonight and I have to prepare a banquet. So get your arse in gear and get it fixed,' the housekeeper retorted.

Gurney led Chardonnay to the bedroom.

'Yeah, there is a faint smell of gas Gurney,' Chardonnay said.

'I still reckon it's where I flushed it out though,' Gurney repeated.

'Just to be on the safe side, let's check the pipe joints anyway,' Chardonnay suggested, tactfully.

'I reckon they're all good. In fact I thought it was one of my better jobs,' he boasted.

Together they did a quick visual check of the exposed pipework near the gas fire.

'Well I'm no expert in gas pipes,' Chardonnay said, 'but it certainly looks OK to me, from what we can see, anyway.'

'Yeah, unfortunately, the majority of the pipes are behind the wainscoting. I'm not going to tear that lot off until we've proved that there really is a problem first,' Gurney said, disconsolately. 'I'll go back to the kitchen and turn the gas back on. See if you think the smell gets worse.'

'OK,' she confirmed.

As he was going down the stairs, he bumped in to Pollen coming up.

'Gurney?'

'Polly?' he said, surprised at seeing her there.

'What are you doing here?' she asked, puzzled.

'I err...am sorting out a...' Gurney paused. Pollen already knew he worked for the Ministry of Disruption. 'You know stuff...what about you?'

'This is my Mother's house. She's the Minister.'

'Oh my God!' The 'penny dropped.' The stories of her Mother's free love in the sixties and the ongoing sex games with her Private Secretary all tied up now.'

Then it dawned on him. He was the mole. He must be the one to blame for jeopardising the MOD. It must have been as a result of his discussions with Polly at the bus stop.

The department's warning, '*walls have ears*,' echoed in his mind.

Obviously Pollen had passed on their secret discussions to her mother, Flower-Hardwoman, in spite of her promise that his secrets were safe with her.

'Why hadn't he linked the name before? Pollen Flower and Flower-Hardwoman, of course.'

Gurney's heart sank. He was the architect of the possible demise of the organisation. Worse still, it could disappear even before he could do his expose`. Whether he had courage to write it or not, his journalistic scoop was disappearing before his very eyes.

It was now more imperative than ever to get hold of the files.

'Well, can't stop. Must get on,' he muttered.

'Yes, umm, see you,' Pollen said, scurrying upstairs. Clearly concerned at his presence in the house.

# CHAPTER 84

As the pair parted, they both suddenly understood the implications of seeing each other there.

Pollen increased her rapid ascent of the stairs, 'Must tell Mother, the Ministry of Disruption are on the premises. Something dire is going to happen,' she thought.

Gurney too realised that unless he stopped Pollen from passing on his presence to her mother, the Ministry of Disruption was, to all intents and purposes, lost. What he would do about it, he wasn't sure.

Quickly he turned and went after Pollen.

'Polly, just a minute,' he called. 'I want to tell you something.'

But Pollen had already reached the top of the stairs and had broken into a trot.

'Polly, please I...Polly,' he called. But as he reached the top of the stairs, Gurney tripped over his feet and went flying.

Pollen was now running along the corridor. 'I must tell Mother,' she thought, increasing her pace.

Checking to see if Gurney was catching her, as she turned a corner in the corridor, she ran into an obstruction, Chardonnay.

'Oh, so sorry miss, but I think Gurney wants to speak to you.'

And before Pollen could dodge out of the way, she was immediately enveloped in a bear hug.

'Let me go,' Pollen wriggled. 'You have no right to stop me in my own house. Let me go.'

At that moment, an out of breath Gurney rounded the corner.

'Oh thank goodness you caught her. She knows who I work for. She's the one who's told the Minister about us at the MO Disruption.'

'I don't know what you're talking about,' Pollen claimed, innocently. 'I'm just on my way into my bedroom to get changed for the banquet. Let me go this instant or I shall...'

The word 'scream', that she was about to say, never left her lips as Chardonnay applied pressure to a 'point' on her neck and she passed out.

'Oh my god, have you killed her?' Gurney said in horror, as Pollen collapsed in Chardonnay's arms.

'No, just rendered her unconscious. Quick give me a hand to get her in the bedroom,' Chardonnay ordered.

'What are we going to do with her then?' Gurney asked panicking.

Together they carried the limp figure into the bedroom.

'You cable tie her hands and feet, while I put this gaffer tape over her mouth,' Chardonnay directed.

'Oh I don't like this. I didn't join the organisation to kidnap people,' Gurney whined.

'It's all part of the training,' Chardonnay said calmly, ripping a large piece of tape off the reel and securing it over Pollen's mouth.

'What training?'

'The unarmed military conflict training, that you will

undertake on future courses. Don't forget, we are effectively a guerrilla force and....'

'Oh I don't like that idea.' Gurney jiggled. 'I think I need to visit the bathroom. I'm a bit of a wimp when it comes to violence,' he confessed.

'You'll soon learn,' Chardonnay added. 'In the end its kill or be killed.'

'Yes but she... '

'She's our enemy,' said Chardonnay completing his sentence.

'We cannot just... Kill her in cold blood,' Gurney said, horrified at the way things were going.

'No, of course we can't,' Chardonnay agreed. 'But we need to smuggle her out into the vans somehow.'

'Oh god! Are we going to kidnap her?'

'Calm down Gurney, You need to keep your head.'

'I can't,' he said, violently shivering.

'Give me those cable ties and I'll do it.'

Chardonnay trussed Pollen up just as she regained consciousness. As she realised the situation she was in, she started banging her feet on the floor.

*'Bang, Bang, Bang'*

Quickly Chardonnay rendered her unconscious again.

'Now listen Gurney. You're going to have to pull yourself together. Go downstairs and find a large laundry basket, so we can get her out of here. Got it?'

'Laundry basket? Yes.' Gurney repeated, although not really aware of what he was saying.

But the slap across his face quickly pitched him out of his fear based trance.

'What did you do that for?' he yelped, holding his smarting cheek.

'Pull yourself together,' Chardonnay said firmly. 'Now go and be quick about it. I can only use this technique once more to 'sedate' her before I have to use a more permanent method.'

'You mean?'

'Yes. Now move.'

# CHAPTER 85

Gurney dashed out of the room as Chardonnay dragged her prisoner over towards the door to prevent any unexpected visitors.

'Damn, how the hell am I going to stop anyone barging in?' she said, discovering there was no lock on the door. 'Well there's nothing else to do but sit here,' she said, lowering her large body against it.

Gurney almost flew down the stairs, desperately hunting for a laundry basket or something on wheels that they could use to transport Pollen out of the building.

Eventually, he came across a hotel type luggage trolley and decided that it would be suitable.

His next challenge was how to get that upstairs and Pollen downstairs.

In fear of discovery, he searched for a lift and stumbled on to a small, old fashioned gated one, which had been fitted as a 20th century addition and was used for transporting guests suitcases to the bedrooms.

As he steered the trolley into the lift, one of the security men, now dressed in a DJ, came round the corner. Gurney's heart stopped.

'What are you doing with that?' the man demanded.

'I... I... Tools. Need to bring my tools down,' Gurney muttered.

'Well make sure you're not too long with it. The guests will be arriving soon and we'll need it for their luggage.'

'Yes OK,' Gurney agreed, self-consciously.

'By the way, you can't ride with it. It's not powerful enough. You need to press the button and walk up the stairs yourself. It's very slow, but it takes the hassle out of moving luggage around,' the guard informed him.

Gurney did as directed and raced up the servants' staircase and waited impatiently as the lift slowly ground its way to the first floor.

'Come on…come on,' he edgily urged the motor.

Finally it arrived with a 'clunk' and he yanked open the metal gate and retrieving the trolley, quickly made his way back to the bedroom.

As he was about to enter, he met the housekeeper coming along the corridor.

'What are you doing with that?' she demanded

'I… Tools. Carrying tools.' Gurney muttered

'Haven't you fixed it yet?'

'No, just testing it.'

'Well, as I told you, I have a meal to prepare.'

'Yes, just checking it now.'

'Well hurry up for heaven sake. This is the last time that I'll be using your firm. It's lucky for you that the guests have been delayed. The road has been closed off. Apparently they've found an unexploded bomb nearby.'

'Yes, sorry,' Gurney grovelled.

The housekeeper went on her way, as Gurney tried to open the door. It wouldn't budge.

'Chardonnay, it's me, Gurney,' he whispered, knocking quietly on the door.

She opened the door quickly.

'Oh this is hopeless. We'll never get her out without

being caught,' Gurney whined, pushing the trolley into the bedroom. Anxiously he looked at Pollen's still figure.

'You haven't, have you?' he asked, fearing the worst.

'No, don't worry. She's still alive,' Chardonnay confirmed.

'The housekeeper is hassling me to get the gas turned on for her banquet preparations.'

'Okay, I'll take this one out to the van, if you sort out the gas then.'

'You won't kill her though will you?' Gurney asked, concerned.

'No, don't worry about her. We need to get those documents and get the hell out of here before they rumble us,' Chardonnay urged.

Gurney explained about the luggage lift and helped place Pollen on the trolley.

'What can we cover her with?' Gurney asked.

'This will do,' Chardonnay said, taking a duvet cover off the bed and laying some tools on top.

Meanwhile, Gurney raced to the cupboard and was relieved to see that the files were still where he'd last seen them. He grabbed hold of the box and checking that he wasn't spotted, ran after Chardonnay with the trolley bearing Pollen.

'Quick, put these under the sheet,' Gurney said giving Chardonnay the box of files.

'Well done Gurney, good job,' she said hiding the box next to the unconscious Pollen.

Gurney's adrenaline was flowing now as he told Chardonnay of his plans. 'I'll go and create a diversion downstairs with the housekeeper, switch the gas on and sort that out the gas fire.'

'OK. Just keep calm Gurney. Be confident,' Chardonnay encouraged.

# CHAPTER 86

Gurney arrived in the kitchen hot and flustered and was immediately interrogated by the housekeeper.

'Well, have you found anything yet?' she demanded.

'Ah.... No, it all looks OK. Tell me again when did you think it smelt the worst?' he asked, playing for time.

'I don't know. Immediately after you left, I suppose,' the housekeeper blustered.

'Only the pipe joints appear to be OK,' Gurney confirmed.

'So what are you going to do?' she demanded.

'I'm going to switch the gas on and check for any leaks with my meter.'

'Well, don't hang around. Get on with it,' she ordered.

'Yes, OK, that was what I was going to do but just wanted to check with you first,' Gurney assured her, mindful of Chardonnay's slow descent in the lift with Pollen.

'Have you brought my trolley back down yet?' the woman demanded.

'No, my colleague is just taking...umm our tools to the van now. It'll be back shortly,' Gurney said, nervously.

'I should hope so too! Taking the trolley without asking. Whatever next?' The housekeeper flounced and went back to her culinary preparations, tutting.

'There was no one I could ask, but the security chappie knew I had it,' he pleaded.

'Well stop wasting time and get on with it. I've got food to cook.'

'Yes OK.'

Unable to think of anymore delaying tactics, Gurney finally switched the gas on again and ran back upstairs.

As he entered the bedroom, he could hear a faint hissing noise coming from near the gas fire.

'What the hells that?' he wondered, kneeling to listen. 'I wonder if I've put a nail in the pipe?'

He retrieved a screwdriver from his pocket, jammed it between wall and wood and started prising the skirting board off. It refused all his efforts. He stood up and pulled harder, but annoyingly a chunk of wood snapped off the top of the moulding.

'Damn, I'll have to patch that up, before the 'Fuhrer' sees it,' he thought.

As the last nail reluctantly let go, he moved the wainscoting away to reveal the gas pipe behind. Then he could see a small hole in the pipe, the slight hiss, became a noisy 'fush'.

'Oh dear, that's the cause of it then. Bugger! I wondered why it was reluctant to go in when I was fixing it,' he said to himself.

Quickly he put his thumb over the hole to stop the leak. He was now in a dilemma. He needed to switch the mains off, but if he took his thumb off the hole, the room would quickly fill with gas. As it was, he was already feeling light headed.

'Chardonnay, where are you when I need you?' he thought, hoping she'd appear.

He wracked his brains to think what he could do to get out of the impasse.

'I suppose I could call for help.' But in the other room he could hear the Private Secretary and Minister were 'at it' again. 'No, perhaps not. They probably wouldn't want to break off their gymnastics, let alone hear me anyway.'

'I've got nothing to plug it with, either. Chardonnay's taken all my tools down to the van.' he thought. 'Well there's nothing for it. I'm going to have to run downstairs and switch it off.'

He was just about to sprint downstairs when he suddenly had a thought.

'Wait a minute. Perhaps I have. I've got some chewing gum in my pocket. I could stick that over it, temporarily.'

Quickly he unwrapped the gum and started chewing frantically to get it soft enough. But the rushing around and apprehension of the situation had dried his mouth and he was having problems trying to get the gum to become malleable.

'Come on,' he urged. 'Bloody hell, this is making my jaw ache.'

After a few more chews, his patience had run out and he stuck the gum over the hole anyway. Unfortunately the pressure from the gas kept blowing it off, but after the fourth attempt he was able to mould it into place and it held.

Gurney rushed headlong from the room and made a 'pit stop' on his way to the kitchen.

The delay was ill timed, for as he got to the top of the stairs, the chewing gum 'blew off' from the damaged pipe.

As he arrived in the kitchen Chardonnay was just

pushing the luggage trolley back, having put a now drugged Pollen into the back of her van.

'Whats the matter Gurney?' she asked, seeing his rushed entrance into the kitchen.

'Hole in the pipe... It's leaking...chewing gum..... What should I do?' he panicked.

'Go and get some tape from my van,' she said, calmly. 'Be careful of the new occupier. And I'll switch the gas off.'

Gurney dashed outside, ran to the van and yanked the door open.

'Tape...tape...now where's the tape,' he said. 'Ah there it is.'

As he reached for the tape, and at the same instant Chardonnay had put her hand on the tap to turn the gas off, a spark from a video recorder, switching on in the bedroom, ignited the room full of gas.

Instantly there was a large explosion which blew the roof off. A fireball rose a hundred feet into the night sky. The force of the blast blew the windows out into the flower garden as the side of the building began to collapse.

# CHAPTER 87

Outside, Gurney was hit by the pressure wave from the blast, which flattened him against Chardonnay's van.

A large piece of flaming debris fell on to his own van and set it on fire.

'Shit! That was close,' he said, startled by the noise of the impact.

'Oh my God! Chardonnay. What should I do? What should I do?' he asked himself. 'What would she do if it was me? She'd come and get me...that's what she'd do,' he concluded.

From somewhere deep inside him Gurney summoned up some courage and without a thought for his own safety, rushed in to the collapsing building, meeting the dust covered housekeeper in the arms of a security man, on their way out.

'Have you seen my mate?' Gurney shouted, his ears ringing from the explosion.

'She was in the kitchen by the main gas pipe,' the shocked housekeeper shouted angrily. 'My banquet! How am I going to prepare my banquet now?' she wailed.

Gurney made his way in to the debris strewn kitchen, peering through the dust and the smoke, as more wreckage rained down around him.

'CHARDONNAY. CHARDONNAY. Can you hear me? CHARDONNAY.'

He strained to hear for a response, but the only noise that came back was the catastrophic sound of a building in its death throws.

'CHARDONNAY, it's me, Gurney. Come on. Answer me.'

Slowly he made his way towards the collapsed outside wall and saw a hand wrapped around the lever of the gas supply. Subconsciously he 'clocked' that the lever was in the off position.

From his vantage point, he couldn't see if the hand was connected to an arm.

With his heart in his mouth, he fought his way over the debris field and headed towards the hand.

As he drew closer, he could see that it was still connected to an arm. But he couldn't see if the arm had a body attached to it.

With herculean strength, he fought his way towards the arm, frantically clearing floor joists from the collapsed room above. Then he found her. To his great relief, arm and body were intact

'Thank God for that. I just hope she's still alive?' he thought. 'Hopefully she's just been knocked out.'

Somehow he remembered the first aid training that he'd received years previously and targeted her neck to find a pulse. 'Yes, she's still with us,' he confirmed with relief. 'Chardonnay, we're going to have to get you out of here. It might hurt, but it'll hurt a damn sight more if this lot comes down on top of you.'

Quickly he lifted the last piece of debris off her.

'Now how am I going to get you out,' he pondered...'I know - the luggage trolley.'

He retrieved the debris strewn trolley and somehow found the strength to drag her dead weight onto the small platform. Quickly he threaded them back through the maze of debris and headed for a gap in the wall.

As he emerged from the damaged building, two security guys ran to meet them, and took the trolley off him.

'Bleeding hell mate, you deserve a medal for that,' one said, checking Chardonnay's vital signs. 'Well, she's breathing. No obvious signs of any broken bones, although she's got a nasty cut to the top of her head.'

Gurney knelt by Chardonnay and held her hand, a tear running down his dusty cheek, leaving a sorrowful tramline. 'I'll get help,' he whispered. 'You'll be OK.'

# CHAPTER 88

Happy that Chardonnay was in capable hands, Gurney rushed back to her van and made an urgent radio call.

'Control Are you there?'

The response was immediate, '*Go ahead the station calling. Please use your callsign. Over.*'

'This is ... um...DO 6.' Gurney said, spotting a label on the radio, 'We are in need of urgent assistance. There's been a big explosion and fire. We have a...an Operative down and a prisoner to take away.'

'*Roger. All noted. Rescue heli is on its way to your tracked location. Over.*'

'Thank you Control...over.'

'*DO 6, for your information, at the moment there is a roadblock to the mansion so no emergency vehicles will be able to reach there until you are lifted. Over*'

'Oh yes control, I nearly forgot. I want to go with the injured person.. umm Is that alright?'

'*DO 6, Yes I'm told in that case one of the crew will recover your van.*'

'Thanks.'

'*DO6, what about the other driver's van? Over.*'

'Control, no need to worry about that. It was hit by burning debris and it's been totally destroyed.'

'*DO6, understood. Control, over and out.*'

Gurney rushed back to Chardonnay's side.

'Don't worry mate. We've called for an ambulance. It should be here soon. Your mate will be OK,' one of the security guards informed him.

'Little does he know,' Gurney thought, as he knelt by the unconscious Chardonnay, 'that ain't going to happen.'

Within twenty minutes the large MO Disruption helicopter was landing at the mansion's helipad.

Having been put in a neck brace by the helicopter medics, Chardonnay was quickly stretchered to its cavernous hold.

Satisfied that she was being cared for by the professionals, Gurney left her side and collected her van. He drove it close to the helicopter and with some help from the crew, guided a whoozy Pollen into it.

'Oh, mustn't forget these,' Gurney said, picking up the cardboard box containing all files about the Ministry.

'Excuse me,' one of the Minister's body guards asked, spotting Pollen being put on board. 'What are you doing with Miss Flower?' he asked suspiciously.

Gurney's heart rate increased at the enquiry. 'We're... um. She was caught in the blast and banged her head, so I put her in the van while I rescued my mate, Gurney lied. 'We'll take her to the hospital too.'

'OK. Just as well the helicopter was around, because the ambulances and fire engines can't get through,' the security guard explained. 'I've just heard that the roads are still closed because of a report of an unexploded bomb.'

'I'm going to the hospital with my mate now,' Gurney explained. 'We'll look after Pollen, I assure you.'

'Yeah, OK. We know the name of your firm, so that when the Police want to interview you, they can get hold of you through them, is that right?'

'Yes that's right.' Gurney smiled at the deception.

The helicopter lifted off from the collapsed building in a cloud of dust. Gurney looked through a window at the burning mansion beneath them as they banked away.

'Pity about that, nobody will see what a good job I did with that gas fire installation,' he thought. The fact that his shoddy workmanship had been the cause of the demise of the lovely building escaped him.

'But at least we've saved the Ministry of Disruption,' Gurney comforted himself.

# CHAPTER 89

The helicopter flew straight to the 'Yorkshire Pudding' building at Elmley and within fifteen minutes had disgorged its passengers.

They had called ahead to get the medical team and the Security Manager on standby to meet them.

Gurney became the focus of attention and found himself directing operations.

His first priority was Chardonnay, he made sure that she was taken to the 'high tech, state of the art' medical facility, where a medical team were waiting to receive her.

An MRI scan later showed no brain damage but she was put in a high dependency ward and closely monitored.

'What are we going to do with your prisoner?' George Beach, the security manager asked, looking at the gagged and 'shackled' semi-conscious Pollen.

'She's the spy. She was the cause of the security leak.' Gurney explained. 'Her mother is the Minister of Defence.'

'But where did she get the information from to pass it on?' Beach asked.

'Don't know,' Gurney lied.

'Right, I'll get on to my boss, John Ripple. Miss Flower will need a bit of memory manipulation to help her forget about us. In the meantime I'll take her to the 'treatment rooms' ready for his interrogation,' he added.

Having sorted out two of his priorities Gurney made his way to an office and telephoned CJ. The phone was answered immediately.

'Carrington Jones,' he announced.

'CJ, its Gurney.'

'Leafmould, good to hear from you. I've been watching events unfold on the plotting table. Looks like it was very dramatic?'

'Yes, I'm afraid there was an explosion and the mansion has been destroyed.'

'So I gather. Are you OK, are you back yet?'

'Yes. We landed back at Elmley a few minutes ago.'

'How is everybody?'

'Chardonnay is being treated for a nasty head wound. I hope she'll be alright,' Gurney said, sincerely.

'If she's in the medical centre, she's in the hands of some very good people,' CJ assured him.

'The minister's daughter was the cause of the security breach, she is back here too, ready for John Ripple to interrogate.'

'I shall be interested to hear who her source of information was so that we can deal with the cause,' Carrington Jones said, coldly.

Gurney felt faint. They would soon know that it was him that told Pollen and it was likely that he would 'disappear' off the payroll.

'And what about the documents she'd got on us?' CJ asked.

'Yes, as directed, I retrieved them before the explosion. Gurney announced, hoping to win some good will to offset his major faux pas. 'And we have a bonus as well.'

'Bonus?' CJ puzzled.

'Yes,' Gurney beamed. 'Inside the cardboard box containing the files, was a wad of pornographic photos of the Minister and Private Secretary in various kinky poses.'

'Really. I shall be pleased to see them. Get somebody to scan them and email them to me please.'

'OK,' Gurney agreed.

'They will carry considerable weight when we drip feed these to the Prime Minister.' CJ continued. 'I don't think she will be in post for much longer when those hit his desk.. Good find, well done.'

'Thanks.'

'By the way what's the story behind the explosion?' CJ probed.

'It appears that there must have been a gas leak after all,' Gurney informed him, being slightly economical with the truth. 'And something must have ignited the build-up of gas.'

'I gather that the blaze raced through the mansion and it went up within twenty minutes,' CJ said looking at a report on his desk. 'Was everybody evacuated in time?' CJ asked.

'Yes, fortunately.'

'D will be very pleased. I'll update her straight away. Well done. Go and have a well-deserved rest. We're very pleased with your efforts and the devastating lengths you went to safeguard the Ministry of Disruption.'

Gurney glowed with pride. Perhaps he'd done alright, after all.

# CHAPTER 90

'D, who's calling?' the woman answered.

'D, it's CJ. I have an update for you.'

'Good news?' she asked, cautiously.

'Yes, very good news. The evidence that the Minister was going to present to the select committee was successfully recovered and will be destroyed.' CJ said joyfully. 'Unfortunately there was an explosion and fire at her mansion.'

'An explosion!' D said, perturbed. 'Have we taken to blowing people up?'

'No. It was an accidental gas explosion,' CJ explained. 'Our fitter appears to have caused a gas leak with the inevitable consequences.'

'Was the Minister in residence?' the senior officer asked.

'Yes. She was found unharmed under a pile of debris,' CJ reported. 'Although she was naked and apparently all she could say was, 'Hee, harr! that was one hell of a ride!'

'Knowing that woman, it doesn't surprise me,' D concurred.

'And her Private Secretary was found nearby, bruised and battered and wearing nothing but a leather harness,' CJ continued.

'Oh, up to her old tricks again was she?' D said

knowingly. 'That woman has been walking the thin line of a sexual deviant for years. God knows how she has got away with it in public office.'

'We have also obtained some pornographic photographs of the Private Secretary and Minister in some Sado Masochistic poses too.'

'Excellent. Have they started manipulating the facts yet?'

'Yes. The Minister's press attaché has denied any scandal and reported that all the Minister's clothes were blown off, due to the force of the explosion.'

'Typical political spin.'

'I believe those porno photos will sound the death knell for her political aspirations anyway,' Carrington Jones concluded.

'Well done CJ. I'm not sure whether your means were quite what I'd anticipated, but nevertheless, it had the right outcome. What about her threats to expose us?'

'The source of the leak turned out to be the Minister's daughter. We've yet to find out who it was that she was talking to, but John Ripple's on the case. We hope to find out later.

'I gather we used a real company as a cover. Can we be traced through the gas firm?'

'No, I think we're in the clear. The one van we used was completely destroyed and the other was the first to go through the newly opened barricaded road, thanks to Eunice's team.'

'And the firm itself?'

'The business that should have been installing the gas fire will be questioned by the police, naturally. Obviously they will deny all knowledge of doing the

THE MINISTRY OF DISRUPTION

job. I'd expect the police will check if any of their staff had been 'moonlighting' too.'

'Right. Did we have any casualties?'

'Yes DO6 is being treated for a head injury, rescued by Leafmould who put his life on the line to get her out.'

'Good man. New isn't he?'

'Yes. We did have some concerns about him at first, but he came through in the end. Leafmould called in the helicopter to evacuate them all and they were quickly taken back to Elmley Headquarters.'

'Perhaps he's another to add to the 'Hall of Fame' for saving the department.'

'I'll see to it.' CJ agreed.

'Anyway. Well done. All's well that ends well.'

# CHAPTER 91

Shortly after Gurney had finished talking to CJ, John Ripple arrived to question Pollen.

'Gurney, as she was your 'prisoner', how would you like to help interrogate the Minister's daughter?' Ripple asked.

'Well I…I'm not into violence.'

'Oh, don't worry we don't use the 'hot poker' anymore. Just ask a few questions and as you know her so well, she's likely to confide in you as a friendly face.'

'Well, I'm not sure,' Gurney edged.

'We need to find out who leaked the information to the Minister to ensure it won't happen again,' Ripple explained.

'I'm sure it won't,' Gurney suggested, almost too enthusiastically.

'How can you be so sure?' Ripple quizzed, suspiciously.

'Well…you know…she probably accidentally dug up the information from somewhere,' Gurney suggested, now starting to panic. 'If we just do the memory manipulation…won't that be enough to safeguard our secrets?'

'Yes, yes of course. But we need to find out the actual source of her information first before we make her forget,' the security man explained.

'Yes, I suppose you're right.' Gurney was now sweating profusely, his heart rate dangerously high. Was he just about to be found out? How would they make him disappear?'

'So you'll conduct the interview with me then?' the security man confirmed.

'Yes...OK.'

Together they made their way through the seemingly endless corridors of the complex to a suite labelled *Interview Room - no unauthorised access.*

John Ripple entered a code in the door access keypad and they both entered the small room. A uniformed attendant stood as they entered.

Gurney took in his surroundings. It was a private hospital room complete with a bed. Over the head of the bed the wall was bedecked with various medical paraphernalia. Next to the bed was a small table and positioned around the pink painted room were several easy chairs.

Pollen was sitting in a lounge chair, her eyes closed.

'Hello, John. Have you come to speak to Pollen?' the nurse asked, extending his hand.

'Yes. Has she been OK?'

'She's still a bit lethargic from the 'infield' injection, but we can fix that very quickly when you're ready,' the nurse explained.

'Great. This is Gurney He's come to help me,' John Ripple said, introducing Gurney.

'Pleased to meet you,' the nurse said extending his hand. 'You're the one who rescued Chardonnay from the collapsing building aren't you?'

'Yes,' Gurney admitted, blushing.

'Well I gather she's doing OK,' the nurse informed him.

'Oh good. Is it OK if I see her later?'

'Yes, I'm sure, John Ripple agreed. 'Now let's get down to business. Have you got the truth drug ready,' he asked the nurse.

'Yes, it will bring her out of her current stupor too.'

The trio positioned their chairs around Pollen and the nurse administered the drug into her arm. Pollen stirred as the needle punctured her skin.

However, within a minute, Pollen appeared fully conscious, stood up and became aggressive, shouting and ranting about Chardonnay kidnapping her.

'Oh dear, that's not supposed to happen,' the nurse said, concerned at the reaction to the injection. I'll give her another one. That should calm her down.'

'Grab hold of her Gurney,' Ripple ordered.

Gurney grabbed hold of the struggling Pollen. 'OK John I've got her,' Gurney confirmed.

The nurse picked up another syringe containing the truth drug and was about to inject it when Pollen twisted and the force of the nurse's impetus put the needle into Gurney's arm instead.

Gurney immediately let go of Pollen and looked in horror at the syringe still in his arm.

'Don't worry,' the nurse said, pulling the syringe out and grabbing another. 'It won't hurt you. You might feel a bit strange. But it will pass.'

John Ripple grabbed Pollen and the nurse injected her with another dose.

Quickly she calmed down and Ripple was able to put her back into her chair.

'What about me?' Gurney said, drunkenly.

'You'll be fine,' the nurse repeated.

'We'll record the interview for analysis later,' he said

switching on the voice recorder. 'Is your name Pollen Flower?'

'Yes,' she said.

'No,' said Gurney.

'Quiet Gurney, please,' John Ripple directed.

'You're going to get double replies unfortunately. The truth drug appears to be working on Gurney as well,' the nurse informed him.

Ripple addressed Pollen. 'Is your mother the Minister of Defence?'

'Yes,' she said.

'No,' said Gurney.

'Did you receive information about the Ministry of Disruption?'

'Yes,' both Gurney and Pollen chorused.

'How did you get the information?'

'Gurney told me,' Pollen divulged to the surprised security man.

'Is this true Gurney?'

'Yes I did, but she said she wouldn't tell,' Gurney blurted.

'I know. But I crossed my fingers so it doesn't count, Pollen confessed.

'I did the same when I signed the official secrets act too.' Gurney added.

'Why did you do that Gurney?' Ripple asked.

'Because I am an investigative journalist and I want to write a scoop about this secret organisation for my newspaper,' Gurney announced to an astonished Ripple. 'The injection has made me feel all funny,' he giggled.

'Right you two, stay here,' Ripple ordered. 'I need to make an urgent phone call.'

'That's good because I like Gurney,' Pollen volunteered, unexpectedly grabbing his arm.

John Ripple left the room and called CJ from a nearby office.

'CJ, we've got a problem. Gurney is an active journalist sniffing around for a scoop, as we expected.'

'How do you know?' the other asked.

'He accidentally got a shot of the truth drug we were using on the Minister's daughter,' Ripple revealed.

'Oh dear! And he has done some good work for us too. Never mind. You know what to do,' CJ proposed.

'Disappear him?'

'No, let's give him another chance. Use the drugs on him first.' Carrington Jones ordered.

'Trouble is, his memory is quite well embedded. With all the training he's had, he's stored a lot of data in his deep cortex.'

'Well, you'll just have to up the dosage and hope it doesn't cause any side effects. CJ suggested. 'He was OK the last time we used it on him, wasn't he?'

'You mean during the dead letterbox fiasco?'

'Yes then. I'd prefer to cope with the fallout of a bad drug reaction to the bureaucracy of making him disappear.'

'Ok. Actually I've got to quite like the guy too. Take it as done.'

Ripple returned and quietly discussed CJ's decision with the nurse.

'I'll prepare the dosages,' he said.

'Right you two. We are going to give you an antidote to make you feel normal again. You'll feel relaxed and wake up forgetting all about this session and the Ministry of Disruption,' Ripple explained.

The pair beamed back at him and giggled as the nurse fitted them both with a skull cap bristling with sensors and a nest of coloured wires.

'What's the funny hat for?' Gurney giggled.

'It's for an electroencephalograph or EEG,' he informed them. 'To look at your brain activity.'

'My Mother-In-Law says I haven't got much of that,' Gurney laughed.

'Great. Can we watch too,' Pollen sniggered.

'Yes of course. After all they are your brains.' He then injected them with the specialist memory altering drug. But the drug had the effect of sending them off to sleep anyway.

However, within a few moments, Gurney had a bad reaction to the injection and started violently fitting.

'What's happening?' Ripple demanded, looking at the convulsing Gurney.

'Unfortunately it looks like the combination of the previous mind drug and the new higher dosage have affected Gurney. I'll get some help.'

# CHAPTER 92

The 'crash' team were at Gurney's side within a few minutes of the alarm being sounded. Ripple stood back and watched as the MOD's consultant neurologist took charge.

Fortunately for Gurney, the consultant was one of the team who had developed the drug and was able to quickly identify a course of treatment that would stop the convulsions, having done so he put Gurney into an induced coma.

Satisfied that after a few days Gurney was strong enough to come out of his coma, the consultant slowly woke him, monitoring him closely as he regained full consciousness.

'Welcome back Gurney,' the consultant smiled.

'Gurney?'

'Yes. That's your name. Don't you remember?'

'No. Where am I? Gurney said looking around.

'You're in a special hospital,' the consultant explained quietly, noting Gurney's responses.

'What am I doing here?'

'You had a bit of an accident,' he lied.

'Is that what's causing the ringing' in my ears?'

'Yes, and you have a few minor burns too. But don't worry, we'll soon have you up and running again,' the neurologist explained.

'Was I a runner then?' Gurney asked naively.

'No, it's just a figure of speech,' the medic informed him, smiling.

Although initially concerned about the bad effect of the drugs on Gurney, CJ was pleased to hear that his overall health had not been jeopardised.

However the drug had been quite brutal with Gurney's memory and the consultant's diagnosis was that it was likely to be a lengthy time before the recovery of any of his background memory.

This meant that his knowledge of the brief time he'd been with the Ministry would likely be lost forever.

Chardonnay, too, had recovered enough to visit a very confused Gurney,

'Are you my wife?' he asked, studying her. 'Your face is familiar.'

'No Gurney, your wife is called Iris. She visited you when you were in a coma. And I expect she'll be back when she is told that you are now awake.'

'What's your name then?' Gurney asked.

'Chardonnay.'

'Chardonnay,' Gurney repeated. 'That's a nice name.'

'I'd just like to thank you for saving my life,' she said quietly, stroking his hand.

'I did?' Gurney questioned, confused. 'How? where? I don't remember.'

'I don't want to talk about it,' Chardonnay said, recalling the warning she'd received from the psychiatrists, not to remind him of the incident, as it might undo the memory blanking treatment. 'How have they been treating you in here,' she asked changing the subject.

'Yes, very well. They are all so cheerful too,' Gurney replied.

'I had the same wonderful treatment too,' she agreed.

'Have you been ill too?' Gurney asked, concerned.

'Yes but not as poorly as I could have been if you hadn't bravely got me out of that building. So thank you again,' she said, kissing his hand tenderly.

Chardonnay stayed with Gurney for thirty minutes until he dozed off again.

'Goodbye Gurney,' she whispered and gave him a kiss on the forehead. 'Nice knowing you.' She left without a backward glance, hiding the tears streaming down her face.

# CHAPTER 93

Gurney remained in the MO Disruption hospital until he had fully recovered and was free from any more convulsions.

As Iris drove them home, she persisted in her interrogation.

'What were you doing to have an accident? ' she probed.

'I told you, I don't know,' he repeated, frustrated at his inability to remember.'

'You weren't up to your old DIY tricks again were you? The explosion at the old mansion bears all your hallmarks.'

'Hallmarks! What hallmarks?'

'DIY... Doing DIY badly. Like when you demolished our house.'

'Did I? I don't remember. I keep telling you.' Gurney said starting to get irritated by her constant questioning.

'Or is it that you say you can't remember, just a convenient way of denying it?' Iris suggested suspiciously.

'No,' he insisted firmly.

'Who is this Chardonnay that sent you the big get well card then?'

'I don't know,' he lied, recalling her goodbye kiss when she'd thought he was asleep.

'No, you wouldn't would you? Iris said, clearly not believing him. 'Oh by the way, the newspaper has sacked you,' Iris added coldly.

'Sacked me! Did I work for a newspaper then?' Gurney queried.

'Yes. Don't you remember? Mother got you a job at the Urbanite.'

'No, I keep telling you. I hardly remember anything.' Gurney said, frustrated at her continual banter.

'Well apparently you were supposed to be working on a secret report.'

'I was?'

'Yes you were. The editor rang and said you wouldn't be able to do your job because of your medical condition.'

'He's probably right,' Gurney agreed.

'So he sacked you. By the way, why have you been leaving notes in the first aid box?'

'First aid box? I don't know what you're talking about,' he said, puzzled.

'Well you needn't worry about it. I took care of them,' his wife explained.

'Why what did you do with them?'

'They shouldn't have been in there in the first place. It's unhygienic. So I threw them away.'

'Oh! It's obviously too late now anyway,' Gurney accepted, but wondered why he'd left written notes there.

'Will you look at this traffic jam,' Iris said, slowing down and joining a queue of cars. 'Damn it. Now I suppose in a minute, you'll be wanting to stop for a wee?'

'No, why would I?' Gurney puzzled.

'Because of your condition,' Iris volunteered.

'Don't know what you're talking about. Condition?' he wondered.

'The need to have lots of toilet stops,' she elaborated.

'Not me. You must have got me mixed up with somebody else,' Gurney insisted.

'Well that's interesting,' Iris replied looking strangely at him. 'I wonder what's the cause of the jam?'

'Over there. There's a dog running loose,' Gurney pointed out.

'Where?'

'Over there. Look. It's a black dog...a black dog! Now why does that seem to ring a bell?' Gurney wondered. 'Where have I heard that before?'

Somewhere deep in Gurney's psyche something stirred. His mind was suddenly filled with a kaleidoscope of images; mermaids, birds, cones, cows, gas fires, explosions.... The blood drained from his face, he became light headed.

'Gurney, are you alright? Gurney!' Iris said concerned.

Meanwhile in the Ministry of Disruption offices, as the country ground to a halt in its normal, highly controlled chaotic way; CJ and John Ripple were congratulating themselves on a job well done.

'I think we did the right thing in not 'disappearing' Gurney Leafmould and I'm sure that's the last time we'll hear about him,' CJ suggested, confidently.

## THE END

# Glossary

Like any large organisation, especially the civil service, the Ministry of Disruption use code words in its everyday business jargon; here is a listing of most:-

| Code | Meaning | Used for |
|------|---------|----------|
| ANPR | Automatic Number Plate Recognition | Used by the Police etc to automatically read vehicle number plates to check for road tax, insurance, stolen etc |
| BCW | Business Code Words | Department that controls MOD business jargon |
| BTS | Barrier to Success | Things that prevent achieving a goal |
| CCTV | Closed Circuit Television | Camera network used to monitor various activities |
| CJ | Carrington Jones | Senior Operational Manager |
| CPS | Crown Prosecution Service | Prosecutes criminal cases investigated by the police. |
| CV | Curriculum Vitae | A persons sales brochure for selling themselves |
| D | Head of Disruption (Organisation) | Similar to 007's M |

| Code | Meaning | Used for |
|---|---|---|
| D2A | Disruption Engineer grade 2A | Rank of Disruption Engineer (Middle grade) |
| D2B | Disruption Engineer grade 2B | Rank of Disruption Engineer (Lowest grade - labourer) |
| DI | Disruptive Index | Target Measurement for Disruption |
| DIY | Do It Yourself | A method of self-construction |
| DJ | Dinner Jacket | Formal suit of clothes for special occasions |
| DLB | Dead Letter Box | Used for leaving and collecting secret messages |
| DO | Disruption Operative | Rank of Disruption Operative (Highest grade) |
| DO in T | Disruption Operative in Training | Rank of Disruption engineer being trained to become a Disruption Operative |
| DO6 | Disruption Operative 6 | Unique Disruption Operative's identity. Also used as a radio callsign |
| DO88 | Disruption Operative 88 | Unique Disruption Operative's identity. Also used as a radio callsign |
| DP | Disruptive Practice(s) | Activities that cause disruption |
| FI | Frustration Index | Used to gauge levels of frustration in any given disruptive activity. (Higher the better) |

| Code | Meaning | Used for |
|---|---|---|
| FLA | Four or Five Letter Acronym | Used by Business Code Words division to explain the limitations of their job |
| FLC | Four or Five Letter Code | Used by Business Code Words division to explain the limitations of their job |
| HAT | Held Awaiting Talks | An example to show the contradiction of ordinary words with three letter codes |
| HR | Human Resources | Used to be called Personnel Groups, deals the administration of personnel |
| ID | Identity | The badge worn for security purposes |
| LDO | Leading Disruption Operative | Foreman of Disruption Engineers |
| M-I-L | Mother-In-Law | Gurney's Mother-In-Law, Delores Eyes. |
| MIS | Management Information System | Used for measuring the effect of Disruption |
| MO Disruption | Ministry of Disruption | Short form for the MOD |
| MoD | Ministry of Defence | Correct abbreviation - note lowercase 'o' |
| MOD | Ministry of Disruption | Confusing abbreviation - which has allowed the Ministry of Disruption to leach funds from the Ministry of Defence budget. |

| Code | Meaning | Used for |
|---|---|---|
| MUM | Minimum Use Methodology | An example to show the contradiction of ordinary words with three letter codes |
| PA | Personal Assistant | Secretary |
| PBA | Personal Bank Account | An example to show the contradiction of ordinary words with three letter codes |
| pigpen | 'temporary' office constructed of free standing partitions | Used in modern open plan offices to create a whole team atmosphere. Replaces bosses separate offices. |
| PNC | Police National Computer | Major computer system used by Police forces to record criminals activities. |
| PT | Personal Target | The desired outcome of a persons activities |
| PV | Positive Vetting | Method of positively checking job applicants background by interviewing their referees and acquaintances |
| R & D | Research and Development | Team that undertake research and development for MOD |
| RARDMS | Road And Rail Disruption Monitoring Statistics | Measurement statistics of Road and Rail disruption |
| SBS | Special Boat Service | Special forces normal marine based. |

| Code | Meaning | Used for |
|------|---------|----------|
| SLA | Six or Seven Letter Acronym | Used by Business Code Words division to explain the limitations of their job |
| SLC | Six or Seven Letter Code | Used by Business Code Words division to explain the limitations of their job |
| TAT'S | Twos And Threes | Used by Business Code Words division to explain the limitations of their job |
| TLA | Two or Three Letter Acronym | Used by Business Code Words division to explain the limitations of their job |
| TLC | Two or Three Letter Code | Used by Business Code Words division to explain the limitations of their job |

# Also by the Same Author

## Godsons – Counting Sunsets

Godsons – Counting Sunsets is a heartening story, charting the stubbornness of the human spirit to let the precious gift of life slip away without a fight to the bitter end.

Multimillionaire Geoffery Foster has been diagnosed with terminal cancer, and has irrationally swapped his luxurious Monaco penthouse for a single room in a Cotswolds hospice in Gloucestershire England.

Determined to maximise his remaining days and impressed by the selfless humanity shown by his hospice nurse, Andy Spider, Geoffery decides to redress his neglected Godfather responsibilities.

Together Andy and Geoffery embark on a journey to track down and improve the lot of Geoffery's three Godsons.

But will resolving the problems of childhood Meningitis amputee Tim, the alcoholic 'drop out' James and the abused husband Rupert, be too much for Geoffery's frail health.

Added to his challenges, a drunken and intimate wedding reception encounter with a former girlfriend comes back to haunt Geoffery as he also gambles with his life in the hands of a woman spurned.

Counting Sunsets becomes the abacus on which Geoffery records his remaining days.

Proving, *'It's never too late to be who you could have been,'* George Elliot.

# The Godsons Legacy

Andy Spider continues to be the glue that cements the three Godsons together as they expectantly await the release of their legacy from Geoffery Foster's will.

But surely even this pillar of society will be distracted from his task when tempted by the radiant beauty of Nadine.

Mesmerised by the exotic Monaco nightlife, his stoic resolve is weakened by lack of sleep and too much alcohol.

Pallbearers wearing Basques, Murder, Blackmail, Fear, Lust, a Motorway Crash, a runaway teenager and police Investigations are the unexpected consequences of Geoffery's legacy as he still controls their lives FROM BEYOND THE GRAVE.

The story is set in Gloucestershire England, near the beautiful Cotswold Hills

# The Godsons Inheritance

The three Godsons have to work harmoniously to place the final piece in the inheritance puzzle for the release of their legacy.

But the wayward Tim makes it a challenging exercise. His self-centred, bloody-minded arrogance means the whole intricate web of relationships is jeopardised. Will his heart bring him back in line or will he still be ruled by his head?

Meanwhile Rupert is continually in fear of his vicious megalomaniacal wife and James is clinging on to life desperate for a liver transplant.

Young army veteran Carrie is haunted by the trauma of active service.

Ben a young carer for his alcoholic Mother inadvertently opens up old wounds by looking for his father. Can fellow young carer Janie help or hinder Ben's traumatic life?

Andy is having a bad time in his personal life, haunted by a late night indiscretion and frustrated by having to coordinate the activities of the three Godsons.

The story comes to a dramatic and exciting conclusion, but is it the end. In this the third book in the Godsons series?

# Unexploded Love

A love triangle is already an explosive situation without the added complication of an unexploded bomb.

But the Luftwaffe's 1944 legacy of a large bomb exposes a burgeoning romance and throws together the three people in the love match.

Trapped in a collapsed hole with a ticking WW2 bomb for company, the love cheat's hope of escape is in the hands of the man he is cuckolding.

Will the frantic race against time succeed? Or will the husband take revenge?

The stark outcome can only be a blast from the past or UNEXPLODED LOVE?

# Gurney Leafmould - The Pied Piper of Calamity

With great DIY aspirations, there is nothing Gurney Leafmould won't tackle – but intent and results are poles apart.

For 'Do it Yourself' means upheaval when Gurney is holding the tools
This is a lively and humorous tale of DIY disasters created by Gurney, a hapless DIYer;

His calamitous CV includes house demolition and fire; a car blaze and a farm inferno coupled together with failed car maintenance and hospital chaos, which are all neatly wrapped in EU red tape. Not to mention a very delicate DIY surgical transplant.
Many wives and partners will recognise some of Gurney's 'attributes' in their own DIY champions.

Willing but incapable, he is a first class prat to his Mother-in-Law but to his long suffering wife, Gurney Leafmould is 'The Pied Piper of Calamity'.

Contains 'Adult Humour'

Lightning Source UK Ltd.
Milton Keynes UK
UKOW04f0647060817
306744UK00001B/18/P